The Landlord and the Wheelchair Child

TERRY JOE GUNNELS

Copyright © 2022 by Terry Joe Gunnels.

ISBN 978-1-959450-47-4 (softcover)
ISBN 978-1-959450-48-1 (ebook)
Library of Congress Control Number: 2022919613

All rights reserved. No part of this book may be reproduced or transmitted in any form or by any means, electronic or mechanical, including photocopying, recording, or by any information storage and retrieval system without express written permission from the author, except in the case of brief quotations embodied in critical reviews and certain other noncommercial uses permitted by copyright law.

This book is a work of fiction. Names, characters, places, and incidents are the product of the author's imagination or are used fictitiously. Any resemblance to actual locales, events, or persons, living or dead, is purely coincidental.

Printed in the United States of America.

Book Vine Press
2516 Highland Dr.
Palatine, IL 60067

ACKNOWLEDGMENTS

To my wife, Shirley Jean (Cookie), ---for encouraging me through 45 years of marriage in all projects I have undertaken. And for spending untold hours proofreading this manuscript for errors.

To my Newest editor, Donje Putnam, whom I have know since she was a teenager and my daughter's best friend. She flooded the printed pages with red ink in quantities that made it look they were bleeding red ink. I thank her.

To all my BETA readers who gave me valuable feedback,

1. To Sterling Norris Monk,---for reading, giving feedback, and finding errors I missed.
2. To Debby Groome Wilkerson,--for her insight on characters, and story line.
3. To Susan Halligan,---who pointed many errors and short comings in my writing. Her honest opinions made the re-writes to the story a definite improvement to the book.

To all others,---for exciting me to move forward with the story and encouraging me to publish.

I give my heartfelt THANK YOU to every person involved with this book.

CONTENTS

Acknowledgments 3
Prologue 7
Chapter 1: Monday…The Wheelchair Girl 9
Chapter 2: Tuesday Morning…Carrie is Sick 22
Chapter 3: Tuesday Evening…The Mysterious Tenant 45
Chapter 4: Wednesday Morning…Surveillance in Unit 143 50
Chapter 5: Wednesday Afternoon…Darcy's House and Val's Place 62
Chapter 6: Thursday Morning…The Phone Call 67
Chapter 7: Thursday Afternoon…Comfort Zone Storage 78
Chapter 8: Friday Morning…The Suitcases 92
Chapter 9: Saturday Morning…Janet 111
Chapter 10: Saturday Afternoon…James has his Humvee Modified ... 120
Chapter 11: Saturday Evening…The Plan 132
Chapter 12: Sunday 5 AM…The Team 145
Chapter 13: Sunday Late Morning…At the Diner and Val 156
Chapter 14: Sunday Afternoon with Daniel 161
Chapter 15: Monday…Daniel's Silver Seraph 165

Chapter 16: Tuesday 4 AM....The Mission 171
Chapter 17: Tuesday Afternoon...At the Compound
　　　　　　to Get Bobby 189
Chapter 18: Wednesday Morning...Darcy's House
　　　　　　with the Griffins 192
Chapter 19: Thursday Morning...Darcy's House,
　　　　　　Hotel, Future Plans 205
Chapter 20: James Sets the Transmitter 224
Chapter 21: Friday Morning...Satchel 235
Chapter 22: Saturday Morning....Daniel Goes Home....................257
Chapter 23: Sunday Morning...Bobby Gets the Big Truck.............266
Chapter 24: Monday morning...Catching Planes............................275

The Landlord's Dead Body

Prologue: About six weeks before today: 283
Chapter One: Monday, The First Day of Construction 286

PROLOGUE

Janet pulled into the parking lot of Black Forrest Village and parked the car in front of one of the apartment buildings. She sat for a moment to rest. It had been a long drive for her and their daughter. Carrie was in the back seat, asleep, and Janet hated to wake her up, but she had to get her out of the car and into the wheelchair.

Janet needed to find her husband because she needed the money. Bobby had left months ago and promised to find a job and send money back to help support her and Carrie. At first, he would send a letter along with the money order. Then there were notes. The money orders became smaller amounts and without any correspondence. Then without warning, the money had stopped. She only knew where her husband was because of the return address on the envelopes containing the money orders he sent. He never explained what kind of work he had gotten.

She hoped to talk to Bobby. Maybe she could get some money, and they could resume a normal life again, but with all that had happened, she doubted it. She didn't want to upset Carrie, so she would take her to the garden area for a while until she could talk to Bobby.

All she had was packed in the trunk of her car. Maybe they could move in together, and she could get a job in this town. Together, they could make enough to live and get the operation Carrie needed to get out of that wheelchair. She wanted, no, she needed to talk to Bobby. It shouldn't take her too long. Bobby said he worked mostly at night, and she could get at least a few things straight in a few minutes. Maybe she and Carrie could at least stay with him until she got a job and could make enough money to get her own place. She didn't know. She was so confused right now.

She laid her head on the steering wheel and rested her eyes for a few moments. She got out and helped Carrie into her wheelchair and walked her around the apartment complex for a few minutes to get up the courage she needed to confront Bobby.

When they got to the garden area of the complex, she bent down to Carrie and talked to her.

"Carrie, Honey. I need to go and talk to someone," Janet said. "It's a nice quiet place here. It shouldn't be too long. Now, you should be fine waiting for me. Do you understand?"

"No, Mommy. I don't know what you mean," Carrie said.

"Don't worry. I'll be back in a little while. I won't be gone too long. Don't worry. No one will hurt you here. Just wait here. Don't leave. I'll be back." She got up and looked down at the child.

"Mommy, don't be long," the little girl called after her mother.

"I won't, dear, and I'll be back before you know it. I promise," she said, walking away, wiping a tear from her eye.

CHAPTER 1

Monday...The Wheelchair Girl

MICKEY WALKED AROUND BLACK FORREST VILLAGE, one of the apartment complexes he and his older sister managed for their father. They took it over when their parents were in a car accident last year, which killed their mother Eleanor, and left their father, Daniel, in a facility, recovering from a severe head injury. Mickey Ray sometimes felt a bit overwhelmed at having the responsibility of the amount of property they managed. Darcy, his sister, managed the office, rentals, and bookkeeping. Mickey oversaw the maintenance. He was just in his mid-20's, and Darcy was a few years older. They accepted their position, and both hoped that their father would someday resume his duties as the owner. Mickey took this walk around the complex almost daily. Even though being targeted at single and young couples, there were a few families with children. He knew the families living in the complex and always greeted the children in the playground area by name.

As Mickey walked the winding paths, he walked toward an area with a fountain in the center, surrounded by small flowering bushes. He saw a child in a wheelchair. Walking up to her, he didn't recognize her as one of the children that lived here.

The little child was transfixed with the fountain and a small bird. She watched the bird flutter its wings in a bathing motion. Sitting down on one of the concrete benches placed here facing the fountain, Mickey watched as the tiny little girl pushed her stringy blonde hair behind her ears and pushed the glasses back up on her nose. She smiled at the little bird flitting its wings. She looked down, brushed the wrinkles out of her jeans, and pulled the long-sleeved shirt around her shoulders, exposing the Disney princess imprinted on the front. He sat on the bench next to her wheelchair and spoke to her, interrupting her concentration on the bird.

"Hello, little one. That bird's beautiful, isn't he?" Mickey said.

She turned to look at Mickey Ray and just stared.

"Do you like birds?" he asked.

She lowered her head toward the ground and nodded.

"Do you know what kind of bird he is?"

She nodded again.

"What kind is it?" asked Mickey.

She raised her head and looked Mickey straight in the eyes. "A Cardinal. How do you know it's a boy?"

"Well, little one, that's an easy question. Some birds have different colors for girls and boys. In the case of the Cardinals, the boy bird is bright red. The girl is a softer red, almost brown or gray."

"Why?"

"That one's not so easy, but there are a lot of thoughts about why. In some cases, the mother bird stays close to the nest to guard the eggs and baby birds. The boy birds look for food and distract predators who want to hurt the babies or eat the eggs. It's a protection for the nest. Some scientists think that girl birds like bright-colored boy birds, so God made some boy birds prettier than others. What do you think?"

She shrugged her shoulders.

"You know, if you told me your name, I wouldn't have to keep calling you 'little one.'"

"Carrie Suzanne Griffin," she said. Again, looking at the ground.

"Wow, what a beautiful name, little one. May I call you Carrie?" Mickey asked gently.

"Yes."

"Do you live here, in an apartment, Carrie?"

"I don't know."

"What'd you mean, you don't know?" he asked gently, now becoming concerned. "Where's your mommy and daddy?"

"I don't know," her voice began to tremble, as a tear dropped from her eye as she continued to look down.

Mickey got up, stepped in front of her, and knelt in front of the wheelchair. Softly, he placed his hand under her chin and raised her head to look at him.

"Have you been here very long?"

"I don't know."

"Did your mother or father leave you here?"

"Mommy said she'd be right back. She told me not to talk to anyone till she got back."

"Has she been gone a long time?" he asked.

"Yes, I think so," she said, nodding.

"It's three o'clock in the afternoon. Do you know what time it was when your mommy left?"

"No. I'm scared."

"I'm sure you are. Are you thirsty or maybe hungry?"

"Yes."

"May I take you and get you something to eat?"

"No. Mommy said to stay here till she got back. I can't leave," she said, with tears now flowing freely down her face.

"Okay, Carrie. I understand. I'll call someone to bring you something to eat and drink. Is that okay with you?"

"Yes. Thank you."

Mickey took out his cell phone and called Sam, one of the workers on-site getting a vacant unit ready to rent.

"Hey, Sam, can you pull yourself away for a while to get something for me?" Mickey said into the phone.

"Sure, Boss. What can I do for you?" answered Sam.

He was one of Mickey's father's oldest maintenance workers. Sam was retired military and helped Mickey keep the other people working when he wasn't around. He was the only full-time worker who could handle almost anything that needed to be done and train the other workers. Although they owned several apartment complexes, Mickey knew that Sam would be working at Black Forrest all week.

"Sam, I'm over at the fountain in the Center Inspiration Garden. A little lady here needs our help, but first, we need you to get her something to eat and drink. Could you also bring something to help her stay warm? It'll be getting chilly here in a while, and she may not want to leave."

"A little lady? I don't understand, Boss."

"You'll understand when you get here. Please hurry." Mickey disconnected the call.

Mickey turned back to the little girl. She was crying now. He wanted so much to lift her from that wheelchair and comfort her, but he didn't know what she had been through and dared not touch her. He was still a stranger to her, and if she had been traumatized, any physical contact might make it worse. He just sat back down next to her and tried to ease her fears. They sat until she had cried out, and he handed her a tissue he carried in his pocket. She used it to dry her now puffy, reddened eyes.

"Carrie, a friend of mine will be here in a few minutes, with something to eat and drink. We'll help you any way you need. He'll also bring something so you'll not get cold. It'll be getting cold as the afternoon gets later, okay?"

"Okay," she answered. "Where's my mommy?"

"I don't know, Carrie, but I'll find out. How old are you?"

"I'm ten and a half years old. I want my mommy."

"I know you do, little one. We'll do our best to find her. Do you know where you live? Do you know your phone number?"

"We used to live at 1600 Johnson Street, but we had to leave there. We don't live anywhere now. That's why Mommy and I came here," she said and began crying again.

Mickey pulled out his phone and dialed. "Dee, please pick up," he said into the ringing telephone.

Finally, the phone stopped ringing, and the voice at the other end said, "Hey, Mickey. What's up?"

"Hey, Dee. I have a problem."

"Okay, hello to you too, little brother," she said back to him.

"I'm sorry to be so abrupt, but I do have a problem here. Look, I found a little ten-year-old child here at Black Forrest Village. She's in a wheelchair, and we don't have a clue where her mother is. All I have is a name."

Taking the phone down from his ear, he again asked Carrie, "Carrie, what's your last name? I want to tell my sister so she can start looking for your mommy."

She sniffed a couple of times, then spoke out. "My full name is Carrie Suzanne Griffin. Can you find my mommy, please?"

"We're trying. We're doing our best, little one. What's your mommy and daddy's name?"

"Mommy's name is Janet Lee Griffin, and Daddy's name is Bobby Michael Griffin."

He put the phone back up to his ear. "Her name is Carrie Suzanne Griffin. Her mother is Janet Lee, and her dad is Bobby, probably Robert Michael. Do what you can, please. It'll be dark in a while. We need to find them and get her home."

"Got it, Mickey. I'll call back as soon as I know something. Bye." Darcy hung up.

He and Carrie talked, and soon afterward, they heard a truck pull up. They looked toward the garden entrance, and Sam walked through with a bag and thermos. He looked at Mickey and then at the little girl in the wheelchair.

"What's going on here, Mickey?" the big burly man asked.

"Hey, Sam. This here little lady's my new friend, Carrie. She's tired, hungry, and thirsty. What did you bring her to eat?"

"I didn't know it was a little girl. I brought what I had left over from my lunch. It's a bologna and cheese sandwich. And all I have to drink is a thermos of coffee. It was warm today, so I had a soda for my lunch instead of my coffee. Sorry, I don't know if kids can have coffee." He handed the bag and thermos to Mickey.

"We'll make do, Sam. Thanks."

"Have you ever had bologna for lunch or drank coffee, Carrie?" Mickey asked.

"I like bologna. Yes, I've had coffee too, but I don't like it unless it has milk and pink sugar," she said.

Mickey looked at Sam for confirmation on the coffee. Sam told him that he had some sugar packets in his truck but no milk. Mickey told him he had some creamer packets and various sweeteners in his truck. Sam left to get the condiments from both trucks while Carrie began eating the sandwich.

Carrie seemed to be getting in a better frame of mind as she ate. "I like bologna. We eat it a lot at home. Sometimes, coffee's all we have to drink except for water. I don't like water, but I drink it a lot."

Sam returned with the packets of creamer and a small bag of various sweeteners.

When Carrie saw the little bag, she pointed and said, "The pink packets, that's what I have in my drinks. I like the pink color packets."

They mixed it up and gave it to Carrie. The sun was beginning to set, and the garden's overhead light lit up with a soft glow. Carrie began to shiver as the temperature dropped, so Sam took off his coat and put it around her. Mickey walked to the edge of the clearing, still in sight of Carrie, and motioned for Sam to come over so they could talk.

"Sam, I don't know what to do here. Do you have any kids from your marriage?"

"Yes, I had two, but the wife got them, the house, the car, and most of my money in the divorce," he said.

"Sorry to hear that, but I don't know what to do. Do you have any suggestions?"

"No, pal, can't help you here. I'd call the police."

"The police and I aren't on good terms."

"Call your sister. She should know what to do."

Just as he said this, Mickey's phone rang. He punched the answer button and held it to his ear.

"Yeah, Dee. What did you find out?" he said into the phone.

"Nothing yet. All the local courthouses are closed for the evening. I can go online, but it's getting late. Have you heard anything about either of her parents?"

"No. It's getting dark, and I might add, cold. I can't leave her here. And I don't want to take her with me. She's scared to go because she believes her mother's coming back. I don't have a good feeling about this. If her mother's coming back, she'd be here by now. No good parent would leave a ten-year-old child alone all day. Especially one in a wheelchair."

"Why is she in a wheelchair? Have you asked her that?"

"No, I felt that when I got to know her better, I would ask that, but I didn't want to approach that quite yet. I don't want to upset her even more than she is already."

"I understand. I agree. I can bring the kids and come there to be with you. I'll bring some food, drinks, and something to keep warm. We'll stay as long as necessary."

"That would be great, Dee. The kids could keep her mind off her mother, but we need to get on this ASAP," said Mickey.

"I also agree with that. I'll be there as soon as I can get the kids ready and pack some food."

Mickey knew that Darcy would be there as soon as she could. Darcy had two children from her marriage, which ended several years before due to spousal abuse. Eight-year-old Cyndi, Mickey's niece, was a pretty little lady with long brown hair like her mother and as sweet as candy. Joel, his nine-year-old nephew, was well behaved but a bit more precocious, and although Mickey would never admit it, Joel was his favorite. He'd bonded with Joel since he was just a baby.

Mickey, Sam, and Carrie sat as they talked. Carrie was bright for a ten-year-old and held an adult conversation reasonably well. Both Mickey and Sam began to shiver, but Carrie was cozy in Sam's coat and seemed content for the moment.

"Carrie, can you tell me how long you've been in that chair?" asked Mickey.

"Ever since the accident."

"What accident? Can you tell me about it?" said Mickey probing further.

"I don't want to talk about it. It makes me sad. I want to play with other kids, but I can't because of this chair," she said again, looking down at the ground.

"That's okay, and we don't have to talk about it now. We might need to talk about it later," answered Mickey.

"I don't want to talk about it," she said, poking her lower lip out defiantly.

"Maybe we won't have to talk about it. We'll see."

Mickey turned to Sam and pulled him aside so they could talk.

"Sam, as soon as Darcy gets here, you can leave. I don't want to be left alone with Carrie. You understand. Don't you?"

"Sure, Mickey. I understand. What're you going to do when Darcy gets here?" he asked.

"Right now, I don't know. I guess we'll wait for a while longer to see if Carrie's mother does show up, but I doubt it. I think we'll call DCS to take her."

"DCS? Do you mean the Department of Child Services? Man, you can't do that. They'll throw her in the system, and I've heard that place is horrible. It's like throwing her to the wolves!"

"I don't know what else to do, Sam."

"Don't you know anyone who could take her for just a few days?"

"No, I don't. We'll wait until Dee gets here. She'll know what to do."

While they waited, Mickey sat in deep thought. He remembered when he was a teenager, and a small child was left alone in one of the apartments. A maintenance man checked on the unit because the occupants had failed to answer the overdue rent notice. They found a little boy about Carrie's age inside the unit. For over two weeks, the child had lived on cereal, sandwiches, and canned soup. Daniel, Mickey's father, called DCS, and the child was taken away and put into the system. The little boy's parents were never found, and he had been transferred from one foster home to another. Mickey heard that the boy was arrested for murder several years later during the commission of a convenience store robbery. Mickey had always felt that if someone had found out what happened to the child's parents, more could have been done to help the boy. As with many children in this situation, the system had failed them. Sure, he knew that some children were taken in by caring foster parents, and eventually, they were placed in permanent homes with good families. He also knew that many foster homes were similar to animal breeders, and the people ran these homes like puppy mills. They took the kids in just for the money paid to them by the city or state. Money is all they cared about, not the kids in their care. The thought of a precious little girl like Carrie being placed in one of these homes almost made him vomit. He felt that he couldn't let it happen.

The Landlord and the Wheelchair Child

He knew that it was probably something they could work out soon, but he knew that any caring parent wouldn't abandon a disabled child like this. He had a horrible gut feeling that something had happened to Carrie's mother. He would find out and do his best to keep this girl out of the child care system.

Sam and Mickey sat and tried to make conversation with Carrie. After about an hour, they were getting cold. They were also running out of things to talk about to the ten-year-old when Darcy finally arrived. She had the kids in tow with blankets and snacks and coffee for the adults with hot cocoa for the kids. Joel and Cyndi made friends with Carrie in no time. Darcy, Sam, and Mickey talked about what to do with Carrie.

Darcy Jean Hill, Mickey's older sister, was a compact five foot five inches. Her dark brown hair hung down over her shoulders so that when she looked down, she could hide her face and mask her feelings. But when she looked up, she could look right into your soul. She had a winning smile that most men found very appealing. She wore only a light bit of makeup which accented her looks without looking "made up." She could be cold as steel or likable as a warm puppy. She was also engaged to his best friend, James T. Bower.

Darcy talked with Carrie for a few minutes and then went back over to Sam and Mickey Ray.

"Mickey, we need to call DCS and get them out here to take her somewhere for the night," Darcy said.

"We can't do that. They'll put her in some foster home, and that'll be that! She's got a mother out there, and we need to find her so that Carrie can go home."

"We can take her back to our house for the night, but first thing in the morning, we WILL call DCS," Darcy said emphatically.

Sam spoke up, "I think you have this now. Do you need me for anything else?"

"No," said Mickey, "you can leave now. As you can already guess, I'll be working on tracking down Carrie's parents tomorrow, so you come on in and pick up where you left off this afternoon. And thanks for lunch you brought to Carrie and for sticking around after your shift today, Sam."

"No problem, Mickey. See you when I see you. I hope everything turns out for the child. She needs some help. I know with you guys, she'll be in good hands," he said as he waved goodbye to Carrie and walked away.

Mickey walked back over to Carrie and knelt in front of her. "Carrie, it's getting cold out here. Why don't we go to your new friend's house for the night?"

"Mommy said to wait here for her. We can't go until she comes back to get me."

"Little one, we'll leave her a note on the bench telling her where you are, so when she gets back, she can give us a call," Mickey suggested.

"She said to wait here."

"I know, but she got held up, and maybe she'll not be here until later. She wouldn't want you to be out here in the cold, now would she?"

"No, I guess not. Mr. Mickey, I have to go to the bathroom. I haven't been since she left."

"I bet you have to go really bad. We'll take you to a place, and Dee here can help you with that. We'll find a warm place to stay until your mommy gets back."

"Okay, but you'll leave Mommy a note, so she knows where I am?"

"You bet, little one," Mickey assured her.

"Can I push her wheelchair, Uncle Mick?" asked Joel.

"I think you better ask Carrie that one, Little Joe," he answered.

"I want to do it," chimed in Cyndi!

Carrie laughed, "you can both do it."

Darcy smiled at all three kids as she picked up the blankets and trash to take to the car.

"I don't think you're going to have a problem with them getting along," said Mickey as he herded the kids together, and they all headed for Darcy's car.

Mickey helped Carrie into the front seat when they got to the car. Then he put her chair in the trunk, and the kids climbed into the backseat.

"Do you think you can get her back out, into her chair, and in the house when you get home?" he asked.

"Sure, no problem. I'll call DCS first thing in the morning. While we are on this subject, why didn't you call the police when you first found her a couple of hours ago? She isn't our problem."

"I know, but she seems like a sweet little girl, and we'll find her mother tomorrow, and it will all be over. You know how many kids end up screwed up after being in the system. It isn't good for them. And besides, when DCS finds out her mother just left her here, they might take her away from her mother."

"Yeah, and maybe that what needs to happen. A responsible mother wouldn't leave a child out here all alone. Especially one in a wheelchair," Darcy said.

"We don't know what or why she left her here. She might have had a good reason. Besides, Carrie said her mom promised to come right back, so it wasn't intentional. We need to find her before the police and DCS get involved."

"Are you coming over to the house in the morning to start working on this?" Darcy asked.

"You bet. I'll be there first thing. I'll stop by the donut shop and bring some pastries for breakfast."

"Bring me a couple of jelly ones. Those are my favorites, Mickey," Darcy added.

"See you in the morning, Dee." Mickey tapped on the window glass and waved goodbye to the kids.

Mickey jumped in his truck and drove to Valerie's apartment. He drove, thinking of when he and Val had become engaged. He thought of her as a friend, a companion, but when someone had called her his girlfriend, and he had denied it, Valerie had gotten her feelings hurt, and he suddenly realized how much he loved her. When she was kidnapped, he thought his world had come to an end. He felt compelled to rescue her. He was willing to give his own life to save hers.

He was tall, and his frame filled out the flannel shirts he wore so often to his job as maintenance foreman of the Christianson Real Estate Corporation. He was strong, had a great set of abs, and worked out in the gym with James, his future brother-in-law. He kept his dark hair short and neat because sometimes he and Darcy had to meet at a bank to explain some financial expenses. He had matured and developed a sense of responsibility since his father had been injured in the auto accident. He was no longer a spoiled twenty-something kid that only worked when he felt like it. He needed to work to protect the property that he and Darcy would someday inherit.

He drove to Valerie's apartment, ready to have dinner and a quiet evening with her, before walking down to the other end of the apartment building to his place. She lived in a small house that burned last year when she was kidnapped. They had both spent much time going to yard sales and thrift stores to furnish her new apartment. Mickey felt it was his fault, so he had allowed her to move into one of his father's apartments, rent-free. When they got married, they would find a place together.

"Hey, Val," he said as she answered the door. He gave her a quick peck on the cheek as he walked into her apartment.

"Hey, Mickey Ray, you're running a bit late, aren't you," she said. "Did you have a problem with something?"

"No problem, but something did come up."

"Tell me about it as I make the salad. When we eat it, I'll put on the steaks for dinner."

Val was pretty with long dark hair and green eyes that sparkled whenever Mickey came around. She had changed in a way that Mickey couldn't explain since she had been kidnapped and James and Mickey had rescued her.

"Pull up a chair while I make the salad and tell me about your day."

The apartment was laid out so when you were at the kitchen table, you could see into the kitchen, so Mickey sat down in his usual chair so he could talk.

"Val, you will never guess what I found today!" he said with a smile.

"What?" she said.

"A little girl in a wheelchair."

"Aww, that sounds sad. How did she end up in a wheelchair?"

"I don't know, but we'll find out. You see, her mother left her and never came back," he said.

Valerie looked up from the salad bowl. "What do you mean her mother didn't come back?"

"Her mother just left this little girl and never came back," he said.

"Why?"

"We don't know. Dee took her home, and in the morning, she'll call DCS and report her to the police."

"Good, maybe her mother will come to get her. What kind of dressing do you want on your salad?"

"I don't care, either Italian or Thousand Island. Whichever you have," said Mickey.

"I have both. I'll put both on the table, and you can do it yourself. What'll you do if her mother doesn't come back?"

"Find her, I guess."

"If she doesn't come back, the police and Department of Child Services will take her. At least you won't have to do it," Valerie said.

Valerie brought the salad plates over, they both ate, and Val put the steaks in the oven to broil.

"If her mother doesn't come back, then James and I could spend a few days looking, just to help out."

"No, you can't, Mickey. You can't get involved in something that doesn't concern you," she said emphatically.

"We'll see. Besides, she'll show up soon. I'm sure. What mother would just walk out on a little child?" said Mickey. He could tell Valerie was getting upset with him, so he changed the subject.

"How was your day at the diner?"

"Let's eat, Mickey. I need to get to bed. I have the breakfast shift at the diner tomorrow."

They ate in silence, and Mickey went home.

CHAPTER 2

Tuesday Morning...Carrie is Sick

Mickey walked in unannounced into Darcy's house the following morning. He did that quite often, but Darcy never said a word about it to him. Even though he had an apartment across town, he spent a lot of time here with her and the kids. Since she and his best friend, James, had gotten engaged, Mickey began to think more seriously that maybe he should knock first, but not this morning. He walked into the kitchen and put the donuts down on the counter. He saw the coffee pot had hot coffee in the carafe already, so he knew Darcy was already up.

Mickey called out, "Darcy, is everyone up?"

"We're up, Mickey. I'm in Joel's room. You can come on back."

Darcy was putting clean sheets on the bottom bunk of Joel's bed as Mickey entered the bedroom.

"An accident?" he asked.

"Yes," she said, "and she kept asking for water all night long. She was wet when we got home last night, and as you can see, she wet the bed last night. That little girl is sick, Mickey. We need to get her to the hospital today."

"I didn't notice it when I helped her in the car last night."

"I'm sure she was embarrassed about it and tried to hide it from you, but she drank then wet the bed. That isn't normal for a ten-year-old child. Maybe she just has a yeast infection or perhaps a urinary tract infection. I don't know, but we need to get her to a doctor right after we get breakfast."

"I hope it isn't anything bad."

"It probably isn't, but we need to get her checked out, so if she needs some medication or professional care, she gets it."

"Where's Carrie now?"

"She's in the bathroom. Joel slept in Cyndi's room last night and let the girls have his room because it has bunk beds in it. Cyndi slept on Joel's top bunk. I'll gather them up and get them to the kitchen for breakfast. While they're eating, I'll call the doctor and try to get an appointment today. If we can't get one, I think we should take her to the ER. I'll also put in a call to DCS."

The kids came in, pushing Carrie in her wheelchair. Mickey pulled back one of the chairs and motioned for Carrie to move into its place.

Carrie looked at the donut on her plate, and her eyes grew large with excitement. "Wow," she said, "Mommy won't let me have donuts."

"I'm sorry to hear that, Carrie. Why doesn't she let you have them?" Mickey asked. "You can have all you want, little one."

"Mommy says it's bad for my sugar," she said as she lifted the donut to her open mouth. She took a huge bite, chewed it, and swallowed, then raised it to her mouth for another bite. She finished it and asked Mickey for another one. He put another one on her plate.

"What did she just say?" asked Darcy.

Mickey looked at Darcy quizzically and answered, "She said, Mommy, says it's bad for my sugar."

Just as he said that Darcy jumped up and grabbed the donut from Carrie's hand before she took another bite. "No, Carrie! You can't have that! It WILL hurt you!" Darcy spurted out. She took the donut and put it back into the box.

Carrie started to cry, and Darcy leaned over and hugged her close. "I'm so sorry, dear. I didn't know, but your mother's right. You can't have that donut. Maybe later. We'll save it for you. We have to see a doctor before you eat another one."

"I want the donut. I like donuts. Please let me have one. I won't tell Mommy that you gave it to me," she cried.

Darcy's heart immediately went out to little Carrie. She now knew what happened last night. Why Carrie was so thirsty and wet the bed.

"Hey, Dee, why'd you do that?" Mickey exclaimed. "One donut will NOT hurt her."

"Yes, it will, Mickey. She doesn't have a yeast or urinary tract infection. She has diabetes! And severely diabetic because your blood gets thick when your blood sugar goes up, and your body tries to thin it down. You get thirsty. Then, your kidneys flush it out, and you have to urinate. Then the process repeats itself. That's why she drank so much and wet the bed last night. We need to get her to the hospital NOW. We need to see what her blood sugar is. It could be potentially dangerous for her. Do you remember telling me last night when Sam brought the coffee, and you said she asked for the 'pink stuff?'"

"Yes, I remember because no kid ever wants that nasty sweetener in the pink packages."

"Right, Mickey, but it's an artificial sweetener. She picked that because she likes pink," Darcy said as she called out to the children.

"Okay, kids, everyone, throw that food down your throat and get in the car. We're going for a ride to the emergency room, NOW," Mickey said.

She helped Carrie into the front seat of her car. Carrie was crying and apologizing, saying she wouldn't wet herself anymore. Darcy tried to explain to Carrie that it wasn't her fault, and she wasn't mad at her.

"Dear, you can't help it. It's okay. We're going to see a doctor to get some medicine if you need it. Then when we get back home, maybe you can have that donut. We'll see. Don't be worried. We want to help you."

Carrie continued to cry, saying, "I want my mommy. When is my mommy coming to get me?"

"She's coming as soon as she can, Honey. We'll find her as soon as we can."

Joel and Cyndi didn't understand what was happening, but they kept quiet in the back seat. Mickey drove to the hospital Emergency Room area where Darcy was getting Carrie checked in. He went over and sat down beside Joel and Cyndi.

Darcy finished checking Carrie in and sat down beside Mickey. She started searching for the phone number of the Department of Child

Services. When she found it, she dialed the number. When someone answered the phone, they transferred Darcy to a caseworker. She explained about Carrie and what happened. They said they would send someone to the hospital as soon as possible.

"I certainly hope we got here before something serious happened to Carrie," Darcy said as she turned to Mickey.

"I do too, but I don't understand why it's so serious that we had to hurry like that, Dee."

"There are a lot of things associated with diabetes that can be serious, for anyone but especially children. Maybe I overreacted, but we don't know her medical history, and it can be deadly if not treated. If her blood sugar gets too high, it could cause severe organ damage, and as you see, she already wears glasses. Eyes are especially susceptible to high blood sugar.

"In adults, high blood sugar can cause heart attacks. That probably wouldn't happen to a child, but as I said, we don't know how serious she is. They can do a simple blood test here, give her some medication, and bring the sugar blood count down, and everything will be fine. We also don't know if she's type 1 or type 2. Type 2 is much easier to control, so that's what we'll hope for at this point."

"I don't understand a word you've said, and I don't understand the difference in type 1 or 2," said Mickey, clearly confused.

"That's not important right now. What's important is we got Carrie here. They'll check her out, and DCS will decide what needs to be done from here. They should take good care of her, and we can continue to look for her parents."

"I wouldn't put any money on them looking for her parents. After what happened with Mom and Pop last year, I don't trust the police department for anything. Maybe we won't have much trouble finding them, and she can go home. I'm sure she misses her parents a lot. I think she's taken this situation very well. I can't imagine a child going without her parents for as long as she has so far."

A man in hospital scrubs came out, looked around, and walked over to Mickey and Darcy. "Are you Mr. and Mrs. Griffin?" he asked.

"No, we're the ones who brought Carrie Griffin in for you to check out," Darcy answered.

"Are you with DCS or the Police?" he asked.

"No, but we…" began Darcy.

He held up his hand as a signal to stop talking. "I'm sorry, but I can't tell you anything because you're not family or an official authority. Carrie is a minor, and her condition's private. I'll wait until the proper authorities arrive." He turned and walked away.

Darcy took a deep breath, let it out, and sighed. She then picked up her phone and dialed the law firm where she worked.

"I'll be right back, Mickey. I must put a doctor in his place. Carrie is now a client of the law firm of Callahan & Johnson, and I'll talk to our client and get her medical records or heads will roll," she stated as she walked again over to the check-in receptionist.

Mickey heard her talking and insisted on speaking with the doctor or someone else in authority. After a couple of minutes, the doctor walked back out the door and began talking with Darcy. Finally, he turned and walked away again. Darcy motioned for Mickey to follow her. Mickey told Joel and Cyndi to sit there, and he would be back in a few minutes. He followed Darcy to an exam room where the doctor and Carrie were waiting.

Carrie was wiping tears from her face as they came into the small room. She reached out her arms, grabbed Mickey, and hugged him tightly as Darcy began talking with the doctor.

"Doctor, this is Mickey Ray Christianson. He is the witness for Carrie. Since she's a minor, she's never without an adult present during any questioning and examination such as the one done here today. We know that she has some health issues. Still, since we don't have access to her past medical condition at this time, we need to know what treatments or medications she might need until we can notify her parents. She will be placed back with her rightful parents or put into the custody of a legal guardian as soon as possible."

The doctor said, "I'll tell you this, as you correctly surmised, Carrie has diabetes. You were also correct to bring her to the hospital this morning because if you had not, I can only say that it could have been catastrophic if her blood sugar had gotten any higher. We gave her an insulin injection to bring her blood sugar levels down. We did draw some blood, and we'll do a few more tests, so at this point, we don't know if she is type 1 or 2. Do you understand the difference, Mrs. Hill?"

Darcy nodded that she understood.

"Good. We'll start Carrie on a medication of Metformin. But you need to check her blood sugar every two hours to see results. If it doesn't stay within proper levels, give me a call immediately. I am only filling in at the ER. I do have a private practice as a pediatrician. I'll work with you in any way to get and keep this little child in good health."

"Thank you, doctor. We'll most certainly be in touch, either here or your practice," said Darcy.

The doctor gave them a prescription for Metformin, then turned and walked out the door.

"Wow, he was rude," said Mickey.

"He was just doing his job, and being in the hospital, he had to be more cautious than he might have been if he was in his own office, so cut him some slack, Mickey."

When they got back out to the emergency room, Betty Crawley stood at the reception desk. She was from the Department of Child Services.

"Hey, Betty," said Darcy with a smile. Darcy had dealt with Betty at Social Services several times at the law office when court cases were pending against a parent that involved children.

"Hello, Darcy. Are you the one that reported the little girl, Carrie, for pickup?" Betty said.

"Yes, how're you doing?"

"Great, Darcy, and you?"

"Fine. Betty, this is my brother, Mickey Ray Christianson. He's helping me on this case."

"Nice to meet you, Mickey Ray," the woman said as she put out her hand for Mickey to shake. She was medium build, with her black and silver hair pulled back and upheld with an old-fashioned hair comb. She reminded him of an old schoolmarm of the nineteenth century.

"Nice to meet you, Betty. I assume that you're from DCS, correct?" responded Mickey.

"Yes, I am."

"Do you have to take her now? We need to keep her for a few days," he said. "There are a few problems we need to work out for her."

"No small talk! I like that. Cut to the chase," she said, smiling and winking at Darcy. "What kind of problems?" Betty asked.

"First, as you can see, she's in a wheelchair," said Darcy. "That might be a problem for you, finding someone that can accommodate her disability. Next, the doctor just informed us that she has diabetes and needs her blood sugar monitored several times a day until they can determine if she is type 1 or 2 so they know the correct medication she needs."

"Are you sure you can take care of her? I know you have a job and two kids of your own, Darcy Jean," Betty said.

Betty knew Darcy from her divorce when her ex-husband had tried to sue for custody of Joel and Cyndi. Betty testified in court that Darcy was a good mother capable of taking care of the kids. Even though Darcy worked a full-time job at a law firm, she managed to be at all school functions, and the kids were well adjusted in school and got along well with the other children, according to their teachers. Darcy also had help and support from her family, including Mickey Ray and their mother, Eleanor, until she died. Mickey had helped and taken up the slack left by Darcy's ex and their mother.

"Certainly, I can. Carrie'll not be a problem. I work from home now. The kids will also help, and they get along with her wonderfully. She'll have a bed of her own and share a room with Cyndi. If she needs medication or a trip to the doctor or ER, I'm free to take her with her medical problems. Besides, it'll only be temporary until we locate her parents."

"I'll fill out the paperwork, but I'll still have to run it by my supervisor and maybe run it by a judge, but that should be just a formality. I don't foresee a problem. What are her immediate needs?"

"The first thing you can do is start the paperwork to pay for this ER visit and her medication, some test strips, and a meter for checking her blood sugar. I have a prescription I need to have filled."

"You did all this without prior authorization from DCS?" Betty said.

"Yes, I did, and it's a good thing I did, or she could have suffered some serious complications as a result."

"Okay, Darcy. I'll fill out the forms for that and get it squared away with the hospital for DCS to pay for it. But next time, call me first."

"I will, but this was an emergency, Betty. You know me better than to think I'd step on anyone's toes at DCS." Darcy smiled at Betty.

Betty thought for a moment, then asked, "Have you reported this child to the police? She was abandoned."

Mickey spoke up, "She wasn't abandoned. Something happened to her mother. We can take care of that."

"I'm sure you can, Mickey Ray, but we need to cross all the T's and dot the I's on this one. So, you need to file a police report down at the police station. Will you do that so that I can put it in my report?"

"Can I wait a day or two, so we can locate her mother?" asked Mickey.

"No. You must do it now. You should have done it last night. If you go to the police station now, I can list it in my report, and all will be fine, but if you don't, the timeline will not match up, and every one of us will have the devil to pay. Understand?" said Betty.

"Yes, Ma'am. I'll do it as soon as we leave here."

"No, leave and do it now, Mickey Ray. You can meet up with them later," she said, pointing at Darcy and the kids.

Mickey nodded and walked out of the Emergency Room. As he walked out, he called back at Darcy, "See ya'll at the diner."

When Betty left, Darcy rounded up her kids and Carrie. It was afternoon, so they went to the diner to get lunch. They went to the local diner where Mickey's fiancé, Valerie, worked as a waitress. When Valerie came to their table to take their order, she said, "Hey, Dee. How're ya'll doing this afternoon."

"We're doing great, and we're all starved, Val."

"Who's this beautiful little girl that's with you this morning?" Valerie asked.

"This is Carrie. She's staying with me a while until we find her parents."

Valerie furrowed her brow and replied, "Find her parents?"

"Her mother left her in the garden area of Black Forrest Village yesterday to run an errand, and she didn't return. So, I'm going to keep her until mom shows up, that's all. No big deal," said Darcy.

"What're you getting involved in now, Dee?" Val asked. "Mickey mentioned her last night and assured me that he wasn't getting involved."

"Nothing Valerie. It's a simple missing person, that's all."

"Yeah, right. I hope so. What can I get ya'll to eat?" she asked without further conversation.

Darcy could tell Valerie was concerned. She could see Valerie's sparkle fade when she was upset. Darcy knew that Val was sad for the little child, but Valerie had her own troubles.

Valerie took their order, turned, and walked away.

They all sat at a large booth at the rear of the room. The kids whispered and were well-behaved. Darcy ordered for the kids, and then sat back and let out a huge sigh as she gathered her thoughts about finding Carrie's parents.

Finally, Mickey came in and sat down. Darcy told him she had ordered for him, and Valerie was already upset with them for getting involved with Carrie.

"How did it go with the police?" Darcy asked.

"Alright, I guess. I talked with Detective Johnson. He's known Pop for a long time. He seems fine. I reported Carrie, Janet, and Robert Michael as their father. None of them are on any sort of missing list. They don't have anything on them. So, they don't know about Carrie. Or at least they didn't know until I told them. Since Johnson is a friend of Pop's, they're going to give us some slack and time to try to find her parents. But I had to promise to stay out of their way."

"Did you make that promise, Mickey Ray?" Darcy eyed him with obvious doubt.

"Well, kind of."

"Did you or didn't you, promise?"

"Yes, I promised," he answered hesitantly.

"But you have no plans to keep it, do you?"

"I'll do it on the down-low. How's that?"

"I hope so. Do you remember the last time the police told you to leave it alone? I think the exact words were…'back off.'"

The Landlord and the Wheelchair Child

"I know, but I'll work low key. I promise, Dee," he said.

"You told Valerie what you're doing, didn't you?"

"I went by her place last night and had dinner. Yes, we talked, and Carrie came up, but I said nothing is going to happen, and I insisted it would only take a couple of days to find her mother."

Finally, she looked at Mickey and shifted a glance toward Carrie. "After the kids went to bed last night, I spent some time on the internet trying to track down her parents." Darcy again glanced at Carrie and mentally noted the child was involved with Cyndi and Joel, so she felt she could talk a bit more freely. "I didn't have much information to go on. A name and an address in an unknown city, is not much to work with since I don't have social security numbers. If her mother left her there and intended to return, she wouldn't be listed with missing persons yet. There's no AMBER Alert either.

"I'm at a bit of a loss to continue an internet trace. Something must have happened to her mother. If she planned to abandon her, she wouldn't have put her so far out of the way as that park area in Black Forrest. She would've left her in a more public place. I don't have a good feeling about things, Mickey Ray. Since Carrie was left in that area, there's probably some connection with someone in the complex. I'll get on that as soon as I get back home. I'll also check the tenant records for anyone from out of town or even out of state. You check the cars parked in the lot in case something happened to Janet Griffin, and her car is still in the parking lot."

"Done," said Mickey. "When I do that, how will I be able to run the plates to get information on the owners?"

"I'll check with James. I think he has some ex-army buddies that work in some police departments, not in this area. The police department can run plates in any state."

"Sounds good to me. I'll walk the parking lot, knock on doors and talk with some tenants. I might be able to get some information from them. If I find out anything, I'll give you a call."

They talked for a few minutes about the kids, and Mickey told Darcy about his visits to their father. Wordlessly Valerie brought their food. As they ate, Carrie seemed to fit in with the group just like she was family. She was well behaved and thoughtful of Joel and Cyndi. Darcy had combed Carrie's hair this morning, so it wasn't stringy and tangled like it was when Mickey found her the night before. She also had on one of Cyndi's pairs of pants and a clean shirt. He could tell she was a wonderful little child.

Mickey paid the bill, and they went out to Darcy's car. He snapped a picture of Carrie in her chair before Darcy loaded her kids into the car. As Mickey picked Carrie up and placed her gently into the front seat, he asked her what kind of car her mother drove.

"I don't know, Mr. Mickey. It's blue. Does that help?" she asked, concerned that it may not help him.

"That helps a lot, little one. If I showed you a picture, would you recognize it?"

"Yes, I think so. The front is mashed in on one side," Carrie added.

"That's great. Thanks, you helped a lot! I'll try to find it, and then we'll find your mommy," Mickey assured her.

"Oh, good. I miss Mommy a lot," she said with a smile.

"I know you do, Carrie. Until then, you can stay with Dee. Is that alright with you?" he asked.

"I guess so," she said, then began to tear up again.

Mickey hugged her close and closed the car door. He walked around the car to Darcy as she opened the driver's side door.

"We need to get on this. I'll start immediately. I think Carrie's handling it well so far, but the more time passes, the more she'll miss her mother. That'll have a toll on her. All children need their parents," said Mickey.

"Yes, you're right. I've got some paperwork I need to get out for the law office. I'll get that done as soon as I can. When you find something, I'll have more information to proceed with the internet search."

He put Carrie's chair in Darcy's trunk and watched as Dee drove out of the parking lot. When he got to Black Forrest, he got out and started walking around the lot, snapping pictures of all blue cars.

He found two with damage, both with damage from minor accidents. One had a "smashed" headlight, and another had damage to the passenger's door. He snapped pictures of both of them and forwarded them to Dee from his cell phone. In a few minutes, he got an answer about the car. Carrie pointed out the one with the broken headlight. Dee took the license plate number shown and contacted someone she knew with the police department, and then ran the plate number. She gave Mickey the car owner's name and sent him a driver's license photo.

Mickey began knocking on doors, showing Carrie's picture on his phone as well as the driver's photo to the tenants who answered. A young woman holding a baby answered the first door. She looked at the picture and told Mickey that she hadn't seen the child or anyone driving the car he pointed out in the parking lot. One by one, everyone that answered said that they didn't know the child in the wheelchair and hadn't seen anyone around or driving the car. On the fifth door, he knocked, and a man in his mid-twenties answered the door.

"Good afternoon, sir. I'm Mickey Ray Christianson. I'm the maintenance man of this complex. Have you seen this little girl?" he asked as he lifted the phone with Carrie's picture for him to see.

The man grabbed a shirt and pulled it around his boney shoulders, and pushed his wispy unkempt hair away as he began buttoning and tucking the shirt inside his ragged jeans. His old flip-flops were several sizes too big for his dirty feet. He ran his hands through his greasy hair and wiped his hands on his jeans. Mickey thought he looked like a weasel. Weasel guy cocked his head. He looked as if he had been awakened from a nap. In the background, Mickey could see an old detective show playing on the TV.

The man barely glanced at the picture, then answered, "No, I ain't seen her. Now, if you don't mind, I'm busy."

"Did you see the person who was driving that car? The blue one, with the broken headlight a couple of doors down?" Mickey asked.

"No, man. I didn't see nobody driving that car. I don't know who it belongs to. Why you asking me all these questions? I gotta go. I'm busy," he said.

"Have you seen this person?" asked Mickey showing him the driver's license photo.

"No, Man. I ain't seen him," he said.

"Thank you, but would you mind just looking at the photo, please?" asked Mickey politely.

"I didn't see nobody! I told you that!"

"Who didn't you see?" asked Mickey again.

"The lady driving that car! I ain't answering no more questions."

"What lady?"

"The one driving that car?" he said as he started to close the door.

Mickey put his foot in the door to keep it from closing. "I didn't say a lady was driving it," Mickey said.

"Well, whoever you're talking about."

"And what car am I talking about?"

"The car with the busted light. Man, you must be deaf or something," the tenant said, agitated by this time as he tried once more to close the door by pushing Mickey's foot away from it.

"Got it. I thought you didn't see anything?"

"I didn't. Now, I tell you, I gotta go to work."

"Okay, sir. Do you live here?" Mickey asked.

"Yeah. Why do you need to know? That ain't none of your business," he said, getting irritated at Mickey.

"Just wondering. Thank you, sir. I'll let you get to work. Have a nice day." Mickey turned to leave, then turned back to ask, "Where do you work, sir?"

"That's none of your business either! Now get out of here. I said I gotta go!" he stated emphatically. "You're just the maintenance man. You said so yourself. So, where I work is none of your business."

"I do hope that information is current and up to date on your rental application. If it isn't, that's reason to cancel your lease and require you to vacate the premises."

"That information is private between the rental office and me, not some flunky maintenance man."

"Yes, sir. That's correct. I'm just the maintenance supervisor. As I said, sir, have a nice day." Mickey smiled, lifted his phone, and snapped a picture of the man. He then turned and walked away.

The man bolted out the door, and grabbed Mickey's arm, then spun him around as he exclaimed to Mickey, "Hey, man! You can't go around taking pictures of people like that."

"I can, and I did. I don't need your permission to take your picture."

"Yes, you do. You can't do that. I'll sue you for taking that picture. You delete it right now!"

"Sorry, I can't do that. I think I'd like another one." Mickey lifted his phone once again and snapped another one.

The tenant pulled back his fist to punch Mickey. Mickey reached up and grabbed the man's arm, twisted it around his back, and pushed it up until the man groaned with pain.

"Hey, you can't do that. I'll have you arrested for assault," he called out between groans.

"I can't do what?" Mickey asked, still holding his arm almost up to his shoulder blade.

"Just go around taking pictures of people without their permission. Man, let go. It hurts. I gonna have your job for assaulting me. I swear!"

"There's no law against taking pictures of anyone. Now, do you want me to tell the police how you assaulted me and I defended myself? We can call the police, and they will ask you a lot of personal questions. Do you really want to do that? I haven't harmed you in any way. Now, can we go back into your unit and talk? How about it?"

"No way, man. You can't come into my house without my permission. I know my rights," he scowled.

"At least you can give me your name and some identification proving you live here," said Mickey calmly.

"Nope. You ain't the police, and I ain't gotta talk to you, so let me go. You show me some ID. I'm gonna call the office and report you."

"That sounds like a great idea. Go ahead. When you do, be sure to give the office manager my name. Then we'll call the police and bring them back with a warrant for your arrest and a search warrant," Mickey said.

"Let me go!" he screamed.

Mickey shoved him forward, and he stumbled and fell onto the lawn. Mickey took out his wallet, removed a business card, and threw it on the ground next to the man. Mickey carried business cards with his name and title of maintenance supervisor. He also had different cards naming him as managing director of Christianson Real Estate.

The man got up, screamed an expletive at Mickey, ran back to his unit, and slammed the door.

Mickey walked to his truck and called Sam, who was getting a unit ready to rent.

"Hey, Sam, can you pull yourself free for a while? Come over to unit 140. I need some help here."

"I'll be there as soon as I can, Mickey. I'm here at Senior Village right now, so it'll take me a few minutes to lock up and drive over there."

Mickey moved his truck to the end of the parking lot and waited for Sam. While waiting, the tenant came out of the unit, got in a beat-up old Ford, and drove away. Mickey snapped a picture of the license plate as he drove by. The tenant raised his middle finger at Mickey as he passed him on the way out of the parking lot. While he waited for Sam to get here, he called the rental office of Black Forrest Village.

"Hello, Susan. This is Mickey Ray. I'm over at unit 140. Can you tell me the tenant's name that's renting that unit? Also, if you will, can you email me his application. I'd appreciate it."

"Sure, Mickey Ray. Is there a problem?" she asked.

"I don't know quite yet. I'm sending you a photo of a car. If you have any information on it, let me know," he said. "I need it ASAP."

He hung up and sent the photo to the office email address from his phone. Sam drove up and parked beside him.

"Good afternoon, Boss. What's up?"

"Hey, Sam," Mickey answered. "We may have a problem with the guy in unit 140." Mickey took a few minutes to tell Sam what happened and the tenant's attitude.

"Well, Mickey Ray, no offense, but at times you do tend to be a bit abrasive. Maybe you just caught him on a bad day."

"Possibly, but I doubt it. He got too defensive too quickly, and I was my wonderful, polite self, I'll have you know," said Mickey smiling sarcastically.

"Does this have anything to do with that little girl you found the other day? How's she doing?" Sam asked.

"Yes, it does, and Dee has her right now. She's doing fine. DCS has given Dee temporary custody until we find her parents," said Mickey. "The guy in unit 140 may have nothing to do with her, but I want to check him out, just in case. I don't like him. I want to go into his unit and look around."

"You know, legally, we can't do that without a twenty-four-hour notice. Even then, if the tenant says 'no,' we can't go in without a judge's permission."

"Sure, we can. Someone reported smelling gas in that area, so we are going in to check it out. That's an emergency, and we need to do that to protect the other tenants and the property."

"Who reported a gas leak?"

"You did, Sam. You were walking the grounds and smelled a gas leak, so you called the office. Then after talking to Susan, you knocked on the door of the unit. When there was no answer, you went in to check it out."

"Did I find anything, Boss?"

"You didn't find a gas leak inside the unit, but you did find one outside, and you fixed it. While you're at it, you might want to check all the units around it just to cover all the bases and our behinds, in case someone complains that we went into their unit without their permission. Be sure to use your gas detection meter. And be sure to write up a full report of the call, repair, and the units you checked. To get the ball rolling, call Susan at the office and report the leak. We'll go into unit 140 first, in case the tenant comes back before you check the other units. After we finish checking that one out, you check all the others to complete the job. To cover ourselves for entry, we need a paper trail. We need written reports on the problem. A real gas leak can be serious, so going into an apartment without someone being home shouldn't be a problem. If someone isn't home, be sure to leave a note on the door telling them we were there and why. That should protect us."

"I'll make sure all bases are covered, Mickey Ray. Is there anything particular we're looking for?"

"Not at this point. I just want to see why the guy was so belligerent, that's all. I'm sure he had something to hide."

Sam picked up his phone, dialed the office, and reported to Susan, the property manager, the potential problem and told her he would check out all units in the general area of the leak. After disconnecting the call, Sam got his gas detection meter. He and Mickey walked over to the door of unit 140 and let themselves in with the maintenance master key.

"Sam, do you still keep latex gloves on your truck?" asked Mickey.

"Of course I do. I use latex gloves when I work on sewers," he answered.

"Good, get each of us a pair to wear, so we don't leave any fingerprints when we search the unit."

"Sure. Got it, Boss," Sam said, turning to go to his truck.

Sam returned a few minutes later with the gloves, and Mickey unlocked the door and stepped inside.

As they stood looking around the apartment, Mickey commented, "It never ceases to amaze me how some people live. Look at this place. It's a pigsty. Half-eaten pizzas are still in the box on the kitchen table. I'll bet dirty clothes are lying on the floor in their bedrooms. Okay, Sam, let's see what we can find. Be sure to look in the closets."

They each split up, with Mickey heading for one bedroom and Sam moving toward the other.

"Yep, this one's a wreck," said Mickey looking around the room and snapping a few pictures with his phone. "There are clothes everywhere. You can't tell which ones are dirty and which ones are clean."

Sam responded from the other room. "This one's not so bad. There's a pile of dirty clothes in the corner, but at least the clean clothes are hanging in the closet. There's a computer in here along with a paper shredder. I'll take a look in the desk drawers."

Sam thumbed through the stack of papers on the bedside table and picked at the pile of shredded paper in the paper shredder beside it. He booted up the top-of-the-line computer on the opposite wall. As it booted up, a log-in screen came on, and he shut it back down, knowing they didn't have time to find a password. Sam took pictures of all the papers on the nightstand and the ones lying on the desktop. He looked in drawers and snapped some photos of the few documents in there.

Sam quickly walked around the unit, snapping pictures with his phone for future reference. Mickey began looking, under furniture, in cabinets, and snapping pictures when something looked strange. They rummaged carefully through papers on the kitchen table and counters. Sam found a zip-lock bag of a white substance in the bottom of one of the dresser drawers in the neat bedroom. He knew what it was but didn't touch it. He took photos of it, then he covered it back up and left it completely undisturbed. Mickey found some printouts of emails to a Robert Griffin demanding payment with an attached threat. Mickey snapped pictures of the printouts. After looking around for almost half an hour, they left as they came, leaving no trace of being there.

"Sam, I'm going to print out these pictures we took. You keep on knocking on doors and checking out the other units for gas leaks. As we discussed, this covers us if someone saw us entering that apartment. Be sure to write up the report and turn it in at the office by the end of the day," Mickey told him.

"Shouldn't we report the drugs to the police? We had good reason for entering the unit."

"What? And tell them we were rummaging through the tenant's dresser drawers? We had reason to enter, but NOT to search it. That's illegal. So even if the police went in, how would we explain finding the drugs?"

"We could take them out of the drawer and put them on the kitchen table. Then when the police go in, they'd find the drugs out in the open!" Sam suggested.

"There are several reasons for not doing that. We saw the email to Robert Griffin. That's Carrie's father's name. That could be a clue to his whereabouts. If we report it, the police will raid the place. It would be on the news, which would make this place look like a drug center. I don't want the bad press. Also, if they don't pick up the guy I met this morning, he could go underground, and we may never find him or Carrie's parents," explained Mickey.

"I'll start knocking on doors and checking for the supposed gas leaks. I guess I'll hear from you when I hear from you!"

"You bet, Sam. Thanks for the assistance." Mickey got in his truck to go to Darcy's and stopped at Valarie's apartment on the way.

On Tuesdays, she got off at two in the afternoon. He knocked, and he heard a voice call from inside the apartment.

"Who is it?" she called.

"It's me, Val, Mickey Ray," he answered.

He heard chains moving and bolts sliding back, then the door opened slowly. Valerie peered through the crack at him. When she saw him, she opened the door and let him in. He folded his arms around her in a firm embrace. "It's only me. I came to check up on you. Are you okay today?" he asked softly. "You seemed upset with me this morning when we came in with Carrie."

"Yes, I'm fine, but I still get scared when I'm alone," she said, trembling.

As she stood there with her head on his chest, he stroked her hair and spoke to her calmly. "I understand, honey. It'll eventually go away, and you'll be your old self again." He put his hand under her chin, raised her head to look at him, then gave her a soft, gentle kiss.

She wrapped her arms around him and returned the kiss lovingly. She backed away and flipped her long auburn hair back across her shoulders and looked up at him with her deep green eyes, and smiled.

She slowly backed away from him and said, "I know I'll be fine, but those nightmares come every time I close my eyes. I feel so awful. Will you take me out, Mickey?"

"Where do you want to go, Val?"

"Anywhere, just somewhere happy. How about going to a nice restaurant to get something to eat? We need to talk."

Even though she worked at the local diner as a waitress, she loved to go out to eat. It didn't have to be fancy, just out around people and food she didn't have to deliver to a table. She went to school taking some college classes at night, but she had dropped out this past semester to take a breather from school.

"We can do that. Do you mind if we stop and visit for a few minutes with Pop and detour by Darcy's before we eat?" he asked.

"Sure, Mickey Ray, we can do that. He's getting better, and I always like talking to him, even when he doesn't remember me," she said.

"It's taken you quite a while, but you have your new place looking good since you moved here."

"Thank you. At least it's good that I had fire insurance. I miss the family pictures I had hanging in the bedroom, and now that you let me move into this apartment, I don't have to mow the yard anymore. You know that I feel like I should pay rent. I don't like living here free!"

"I know, Val. We've talked about this before."

"Let's go, Mickey," she said as she grabbed a sweater out of the closet.

When they got to the rehab center to see his father, they went to his room. Daniel had been staying here since his accident several months ago. He still had memory problems, but Mickey visited him several times a week and talked about past experiences and memories. The time they spent together was therapeutic for Daniel, and it always lifted both of their spirits. Daniel was responding well, and Mickey enjoyed seeing his father.

Daniel was sitting in a chair facing the window. He was looking at a squirrel in the tree just outside the window. Daniel didn't know that Mickey and Val were there until Mickey spoke.

"Hey, Pop," Mickey said as he and Valerie entered the room.

He turned and saw Mickey and Val standing in the doorway. He hesitated, then spoke slowly. "Hello, Valerie. Hello, Mickey Ray. How're both of you today?"

Valerie blushed. "Gosh, Mr. Christianson, you remembered me! That's so good."

"Well, I get a little better each day, Valerie. I don't know how I could ever forget such a beautiful lady like you, my dear," he said with a smile.

He turned toward Mickey and said, "I love it when you come to visit with me. And especially when you bring such lovely ladies to see me." Then he gave Micky a wink.

"Thanks, Pop. She is beautiful, isn't she?" Mickey winked back.

"Stop it, both of you. You're embarrassing me!" She continued to blush and giggled.

Daniel motioned to the two chairs in the room. "Please, sit down."

"I'm in physical therapy, Valerie. I hope to be able to walk again in a few weeks. By the end of this week, I hope to be at least using a walker."

"That's great, Pop. You'll go from walker to cane and then walking without any help," said Mickey Ray.

"I certainly hope so, son," Daniel said.

They talked for a few more minutes, and Mickey sat back as Val and his father talked. They were smiling. It was the first time they had both smiled in months. Mickey felt that progress for both of them was finally showing. Maybe soon, they would both be their old selves again.

After spending almost an hour with Daniel, Mickey and Val left. They went to an Italian restaurant and ate pasta until they were both stuffed. They had a glass of wine, and their troubles seemed so far away.

"We need to talk more about that little girl."

"No, we don't. I'll find her parents in a day or so, and we'll never hear from them ever again."

"But what if you don't find them?" asked Val.

"We will."

"You don't know that, Mickey Ray," she explained.

"Sure, I do. Who would leave a little girl in a wheelchair all alone if they didn't intend on coming back to get her?"

"That's exactly my point, Mickey. No one would. Something has happened to her mother!"

"Okay, so what's your point? I'll find her!"

"It won't be that easy."

"You don't know that, Val."

"The fact that it's been twenty-four hours or more and the police haven't had any reports of a missing child. A good mother wouldn't do that. Common sense means that something's happened to her mother."

"I'm taking you home now, Val. You're getting upset and unreasonable."

"You're getting involved in something that isn't your business, Mickey Ray," she said. "Something isn't right, and I don't like you getting involved."

"I can't just throw her out or not try to help her."

"Why are you doing this, Mickey? The police do that. It isn't your job," she said, now raising her voice.

Mickey raised his hands in a stop motion. "Shh, Val, please don't raise your voice. We don't want the others here to hear our troubles."

"Mickey, we need to talk about this now. You're getting involved in things you should stay out of," she said with a trembling voice.

"I'm trying to help a little girl, Valerie. Don't you understand?"

"Mickey, you can't help every waif that crosses your path!" she said in a softer voice now.

"I'm not, Val...."

"Yes, you are, Mickey. I've been thinking. I think we should postpone our engagement."

"Hold on, Valerie. Are you still seeing the counselor I recommended?"

"That's not the issue here, Mickey, and you know it!"

"Yes, it is. It would be best if you kept seeing the counselor. He'll help you get past your problems," he said softly to keep others in the restaurant from hearing their conversation.

"I don't need to keep going to a counselor. He isn't doing anything. I can't sleep, and when I do, I still have nightmares. I still get scared when I'm alone."

"Valerie, you need to keep seeing the counselor. These things take time. You can't heal overnight," he said, reaching across the table and taking her hand.

"I'm not crazy, Mickey Ray. I don't need to see a shrink anymore. He isn't helping. I need more space. I don't need this pressure," she insisted.

"Of course, you aren't crazy. I know that. No one has said or even thinks that you're crazy. You need help with dealing with your fears. That's all."

"Fears! Fears! You have no idea what I went through, Mickey Ray. I thought I was going to die. I wake up in cold sweats that someone is going to sell me to some crazy sex pervert! You are getting right back into it with that little girl, Mickey."

"I'm just going to help her find her parents. Nothing will happen. I Promise."

"You can't make a promise like that, Mickey Ray Christianson. You know you can't! I can't deal with this anymore!" she said, slamming her hands on the table and standing up. "I don't want to get married now!"

"You don't mean that, Valerie. I'm taking you home now, Val. You are getting upset and unreasonable," he said, putting down his silverware and motioning to the server. Mickey felt very uncomfortable now because everyone in the restaurant had eyes on them.

The server came over, and Mickey asked for the check. When he left, Val sat back down.

"Are you breaking up with me?" he asked quietly so as not to attract attention again.

"No, I'm not breaking up. I'm not even calling off the wedding. I just need some more time. It would be best if you got your priorities in order. You choose me or this savior complex that you have to help everyone!"

"What happened last time was not my fault, and I had to do what I did to save my family and you, I might add," he said defensively.

"I understand that, and I sort of agree, but even then, you should have called the police and let them handle it. You and James stormed that place like you were in a war zone. James is trained for that stuff. You're not, Mickey Ray Christianson."

Mickey sat looking down at his lap like a chastened child. He didn't know what to say.

"Mickey, I love you so much, but I was terrified. I thought I would die. True, you and James came and rescued me, but...."

"But what, Valerie? I did what I had to do. I had to do it, and I would do it again. It was a one-time experience. It'll never happen again. I promise."

"You can't promise that," she said.

"I can. How many times has something like that happened? People have rental properties and apartment complexes all over the country, and this has never happened. It won't happen again.

"You need to get back into counseling to help you through it. If you want to postpone the wedding, that's fine. It'll give you more time to get things straight. I understand," Mickey said calmly.

"I'm not crazy, Mickey! I don't need counseling. I need all this stuff to go away. Just take me home, now. Please, Mickey?"

Mickey paid the bill. They rode on in silence until Mickey pulled into the apartment complex where they each lived.

"Valerie, are you sure you want to cancel the wedding?"

"No, Mickey. I told you, I don't want to cancel it. I want to postpone it for a while. I still want to get married, but not anytime soon. NOT NOW." Val got out, slammed the door, and walked to her apartment.

Mickey was shocked but hoped that Valerie would come around and change her mind. He had to get out of the mood he was in right now. Seeing Dee and the kids would make him feel a lot better. First, he'd take a ride. He loved driving through the countryside around Bridgeton. It relaxed him and helped him clear his mind.

CHAPTER 3

Tuesday Evening...The Mysterious Tenant

AFTER LEAVING VAL AT HER APARTMENT and going for a drive, Mickey went to Darcy's house. He still felt upset, but he would shake it off. Knocking on the door, he called out to Darcy, waiting for an answer.

"I'm back here, Mickey. In my office. Come on back," answered Darcy.

As Mickey walked down the hallway to her office, he noticed that both children's bedrooms were empty.

Darcy was sitting behind her office desk, and James was sitting in front of her. "Where's Carrie?" he asked.

"Mickey, have a seat. James took everyone to one of Cyndi's friend's houses to play for a while."

James Bower, Mickey's best friend, was engaged to Darcy. He was ex-military and got out on disability after being burned over a large percentage of his body sustained during a mission. The injuries included his hands, arms, and face. He lived at the Senior Apartment Complex owned by the Christianson's. Although he was in his late twenties, he was allowed to live in the Senior's Complex because most of the other residents were retired military, and they considered James one of their brothers in arms. Although he wasn't in their actual age group, they took him under their wings.

James had a soft spot for children, and Darcy's two kids loved him, despite his scarred face. When he wanted to be in public several times a week, he would dress up as a clown to hide his scarred face. James would apply full face paint and entertain kids at the local mall by doing magic tricks and making balloon animals. He had skills he learned in the military and had contacts that had gotten Mickey and Darcy out of a deadly situation just a few months before.

"Hey, James. What brings you here?" asked Mickey.

"Nothing particular. I just stopped by to see Dee for a few minutes. I see Dee has a new house guest," James said.

Mickey smiled at James. "Yes, she does. She's a sweetheart, isn't she? I hope we can help her find her parents."

"I hope so too. I'll help you any way I can, bro," James answered.

"Let me fill you in on what happened today," Mickey said. He proceeded to tell them about the guy in unit 140 and how he responded to Mickey's questions.

"Why didn't you call the police to have him arrested for drug possession?" James asked.

"It would be inadmissible in court because of the way we found it. Without that, the police have no case. Also, I want more information from him. If he's in jail, we get nothing. If he skips town, we get nothing. James, do you have any equipment to bug his apartment?"

In mock surprise, James put his hand to his mouth. "Why Mickey Ray, that would be illegal!"

"I won't tell if you don't, James," Mickey said.

"Deal. What do you want? I can get bugs for his apartment, landline, and even his cell phone. It might cost a couple of hundred, but that's easy and not all that expensive."

Mickey knew that James had ex-military contacts. He could get strictly illegal supplies on the black market and knew men that had served in similar capacities. In short, James knew people.

"Great. Get what you can, James. Let Darcy know how much you need to buy it. Did Susan forward the application on the tenant in unit 140?" Mickey asked Darcy.

"Yes, she did. His name is Alan Halston, and he's from Raleigh, North Carolina. He put on the rental application that he was a route salesman for

TOPLINE auto parts. They're an auto parts wholesale company. I called the company, and the number was disconnected. I checked with the local courthouse for a business license for that company, and it doesn't exist."

"We have all applicants checked out. The office manager is supposed to check these people out. Why didn't they catch it?" Mickey asked.

"Most of the time, background checks are not that in-depth. Some people don't have regular jobs or bad credit, or maybe they've been put out of their last apartment or just moved out in the middle of the night. If you don't take them to court, there is no legal record of their poor paying record. They lie on their rental application so the landlord will rent to them. It happens all the time. Rental agents do a cursory check, and that's about all. People give their friend or relatives' addresses or phone numbers as their place of employment or as their last landlord. When the rental agent calls to get a reference, their Uncle John gives them a good reference so that we'll rent to them," Darcy explained.

"I never realized that. I just did what Pop told me to do on the maintenance end," Mickey said as he shrugged his shoulders.

"Yes, that's the part that most people don't understand," Darcy said. "Managing property is a lot harder than it looks. Now back to the situation at hand. They did run an internet check on Alan Halston, and there was no adverse information on him listed. So, that may be why his application was accepted."

Darcy continued, "The person listed as the car owner is Beverly Griffin. I searched for that name also, and she seems to be the sister of Robert Griffin. We have a connection, guys. We don't take photos of tenants when they move in, so we don't know if the picture you took, Mickey, is our registered tenant or just his roommate. I can't find a picture of Robert Griffin or Alan Halston."

Mickey said, "If this guy had just answered my questions about the photos, and the car, I wouldn't have suspected anything, and we wouldn't be here. When he immediately got belligerent and defensive, I knew something was up. When we found the email with Carrie's father's name and the drugs hidden in a drawer, we decided we needed to take other action."

James spoke up, "When do you need the eavesdropping stuff? I can probably get it tomorrow. There's nothing special about any of that kind of equipment. We can listen to everything there by noon tomorrow afternoon if I pick it up early enough. Do you want a GPS tracker for his car? Last time you used an old cell phone. It worked, but I have to admit, it was kind of lame."

"Lame maybe, but I didn't have access to things like you do. It was creative, and as you pointed out, it worked," said Mickey defensively.

Darcy intervened, "Okay, boys, let's not argue. You're both pretty innovative. We need to move on this. Right now, Carrie is homeless, and if we don't find her parents, DCS'll take her and put her into the system and permanent foster care. We don't want that."

"I agree," said Mickey. "James, you get the equipment, and I'll check with Sam and see if we can get some extra help to stake out the place 24/7."

James spoke up again, "Mickey, I can get some guys to do that. They're trained for that kind of activity and can blend in the scenery."

"That's good, James, but we don't need an ex-Navy seal team. We just need some guys to sit around, not be seen, and notify me when weasel guy leaves the place," said Mickey.

"Right, and when 'weasel guy,' as you call him, does move, you want someone that can follow him unobtrusively, and get proper and accurate information back to you, right?" retorted James.

"Who are these guys you're referring to? When you were in the army, did you work for Black Ops 'R' Us? Guys like that cost a fortune. We don't have that much cash right now. We're still recovering financially from the incident we had last year!"

"Mickey, there's a little girl without her parents right now. These guys will go to hell and back for a child. I can get a discount, and you can put the fees on an account. They understand things like this. Last, they're my brothers. They owe me," James said as he looked Mickey straight in the eyes.

Mickey shook his head like he was trying to clear some mental cobwebs. "You never cease to amaze me, James. Now, these guys have 'accounts?' Do they have tax ID numbers and send me a bill each month like I just shopped at a retail store? Whatever they might charge, all I need is a couple of guys with a car and a cell phone. On this, thanks,

James, but I can get someone cheaper that I can afford and not run up a huge tab."

"Suit yourself, but remember, bro, you get what you pay for." James sat back and folded his hands.

Darcy sighed, watching the face-off between her cocky brother and her fiancé.

"Mickey, now, if you guys are finished showing off your plumage like a couple of peacocks, let's move on. James, if you can get the equipment we need, please do it. Mickey, whatever calls you need to make to get some people to stake out unit 140, then you do it."

"Got it," said James.

"I'll get right on it, Dee," said Mickey.

"Good, now both of you get out of my house. I have to give Carrie her medication, come back here, get some legal work done for my employers and send it to them before morning so I can get a paycheck."

James and Mickey left Darcy's house intent on their assignments.

CHAPTER 4

Wednesday Morning…Surveillance in Unit 143

THE FOLLOWING MORNING ON HIS WAY to follow up on last night's visit with Darcy, he decided to stop and see Daniel. Mickey went straight to the rehab facility where his father had been living since his accident last fall.

When he reached Daniel's room, Mickey saw his father sitting in a wheelchair, looking out of the window.

Daniel turned and smiled. "Hello, Mickey Ray. It's great to see you today."

"It's a great day, Pop."

"I'm going to Physical Therapy, but my mind still isn't clear. There's so much I don't remember."

"I know, Pop, but hopefully, in time, it'll all come back," said Mickey.

"I just don't know. Today's a good day, but tomorrow, I may not remember what day it is or where I am."

"Don't worry about it, Pop. I'll come to see you every day, and we'll work with you and help you get better so you can go home again."

"Mickey, I do miss Eleanor. I hope she's doing fine now. Is she getting better too?"

"No. You don't remember this, but Mom's gone. She has been gone for about six months."

"Would you take a minute to tell me again what happened to her? I know you have told me several times, but just one more time if you don't mind."

"Sure, Pop. You see, this group of people insisted that you help them in a human trafficking ring they had going in this area. You didn't know exactly what they wanted, but you knew it was wrong, so you refused to bow to their demands. When you refused, they put out a contract on you. They hired someone to cause an accident. Instead of killing you, Mom was killed. You were injured and came to this facility to recover. James and I put a stop to the business, and most of the people are dead now. We got justice for Mom."

A tear formed in Daniel's eye and ran down his face. "Right, you keep telling me, and I keep forgetting. I miss her, son."

Sitting down in a chair in front of his father, Mickey said, "I know, Pop, me too. I don't mean to upset you by continually telling you that, but it helps you remember things so you can get better."

"I need to know all the things I forgot. We need to find out who killed your mother so I can go home."

"We already took care of that too, Pop. You can go home as soon as you remember a few more things so that you can take care of yourself."

"Darcy'll be coming by maybe later today. She wants to bring Cyndi and Joel to see you too."

"Cyndi and Joel? They're such wonderful children," he asked, clearly confused but determined to remember his grandchildren. "Never mind, Mickey Ray. I remember them. How're they doing?"

"Yes, Pop, they are good kids, and they are excited to see you too."

Mickey and Daniel talked a few more minutes before Mickey had to go so he could make arrangements for someone to watch unit 140. He hugged his father, and he left. Daniel was drying tears from his face. Daniel was crying most of the time when Mickey left. Daniel was trying so hard to remember his past. His memories of Eleanor and the 35 years of marriage with their two kids were fuzzy and disjointed. Mickey tried to be positive and supportive of his father even though Daniel's memories were scrambled and fragmented. Mickey hoped his father's memories would return someday.

Mickey left the facility and drove to the diner. While waiting for his order to come up, he reached into his pocket, took out his phone, and dialed.

Mickey said, "Hey Glen, what's up, man?"

"Hey, Mickey. Not much is happening here. What's going on with you?" came the answer.

"I need some help for a couple of days. You busy?"

"Sorry, Mickey Ray. I can't help you out. I fell and broke my arm at a job a few weeks ago, and my arm is in a sling for a few more weeks. Maybe I can hook you up with a friend of mine instead," he said.

"Glen, I don't need your arm, so you can still help me. I was hoping you could keep an eye out on a place for me. Watch and see who comes and goes. You know what I mean. Surveillance job. And I could still use your friend. I need it staked out 24/7 for a few days, maybe a week. Interested?" Mickey asked.

"That's right down my alley. I'll give George a call. He could use the work also," he said enthusiastically. "I'll call you back, Mickey. Thanks."

Glen had helped Mickey and Sam for a while to maintain the property until his parents died in a plane crash a couple of years ago. He got a small inheritance that helped him with basic living needs, but he was always looking for a few bucks to help out. As long as Glen had a few dollars in his pocket, he avoided work, but when the money ran out, he called Mickey for a few odd jobs here and there. He hung around with another friend, George, that also helped doing unskilled day labor. Neither man was skilled but could be reliable for short, simple jobs.

About halfway through his lunch, his phone buzzed. He picked it up and taking a quick look at the screen he saw it was James.

"Hello, James."

"Hey Mickey, I have the equipment you want. We can install it anytime you're ready. I have three GPS's that we can install on cars, five wireless mics to go in the unit, and a high-power wi-fi range extender. We can use a nice piece of equipment to scan his phone and clone it. If we get close enough, we can get all the information, including contacts installed on it."

"How close do we need to be to get it?" asked Mickey.

"About four feet. And no other cell phones around to interfere," James said.

"Wow, that's pretty close. That may not be so easy."

"Piece of cake, Mickey Ray," James said confidently. "You just need to know someone that knows what he's doing."

"I still can't figure out how all this ties into Carrie, her mother, or her father. I'd still like to know where Carrie's mother is and why she left her out in the park that night. I think something terrible happened to her. A good mother doesn't do something like that and not come back."

"True. I agree, Mickey Ray. The tie-in is that email you found, and then we can get more info on her parents. We need to be patient. Something kept Carrie's mother from coming back to get her the other night. As soon as we find out why she left Carrie, we can find her. If we act too quickly, we'll scare them off. They might take drastic measures. Easy does it, bro."

"I'm here at the diner. Come on by, and we can go take a look to determine if we can put the bugs into place." Mickey disconnected his phone and placed it on the table.

Mickey got a refill on his drink. A short while later, James walked into the diner and sat down at the table with Mickey.

"I wish we had a vacant apartment closer to unit 140, but the closest I have is 143, across the street. Will your equipment broadcast that far?" asked Mickey.

"Yeah, across the street will be perfect. It's state-of-the-art stuff," said James.

"Visual is fine. We can see the unit from that distance, but we still need a good zoom on the camera to get good clear pictures."

Their server brought them each a drink to go. They left the diner and drove to Black Forrest Village.

They drove past unit 140 without stopping. The blue car with the broken headlight had not moved. The Ford that the weasel guy had driven previously was parked in front of the unit. They parked in front of unit 143 and let themselves inside. James walked around the apartment while Mickey looked out the window at the entrance to the unit where the weasel guy lived.

James came back into the living room and commented to Mickey, "These places pretty much all look the same, don't they?"

"Yes," answered Mickey as he continued looking through the blinds on the window. "They're cheaper to build that way. Also, when a person sees the model apartment, they know what the apartment they're renting will look like."

Mickey turned and looked around. "We can set up in here. We'll get a coffee pot for the kitchen, some bathroom supplies, maybe a few snacks for the guys to nibble on. I'm sure a stakeout's a boring job."

"Yes, they are, and sometimes you aren't in a nice, comfortable apartment. Did you find someone to watch?"

"I called a guy that used to work for me. He isn't always the most motivated person as far as employment, but he'll do fine when he needs money. All he has to do is look out the window and take a few pictures when someone comes and goes. It isn't rocket science."

"We can put a wi-fi range extender/transceiver on the front wall of the building. It'll act as a repeater for the wi-fi signal. We'll be able to detect the phone signal when someone dials out, but we may not be able to tell him from other calls in the building."

"What's a repeater? And won't that be a bit obvious?" asked Mickey.

"A repeater picks up a signal, amplifies it, then resends it back out. They work on most things, but they must be tuned to a certain frequency. Cell phones and wi-fi, TV, and radio are all on different bandwidths. This one is multi-band, so it'll pick up a cell phone and wi-fi signals. Mounting it won't be obvious if someone's working on the entire front of the building, especially on a tall ladder. They start at one end of the building, do something that looks like real work, then work to the other end. Put the repeater on when in position. Simple."

Mickey thought for a moment, then said, "Sounds about right. I'll call Sam to bring a ladder and place the equipment in a few minutes. In the meantime, we can keep an eye on the front until he leaves."

"After he leaves, we can go in and place the bugs. We can set up the monitoring equipment now, then come back later when the crew arrives to use it," said James.

They began setting up a folding table, a recorder, a small telescope, and a tripod with a mounted camera. James set up a receiver unit to monitor all cell phone calls.

Sam arrived in a few minutes and placed his ladder on one end of the building after going to unit 143, where James gave him the equipment. In about half an hour, Sam had completed his fake work. He had mounted the kit on the front of the building as Mickey had instructed. While Sam was loading his tools into the truck, the skinny weasel guy came out, got in his car, and drove away.

Seeing the guy in unit 140 leave, Mickey and James went into the apartment and placed a wireless microphone in each room. Soon after that, Glen and his friend, George, arrived at the unit. Mickey introduced them to James, and they familiarized themselves with James' equipment. They also brought an air mattress, a couple of sleeping bags, and food to keep in the fridge.

Mickey laughed. "You're prepared, aren't you?"

"Yeah, man," Glen answered. "You said you wanted that apartment covered twenty-four hours a day for the next few days, so we came prepared. You pay us for a twenty-four-hour day, and we decide the hours we each put in and split it accordingly. Also, we don't have to leave since we'll eat and sleep here until you kick us out. How's that for efficiency, chief?"

Mickey laughed, "Glen, sounds like a plan to me, but if you're going to live here, you clean up after yourselves. I don't want to send in a cleaning crew when you leave. You leave it as you found it, or I'll take cleaning fees out of your pay!"

Glen put out his hand for Mickey to shake and said, "Deal, my friend. Now, how long are you estimating that you need us."

"I hope only a couple of days, but I'm sure we can wrap this thing up in a week."

Mickey's phone rang, and when he answered it, he listened, shook his head, and said to the caller, "Okay, I'll be right there."

Mickey turned to James, "Since you're riding with me, let's go. That was Sam. He needs me to come over to unit 195. It seems that the tenants skipped out and trashed the place."

They drove one block to unit 195, where Sam was waiting for them. When James saw the unit's condition, his eyes popped open, and his jaw dropped in astonishment. It was a disaster. James couldn't believe that people could live like this and then move out and leave it in such a filthy condition.

Sam was standing in the living room area with his hands on his hips, shaking his head. "Hey, Boss. I know what we need to do. I just thought you should see it before I get some guys over here to clean out this crap."

"Sure, Sam. Do it. Let's get this place back on the market as soon as possible."

James looked around. "I bet you hate seeing one as bad as this, Mickey."

"Landlords deal with this all the time. This one, as bad as it looks, isn't all that bad."

James shook his head. "I don't understand. They left half their furniture here. There's a huge couch. I looked in the bedrooms. They left both sets of mattresses and bedsprings and a large dresser with the drawers lying upside down on the floor in one room. Filthy clothes are lying all over the floor. The stove is covered in grease, and the refrigerator looks like a science experiment. How do you deal with it?"

"Most tenants are like this. They don't have much, so they don't know how to care for themselves or others. They're users. They stay in a place until they destroy it, then move on to another place, and it starts over. Couches and mattresses are large items. When they move, they put all they can into the back of their car or borrow a friend's truck. This stuff doesn't fit into a truck bed or a small trailer, so they leave it. Someone gives them another one, or they buy more at a used furniture store or garage sale. Many times the tenants don't even have bed frames. They put the mattress on the floor. It's also the perfect time to weed out their old clothes, so they pack what they want and leave the old. They figure they'll not get their security deposit back, so they don't clean it up. They just walk out, and most of the time, they don't even pay the last month's rent."

"Is everyone like this?" James asked.

"There are exceptions, of course, but most are like this. Good tenants who take care of a unit are rare and hard to find. You better take good care of them when you get a good one. The sad thing is, if tenants would take care of the unit and clean it when they leave, they'd get their deposit back. We refund thousands of dollars to tenants every year. People rarely leave a unit clean. More often than not, it looks like this. Even good tenants sometimes leave a unit like this."

"How much does it cost to get a unit ready to re-rent."

"Let's see. It'll cost a couple hundred to get some guys in here with a truck to move the furniture out and haul it to the dump or put it in the dumpster. We then get a cleaning service to clean the unit, which includes that nasty stove and fridge. Next a carpet service to shampoo the carpet, if we don't have to replace it. Then a pest control to spray for roaches, and last, we have to paint the entire apartment. All of that will be charged to the tenant, except for the painting. Add to that the lost rent during the repair time. So, it costs us two, maybe three thousand dollars for each vacancy."

"Can't you take them to court to recover the cost?"

"Sure, you can take them to court, but most of the time, you can't collect. It's just lost money that the landlord absorbs."

"Wow, I never realized all the headaches you put up with, Mickey."

"That's why many rental property owners are selling to investment companies. Private people either can't afford the costs or just can't take the aggravation, and they get out from under the problems. Let's get out of here, so Sam can get started."

James got out when Mickey took him back to his Humvee at the diner. "Wow, it was a real education on the rental business. I guess I'll not be getting into the rental market anytime soon. For now, all we can do is wait for word from your friends on surveillance. Hey, you want to work out at the gym for a while? We haven't gotten back into our routine since we got back from our last trip."

"That sounds good to me, but I have a few errands to run. I'll meet you at the gym first thing in the morning."

Mickey drove along, and his mind wandered to everything that had happened in the past few months. He took some of the back roads he drove when he wanted to clear his mind. He looked around at the foliage on the evergreens and the bare branches of the other trees. It would be early spring in another month, and the sun shined through the bare branches peeking through the scattered clouds that hung over the winding road. Even though it was the same road, the view looked different to him. He felt different now. It wasn't as relaxing as it used to be. He knew what made it different. His innocence was gone. He felt like a child that had finally realized there was no Santa Claus. The wonder of the world had gotten real. Someone had killed Mom, and Pop was in rehab. Everything had changed. He had changed.

James had told him the events that happened a few months ago would change him, and James was correct. Mickey Ray was now a man. In some ways, he was a veteran in many areas of life. Last year at this time, he was just a maintenance person for his parents' property. Now he and Dee were the managers of several million dollars of rental property. Pop was no longer in charge. Before, Mickey Ray did what his father told him to do. Dee handled the legal and bookkeeping part of the management, but Mickey now made the everyday decisions. He now decided when to replace an appliance. A simple word from him determined if a carpet should be replaced or cleaned. Should he have the tree whose branches hung over the roof of a building trimmed or just cut down the entire tree? He also decided when to hire extra help and what they should be paid depending on their skill. Last month, he got proposals on a new roof on one of the apartment buildings. He had never done that before. After many phone calls and negotiations with contractors, he authorized a thirty-thousand-dollar roof replacement.

He and Darcy had meetings about various tenants. Who they would evict for non-payment of rent, and who they should give more time to get their finances in order? Who should they take to court for back rent? Who they should forgive their debts? As expenses went up, they had to increase rents. Which tenants could afford increases and who could not? Either way, they had bills and upkeep costs that seemed to rise constantly.

To help with cash flow problems they had incurred during the past year, he and Darcy had met with bankers to arrange for a ten-million-dollar loan to get them on stable financial ground since their parents' accident. He had to submit a resume' stating his maintenance qualifications in conjunction with Darcy's ability to manage the office and financial duties. Another first for him, and though he would never admit it, it frightened him to sign such a considerable loan amount. Releasing Pop from all responsibility was the result of signing the loan papers. Now, he and Darcy were millions of dollars in debt. He now lived in a different world.

It seemed that life had gotten exponentially more complicated. His countryside rides would never be the same.

Mickey went to visit with Daniel again.

"Hey, Pop. How're you doing?" he said enthusiastically.

"I'm doing fine, Mickey Ray. I'm not sure, but weren't you here earlier today? Sometimes, I get time mixed up. I still get confused," Daniel said, not quite sure if he was correct.

"Yes. I was here earlier. I know you're having a good day, and I wanted to spend some more time with you. I hope that's okay."

"Mickey Ray, you know that I always look forward to you coming to see me. I'm looking forward to getting back home. How is Eleanor doing? Is she getting along and recovering from her injuries too?"

"She's doing fine, Pop." He didn't like lying to his father like that, but sometimes, he felt that when Daniel was having a good day, he didn't want to spoil it by telling him that his wife of thirty-five years was dead. He just answered him and changed the subject. "Hey, Pop, it's a bit cold outside, but if you want, we can get your coat, and I'll be glad to take you for a spin."

"Sure, son. I'd like that. My coat's over there in the closet. I'll need some help putting it on since I'm in this wheelchair," he answered.

"No problem," Mickey said as he opened the closet door and reached for the heavy coat. He had brought that to him a few weeks ago so he could take his father outside.

He helped Daniel with his coat and then grabbed the chair's handles and wheeled him to the front desk, where Mickey informed the on-duty nurse that they were going for a walk.

She smiled at Daniel and said to him, "Mr. Christianson, you have a wonderful family. They're so considerate to visit so often. Do you remember your daughter coming by with your grandchildren?"

"Yes, I do remember. Didn't Darcy have a little girl in a wheelchair with them? I don't remember who she was," he asked.

"Yes, sir. She's just visiting with your daughter." The nurse was surprised that he remembered Darcy's visit and the little girl in the wheelchair. "That's great that you remembered that." She gave Mickey a wink and a thumbs-up sign.

"Pop, let's take a run around the garden," he said as he gently pushed Daniel's chair toward the door. When they got outside, Daniel pulled the coat tighter around his neck.

"At least the sun's out, and it feels warm on my face. Tell me again what happened to Evelyn, son."

"The sun is nice and warm, Pop. I'll tell you some other time about Aunt Evelyn. We've discussed that several times. Let's enjoy this beautiful day right now. You know that little girl that was here with Dee yesterday?"

"Yes, I remember her. Why's she in a wheelchair, Mickey?"

"I don't know yet. She's such a sweet little girl. Her name's Carrie, and we don't want to upset her right now by asking her too many questions. When she feels more comfortable, I'll try to get some more information from her. We're trying to find her mother. She says her father left them some time ago, so until we find one of her parents, she's staying with Dee. James and I are looking for her mother."

"That's nice that you're trying to help her, Mickey Ray. I like it when we can help people."

Daniel still spoke slowly since his injuries in the accident, and now he still rarely used contractions in his speech. Sometimes if Mickey talked too quickly, his father would furrow his brow and cock his head like a dog questioning what he saw. Mickey knew that his father was trying to process what he was saying. Mickey tried to speak slowly so he could understand. Mickey Ray was patient when talking to his father, and he was elated to see his father's progress.

Mickey talked with his father for a few more minutes, speaking slowly to keep his attention. Occasionally, Daniel would smile and nod his head as though he understood. Mickey didn't know if Pop caught everything, but his father's smile meant so much to him that he kept talking. Finally, he said that they had to go inside. Mickey had to go back to work, and the longer they stayed outside, the colder it seemed to get. He wheeled his father back inside.

He hugged Pop goodbye, and as he did so, he whispered in his ear, "I love you, Pop."

Daniel whispered back, "I know you do, son. I love you too."

Mickey Ray Christianson walked out of that building today, sad that his father was in a wheelchair but happy that Daniel had the best day he had in months. He needed to talk to Darcy again, so he turned the truck towards Darcy's house.

CHAPTER 5

Wednesday Afternoon... Darcy's House and Val's Place

When Mickey got to Darcy's house, as usual, she was in her office and on the phone. She motioned for him to take a seat.

When she hung up, she greeted him with, "Mickey, what's up?"

"I just left the rehab place where Pop is. I'm sure soon they'll boot him out of there," he said.

"And?" Darcy responded.

"Where's he going to go, dear sister?"

"I don't know. I haven't had time to give it any thought."

"I understand, but maybe you need to take some time," he said.

"We'll deal with that when the time comes, Mickey," she said.

"I think we need to deal with it now, or at least in the next few days, possibly the next week or so."

"You think it'll be that soon?"

"I do. I know you have a job, but so do I, and you have the kids, and now you are also taking care of another disabled person. We need to address this soon."

"What do you have in mind?"

"Dad can't live alone yet. I don't have room in my apartment."

"So, you are suggesting that he come live with us?"

"Yes, but before you explode, hear me out," said Mickey.

"Go on."

"You and the kids move back home. I mean to Mom and Pop's house," he said, then sat back in the chair and waited for her reaction.

She sat quietly, thinking about what Mickey had just said. "What do I do, move back into my old room when I was a little girl?"

"No, of course not. You move into the master bedroom, where Mom and Pop slept. Joel can take my old room. Cyndi can take your old room. When Pop comes home, he can take the downstairs guest suite. It has a bedroom, a sitting area, and a full bathroom. It's perfect."

"Do you think Daddy will want to move into that area? What if he wants his old bedroom back?" she asked.

"He can't even get upstairs. He's still between the wheelchair and a walker. He can't live alone. At least not yet. I think he'll understand and agree. Someone should get the use of the house, and when you and James get married, it'll be perfect for both of you," Mickey said with pride.

"What do I do with my townhouse?"

"I'll move in, and when Val and I get married, we'll both live here."

"Sounds fine with me, but you gotta run it by Daddy," she said. "Speaking of getting married, when are you and Val going to get married. After all, you've been engaged to her for quite some time."

"Yeah, about that. She has decided to postpone the marriage."

"For how long, Mickey?" Darcy asked.

"I don't know. She didn't say. She just said she wanted to postpone it."

"Why?"

"She's still having some personal problem over what happened to her last year. She says that she doesn't like that we are getting into things that aren't our business. She's scared that something like that will happen again," he said sadly.

"When did she decide this, and why didn't you tell me?"

"So much has been going on, I didn't have time to tell you. I think it'll pass, Dee. She'll change her mind. It'll be fine."

Darcy leaned back in her chair and said, "Don't be so sure, Mickey. We all went through a lot last year, and it changed us. Valerie hasn't been able to cope with it as well as we have. Maybe you can recommend some counseling for her."

"I suggested that Dee, but she thought I was calling her crazy," Mickey said exasperatedly.

"We all know that she isn't crazy, but sometimes people need some help adjusting to things. Can you bring her by here sometime? Maybe I can talk to her, you know, girl to girl."

Mickey rubbed his hands over his face, trying to relieve his stress right then. "I'll try to get her here, but if she even thinks that the reason I'm bringing her here is for you to talk to her, she won't come."

"I understand. Bring Val by like you're coming by for a short visit."

"I'll try that. I don't know if it'll work, but I'll try it," he said, getting up from the chair. "I guess I better get to work, and I'll bring up the idea to Pop of you moving into his house. I try to see him every day, or at least every other day." With that statement, Mickey got up to leave. As he got up, he asked, "Speaking of getting married, have you and James set a date yet?"

"No. I haven't had time to do anything, but I'm sure it'll be in a few months. Whenever it is, it'll be just a few friends and family. Planning a big wedding is too exhausting, not to mention expensive."

He nodded approval and left Darcy's house for home and a stop at Val's unit at the other end of the building he lived. When he knocked on her door, he could hear her television playing and waited for her to answer. Finally, after the third knock, he started to get his master key out when the door opened just a couple of inches and heard her voice.

"Who is it? Oh, Mickey, it's you. I didn't expect you," Valerie said.

"I know, but when I pulled up into the lot, I thought I would come by for a few minutes. Do you mind?"

"No, I don't mind. I wish you had called first," Valerie said as she closed the door to take off the security chains. She opened it again wide enough for Mickey to enter.

"I'm sorry. You've never asked me to call ahead," he said, a bit concerned.

"I guess I haven't. I didn't mean you can't come over. Sure you can. I just wasn't expecting anyone. That's all."

He pulled her close to him and kissed her. She didn't respond and pulled away.

"What's wrong, Val?"

The Landlord and the Wheelchair Child

"Nothing. Can I get you something to drink? I've got soft drinks or juice. I know you don't like water, but if you want that, I'll get you a glass."

"Sure, how about a cola. I just wanted to come by and tell you my latest idea," Mickey said as he sat on the couch.

"I'd like to hear it. You can talk while I get your drink," she said, walking into the kitchen area.

"I just left Dee's house and ran it by her. She likes it, so I thought I would run it by you. Okay, you know that Mom and Pop's house is sitting vacant now and has been for the past few months while Pop's been in the hospital and rehab."

"Yes, that's such a shame to sit vacant," she said, handing him a glass of cola.

"I think it would be a great idea if she and the kids moved into the main house. When Pop gets well enough to come home, he can move into the downstairs guest area, then Darcy and the kids can have the upstairs bedrooms. It's a perfect arrangement. I move into her townhouse. When she and James get married, they have a nice place with plenty of room, and when you and I get married, we have a place big enough when we have kids! Isn't that a great idea, Val?" Mickey said happily.

"I don't know, Mickey. What does your dad say about it?" she asked.

"He'll love it. Pop knows he can't live alone, and if he could, he doesn't need a house that huge. You know how big that house is, it's five bedrooms upstairs, and that isn't including the guest suite downstairs."

"I don't know, Mickey. Maybe I don't want to live in Darcy's house. Perhaps I want us to get our own house."

"Why not? It's perfect, Val!"

"I don't know, Mickey. I just don't know what I want right now. I told you we can't get married right now. That's way off in the future."

"What's wrong? What did I do? I don't understand," said Mickey, confused.

"Mickey, I love you. You know that, but I just want to be alone right now. Please!"

"Okay. I'll leave, but I don't know what's been wrong with you lately. You're not acting right."

"Please, Mickey. Just leave. Maybe you can come back tomorrow, and I'll feel better."

"No problem. I'll leave. I love you too. I wish you'd just talk to me. That's all."

"I will but another day, Mickey, we'll talk. I promise."

It was still early afternoon, so he decided to go and check on the empty apartment that Sam was working on and maybe help him. He needed the exercise to help calm himself. When he got there, Sam was beginning to paint. Mickey grabbed a paint brush and started to work.

Sam said, "Mickey, something must be wrong. I don't mind you being here, but lately, you have had a lot on your plate and haven't had time to help with the maintenance like you used to do."

"I'm fine, Sam. It does me good to get down in the trenches with you sometimes. I'll trim if you want to roll the walls."

"Sure, Boss. Always glad to have you here. Is it okay if I turn the radio on?"

"Of course, Sam. Anything that makes you happy," said Mickey.

At quitting time, Sam packed up his tools and left Mickey working, painting another room. Mickey continued painting. He liked to paint. It relaxed him. It didn't take a lot of thought, so his mind could wander, and he could forget the cares of what was going on around him. He finished painting the room at one o'clock in the morning, cleaned up the tools, and left. He was tired and sleepy, but he felt good.

CHAPTER 6

Thursday Morning...The Phone Call

MICKEY MET JAMES AT THE GYM on Thursday morning. They did a full workout rotation and then hit the showers. Afterward, they went to the diner for breakfast.

"Mickey, what's wrong? You haven't been yourself all morning. I didn't say anything earlier because you were so intent on the workout that I knew something was wrong and thought maybe you needed the sweaty workout to work it out. You didn't, so it must be very personal."

"Well, to be honest, it's Valerie," said Mickey.

"Can you tell me? Maybe I can help," said James taking a sip of coffee.

"Sorry, my friend. This one you can't help. Val's been acting differently the last few months," Mickey said, looking at James, then turned and looked out the window of the diner.

"What do you mean? Talk to me, Mickey," asked James.

"It is all because of what happened to her last year."

"I don't understand. I thought that after this time, Valerie was getting over it."

"I did too. I can't explain it. She's just different. She said she wants to postpone the wedding. She got mad when she found out that we're trying to help Carrie. Then she got angry again and asked me to leave her apartment again last night."

"What does she expect you to do? And what do you mean she asked you to leave and postpone the wedding?"

"I told her that Darcy might move into Mom and Pop's house, and I would move into Darcy's house, and when we got married, she would come to live with me in Darcy's house. She said she wants to postpone the wedding.

"She got all weird. I don't know. She just asked me to leave, so I did. I don't know what's going on in her head. She doesn't want me to get involved with anything like this. She's afraid that something could happen like the last time. She wants me to turn Carrie over to the police or DCS."

"I'm not a counselor, and I have my own demons that I constantly grapple with," said James. He added, "The other day, I read a quote from Rose Fitzgerald Kennedy. She once said, 'It has been said, "time heals all wounds."' I do not agree. The wounds remain. In time, the mind, protecting its sanity, covers them with scar tissue, and the pain lessens. But it is never gone."

"Who was she?" asked Mickey.

"She was President Kennedy's mother. Do you ever pick up a book?"

"Sure, I do, but I don't like history and stuff like that. And in school, we never studied the lineage of the Kennedy family. What does that have to do with Valerie?"

James rolled his eyes at his friend. "You need to spend a bit more time in some real books. It means that Valerie may never get over what happened to her, but she will be able to cope with it over time. I still wake up with night sweats and have nightmares, but I've learned to put it in the back of my mind. Valerie hasn't learned how to do that yet. She needs to go back to therapy. She's not crazy, but she is still sick."

"I know. But I see her getting worse, not better. I love her, but I don't know how to help her," Mickey said, holding his cup like he was warming his hands in the cold.

"I understand, my brother. Be patient. It'll take time," James answered.

Pauline brought their orders, set them on the table, and then refilled their coffee cups.

"Mickey, what're you going to do with Carrie when we find her parents?" asked James as he took a bite of his eggs.

"Don't know, James. We don't know the story, but at this point, I suspect Carrie's father is into something he shouldn't be involved in."

"True, but that doesn't mean he's in it voluntarily. You know what I mean, like those guys tried to do to you last year."

"Good point there, but being in the rental business, I tend to have a jaded view of people. I assume the worst until they prove their intentions," said Mickey.

James laughed then said, "So, now, in your mind, people are guilty until they prove themselves innocent?"

Mickey thought for a moment, "I guess you're right, but it wasn't always that way. When you get burned so many times, you're wary of everyone. Hey, when are we going back to your cabin and hone our skills?"

James sat back in his seat with arms folded. "Hone our skills? That was a one-time thing. I hope we NEVER have to do something like that ever again!"

"I know, it was grueling but exhilarating at the same time."

"Look, you don't know grueling, but we can go back out there sometime to just get away for a couple of days."

"Sounds like a plan," Mickey responded.

"How's your father doing? I heard from Darcy that he's doing better the last few weeks."

"He's doing better. He has his good days and bad days. One day he's talking normally. His memory is improving almost daily. He's still in a wheelchair, but he can walk short distances with the walker. I think he'll be walking on his own in a few more weeks."

"The brain, or mind, if you will, is a wonderful and mysterious part of us. Your Pop may never be the same, but then again, he may make a complete recovery. I hope he'll be well enough to be at Darcy's and my wedding," James said as he looked down at the drink sitting in front of him like it held some secret that it could divulge.

"We all pray for that to happen," Mickey said as his cell phone rang. "Hello," he said as he put it to his ear. "Yes. That's good. Did you put the GPS on the car last night when it came in? Okay, good. When did they leave? Did you see who was driving? You are sure it was from that unit and not another unit nearby. Thanks, Glen. James and I'll head out now and follow. You stay there and keep your ears and eyes open. Later," he said as he clicked off and put the phone back on the table.

He looked at James and said, "I guess you heard. They just left the complex, and they're heading in our direction. They might still turn off along the way, but we can watch them on our phones since we're linked up with the GPS. They got some clear pictures of the man as he came out of the building and got into the car. He said they did get some cell phone traffic late last night, but it was from several different sources, so they don't know exactly when one was from that unit. They can't listen in yet, since they don't have the specific phone isolated. That's pretty much their limit."

"They did well considering their limited knowledge. I'll call and see if we can get someone over there to isolate the frequency."

"If we're going to tail them, we better take care of the check and pull out," Mickey said as he got up and threw some money on the table and motioned to the waitress.

As she walked over toward them, Mickey said to her, "Pauline, I left some money on the table that should cover the bill and you. We have to go. See you later."

"Thanks, Mickey Ray. You and James have a great day," she answered as she was busing the table.

Mickey got into his truck as James climbed in the other side. James opened his phone and clicked on a GPS app linked to the GPS mounted on the car parked at unit 140.

"They're headed in our direction. If they don't turn at the next intersection, they'll pass right by us. All we have to do is sit here and wait. What if they stop here? It's still early, and maybe they'll stop here for breakfast," said James looking at the screen on his phone.

"I'll punch the number of the diner but not connect the call unless they stop here," answered Mickey.

"They just passed the last intersection and should be here in a minute or two. Yeah, they're getting closer, wait, they're way down the road," James said as he squinted into the distance at a vehicle coming toward them. He pointed his finger at the car and looked at Mickey.

The car turned and pulled into the parking lot, and stopped.

The Landlord and the Wheelchair Child

Mickey punched send on his phone and drummed his finger on the steering wheel, waiting impatiently while it rang at the other end of the line.

"Hello, Pauline?" he said when she answered. "This is Mickey Ray."

"Hey, Mickey Ray. I can see you from here. Ya'll haven't even left the parking lot. Are you okay?"

"Thanks, we're fine. Could you do a favor for me? There's a guy that just pulled into the lot. He'll be coming in, in just a minute. Would you seat him by himself away from anyone else? Then, we'll come back inside shortly after. We need for you to seat us right behind him, but this is important. DO NOT ACT LIKE YOU KNOW US! Act like we're total strangers. Can you do that, please?"

"Sure, I can, Mickey Ray. Can you tell me why?" she asked.

"I'll tell you later. Just please help me out now! I don't want him to suspect anything. Remember, seat us behind him."

"Here, he comes. I'll do exactly what you asked."

"Thank you so much, Pauline." Mickey hung up his phone.

They watched the man enter the restaurant and approach the register at the inside of the entrance. After a moment, Pauline led him to a table in the corner near the front of the diner. They could see her through the window as she walked back to the register and picked up the phone. He saw her turn away from the man as his phone rang.

"Mickey Ray?" she said when he answered.

"Yes, Pauline?"

"He put in a to-go order. What should I do? Are ya'll still coming inside?"

"Give him a complimentary cup of coffee for his wait. Then, after we're seated, go back into the kitchen. Come back out to the table and tell him that the cook messed up his order, and it'll take a few more minutes to cook it again. Bring him a Danish for his trouble, and tell him that the entire order will be on the house if he waits. Of course, I'll pay for it when we leave."

"You got it, Mickey Ray."

"Thanks, Pauline. You're a doll!" he said as he disconnected the phone.

They waited in the truck for a few moments, then proceeded inside. Pauline came to them and seated them behind the man. James sat with his back to the adjacent booth, and Mickey sat across from James, looking at the man's back. Pauline took their order and left without any sign of recognition as Mickey had asked. They asked quietly that their meals also would be made to go. They sat making small talk until the man picked up his phone and dialed. When Mickey saw this, he motioned to James. When the man placed the phone up to his ear, James pulled out an instrument the size of a deck of playing cards and pushed the buttons on the front. Then James held it close to his chest to be as close as possible to the man's phone. There were two small lights on the little box. One light was red and flashing, and the other was dimly lit green. After a few moments, the red light went out, and the green light glowed bright and steady. James nodded his head slightly to let Mickey know the instrument had synced with the man's phone. He shut it off and placed it back into his pocket. They motioned for Pauline to return to their table.

When she arrived at their table, she had a small bag with their order. Mickey took the bag, pressed a fifty-dollar bill into her hand. He thanked her and quietly said, "You did great! Keep the change."

They got up and walked out to the truck, and waited for the man to leave. Mickey checked his phone and opened a picture taken by Glen when the man left the apartment. He looked at it and forwarded it to Darcy and Susan, the apartment manager, to confirm that he was the man who had rented the apartment. After a couple of minutes, Mickey got a text from Susan that he was not the person listed on the lease. Neither was weasel guy. She had no idea who they were.

"What do you do when something like that happens, Mickey?" James asked.

"It all depends. If there are no problems, we let things slide for a few months. If they continue to pay the rent without any trouble, we approach them and ask them to sign a lease to make things legal. Sometimes people move in, and the last tenants move out without notifying us. The new tenants don't tell us because they don't qualify to rent the apartment more often than not. If there are problems, we get a warrant and evict them."

"Wow, there sure are a lot of rules you have to follow. If you own it, can't you just set them out?"

"No, it takes a court order, which can take one to three months for an eviction. Hey, here comes our man. Let's get ready to roll," Mickey said.

Since they had a GPS tracker on his car, they didn't need to stay within sight of it. The guy headed straight back to the apartment complex and returned to unit 140.

"Well, this trip was a dud," said Mickey.

"No, it was golden. We got the phones cloned. Now when he gets a call, we can listen in, or even, if we want to, we can answer and cut him out. Now we have the best information line that we can get, other than the internet and emails. Let's get back to the surveillance unit and clone that phone. We link them up, and we're good to go."

They pulled into the complex, parked near the entrance so the truck wouldn't be recognized if someone looked out the window. They got to unit 143 and let themselves inside.

"Hey, Glen. How's it going?" asked Mickey as he stepped inside the room, followed by James.

"Hey, Mickey Ray. It's boring just sitting here looking out the window. It's mind-numbing. I should ask for a raise," he said.

"Raise? I should make you pay me for letting you stay here, complete with all utilities and even snacks. How many jobs would pay you to sit on your butt!" Mickey laughed and slapped Glen on the back.

"Yeah, yeah, you're right. I'm just kidding anyway."

"I know you were. What's been happening? Have you seen anything interesting?"

"Only what I already told you about, Boss," he said, then put the binoculars back up to his face to continue watching across the street.

James tapped Mickey on the shoulder. "Why don't you give the guys a break and let them have a couple of hours out of the house to loosen up. You know what I mean," as he raised his eyebrows.

Mickey nodded back to him knowingly. "Where's George?"

"He's in the backroom getting some shuteye. He took the night shift last night."

"Why don't you get him up? Both of you take a break and get out of the house for a while?"

"If you insist, but I don't think George cares. He's asleep anyway."

"Glen, wake George and take a hike. Be back here in two hours."

Glen got the subtle order, got up from the chair, handed Micky the binoculars, and left the room. Glen came out of the back bedroom with George in tow, grumbling to himself, and they left.

"I need the equipment that's locked up in the trunk over there in the corner. I didn't want Glen and George to see what was in it. I don't know them, so I don't trust them. Nothing personal against your friends," James said.

"I fully understand. No offense taken. And for the record, they aren't my friends. I just use them for odd jobs, that's all."

James unlocked the trunk. Mickey looked into it and saw several kinds of instruments he didn't recognize or understand their function. James took out a box about the size of a cigar box and plugged it into a wall socket over the counter in the kitchen area. He took out a cable about three feet long and plugged one end into the box on the counter. He took the small box with the lights he used in the diner from his pocket and plugged the other end of the cable into it. James then turned on both boxes. Red lights on the boxes lit up and blinked. After a few moments, both lights turned green. James shut off the boxes and unplugged the small box. He took out a cell phone and plugged it into the same cable previously plugged in the small box. After about thirty seconds, the light on the larger box turned green again, and James unplugged the cell phone. He packed up both boxes and put them back into the trunk.

He turned to Mickey and said, "We're now synced with his phone. We can listen or interrupt any call placed to or from his phone."

"Where can you get something like that, and is it legal?"

"That's need to know. It's only borrowed, so we need to take care of it. It is ungodly expensive to replace. That's another reason why we needed to be alone."

"I've told you before, James, sometimes you scare me," Mickey said.

"Yeah, it's a good thing you're my best friend and almost family," James added.

As he stood there with the phone in his hand, it rang. Mickey just looked at James for instructions.

James said, "Since I already have it in my hand, I'll show you how it works. First, you mute the mic. When the other phone is answered, it'll stop ringing. We can listen privately or put it on speaker. Also, it automatically records the conversation, so we can put it down and grab some shut-eye and still get all the calls."

James walked over to a chair, sat down, and placed the phone on a small table beside him. The voices came out loud and clear.

"Hey, Satchel, have you talked with Bobby?"

"Yeah, he doesn't have the money and says he has no way to get it, so I made a deal with him. If he makes ten trips for me, we'll call it even. That comes out to about a thousand dollars a trip," said the person on this end of the phone.

"That's cheap. Sometimes you pay your transporters several times more than that in cash."

"True. But he was a bit hard up and ready to deal. What about his old lady? What've you done with her?"

"We have her locked up safe and out of sight. The only problem is she keeps screaming about some kid she has."

"What kid?"

"I don't know. She just says the kid needs medication, and she left the kid somewhere outside. We looked but can't find the little brat."

"You said, she, so the kid's a girl. How old is she?"

"I don't know. I think she's little. She can't identify anyone."

"You find that kid and make sure she doesn't identify anyone. You got me? When this is over and he pays his debt, we can dispose of him also. Tie up loose ends. Understand?"

"I know what you mean, Satchel."

"Where is the crazy lady now, Neal?"

"She's in one of the storage units, sedated."

"What if she sobers up? Is anyone there watching over her?"

"No. Right now, I don't have anyone to do that. Don't worry. I pumped enough stuff in her, so she won't wake up before I get back. Satchel, we know what we're doing. She's in the one we soundproofed way back. No one could hear her if she screamed her guts out," Neal said.

"Can you get that loser brother of yours sobered up to look after her?" Satchel asked.

"No, not right now. Carson still needs some more time to get straight, but I'll see what I can do. Speaking of Carson, he said someone was here the other day asking about that car in the lot. I don't know, but I suspect it was the lady's car."

"So, what does that have to do with us?"

"Carson said he was asking a lot of questions about the guy that's renting this place. He wanted identification and proof that Carson's the legal tenant."

"What guy? What's his name?" asked Satchel, not concerned but cautious.

"I don't know. I wasn't here, but Carson said the guy said he was the maintenance guy. That's all I know."

"Call the office, report a problem, and see who shows up to fix it. Let Carson identify him. Look, I have to get back to some other business. Don't worry about who lives there. The original tenant is never going to reappear. I guarantee it. If they're concerned, you can say he left, and he'll be back in a few days. Problem solved." Satchel hung up without a response from Neal.

Mickey grabbed his phone and called Susan at the office. "Hello, Susan, this is Mickey Ray. A man from unit 140 will be calling about a problem. Do not mention me. Say that Sam is the maintenance supervisor, and send him. Tell Sam what I just said. He'll know what to do."

They turned on the receiver to listen to the bugs they placed in the apartment. They heard Neal walking around and then some rustling noises.

"Hey, stupid. Wake up." More rustling sounds.

"Leave me alone," came a voice slurred from sleep.

"Get up. I need your help. Satchel says you need to watch over the girl we're keeping."

"Why me? I ain't done nothin. I don't even want to have anything to do with that retard Satchel."

They heard what sounded like a slap and then a noise that was surely Carson falling on the floor.

"Hey, why'd you do that? I've got a headache. I need to sleep," Carson whined.

"All you have is a hangover. Furthermore, I don't care what you need, moron. I need you to get up. Get your sorry self dressed and come with me! Now move!" Neal said.

More rustling. Mickey and James assumed it was bed covers. They looked at each other and shook their heads. There was movement and a thump, and then Carson cried out.

"Ouch, that hurt!"

"What'd you do, idiot?"

"I hit my head on the dresser," he answered.

"You, Jackass. Get dressed. We leave in five minutes. You be dressed or go in your birthday suit. Hear me?"

"Yeah. I hear ya."

Mickey and James scrambled to get their coats on and leave the apartment to get ahead of Carson and Neal at the complex entrance.

CHAPTER 7

Thursday Afternoon...Comfort Zone Storage

The car with Carson and Neal pulled out of the complex, followed far behind by Mickey Ray and James. They looked much like what Mickey imagined. Carson was just as he had seen him before, but Neal was tall, a bit more heavyset than Carson. While Carson had wispy hair, Neal's hair was thick, wavy, and dark-colored, and he wore horn-rimmed glasses. Mickey drove, and James did a search on his phone for storage warehouses. There were three in the city limits of Bridgeton.

"Mickey, these three sites are listed online. High Wall Storage, Elite Storage, and Comfort Zone Storage. My guess is they would go to Comfort Zone because it's closer and has insulation in most of the storage compartments. It even has a freezer section. The freezer section will have added insulation to keep the temperature cool inside. To do that, they need a lot more insulation, which will make it more soundproof."

"You're probably right. If we lose the signal, we'll have an idea where they're going." Mickey looked over at the screen on the phone with the GPS reading. As he looked, he saw where Carson made the next turn about two blocks down the road. As he approached the side road, he turned on his signal.

"It looks like he's going to Comfort Zone Storage," commented James.

"Yep," said Mickey as he slowed down. He saw the taillights light up down the road, so he pulled off into a convenience store parking area. The car ahead made a right turn, and Mickey slowed down even more, giving the car time to pull into the facility. Then Mickey sped up and moved up to go by the storage facility. As they passed, they looked to get a layout of the buildings. There was an eight-foot chain-link fence around the entire area. A small two-story building was used as the rental office and resident manager's living quarters in the front, and a security gate lowered across the driveway. It was similar to most storage facilities. The buildings were built parallel, with letters and unit numbers from 1 to 20 on each roll-up garage door. As Mickey drove slowly by, James looked down each row, looking for the car. Near the end of row three, they saw the car sitting in front of a door labeled C-18. As one man entered, the other would look around, then lift the door and lower it when the other entered.

"Did you get the unit number, James?" Mickey asked.

"Yeah, I got it. We can come back later and find out what's in that unit," James answered.

"We can't do anything until after they close. We'll go back, and you can get your Humvee, and I'll go see Pop."

James shook his head in approval. "I'm glad to hear that. I hope he has a full recovery."

"Thanks. I hope so too."

"If we stick around and wait for these guys to leave, we can go into the office like we want to rent a unit and get a map. We can get an idea of some of their things, like security, heat, and A/C in the units. Then we'll have an idea when we come back what we might encounter."

"Good idea. We'll wait here until they leave," said Mickey as he pulled into the parking lot of another convenience store about a mile down the road from the storage units and shut off the engine. Mickey leaned back in his seat and closed his eyes.

They sat quietly for a few minutes as James kept watch for the car to come back this way. James turned to Mickey and said, "They may not come back this way, Mickey."

Without opening his eyes, Mickey answered, "I know, but we have a fifty-fifty chance they will."

"Right. Hey, Mickey, we talked about Val, but how are you doing since all that crap happened? You seem to be dealing with it pretty well."

"I still have nightmares about what we did that night. I don't know if I'll ever get over it."

"I told you that the entire thing would affect you. You're no longer innocent, Mickey. Killing someone, even in self-defense, changes a person. It changes you in a way that you can't describe."

"I don't like it. I didn't like it then. I don't like it now," said Mickey.

"Tell me about it. I see the result of evil every time I look in the mirror. Sometimes I hate myself. Sometimes, I hate the people that did this to me. Sometimes I hate the world in general. The best thing that's ever happened to me is your family. You, Darcy, her kids, all of you have been my saving grace. You need to be patient with Val. You have no idea what she went through. She needs time, and even then, she may always have flashbacks of that time."

Mickey just sat, unmoving with his eyes closed. He knew what James was talking about. James was wounded in Afghanistan when his team was ambushed, and he was left for dead with burns all over his body, including his face. When he was found, he was airlifted to a field hospital. After coming back home, he was discharged from service with full disability. Darcy loved James despite his disfigured face, as did both of her children. Last year, after James and Mickey had destroyed a human trafficking ring and rescued Valerie, Darcy had asked James to marry her.

"Hey, Mickey, do you believe in God?" James asked.

"Sure I do." Mickey opened his eyes and looked at James. "Why would you ask that?"

"Just wondered. After what I went through in the army, and what I saw, I don't believe anymore. I used to, but not anymore. How could a good and loving God let things like that happen to people?"

"I don't know, James, but I believe."

"Why?"

"I don't know why. I just do. Nothing and no one can make me not believe in God. I also believe in the devil. He causes all the evil in the world. He messes up all the good in the world."

"If there's a God, why does he let this crap happen, Mickey? Why doesn't he stop it?"

"I don't know why. He has His reasons. I don't understand it. I believe He has a plan for everything, but I don't know what that plan happens to be. I believe it'll all turn out in the end. He knows what He's doing," Mickey said as he leaned back in his seat and closed his eyes again.

"Well, I think that maybe…Hey, they're coming back this way. You want to follow them?" James said as he looked down the road at the oncoming car.

Mickey popped his head up and started the truck.

"No, we'll go to the office and check out the things like you suggested."

Mickey pulled out of the convenience store parking lot as the car passed in front of them. "What made you bring up God, anyway?"

"Dee asked me to go to church with her and the kids," James answered.

"Are you going to go with them?"

"I don't know," he answered pensively.

"Well, go with them. Our whole family believes in God. It'll make her happy."

"I'll think about it," James said.

They pulled into the storage unit parking area outside of the fence, beside the security gate, and walked into the office.

"Good afternoon. How may I help you?" said an elderly gentleman.

"Good afternoon to you, sir. We'd like some information on your storage units," Mickey asked as James looked around at the posters on the walls.

They showed smiling people inside rental trucks passing boxes to women and children placing items in a storage unit. These pictures gave the appearance that families were enjoying putting their personal belongings into storage. Other posters gave sizes of units, including a map showing which ones had heat and air conditioning. One sign showed moving and packing supplies with prices. It listed things like boxes of various sizes, packing peanuts, sealing tape, bubble wrap. Another one showed moving equipment and rental rates like hand trucks, padding blankets, dollies, and even trailers and moving trucks. The man asked what they wished to store so he could make some helpful suggestions.

"We have a great selection of units. We have climate-controlled units. We have all sizes of units. We have parking spaces in the back if you have things like a boat, camper, or RV. We can store just about anything you might have, except, of course, dangerous materials.

"Again, how may I help you?" he asked.

James spoke up. "My friend here is moving out of the area, and he needs a unit to store a two-bedroom apartment for about six months. We don't need any climate control. Do you have a map of the complex showing the units and sizes?"

"Why yes, I do have one," he said, reaching under the counter and pulling out a large colored map of the entire storage facility. "As you can see, Buildings A and B have the climate control units. Buildings C, D, and E have no climate controls. Building E also has some small units that you access from walk-in doors to the inside hallways. They are the ones where you may need something like a large walk-in closet to store boxes but not necessarily large enough for furniture." As he spoke, he moved his hand over the areas of the map.

"What kind of units are in this area?" said James as he pointed to the layout of Building C. He moved his hand and waved it over the general position of C-18 and units surrounding it.

"Oh, that area's for large size units 8 x 14 and 8 x 16 feet. They're all taken right now, but we have some spaces open across from it in the D section. Would you like to see one?" the gentleman asked. "If you have a two-bedroom apartment, you might need a medium-sized space. That is unless you can pack well and don't have any very large furniture, like those big sectional couches, if you know what I mean," he added.

"What about security? Do you have any outside cameras, or maybe even a security guard?"

"Yes, we have cameras at the corner of each building, and I walk the grounds several times during the day. As you can see, you need a code to drive in so unauthorized vehicles can't come in through the gate. We do have large floodlights over the entire area at night. I close and lock the front gate at 10 PM each night and open at seven each morning. We have barb wire on top of that fence around the lot to prevent anyone from climbing over. We've never had any problems with any theft or vandalism. If there is a problem, I live right above the office," he said, pointing his finger up.

"Thank you, sir," Mickey said as he took the map and put it in his pocket. "I have a couple of weeks to decide what I need to keep and what to dispose of. You've been very helpful, have a nice day." Mickey turned and walked to the door, followed by James.

"Hey, you want to go with me to see Pop?" Mickey asked when they got back into the truck.

"Yes, I haven't seen him for weeks, Mickey."

The nurse told them Daniel was having a lucid day at the rehab facility where Mickey's father was staying. He was standing, holding onto a walker for support to greet them when they got to his room.

"Hey, Pop. You're looking great today!" said Mickey when he saw his father.

"Thanks, Mickey. I'm feeling great too. Hey, you brought James," Daniel said when he saw James standing behind Mickey.

James stepped around Mickey and put out his hand to shake Daniel's.

Daniel smiled but shook his head. "Sorry, James. I need to hold onto this four-legged crutch for a while longer," nodding his head down at the walker.

"Excuse me, sir, I didn't mean to…" James stammered.

"Don't worry about it," interrupted Daniel. "Maybe we can shake hands next time you visit. I'm working hard to cut ties with this walking assistant," he said, referring to the walker. He turned toward a chair, slowly walked over to it, and sat down shakily.

James and Mickey sat in the other two chairs in the room.

"I'm so glad you're doing well, Mr. Christianson," said James.

"Thanks, James. How're you and Darcy getting along? I understand you plan on putting a ring on her finger sometime soon," he said. "Both of you are getting married, am I correct?"

"Yes, sir. I am looking forward to it. We're looking at houses to purchase as soon as we set a wedding date."

"And what about you, Mickey. Are you looking at houses yet?" Daniel asked, looking at Mickey.

"Not yet, Pop. We're going to take a while to do that, but since you brought that up, we're hoping that you can get out of here and come home."

"Yes, I'm looking forward to getting out of here too," Daniel said, agreeing. "Would you mind if Darcy and James moved into my house when they get married, Mickey?"

"Of course not, Pop. They're welcome to it. I already talked to Dee about that. She and the kids could move in now, so they would be there to take care of you when you come home."

"That sounds fine to me, Mickey. You understand that Darcy already has two kids, and I'll most certainly take care of you, Mickey. Maybe we can build one together. That way, you could design one just like you want. I could just move into the Senior Village, maybe into James' unit. That would be good enough for me."

"No, Pop. Dee and the kids will move into your house now, and you can move in with them," said Mickey.

"That's very generous, Mickey, but we couldn't take your dad's house," James said, embarrassed and looking down at his feet.

Mickey turned and interrupted James. "Pop, that would be a great idea, but I don't think that you should be living alone yet. If you moved into the guest area in your house, Darcy and the kids could have the upstairs and take care of you until she and James get married."

"I shouldn't speak so freely right now. Mickey, you, James, and Darcy need to get together and work it out," said Daniel.

"Sir, Mickey has just as much right to that house as Dee and I do," James added.

"That's true, but I'll take good care of Mickey Ray, James. Don't you worry about that! Is that acceptable with you, Mickey?" he said as he turned to Mickey.

"Sure, Pop, I know you'll take care of both of us equally. But right now, you need some home care, and it would be great if Darcy moved in now and prepared that area for you to live when they allow you to leave here."

"Sir, if you would permit me to make a suggestion?" James said.

"What is it, James?" asked Daniel.

"Why don't I just buy out Mickey's half of the house since it'll be half his anyway?"

"No. You and Darcy will take possession of my house, and Mickey and I'll work out an equal settlement for him. Mickey Ray, is that okay with you?"

Mickey shook his head, "I'm not sure we're all on the same page right now. Sure, Pop. I'd be very happy for James and Darcy to have the house. We can work something out. I just think that Darcy should move in right away. You'll be leaving here probably in a week or two," Mickey said.

"Mickey, it's fine if your sister wants to move in now. That sounds like a wonderful plan. You help her with it."

"I will Pop. I'll get on it right away."

They talked about several things, and Mickey decided it was time for them to go. They said goodbye to Daniel and left the facility.

As James and Mickey walked to the truck, James said to Mickey, "Hey, bro, do you think your dad was clear-headed today?"

"It was a bit confusing at times, but I think he knew exactly what he was saying. I believe he was in his right mind about everything he said, especially about the house. He meant it, and I'm in full agreement with him. As far as I'm concerned, the house is yours and Dee's. I do love that giant garage for the cars," said Mickey.

"Yeah, that's a pretty awesome garage. We can work out something. We live in the house, and you can have the garage."

"We need to get the furniture moved and get the house set up so it'll be ready when Pop is ready to come home," answered Mickey matter of factly.

"We'll see. We have to get ready to go back into that storage unit later tonight. We know there are cameras, and we can find a way outside of their viewing range. Let's go to Dee's house and kill some time until we can get inside the fence after closing."

They went straight to Darcy's. As usual, Mickey walked right in and called out, "Anyone home?"

"Back in the office, Mickey Ray," Darcy returned his greeting.

As they walked back, they stopped to hug and kiss the kids, including Carrie. They continued to Darcy's office and sat down. They told her what they had found out during the day and informed her that they intended to return tonight.

After a bit of small talk, Mickey told Darcy they had gone to see Daniel. He told her what Daniel had said about giving her and James the house. She was astonished at his lucidity and questioned the wisdom in that decision.

"It doesn't need to be done until we're married. We'll keep in contact with the doctors about Dad's mental progress and state until then. When the doctor says Daddy can make a financial decision like that, we'll consider a deed transfer. We do nothing until then," Darcy said.

"Okay. Pop needs a place to live when he's discharged from rehab, so we need to get on this now. It would be best if you moved now, and the legal stuff you can do later. He could be discharged in about a week."

"I still have some more paperwork to do for the law firm, and that'll take about two hours."

Mickey and James went back into the living room and talked until around eight PM. Then they put the kids to bed.

They left to go by James' apartment when it got late enough. They needed supplies to get into the storage facility.

As James laid out a few items on the table, Mickey picked up and put on some black pants, shirt, and stocking cap to put over his head. The pants had lots of pockets in which to put things they might need.

They each picked out wire cutters and small pieces of wire to repair the fence after exiting the premises and the small digital camera. Mickey took a lock pick gun. Both had earbuds for communication in case they got separated and a small pocket-sized flashlight. After checking their gear, they got James' Humvee and drove to the same convenience store near the storage facility. The store was still open for business, so they parked away from the parking lights as much as possible.

After waiting until no one was coming or going out of the store, they got out quietly and locked the doors of the Humvee. Walking behind the building, they scoped out the area to continue toward the storage facility, out of sight and off the road. They walked through an open field, behind two other businesses, until they got to the back corner of the storage building's fence area. Picking a place in the fence with dim lighting, James took out the wire cutters and clipped an opening in the fence just barely large enough for them to crawl through it. When possible, they tried to stay close to the buildings and out of sight of other businesses and the road just in case someone drove by and looked their way.

James crept slowly, looking around from one corner of a building to another. He stopped, looked, and moved forward. He stopped and motioned for Mickey to stop. He pointed to the corner of the building ahead.

"Those cameras are not directed accurately to see everything. They're leaving huge blind spots we can hide in and move around the field of view," said James.

Mickey saw a pinpoint of light very similar to the sensors mounted at the base of garage door openings. James took out an aerosol can and sprayed it. In the dark gray smoke, a thin red line emitted about two feet from the pavement about knee level. They both looked around. At the corner of the building, Mickey spotted a camera and pointed it out to James. James motioned to Mickey to move back.

Two words came over Mickey's earbud, "Abort. Now!"

They quickly retraced their steps, but instead of returning to the Humvee, they backed off from the fence to the edge of the field behind the storage facility.

Mickey whispered to James, "Cameras and laser security. The old man didn't tell us about the laser units. What do we do now, James?"

"We wait to see if we triggered any other security we don't know about. He didn't know us, and it's conceivable that you don't go around giving your security secrets to everyone that walks in."

"True, but wouldn't you want customers to feel safe by exaggerating your security instead of minimizing it?"

"Maybe. Let's just wait and see if someone comes to check it out. If they do, it should be any minute now."

Mickey waited while they lay there in the grass, and James kept looking through his binoculars, sweeping the area.

"Mickey, those cameras are dummy ones. The real security is those laser sensors we almost tripped."

"How can you tell the cameras are dummies?"

"Easy. First, the cameras don't have coax cable connections, and they aren't wireless because they don't have antennas. If they were wireless, they would be battery operated, which means they would either have a power connection or a small solar panel for charging during the daylight hours. So, they're dummies. That's good for us because the lasers are easier to get past. If someone doesn't come in a few more minutes, we can go back in."

"Got it. You say the word." Mickey lapsed back into silence.

Finally, James tapped Mickey on the shoulder and motioned him to follow. Climbing back through the fence opening, they proceeded back to the area where the sensors were located. The sensors were just high enough it was difficult to step over, so they laid down and crawled under the beam.

When they got to Building C at the opposite end of the road, near unit 18, Mickey took the lock pick gun out of his pocket and got it ready to use. James took a lookout position and watched until Mickey picked the lock and started opening the unit door. Mickey quickly and quietly moved to the door. It was a huge door almost ten feet high and ten feet wide, like the doors used in warehouses and truck garages. Mickey saw the door had a super heavy-duty lock that he wasn't sure even his lock pick gun could open. He slipped the tool's pins into the lock and pulled the trigger numerous times. Each time he pulled the trigger, the small tool clicked. To Mickey, it seemed like an actual gun going off. In reality, it was a low metallic click that could only be heard a few feet away. Mickey's heart pounded as he patiently waited for the lock to click open. He worked and worked, but it wouldn't open. He wasn't a locksmith and didn't know that much about locks, but he knew this was a significant security type of lock. Mickey turned and motioned to James to come to the door.

"This lock's too complicated for this tool. It won't open it. I've never tried to pick a lock like this. I've only used it for residential locks."

"Keep trying. I want to get in here without anyone knowing. I don't want to break in. We don't want these people to know anyone's on their trail," James said.

"Can't you do it?" Mickey asked quietly.

"No, we didn't pick locks. We kicked in doors. Hurry up! We can't stand here all night. Someone will see us."

"I'm trying. Be patient. I'm doin' the best I can," said Mickey, obviously very frustrated.

Finally, just as Mickey was ready to quit, the lock dropped open. He lifted the door quietly, and James ducked under it, and he rolled it back down as quickly and quietly as possible. They turned on the single overhead light in the unit and looked around. The space was huge and probably continued from one side of the building to the other side, which also had a garage door. If necessary, and if both doors were open, it could be used as drive-through storage. It was about twenty feet long by 12 feet wide, packed with boxes and several large crates marked "medical equipment."

As they began walking around the unit, they pulled rubber gloves from their pockets and put them on to not leave fingerprints on anything. They looked at the labels on the boxes. Several boxes were labeled "Portable X-ray Machine," "Portable EKG." Larger wooden crates had CT Scan Machines, and the largest one in the corner was labeled Open Magnetic Resonance Image Machine. In another corner was another large container labeled "Portable CT Scanner." It was all medical equipment and supplies. The room was filled almost to the ceiling. They moved boxes around to get an idea of what was there.

Hidden behind all the boxes against the back wall were two medium-size suitcases. They moved them aside, and Mickey snapped pictures of the labels on the side of boxes and crates.

"What good is the medical equipment?" asked Mickey.

"I don't know. Maybe they plan to ship it out of the country. Some countries where this stuff's rare and very hard to get is worth its weight in gold. There are two portable X-ray machines over here," James said, pointing at boxes in the corner. "What's in those two suitcases?"

"I don't know. I just moved them out of the way to get to some other stuff."

"Check them out," said James.

Mickey picked up one, put it on top of the box in front of him, and clicked the case open. When it opened, they stared for a few moments, and then they just looked at each other in shock. In it was cash. They each picked up a band of bills and rifled through them. They were all one-hundred-dollar bills. They closed it, and Mickey picked up the other. It also contained cash, but it had fifty-dollar bills.

"What should we do with it?" Mickey asked rhetorically.

"Take it, Mickey. Take it," James whispered.

"Are you sure? What if we get caught?" said Mickey.

"What do you think will happen if we get caught in here! Besides, we can figure that out later. I'm sure all this stuff is stolen. They don't store medical equipment in public storage units like this. Some of this stuff is government-controlled. Not just anyone can buy this stuff. Common sense would tell you it's stolen. By whom and where it's being sold is the question. The money is stolen, or it's used as cash for transactions. If it were legal, it would be in a bank somewhere, not in a storage shed. Do you think they're going to call the police? I don't think so. Let's go. We'll decide what to do with it later. I just don't know why it's stored in a storage unit. That is inadequate security for such a large amount of money."

"Yeah," said Mickey, "but if no one knows it's here, theoretically it's secure. People don't usually store really valuable stuff in a storage unit like this. People usually store old furniture, clothes, things like that. Not cold hard cash, in a briefcase!"

"We still need to find Carrie's mother and father. Let's go before someone finds us here."

Mickey got out the camera and started recording. First, they recorded the interior of some of the boxes showing the merchandise. Mickey shot some video of the side of the crates to displaying the shipping labels. Then they tried to place the boxes back in the exact location they found them. That way, if someone came in, they may not notice the briefcases were missing. They each grabbed a suitcase. James slowly opened the door and peered outside, and pronounced it all clear. They went out, shut the door videoing the entire scene to show the unit number, C-18. Mickey was careful to make sure that neither of them was in any of the recording frames. Mickey put the padlock back on the door and snapped it locked again. They snaked their way back to the store and got back in James' Humvee, and left. They drove by the facility entrance and took a quick video of the sign in front showing the facility's name on the way out. Neither spoke as they rode in silence.

When they got back to James' place, they agreed to meet at the diner in the morning. Mickey got in his truck and drove home. As Mickey pulled into his parking space, he looked at the last apartment. It was Valerie's unit. It was dark.

"Why wouldn't it be dark?" he thought. "It's after three AM. All sane people not working the graveyard shift would be in bed." He needed to get into bed. He and James needed to decide what to do later on this morning. All that money! Wow! What, why, and who is using it, and why did they put it in a low-security storage unit? They would work on that tomorrow. He got out, went inside his apartment, and went to bed. He was wired but finally fell asleep.

CHAPTER 8

Friday Morning...The Suitcases

When Mickey got to the diner, he ordered for both himself and James. Valerie waited on him and took his order.

"Hey, what're you and James going to do today?" she said seriously.

"We're still working on trying to find Carrie's parents. We've got a couple of leads, and we're going to look at how to pursue them."

She turned and walked away. Mickey could tell she was still upset with him.

James came in and sat down at the table. Mickey told him he had ordered for both of them.

"Mickey, after you left, I counted that money," he said softly so no one else could hear. "There's two and a half million dollars in one case—all in one-hundred-dollar bills. The other one has fifty-dollar bills and has one and a half million. In total, there's four million dollars cash in those two cases," he said.

Valerie came back over and put both cups on the table and poured coffee in them. "I'll bring back some cream and sugar. Your orders will be here in a couple of minutes. How've you been, James?"

"Doing great, Val. How about you?"

"Good. You haven't been around to see us here for several weeks," she said.

"Sure, Val. I've just been busy, that's all."

Valerie walked away to wait on another customer, totally ignoring Mickey.

"Are you and Valerie still having problems? She completely ignored you," asked James.

"Yeah, I told her we were going to find Carrie's parents, and she's still mad with me about it."

"Sorry to hear that. I have an idea what we can do with the video," James said.

"What about the money?" Mickey asked.

"That can wait. No one knows we have it. We need to concentrate on the video. We need to send it to the police," James whispered.

"Why? What good will that do us?"

"It'll provide a smoke screen and divert attention away from the money."

"How do we do it without it being traced?" asked Mickey.

"We can't do that exactly, but we can divert the source. We could go to a public place like a library, or go somewhere like a coffee shop with free wi-fi. Or, this one is good. Go back into their apartment and use their computer!" said James with a satisfied smile.

"No, we do that as a last resort. I don't want the publicity at our apartments," Mickey said, shaking his head. "Besides, what good will it do for us? How will it help us find Carrie's parents?"

"When that happens, it'll make them very nervous. They probably have bosses higher up, and the bosses will NOT like losing that kind of money. Of course, the police won't find any money, but they'll get the blame for taking it along with the merchandise inside the unit. The whole thing will take the heat away from an external theft, which is us. They won't even try to look elsewhere."

"Again, I ask how will that help us find Carrie's parents?" asked Mickey again.

"I don't know. I haven't gotten that far yet."

"We need to address that situation. That's what started this whole thing. We need to find Carrie's parents. What about this? We call them and tell them we have their money and demand an exchange for Carrie's parents?" Mickey suggested.

"Bad idea, Mickey. The money exchange is the weak point of any kidnapping for ransom situation. Most of the time, the kidnappers take the money and kill their victims."

"You know that saying about people who defend themselves in court has a fool for a client?"

"Yes, I've heard it. What does that have to do with this case?" asked James.

"Why do they say that?"

"I have no clue, Mickey. And what does that have to do with this situation?"

"They say that because they're too close to the situation. They're emotionally involved. You never work a case if you are emotionally involved. That goes for any negotiation, court cases, and even policemen in criminal cases."

"So, what's your point?"

"We can negotiate because we're not personally involved."

Valerie brought their food and placed it on their table. "Do you need anything? Syrup for the pancakes, butter, jelly for the toast?" she asked.

They both looked down at their plates. "All of the above and a coffee refill," said Mickey.

"Be right back," she said and walked away.

They waited until Val left and continued their conversation.

Mickey ignored James' comment and changed the subject back to the situation. "We need to get another burner phone, so they can't trace our call."

"That's not a problem. I can get one as soon as we leave here. Where do you want to meet to make the call?" said James.

"How about at the apartment where we have the surveillance set up?"

"Sounds good to me. Let's eat. Then I'll meet you there in two hours," James said, looking at his watch.

They ate, left enough money on the table to cover the food and a generous tip for Valerie. Mickey waved at her as he walked out. "Catch you later, Val," he said.

She gave Mickey an icy stare.

Mickey went to see Pop. When he got to Daniel's room, Daniel was sitting on the side of the bed, fully dressed, looking at his walker.

"Hey, Pop, how're you doing today? Do you need some help getting up?" he asked.

"Hello, son. Yes, I think I do need some help. Just help me stand. I can take it from there," Daniel said with a smile.

Mickey moved over beside him and gently helped his father stand and grab the walker. He felt so happy that his father was cheerful and in a great mood. They began slowly walking out of the room into the hallway. As they walked, Daniel talked. He talked about the weather outside. Once again, he mentioned Mickey Ray's mother, Eleanor.

Daniel got melancholy for a few moments as he referred to his deceased wife. "Mickey Ray, I remember your mother, but I try not to think about her too often. It makes me sad, and I haven't felt happy for so long. Slowly I remember what happened. I can't remember it all and don't know all the details, but I'm trying."

"Pop, you don't need to think about that now. All you need to think about is getting stronger so you can get back home."

"You're right, Mickey, but I want to remember your mother. It hurts to think of her as gone, but still, the memories are happy ones."

"I know what you mean, Pop. I think of her a lot, and it makes me sad also. We need to remember but try to live in this moment. Don't let the past define our future, Pop."

Daniel stopped walking. He turned and looked at Mickey. "When did you get so wise, son?"

"You wouldn't believe what's happened in the last few months. Now isn't the time, but I'll fill you in on all the details as you get better."

"I still get my memories mixed up at times. One that confuses me sometimes. Did I tell you that Darcy and James could have my house when they got married?"

"Yes, you did, Pop."

"I didn't mean to slight you, Mickey. Are you okay with that?"

"Sure, Pop, I think that's a wonderful idea. You didn't slight me. You told me that you and I could design and build a house together. So, all's well. I'm good with it."

"That makes me feel a lot better. I wasn't sure if I said that or not, and if I did, I didn't want you to think I'm leaving you out."

"Nope, you didn't. It's all good, Pop. Hey, I have to meet James about a business deal. I have to go now. Let's get you back to your room."

"That's fine, Mickey. You can leave. We're in the solarium room. It's peaceful and has a wonderful view. I'd like to stay here for a while. You go. Meet James. I'll see you next time."

"I'll stop by again soon, Pop."

"You always brighten my day. You know that, don't you, Mickey Ray?"

"Seeing you get better brightens my day, too. Later, Pop," Mickey said as he waved goodbye to Daniel.

Mickey went out to get into his truck when his phone rang. It was James. "Mickey, it just hit the fan. One of your guys in the surveillance apartment called. Someone went to the unit and found out the money's missing, and they're burning up airways on the cell phones. Several others are in on this business. Your guy, Glen, told me that the guys in the apartment are afraid to call their bosses and try to decide who knows about the money and who gets the blame. If something doesn't break, then heads will roll."

"I'm on my way. I should be there in fifteen minutes. Is there any activity such as people coming or going out of the apartment?"

"They didn't say, but I doubt it. If there was, I'm sure Glen would've said something."

"Is the GPS still online?"

"Yes, it'll be active for weeks. I got the burner cell phone like we agreed on. See you in a few," James said and disconnected.

As Mickey drove, he called Darcy to check on Carrie. When Dee answered, he asked how everyone was doing. "Everyone is fine, but Carrie's missing her mother. She's been crying all morning. She cries herself to sleep and then starts all over again when she wakes up. I can't get any work done for the law firm."

"Aren't the kids helping keep her occupied?"

"They're doing the best they can, but she misses her mother, and they can't replace her. When a child misses her mother, it's a difficult situation to deal with."

The Landlord and the Wheelchair Child

"I'm sorry, Dee. I wish I could help."

"Thanks, Mickey, but there isn't anything you can do. We'll just do the best we can to make her feel comfortable and loved right here."

"I'm here at the apartment, and I've got to go in and speak with James. There's a situation we need to deal with. I'll tell you about it later."

When Mickey got to the apartment, James and Glen were listening in on a conversation that was going on right then across the street. The equipment was recording everything as they listened to the cell phone conversation.

A voice screamed through the speaker.

"No!" said the voice, which sounded like Neal, the one they heard on the phone yesterday.

"I've looked everywhere. It isn't here," said a voice at the other end of the line. The voice sounded like Neal's brother, who lived in the apartment, referred to as Carson.

"Did someone break into the unit?" said Neal at this end of the line.

"No. The lock didn't look broken. I don't know."

"Then it must be someone that had a key, right?"

"I don't know, Neal. I don't know!" he screamed. "Someone has another key, but I didn't give one to anybody. What're we gonna do, Neal?"

"There are only two keys. You have one, and I have the other. If the money's missing, then YOU took it!"

"I didn't take it, I swear! I wouldn't do that, Neal. You know me. Man, we're gonna get killed over this. I mean literally killed. We're dead men, man."

"Shut up. Don't talk like that. If it wasn't you, and it wasn't me, someone else knows and took it."

"Who else knows, Neal? I didn't tell nobody. I mean nobody! I would never do something like that. You know me, Neal."

"We agree on one thing. That is, we're in pretty deep, and we need to figure out what happened before Satchel finds out, or we're toast. Get back here, Carson. NOW!" he said and disconnected.

James was sitting in a folding chair beside the table with the speaker and equipment on it. "Well, my friend, I think we got their attention," he said.

Glen looked at Mickey, then back at James. "They mentioned money. What money are they talking about?" he asked.

James said, "Don't know, but whatever it was, it must be a lot."

"You guys went into that unit last night, didn't you? You know exactly what they're talking about. Come on, now. I may not be as smart as you guys, but I'm not stupid! What's going on?" Glen insisted.

Mickey spoke up first. "True, Glen. We did go in there last night, and we found some stolen merchandise. It looked like it was stolen either from a warehouse or maybe a hijacked truck. We don't know where it came from, but it's worth a lot of money, and they know someone took some of it. Right now, the less you know, the safer you are, so don't ask questions. What you don't know can't hurt you, understand?"

"Yeah, I guess so, but I don't like being in the dark," he said.

"I don't blame you. If I were in your position, I might feel the same way, but you're getting paid and paid very well, I might add. Just keep your eyes and ears open and your mouth shut. Take your pay when this is over, and you'll be safe and have a pocket full of money. Can I trust you, Glen?"

"Sure, you know you can trust me, Mickey Ray," he answered.

"Is George asleep in the back bedroom?" Mickey asked.

"No, he doesn't come in till 8 o'clock. He does night shift."

"Okay, you can read him in, but he is under strict silence also. What you heard is some serious stuff, and from this point on, we're dancing around a landmine. If anyone finds out we know anything, we could be killed, got that? I mean, just as you heard them talking on the phone, we could be killed if they find out we're listening in on them."

"I got it, Mickey Ray, but you haven't told us anything so far. Can't you tell me at least what this whole thing is about?"

"I can tell you this, Glen. A few days ago, we found a little girl in the garden section of this complex. She was waiting for her mother to return to pick her up. It seems that the mother was taken as security to ensure the father would settle some debt he owed by making some kind of deliveries for them. We believe that even when he makes the delivery, they'll kill them both. They found out that there's a child somewhere, but they don't know where. That's what you can tell George. That's all you tell him because that is all you know. Understood?"

"Yeah, Mickey. That's all I know. Nothing else," Glen said.

"James and I followed them to one of the units they rent in hopes of finding the mother and maybe the father. Instead of finding them, we found some of their merchandise, and we took some of it. Now, they want it back, but as I said, they don't know who we are or how we got onto them. If they find out, they could kill us for getting involved. We believe these are some nasty people. That's all we know."

"Wow, that is seriously deep, Mickey Ray. What're you planning to do?" Glen asked.

"We don't know right now, but we are going to try to get both mother and father out alive and reunite them with Carrie, the little girl. Can I count on you and George keeping quiet about this? I mean it, when we get them free, we'll take good care of both of you. You know me well enough to trust me, right?"

"Sure, Mickey Ray. I trust you. We'll keep quiet. I promise."

"Good. Glen, why don't you take a drive to get out of the apartment for a while. Take the rest of the day off. You said George would be here tonight at eight. Give him a call and tell him he doesn't need to come in until midnight. We'll take the rest of your shift and the first few hours of his. Be back here to relieve George in the morning."

"Sure thing, Mickey. Thanks, Boss. My word, quiet!" he said, raising his finger to his lips. He turned and walked out the door.

James sat and watched the entire conversation without saying a word. He spoke up when Glen walked out the door. "Do you trust him, Mickey Ray?"

"Only so far. He's trustworthy to a degree, but I wouldn't trust him with the knowledge we're sitting on four-million-dollars. He might sell us out for a huge cut. I guess that means NO. I don't trust him. Now, do you have any ideas what we should do?"

"Nope. Not a single one. Let's sit here and think about it and wait for another frantic phone call."

Mickey had just dozed off when James called to him. "Mickey, wake up. I just thought of something."

As Mickey was waking up, he felt James grab and shake him violently, "Wake up. We got it all wrong!"

"What do you mean? What're you talking about? Got what all wrong?" he said as he looked at the clock. It was around nine o'clock and black outside as pitch.

"We went to the wrong unit to get Carrie's mother. I mean, she's still there. We missed her. We went to the wrong unit!" James said excitedly. "Get up. Splash some water on your face. We've got to make another run on that storage place."

Mickey sat up and rubbed his face, fully awake and ready to listen to James. "Okay. Tell me this great revelation you had. I'm awake now."

"When we heard them talking before, they said they had to go and watch the woman. I assume it was Carrie's mother, right?"

Mickey nodded.

"We only saw them go to C-18, where we went later that night to the storage place. We didn't see the other unit they went to."

"How do you know they went to another unit?" asked Mickey.

"We don't know, but we sat down the road for several minutes, waiting for them to drive back out onto the road. All they needed to do was check on her, give her some food and more water and make sure she was still alive then and leave. It would take only a few minutes, and we sat through the whole thing."

"Okay. What do you suggest we do?" asked Mickey.

"We go back down there tonight and open up the right one and get her out."

"Lots of holes in that plan. First, we don't know which unit she's in. Second, they'll know we got her out and possibly kill her husband if we find the right one. That's NOT a good solution."

"We don't know exactly which one, but we have a map of the building layout that shows which units have climate control. They'll have the soundproofing they mentioned. We go down the line until we find the right one. We get in and out the same way we did last night," said James as he paced back and forth across the room.

"We get her out, but then what about the husband?"

"We negotiate with them to get him out. We have four million dollars of their money! They'll be glad to trade him for the money." It was evident that James was getting excited now.

"Like I said before, Mickey, the hand-off is always the weak link in any hostage situation."

"True, we'll just have to think of some way to make it viable for us. Unlike the FBI and the police, we don't have any rules to follow. We can do anything we want to do."

"When do you want to go in?"

"Anytime you're up for it," said James.

"Not tonight. Neal and Carson won't do anything yet until they decide what to do about the money. They don't have any clues about us so far. We can wait just one more day. That also gives us time to put together a plan," Mickey said thoughtfully. "We might be able to make it work. We just need to plan it carefully. We've had the bug receiver turned off, but it's still been recording what they say inside the apartment, right?"

"Yes, it's motion operated to record everything even when the receiver isn't on. We can listen to the recording anytime we want. It might be a good idea if we listen to what the 'dumb duo' have to say before we make a plan."

"I agree. Turn it on."

James reached over to the table and turned a knob, and the receiver boomed to life. They listened as the profanity flew from the speaker box. James and Mickey could tell that the men at the other end of the transmission were sick with fear.

Mickey grimaced as they talked. "What the f*** happened to it?" said the voice they knew to be Neal.

"I don't have a clue. You've been there lots more times than I have. I bet you took it!" said Carson.

"Look here. You know I didn't. I'm not that STUPID. You had better bring it back, or we're both dead men!"

SILENCE at the other end of the transmission.

"Do you hear me? Did you hear what I said!"

"I heard you, but I didn't take it, and you know I didn't. So shut the ***** up at me!"

"WHAT ARE WE GONNA DO, NEAL!" Carson screamed.

"SHUT UP, SHUT UP, SHUT UP. Let me think. I don't know what we're going to do. Give me some time."

James smiled, nodded, and reached over and picked up the burner phone. Mickey looked at him questioningly, but James moved his fingers to his lips and "shushed" Mickey. He then dialed a number.

They both heard a phone ring through the receiver. James reached over and turned down the volume so they wouldn't be an audio feedback squeal. They heard a voice through the speaker.

"Hello?" said Neal.

James could hear Neal's voice through the cell phone. "Hello, Neal?"

"Who's asking?" he answered.

"That isn't important right now. I will answer you, though. I am the person who has your money!" James said calmly.

"Who the f**** is this!"

"First, you had better clean up that mouth of yours, or I'll go on a spending spree, and I may not stop until I have spent a lot of this wonderful cash I have."

"Who is this, and where are you?"

James became more firm this time as he spoke. "You listen to me. If you don't want Satchel to send someone by to blow both yours and Carson's head clean off your shoulders, you better shut up and listen."

"Okay, then," Neal said. "What do you want? What've you done with the money?"

"Let's get this straight. I ask the questions here, and you give the answers. Do you understand me?"

"Yes. But I want...."

"SHUT UP, AND LISTEN," James said even more firmly as he picked up a pencil from the table and wrote on a tablet.

"You don't get to ask any questions. I ask them, and you answer. Have you ever watched any cop or lawyer shows?" he asked to buy some time. There was silence at the other end of the line. "I asked you a question, Neal. Answer with a yes or no."

"Yes," Neal answered.

"Good. Now, do you know one of the first rules a lawyer learns about asking a person a question on the witness stand?"

"No," said Neal shakily.

"Don't ask a question you don't already know the answer to. Have you ever heard that, Neal?"

"I'm not sure. I think I have," Neal answered.

"Now, this is what I'm going to do. I'm going to ask you some questions, and you will answer truthfully. I will already know the answer to that question, so you better answer honestly, or I'll know you're lying to me. Got it?" James said.

"Um, yeah, I guess so."

While James was talking, Mickey had read the note and was following James' instructions. He quietly slipped outside and around the corner where James had parked his Humvee. Mickey retrieved a pistol from under the front seat and screwed a silencer onto the barrel. He had the earbud they had used in the past plugged into his ear to hear and continue following James' instructions. Mickey told James that he was in position behind a shrub across the street right in front of the apartment's front picture window. The drapes were drawn shut, so he couldn't see inside.

"Let's start by setting a baseline. Do you know what a baseline is, Neal?" asked James.

"Yes, I think so," he said.

"When you take a lie detector test, they ask some questions to calibrate the machine, so they know when you're telling a lie. We are going to do the same thing. Now, I'll give you a sample of what can happen if you lie to me. Because these first questions, I already know the answers to. Understand, Neal?"

"I understand, you jerk. What do you want? What's all this crap and stupid directions…"

James quietly told Mickey to put a shot into the front window high enough not to hit the men in the apartment. As Neal started ranting, the front window shattered with a loud crash, and a lamp toppled over as the bullet continued across the room, hitting it and burying itself in the wall. Up to that point, Carson had just stood listening to Neal on the phone. When the window shattered, they both dropped to the floor. Glass shards sprayed across the room, covering both of them, and the phone flew from Neal's hand. Knowing they would both be lying on the floor below the window, Mickey took that opportunity to slip back into the hallway and back upstairs to the surveillance apartment. Mickey and James both smiled at each other.

In a few moments, Neal was back on the phone. "What the f****? I mean, why'd you do that, man? The rental people will make me pay for that!"

"Let me start by saying, I want you to be respectful to me. Stop the disrespectful attitude. I told you I have to calibrate the machine, and I also want to show you what might happen if you lie to me. Are you ready to answer my questions now?"

"Yeah, I'm ready."

"I assume that both of you are on the floor since that shot?"

"Yes. Yeah, where'd you think we'd be since you're shooting at us?" Neal said, exasperated.

"Good. First question. Give me your first, middle, and last name. Remember, I already know it, so don't lie to me!"

"If you already know it, what a stupid question…."

"Take cover for a second round. I'll not tolerate disrespect. This one will be in the radiator of that piece of junk car of yours, and…"

"Okay. Okay. It's Neal Oliver Sadowski and Carson Basehart Sadowski."

"Good. I got a good laugh out of your middle name. Oliver. And why would parents give a little kid a name like Basehart? Your mother really didn't like Carson, did she?"

James told Mickey to go out and put a round into the radiator anyway as they were talking. James needed to ground them for a while.

"Next question. Where did you get the merchandise in the storage unit C-18?"

"Our boss got it. They hijacked a truck, brought the stuff in several pick-up trucks, and put it in that storage unit."

"You mean Satchel, don't you, Neal?"

"Yes, him and some others."

"What's Satchel's last name, Neal?"

"I don't remember."

"Oops, wrong answer! There goes the radiator in your car, Neal."

"Okay. Okay! It's Binghamton. That's all I know, honest. Really. That's it."

"Let's keep it honest here, Neal," James said.

"What unit is your lady hostage being kept? You know who I'm talking about. Janet Griffin."

"She's in E-15," Neal said.

"What was that, Neal?"

"No, wait, not 15. I mean 13."

"Make up your mind, Neal. Your life may depend on it."

"It's 13. She was in 15. We moved her to a smaller unit. It had better soundproofing."

"Do you want your money back, Neal?"

"Yes, I do. Please let us have it back. What do you want?"

"What kind of drugs are you giving her, Neal, to keep her drugged up?"

"Sleeping pills. That's all we have."

"Do you expect me to believe that with all the money you have, all you are giving her is sleeping pills! Give me a break, Neal. I think we need to flatten a couple of your tires," James said condescendingly.

"No, please don't do that. Honest. That's all we gave her. Satchel said not to waste any product on her, and they're cheap. It kept her asleep. That's all we wanted to do," pleaded Neal. "We didn't want to hurt her."

"I want you to tell me where Robert Griffin is being held, Neal," asked James calmly.

"I don't know that."

"Oops again, Neal. There goes your back glass," James said and motioned toward Mickey, who was standing by the door with the gun still in his hand.

Mickey went out and put a bullet into the car's back glass and ducked back into the apartment. Each time he went out, he looked around to see if anyone was around or peeking out of a window. All was quiet. He knew this would be impossible to do if there wasn't a silencer on James' gun.

"Would you like to peek out your window to see what a thorough job my partner is doing to your car, Neal?"

"Ah, um, NO. I'll take your word for it," he said. Carson was still lying face down on the floor in complete silence and shaking almost uncontrollably.

"Now, do you want to tell me where they're keeping Robert Griffin?"

"Honest, man. I don't know. Really, don't you think I'd tell you if I knew? I DON'T KNOW. I'm telling you the truth."

"Let me process your answer. I need to think about it for a while. You may get up from the floor now. I have a man stationed hidden outside your front door. He has a high-powered rifle, and if he sees you at the front door, he'll drop you right there. Do you hear me, Neal?"

Silence.

"Do you hear me, Neal?"

"Yeah, man. I hear ya! Are you going to shoot us when we get up?"

"No, only if you try to leave that apartment. Also, no phone calls. Understand? No phone calls. We'll know if you dial out."

"Got it. No leaving, no phone calls."

"I need to think about it. I'll get back to you in the morning. Stay put, one other thing. No peeking out the windows, not even the back windows. If you do, then the person at your back window will take you out. Got that also, Neal?"

"Yeah, we got that too. No leaving, no phone calls, and no looking out the windows. When can I expect to hear from you?"

"I would say, by noon tomorrow, Neal. Why don't you and your dippy brother get some sleep? We'll be in touch." James pressed end on the phone. He placed the phone on the table, looked at Mickey, and smiled.

Mickey said to him, "We don't really have a man hidden somewhere watching the apartment, do we, James?"

"No, but they don't know that, and I'd bet you a million dollars, they won't try to look out and see."

Mickey had to let out a laugh at James. "I keep telling you. I'm glad we're on the same side. You scare me, James."

"As long as they're scared, that's all I want right now. Now, let's go get Janet out of that storage unit while it's still dark."

They made sure the bugs were properly working and all equipment was in order, then they left the apartment to go to the storage unit to get Janet, Carrie's mother. Mickey called Glen and told him they were leaving surveillance. He and George should carry on until they get back sometime tomorrow. Since they had been going into situations where they needed night gear, James kept a basic kit in his Humvee in a secret compartment in the back. They drove to a dead-end road and suited up before going to the storage units. When they got there, they left the Humvee at the exact location they parked the last time. The convenience store was still open, and they parked beside the building out of sight of the cashier inside. Mickey and James got out and proceeded down the road to the storage area. When they got to the part of the fence, they quickly saw that no one had seen the cut in the fence. The repair they made was adequate and wouldn't be noticed under casual visual conditions. They opened it back up and crawled through and quickly went to unit number E-13.

Mickey got out his lock pick gun again and quickly had the lock popped open. He removed the lock, opened the roll-up door as slowly and quietly as possible, and moved it back down as soon as they entered. As they did so, the odor of body sweat and toilet smells hit them in the face. They clicked on a flashlight when they closed the door and looked around the small storage unit. Overhead was a light with a switch on the wall next to the right of the door. Since the door was closed, they felt it was safe to turn on the overhead light. There she was, lying in a corner on a dirty blanket. In the other corner was a chemical toilet and a roll of toilet paper. That was causing most of the odor since the toilet had not been emptied and cleaned in some time. There was a pile of food wrappers and empty water bottles beside the woman and her blanket bed. She was sleeping, and they were sure she was drugged to keep her docile.

James went over to her and shook her. She moved groggily, and he shook her again to wake her.

"Janet. Wake up. It's time for you to go home," he said quietly.

"What?" she said softly with a slur.

"You have to get up. We need to get you out of here," James added as he shook her.

Mickey took one bottle of water, poured it on his hand, and rubbed it on her face as James tried to get her to stand. "Janet, you have to get up and walk. Come on now. We're here to help you."

"I can't go. I need to let Bobby do what they want so we can get money to help Carrie," she said.

"We have Carrie. She's okay. We'll take you to her. Help us get you out of here. You need to walk. Help us out here, Janet," James coaxed.

She tried to stand up, but her legs kept giving out, and she would stumble. James would move her closer to the door.

"That's good, Janet. You're doing great. Move one foot in front of the other, Janet, slowly. You're doing fine," he kept saying.

"I'm trying to do what you say. Who are you? What happened to your face?" she said, referring to the scars on James' face.

"That, my dear lady, is a long story. Let's get out of here, and I'll tell you all about it."

"Are you going to hurt Bobby?"

"No, we're going to help you, then we'll find Bobby. When we find him, we'll help him. Now, Mickey's going to turn out the light, open the door, and we are going to get out of here as quickly and as quietly as we can. Do you understand me?" James said.

When she didn't answer, James nudged her out the door and asked her again. "Stay with us, Janet. You need to move along quietly. Follow my friend in front of us. I am going to lock the door now. Be quiet."

She stood looking around and up at the lights up and down the rows of buildings. "Wow, it's bright out here. Is it nighttime?" she asked.

"Yes," said Mickey as he gently pulled her closer to him and supported her so she wouldn't fall. He pulled her to the back of the storage facility then toward the cut in the fence. She frequently stumbled as she walked. They helped her crawl under the laser sensors at the corner of the building.

When they got to the opening in the fence, they made her get down on her hands and knees and crawl through. Mickey was in front, then Janet with James in the rear. When they all climbed through, Mickey helped her get back up while James made the repairs to the fence so it would again look almost secure. It took about ten minutes to get back to the Humvee and get her buckled into the back seat. Mickey got in back with her so that he could look after her. James drove them to Darcy's house.

Mickey called Darcy and told her they were on their way. It was after midnight, and Mickey knew the kids were in bed asleep. He told her not to wake them so they could get Carrie's mother woken up.

When they got to Darcy's house, she came out and helped get Janet inside the house without curious neighbors knowing what was happening. They got her inside and put her in the bed in Darcy's room.

"I changed the sheets before you got here. Do you know what she's on?" Darcy asked.

"Our source says they only gave her sleeping pills," Mickey said.

"Who is your source, Mickey Ray?"

"The guys that were keeping her."

Darcy cocked her head sideways and put her hands on her hips, "And you believe them? Are you nuts, Mickey?"

"If you had been there and heard James talking to them, you'd believe them too. James was awesome!"

James came out of the bedroom. "Okay, Dee. You should stay there with her. She should be okay after the pills wear off, but watch her just in case. We have to go. We still have some more work to do. Now we have to find her husband. One more thing, if you could run an internet search on these people, that might help us."

Mickey handed her a piece of paper with the names Satchel Binghamton, Neal Oliver Sadowski, and Carson Basehart Sadowski written on it.

"Who are these people?" She asked as she looked at the names on the piece of paper.

"They're some terrible people, but to be more specific, they're two brothers that were watching after Janet, and the guy on the bottom of the list, Satchel, is their boss."

Mickey and James got back in the Humvee and headed back to the apartment complex to check on Neal and Carson. They pulled into the complex, and they walked around the building and into the entrance hallway of the surveillance unit.

George was sitting in a chair reading a magazine. "Hey guys! What's up?" he said.

"Has anything been happening across the street?" Mickey asked.

"Not a thing. It's been quiet as a graveyard, Boss."

"Good," said James.

"Really? I mean, I thought you wanted something to be happening," George said.

"Not this time. Right now, we want quiet. We didn't want anything to happen while we were gone. It's 4 AM. Is Glen going to be here to relieve you at 8 o'clock?" said Mickey.

"Yes, he'll be here. You need me to tell him something for you?"

"Not unless you hear some chatter on the phone or if they try to leave the apartment. They shouldn't do either until at least noon today," said Mickey. "James and I'll be back later. We're going back to his place and get a couple of hours of sleep."

CHAPTER 9

Saturday Morning...Janet

MICKEY SLEPT ON JAMES' COUCH FOR the rest of the night. When he did get up, he stretched and smelled coffee. He walked into the kitchen area and saw James sitting with a coffee and a Bible sitting on the table in front of him.

"Don't you ever sleep? You were in here last night when I crashed on the couch," Mickey said.

"I don't sleep well anymore. When I do, I have nightmares about my time in the military," James said matter of factly.

"Been doing a little light reading, I see," Mickey said, pointing at the Bible.

"Yeah, but I don't get it. It's complicated," James said, shaking his head.

"At times, it can be very complicated, but the more you read, the better it gets. What part have you been reading?"

"Job. It's about this guy that seems to love God, and God lets the devil take everything away from him. I don't get why a loving God would allow that. Seems cruel to me."

"Wow, you picked a super serious one to read. A lot of people don't get that one either. Why not start with the book of Matthew in the New Testament?" Mickey suggested.

"You think that one's better?"

"I know it's better. Just try reading it," Mickey said, looking at the clock on the stove. "I guess it's late enough to give Dee a call and see what she's found out on the list of names we gave her."

Mickey dialed the phone, and Darcy answered. "Hey, Dee. Have you run any checks on the names we gave you earlier?"

"Good morning to you, little brother!" she answered. "No, I haven't. Janet's up and is sitting with Carrie. They had a big cry fest for almost an hour. She's still groggy and is sick to her stomach. She hasn't been able to eat a mouthful of food without throwing it up. I think it's a side effect of the number of sleeping pills they gave her.

"All in all, she's fine. Carrie is ecstatic about having her mother back. As soon as she gets a bit more clear-headed, we'll talk. Maybe I can find out more information so that you can find Bobby. Are you guys coming over here today?"

Mickey answered, "Yes, but we need to go back to the apartment where Glen and George are watching. We have to clear up things with Neal and Carson."

"What do you mean…clear things up, Mickey? Aren't you done with them now?" she asked.

"Nope. Not by a long shot. We need more information from them so we can find Janet's husband. I think James can get that information, or at least get a lead for us to follow. Also, they have a storage locker full of stolen merchandise. We need to get that reported to the authorities so that they can take possession of it. Dee, we can stop by but can't stay long. We have a LOT of work to do. See you later." Mickey disconnected the phone and turned to James.

"If you're finished with your Bible lesson for the day, let's head over to the surveillance apartment and check things out there. Then we can go over to Dee's house and check on Janet and Carrie."

"I'm ready when you are."

James walked behind him and added, "What're we going to do with the money, Mickey?"

"We're going to keep it," he said.

James walked out of the door and set the deadbolt. "Shouldn't we turn it into the authorities?"

"Normally, I'd agree, but it's stolen money, and we aren't even sure if it's stolen. Maybe it's just profits from selling the stolen merchandise. It isn't like whoever is running this operation is legal, and they can't keep it in a bank. If we turn it in, the government will keep it. If it was, let's say, taken from someone, or a bank robbery, or something like that, I would say return it." He waited for James to use his remote to unlock the Humvee door, then he got in the passenger's side.

James remained silent for a time as he walked around the vehicle and then got in on the other side. "Okay, we can hold onto the money, and try to find out if it was stolen, say from a person or a business. Then if nothing is reported taken, we keep it. Deal?"

"Deal," said Mickey.

As they headed toward Darcy's house, James went through a fast-food restaurant and got a couple of biscuits that they ate on the way. They rode in silence as they headed toward Darcy's house. When they got to Darcy's house, Mickey walked up to the door and knocked. He waited as James followed him up to the door.

"Since when did you start knocking at Dee's door?" James asked.

"Starting now. There are four females and one little boy in there, and I don't want to walk in on anything," Mickey answered.

"Good thinking!" said James just as the door opened.

"Hi, Uncle Mickey," Cyndi said as she moved aside, letting both of them inside. "Hi, James."

"Good morning, my little girlfriend," said James with a smile.

Mickey walked into the kitchen, where everyone was sitting. Darcy and the kids were all sitting around the table in front of empty plates. Darcy and Janet both had a cup of coffee in their hands.

"Hey there, boys," said Darcy.

Janet spoke up, "I guess I owe both of you a sincere thanks for rescuing me and probably saving my life. You're Mickey," she said, pointing at Mickey. "You're James," she said, pointing at James. She got up and hugged both of them.

"It was our pleasure, Janet. Carrie here needs her mother," said James.

Mickey filled two cups of steaming brew from the coffee pot. "Now we need to find your husband, Bobby," he said, then handed one of the cups to James.

"Do you know where they're keeping him?" James asked.

"No, I don't know. I wish I did. I don't know if he's still even alive."

James spoke up, "He is because you are. I mean, if they no longer needed him or if something happened to him, they would most likely have killed you. You were the leverage they used to get him to do what they want. Do you know what they wanted?"

"No, not really. Bobby left Carrie and me a few months ago to get a job driving trucks so we could afford the operation and medication for Carrie. The accident that caused her to be in that wheelchair was his fault."

Darcy turned to the kids. "Why don't you kids go play in your room and let the grownups talk. Okay?"

"Sure, Mommy," the kids said as they got up and left the room.

When the kids left the room, James sat down across the table from Janet. "Now, Janet, to help you, we need the story from beginning to now."

"Why do you need to know? Just let us leave. You've done enough," she said as she looked down at her coffee cup.

"We need to know because Mickey and I both have spent a lot of time to find and rescue you, and Dee here has spent the same on taking care of your daughter. You owe us at least an explanation. If it weren't for all three of us, you might be dead."

"Yes, that's all true, but we aren't, so just let Carrie and me leave," she said a bit more firmly. "To be honest, I wish Bobby would die. I hate him!"

"Not going to happen, lady. We're going to find Bobby and get him out of this mess. What the two of you do when he's free is your business. Now start talking, or we'll call the police and tell them everything we know," James said as he drummed his finger on the table.

"No! You can't call the police. They'll take Carrie from me!" she said, beginning to cry.

"I don't really care, Janet. Right now, we're looking out for Carrie's best interest, not yours. Now, either talk, or I'll make that call. You can start by telling us why you hate Bobby."

James sat for a few moments as Janet sat still staring at her coffee cup. When she didn't respond, James reached into his pocket and withdrew his cell phone.

Janet jumped up and put out her hand in a "stop" gesture. "Alright. I'll tell you. Just don't call the police, please."

"Before you start, we have to tell you that when we first found Carrie, we reported all we knew to the Bridgeton police," said Mickey.

"Oh, no. I'll lose Carrie. They'll take her away from me. I don't know what I'll do without her. I wish you had left me in that storage unit to die." She sat back down, placed her head on the table, and began to cry.

"Hold on for a minute. After this is over, we can fix this, but we need to know where Bobby is and how we can get him out. Then we can figure out how to make everything okay with the police, Janet," Mickey said.

"But if they think that I left Carrie on purpose...."

"Hold on now, Janet. We now know you didn't leave her on purpose. We do need to know how to get Bobby out so we can explain everything to the police, and they won't pursue this any further," added James.

Darcy nodded her head in agreement with James. "They are correct, Janet. We can get it all straight with the police, but we need to know the entire story."

Janet took a deep breath and started talking. "Several years ago, after Carrie was born, we found out she had diabetes and needed medication and constant visits to the doctor to control her condition. Bobby worked a lot of overtime to pay for it. We didn't have insurance, and he started taking side jobs for some guys he heard about. I don't know exactly what he did, but it was illegal. He began drinking. It got worse. He stayed drunk when he wasn't working, and he worked a lot. Finally, his drinking began to affect his legitimate job, and he got fired. After that, he started skimming off the top of his part-time job. He got caught. They threatened to kill him, and he just left one day. He disappeared. He left Carrie and me high and dry."

Mickey interrupted her, "You mean that his employer threatened to kill him for skimming a few dollars from his boss?"

"Yes," Janet said.

"How much did he take?" asked Mickey.

"I don't know the exact amount, but I think it was several thousand dollars."

James said, "Mickey, people rob convenience stores and kill the workers for far less than that. Look at the pizza drivers that have been robbed and beaten, shot, or stabbed for less than fifty dollars. It's not unheard of for people to be killed over an insignificant amount of money. It also depends on who he was working for, and my guess is they weren't exactly upstanding businessmen."

"I never thought about that. You're right. Go on, Janet," said Mickey.

"We had a mortgage to pay, but I only worked part-time and couldn't pay all the bills. After a few months, we got behind in payments and lost the house. I went on food stamps and applied for government programs, but it wasn't enough. We lived with friends until they asked us to move. We lived in our car while I tried to find Bobby. I looked for him until finally, I found him here. He was staying here, in Bridgeton. He was living with a guy named Alan Halston. I went there looking for him and explained who I was. They took me and put me in that place where you found me. Eventually, I lost count of the days I was locked in there, and one night you came and got me out. That's the whole story. Honest. That's it." She took a deep breath and leaned back in the chair like she was exhausted from telling the story.

"Tell us about the accident that injured Carrie," asked Mickey. "She refuses to talk about it. I suspect that it brings back awful memories for her."

"Yes, I guess it does," Janet said as she regained her composure. "Bobby was taking Carrie out to get some ice cream. She doesn't get any very often because of the sugar content, so it was a special treat. As usual, Bobby had been drinking, ran a stop sign, and the car was hit by another vehicle on Carrie's side. It broke both her legs, and she'll never walk again unless she has a series of operations. Soon after, that's when Bobby got caught skimming the money, and he left."

"Okay, first," said James, "we're not going to put you out. We're going to find Bobby. If he's still alive, we'll get him out. We'll give you enough money to leave this area and get a new start. We expect you and Bobby to work out your differences. We can't help you if you don't help yourself. Understand?"

"How are you going to do that?" she asked.

"Don't ask questions. We'll get you to safety. That's all I'm going to say," James said. He turned to Mickey. "We have to go now. We told Neal and Carson we'd get back to them before noon." James stood up.

Mickey stood with him and left to tell the kids goodbye. James spoke with Darcy for a couple of minutes, and she said that she should have some information on the names in a couple of hours. That might give them some helpful information. Darcy followed them out to the Humvee.

"James, you told her that you'd give them some money to get them started. Where's this money coming from? You know Mickey and I don't have enough money to give them."

"We'll work that out. Don't worry about it right now, Dee. We know what we're doing."

"When it comes to the money and finances, I need to know what's going on, James," she said sternly.

"Trust me. We'll work something out."

Darcy shook her head in resignation. "When it comes to handing out money to strangers, I hope you have something up your sleeve. And Mickey better not be part of it."

"God will provide, Dee. I know he will," said James.

She looked at James questioningly, "I don't know what you are up to, but I do know you don't even believe in God, so don't give me crap like that, James T."

When they got into the vehicle and drove away, Mickey looked over at James. "Hey, man, you almost stepped in it back there. When Dee starts calling you James T., you better watch out. She knows something's up, and she'll sniff it out faster than a bloodhound on a trail."

Mickey called a local restaurant and ordered two meals to be delivered to Neal and Carson.

When they got to the surveillance apartment, the food delivery car arrived at Neal and Carson's apartment. Mickey and James went into the surveillance apartment before the driver went to the door across the parking lot. James quickly called Neal and told him to answer the door and give the driver a generous tip. He also told him to call the office and tell them about the broken window. Tell them someone threw a rock through it, and it needs to be fixed.

After the phone conversation, Mickey asked Glen if any phone calls came for Neal. Glen said that only one had come in, and he believed it was from the guy they called Satchel. Mickey turned to the recorder and turned it on to listen to the conversation.

"Neal, have you been to the unit and checked on the stuff and the woman?" the man called Satchel said.

"Yes," Neal said. "We go by there every day. Why you askin'?"

"Just checking. Don't want anything to go wrong," Satchel said.

"Nothin' is going to go wrong. We're okay here."

"Bobby's making the first run. He wants to see his wife. I told him he could see her after he makes at least two runs. I also told him he has to make eight more before we let them go. Little does he know that the last run will be the last one he ever makes, anywhere!" Satchel laughed at his joke.

"When's the next one, Satchel?" asked Neal.

"When I set it up. It might be another week. I don't know. It isn't like they make nightly runs. Why do you care? You're getting paid enough."

"Yeah, I know. We're happy with the pay. We like to know what's going on, that's all."

"Don't ask questions. The less you know, the better I feel. Got it?"

"Yeah. We got it."

Satchel disconnected without saying goodbye. Glen said, "That call came in this morning. That's the only thing that's happened."

Mickey, James, and Glen made small talk for another fifteen minutes, and James redialed Neal.

"Hey, Neal. Did you and Carson like the meal we sent to you?" asked James.

"Um, yes. It was great, thanks."

"We aren't the monsters you may think we are. Now, I know another shipment is coming through, and I want to know where and when. By the way, have you called the office yet on that broken window?"

"No, we just finished eating. I don't know if I can get that information for you. I can't ask any questions of Satchel. He doesn't like me asking questions."

"I said to find out. I didn't ask what you could and couldn't do, Neal," James said with a definite tone of authority.

"You can find out when and where, or we might have to give you some more incentive. Do you know what I mean, Neal?"

"What kind of incentive?"

"We'll figure something out. How many fingers do you have, Neal?"

"Ten," he said.

"My, my, my, that's way too many. You don't need that many. How about you give me a couple, Neal?"

"No, please. I'll find out. Give me a couple of days?"

"You have twenty-four hours, Neal."

"I need more time than that, please!"

"Don't leave the unit, but you may now make outgoing calls. Don't try to give out any coded distress messages. I will know if you even try to pass a distress call. I will send someone, and all they will rescue is your dead body!" James disconnected the call. He turned to Mickey and smiled. "I thought he needed a little incentive to get us information and keep his mouth shut."

Glen looked at Mickey, then back at James. "Would you really do that, James?"

"Don't test me, Glen. And, I might as well say this to you. Keep your mouth shut, now and forever. If you even say a word to George or anyone else, they'll not even find your body."

"I won't say a word to anyone. I promise," Glen said and crossed his heart as a kid would do on a schoolyard playground.

Mickey placed his hand on Glen's shoulder and said, "James will be your best friend or your worst enemy. I know. We've been friends since high school. Just don't test that statement."

"I won't, Mickey," he said very clearly, now afraid of James.

"Now, here's a prepaid credit card. Call the restaurant twice a day and order food to be delivered to them. DO NOT order anything for here on this card. I don't want any connection between them and us, not even a credit card or delivery service. Here is two hundred dollars cash. You may order take-out or delivery for yourself and George with this cash. Do not order anything from the restaurant that delivers to them. We have some errands to run. Call me if anything happens, or they get any other calls."

CHAPTER 10

Saturday Afternoon...James has his Humvee Modified

JAMES TOOK MICKEY BACK TO HIS apartment to pick up Mickey's truck. They agreed to meet later that afternoon.

In the meantime, Mickey had several hours to spend, so he thought he would take Pop out for a ride. He went to the rehab center and asked the head nurse to take Daniel on an outing. She agreed and said it might help his memory. When he went to Daniel's room, he was sitting in a chair watching the television.

"Hey, Pop. How're you today?"

"I'm fine, Mickey Ray. How're you?"

"Great. I had an idea. How about us going for a ride around town?" said Mickey.

"Will they let me do that? I'd love to do that," Daniel said.

"I've already cleared it with the head nurse, and they'll help you get into my truck. We can drive around some of the familiar places and see what you might remember," said Mickey, now helping Daniel stand up and into his wheelchair.

An orderly helped Daniel into Mickey's truck and they headed toward Daniel's home. As he drove, he pointed out some of the landmarks of the town. Daniel recognized some, others he didn't, but Mickey felt they were making progress and was pleased. Finally, he pulled into Daniel's home. As he drove up into the entrance road, Daniel smiled.

Mickey turned toward his father and said, "Looks good, doesn't it, Pop?"

"Yes, son. It does. I like it. Can we get out and walk around? Can I go inside?" he asked.

"No, Pop. Not today. We didn't bring your wheelchair. We can drive around to the back of the house so you can see that area also. Would you like that?"

"Yes, I wish I could get out and look inside the garage at the cars."

At that moment, Mickey felt a stab in his heart. All the cars were now gone. A few months ago, Aunt Evelyn sold Pop's entire collection to an unknown out-of-state buyer. Pop loved those cars. Some Daniel bought and restored, others he purchased in mint condition, but he treasured each one.

"Is the Corniche we restored in there?" Daniel asked. "I really enjoyed the time we spent together restoring that old Rolls Royce."

"It was some fun times, wasn't it, Pop. Some of the best times of my life. Maybe we can find another car to restore together."

"That would be fun also. What would you like to do next time, Mickey?"

"I don't know. I'll think about it, and we can decide together. You picked out the Corniche. When we finish it, you can take that one since I got the last one."

"We'll see. We have a lot of time to make up our minds on that one, Mickey."

"That we do, Pop. I guess we had better get you back to the rehab center. We can do this again soon, and next time we'll bring the wheelchair so you can go inside and look around."

Mickey headed back to the rehab center to drop his father off. It was a great afternoon with his father.

After dropping Daniel off, he headed back to James' apartment. They needed to find out where Bobby was being held. Maybe another conversation with Neal was necessary. When he got to James' apartment, James was walking down the sidewalk swinging his arms. Mickey pulled into a parking spot, and James walked over, still swinging his arms.

"What's with all the gyrations, James?"

"I just got back from a run, and I'm walking the last block and cooling down. Swinging my arms helps to limber them up. Got time for a short workout?" James answered.

"No, we have to find out where Bobby is before they find out Janet's gone. Neal or Carson takes her food and water each day, so they'll find out soon enough she's gone. If they report it to Satchel, then they might kill Bobby. We need to move fast."

"If Satchel has Bobby, then we need to find out where Satchel is and make him tell us. Until then, we can tell Neal that we'll take over taking care of Janet. We don't have to tell them we already have her," said James. "Let me go back in my place, shower, and change, and we can have another talk with Neal. Wanna come inside and wait?"

"Sure, got anything to drink?" Mickey asked as he got out of his truck.

"Water."

"Nope. I'm not that thirsty. But I can read one of your gun magazines while I'm waiting," he said as they both walked into James' apartment.

Twenty minutes later, they were going back to the surveillance unit across from Neal and Carson's apartment.

When they pulled up, they noticed Sam taking measurements of the broken picture window on that unit. He looked at Mickey and discretely shook his head, and nodded at the window. Mickey shook his head "yes" in response but kept on walking into the surveillance unit.

Glen and George were both sitting, talking about the broken window across the street when they walked in.

Glen looked at Mickey and asked, "Hey, Mickey. Do you know anything about that?" he asked.

"Yes. They reported it this morning. Someone put a rock through it last night. Why do you know anything?"

"Nope. We thought you might know something, that's all."

"I know that we must pay to fix it, and those large windows aren't cheap. If it happens again, maybe we should put up more security lights or some cameras."

James coughed a few times to cover up his laugh. Then he told both Glen and George they could take a break for a while. They didn't have to come back until around ten that night. They got up and left the unit. Just as they left, Sam walked in.

"Hey, Mickey. What happened over there. I know you had something to do with it, and that's why I didn't say anything outside. I asked them to come outside and take a look and maybe point me in the direction that the rock came from, but they wouldn't get near the door. I don't know what you did, but you scared the devil out of them."

"Yeah, Sam, and that's exactly what we wanted. Take your time fixing it. Keep coming back to check on it and them. Just let them think you are an efficient and caring maintenance person. Tell them you have to order the glass and it'll take a few hours. That will put it around quitting time, then tell them you'll come back tomorrow and put up some plywood to secure it."

Sam got a serious look on his face. "Boss, tomorrow is Sunday."

"I know. I'll pay you double time if you'll come tomorrow," Mickey said.

"You got it, Mickey Ray," Sam acknowledged, then turned and left.

When Sam left, James laughed out loud, "You are slick. I'll give you that, Mickey. You know when to talk and who to talk to. Good idea keeping even Sam in the dark, and I'd trust him a lot more than Glen and George. And you even offered him double time. You're a good boss, Mickey Ray!"

"I do trust him more, but the fewer people who know, the better for them and us. Let's give Neal a call and see what he knows," he said as he handed James the phone.

"Neal, how are you doing today?"

"Fine."

"I got word that you called the office, and they sent someone to repair your window. Are they doing a good job for you?"

"Yeah, they're doing it okay. It won't be fixed for another few hours. The guy said he has to order the glass from a local glass shop, and he'll be back to check on us."

"Good. It sounds like the people that own this place are very efficient. I wouldn't let anyone inside except the maintenance personnel, Neal. Now, we want to get in touch with Satchel."

"No, please don't do that. We need to go take care of some business too. Can we leave? Just for an hour or two. We really need to do something."

"No, Neal. You can't leave, but don't worry about the business. We'll take care of that for you. You need to take care of someone, don't you? We will take care of her for you. You needn't worry about her anymore."

"Please don't hurt her. We'll do anything you ask, but don't hurt her. Satchel will kill us if something happens to her."

"I promise I won't hurt her if you continue to help us. Will you do that?"

"Sure. Anything you say. Just don't contact Satchel!"

"We need to contact him. Where does he live?"

"I can't tell you that. Please!"

"Neal, I need to know that, and you will tell me, or I will drive to your apartment and begin taking fingers until you do tell me. Now, if you tell me now, I'll let you keep all your fingers."

"If I tell you, Satchel will kill me. Losing a finger is better than dead!"

"Let's see. If I tie you down and cut off both your thumbs, then if you live, you'll never be able to pick anything up with one hand. If no one finds you in time, you'll bleed to death slowly and painfully. So, as a show of good faith, I promise not to tell Satchel how I got his address. So, if you cooperate right now, you will keep all your fingers, and maybe Satchel will let you live. Deal?"

"Yes, thanks. Anything you say."

"Good. Talk to me. Give me the address."

"It doesn't have an address, but I can give you directions."

"Talk to me, Neal."

"First, you know route 143 north at the Interstate exit?"

"Yes."

"Go past the big lumber yard exactly three point two miles and turn right onto the dirt road. Go all the way to the end. His house is down there at the end."

"What about security, Neal?"

"I don't know. I think he has a big dog. I don't know much about dogs."

"What about cameras or perimeter security?"

"I don't know what you mean!"

"I mean alarms, you idiot! I should have you shot for being so stupid!"

"No, let me think for a minute. He has an alarm switch on a post just before you get to the house. It is kind of hidden, but if you know it's there, you can see it just before the house gets into view. If you see the house, you've missed the alarm box. I swear."

"What is the alarm code, Neal?"

"It's one, nine, eight, four."

"Good. Now tell me where Bobby is!"

"I don't know, honest. Maybe he's at the warehouse."

"Why didn't you tell me this the last time I asked you?"

"I don't know. I forgot. I still don't know if he's really there."

"Last question, Neal. Where's the warehouse?"

"It's not really a warehouse. It is a huge barn-like building behind Satchel's house."

"If they have a warehouse, why do they have rental spaces?"

"For the overflow. Sometimes he gets so much merchandise, and he needs extra space. Sometimes he uses it for deliveries. He rents a space, and instead of meeting the buyer in person, he tells them where the unit is, and they pick up the stuff themselves. Usually, the payment's made the same way. Except he rents just a tiny space and puts a box of money in it. That way, it can be in a different space all the time, and no one knows where it is. They place the money and put a combination lock on the unit. The buyer calls and Satchel tells them where to leave the money, and he gives them a combination of the lock. Then he sends someone to get the money, and Satchel calls them back with a unit number and combination of where the merchandise is located. That way, no one meets in person. It's simple once you get the hang of it."

"So, where does Bobby come in?"

"He's making some pickups and deliveries for Satchel right now. He's only temporary."

"How temporary? How long do you plan on keeping him?"

"I don't know. That isn't part of my business. Satchel only knows that, and he don't tell nobody much. He's a kind of need-to-know person, know what I mean?"

"Yes, I know what you mean."

"Is Bobby in the house or warehouse?"

"I don't know. Probably in the warehouse. Satchel has a couple of rooms in there for situations like this."

"What do you mean, situations like this?"

"Why so many questions. I don't know everything that happens. All I know is if someone, a driver, comes into town and maybe needs to leave from the warehouse early or something like that, he gets to stay in one of the rooms in the warehouse. Satchel doesn't usually let drivers get out. They have to stick close so they can be ready to roll at a minute's notice."

"Where does he get his merchandise?"

"I don't know that either. We just do what Satchel tells us to do."

"Have you ever killed anyone, Neal?"

"No, never."

"That lie will cost you one finger. You'll probably live with one finger bleeding, but not two. You'll bleed out before someone can stop it. Now, I ask again, have you ever killed anyone? Now, let me say to you, I have killed lots of people, and one more will not make any difference to me."

"Okay, yes. I did kill one person, but it was in self-defense."

"Uh, huh. Yes, and you expect me to believe that."

"No, I mean, yes. The guy tried to kill me, but I got to the gun first and…"

"Shut up, Neal. I don't care. Shut up before I send someone to bring that finger you owe for the lie you told."

There was silence at the other end of the line. "Neal, do you hear me?" said James.

"Yes, I hear you."

"Now, this is what I want you to do. Stay right where you are tonight. Then tomorrow morning at eight o'clock, you may leave. Hear me, Neal?"

"Yes," was the one-word answer.

"When you go outside, you're to take the license plate off of your car. It's no good now anyway. You'll call a cab to take you to the storage facility where Janet Griffin is being held. There'll be some money there for you and Carson. At the office, will be a set of keys to a car out front at the gate. You'll then put the plates on the car we have provided for you. We'll leave the car title and the money in the glove compartment, and you may title it in your name where ever you wish to live. There'll be enough money to get you far from here. If you call anyone or stop anywhere in the city limits, we'll know. You will NOT come back. You will NOT pass go. You will NOT collect any more money. You will disappear. If you ever return here, I will personally hunt you down and put a bullet into that tiny brain of yours and Carson's. Do you understand me? I give you my word, I'll not tell Satchel you told me anything."

"But what about the lady?" asked Neal cautiously.

"She's no longer your concern. Understand, Neal?" answered James.

"Yeah, I understand."

"That's what I'll do for you. Is this all clear? I'm giving you a second chance at life. Trust me, we both know Satchel wouldn't do this for you. Do you know why I am doing this for you, Neal?"

"No."

"Because I'm a nice guy," said James calmly. "Any questions, Neal?"

"No."

"Good. I'll pull the guards off of you at eight in the morning. One will follow you unobtrusively until you get out of town. We'll know if you don't continue going. Understand, if you turn around, you will die!" When James stopped talking, he disconnected the call.

Mickey took a deep breath. "Do you think they'll do it?"

"I know they'll do it. Now we have to get them a car to drive. We'll use some of the cash we got the other night."

"How much do we give them?" asked Mickey.

"I don't know. How about five grand?" said James.

"That's a lot."

"Yes, but if we give them enough, we won't have to worry for a long time for them to return. At least not until the money runs out. Even your Bible says in Proverbs 26:11 Even a dog returns to his vomit. They'll be back."

"Are you going to tell Satchel how you got the information?"

"Nope. I promised I wouldn't tell."

"You know that when Satchel finds out they've skipped town, he'll assume they took the money. And if he finds them, he'll have them killed. When they run, they'll be signing their death warrant."

"Don't care. Not my problem. I'm giving them a chance to run. What they do with that chance is no concern of mine. Now let's go find a car for the boys across the street."

"Man, you are one cold dude."

"Look at what they did to Janet and would have done to Bobby if they were ordered to kill him. They have no soul. They're as evil as anyone in Satchel's organization. They're just dumber than most of the others. For two cents, I'd have killed them myself. This way, they have a fighting chance."

"Where should we go to find a car?"

"I don't care. We need to go by my place so we can get some cash to pay for the car and give those dopes five grand."

Mickey drove to James' apartment and waited in the truck while James went in to get the money.

"Stay with the small private dealers. A name-brand dealer will want all kinds of information and stuff. Since this is a cash sale, they don't need anything from us but greenbacks," James said.

Mickey drove around town until he got to "Bubba's Used Cars and Trucks." Our motto is: Cash is King. We give 10% cash discount on all our vehicles, complete with a 30-day warranty. Mickey pulled in and parked. They picked out a reasonable-looking vehicle, paid the lot owner, and walked out with the keys. Mickey called Sam and told him to meet them at the local fast-food restaurant. When Sam got there, Mickey told him what to do.

Sam was to go to the storage facility, give the little old man the keys to the car, and tell him when Neal and Carson came in, he was to give them the keys, and Sam would give the old man a one-hundred-dollar bill for doing this. The two men would be in around eight-thirty tomorrow morning. Mickey gave Sam the keys and the hundred-dollar bill. He was to give Mickey a call when this was done.

As Sam was leaving, James said to him, "One other thing, Sam. Tell them it is compliments of the Mongoose!"

"Okay. Is that supposed to mean something to them?"

"No, they won't get it."

When Sam walked out, Mickey said to James, "What's this Mongoose thing?"

"I don't know. It just sounded good when I said it. You do know what a mongoose is, don't you?"

"Sure, it is a little furry animal that kills snakes…Okay, I get it…It kills snakes, and you kill snakes."

James showed a big toothy grin. "You got it, little bro. Let's have a piece of apple pie and a milk shake. My treat."

After about 30 minutes, Sam called and told Mickey he had done it, and the old man was ecstatic about the hundred-dollar tip. Sam said the old man told him he would deliver car keys all day long for tips like that. After that, they got up and left the restaurant.

"Great, now all we need to do is to get Bobby out of that warehouse, assuming he's there," said James.

"Since you know how to do all that, we'll go to your place," said Mickey as he headed in the direction of James' apartment complex.

"Mickey, do you mind following me over to drop the Vee off at the garage to get some work done on it?"

"I don't mind. What's wrong with it?"

"Nothing. I just want to have some modifications, that's all," James answered.

"Sure. I'll follow you there," Mickey said as he pulled into the parking space next to James' Humvee.

James drove to a locally owned used car lot, proceeded around to the back, and stopped in the front of a garage door of the automotive repair area. The door opened, and after James drove inside, it closed again. Mickey parked and went into the entrance door with a sign that said, "Customer Service Entrance."

Mickey went inside and looked through the interior glass door and saw James and a tall muscular-looking man with a Vandyke beard talking. They were waving their hands over the rear end of the vehicle.

Mickey opened the door and started to walk into the service area when the man looked directly at him. He put a hand up in a stop signal and called out to Mickey.

"Sir, please don't come back here. It's an employee-only area. I'll be with you in a few minutes."

James spoke up, "It's okay, Logan, he's with me." Then he motioned for Mickey to come over where they were standing.

The man put out his hand to shake hands with him. "Hello, how are you?"

James nodded from each man, "Mickey Ray, this is C. Logan King. He owns the place." Then he turned to the man, "Logan, this my friend, Mickey Ray Christianson. He's the one I told you about that's looking for a replacement Rolls Royce. His last one was torched and a total loss. I thought maybe you could help him out."

"Sure, James. I can help him," he said.

Mickey said, "I don't know what I want right now, sir."

"Call me Logan. I'll look around if you can give me some guidelines to look for. You want a new one, restored antique or a do-it-yourself project?"

"As I said, I don't know. I'm open right now. As much as I enjoyed helping my dad restore the last one, I don't know if I want to go through that again. Maybe a bit newer one. Do you work on them?"

"Nope, but I can learn if you need some help occasionally. I'll help you in any way I can. They're radically different than most cars on the road today."

James said, "His last one was a Corniche, but maybe now he would like to move up. How about a newer one that he can buy and ride, not spend years and tens of thousands in restoration costs?"

"Fine, I'll keep my eyes out for one for your friend here," Logan said as he wiped more grease off his hands.

"Now back to the Vee," said James. "Can you put in a bulletproof rear glass and some armor plate in the doors? Also, I'd like a bulletproof windshield and run-flat tires. Are they doable?"

"Yes. I can install an armor-up kit. It essentially puts armor around the vehicle. It'll give you bulletproof glass and light armor on the doors, which will stop basic pistol rounds and some light rifle rounds, but it isn't a full armored vehicle. It will cost, but if you want it to be entirely bulletproof, I suggest trading it for an HMMWV which is the full military version. They'll stop an RPG."

Mickey asked, "What's an RPG?"

"Rocket Propelled Grenade. I don't think I'll ever need a military Hummer, but I would like some basic protection," James said.

Logan looked at James and nodded toward Mickey. "Is he read into the situation?"

"Yes, he's up to date," James answered.

Mickey said to James, "I guess Logan's another one of the contacts that I'm just learning about?"

"Yes, he is. He helps with transportation."

"Fine. Do you want it?" Logan asked.

"Yes, and I need it yesterday," said James.

"Of course. I'll order the kit and have it brought in by truck tonight. Same as always. COD."

CHAPTER 11

Saturday Evening...The Plan

Mickey sat down on James' couch and dozed off while James went on his computer to get a google map layout of the place that Neal had described that Satchel owned. He printed it out and studied it for a few minutes. Then he walked over and shook Mickey.

"Mickey, wake up," James said as Mickey shook his head and rubbed his face in an attempt to wake up.

"Did you find something?" he asked.

"Kind of."

"What do you mean, kind of?"

"Just what I said. Kind of. I found the place. The house is visible on the map, but the barn isn't that easy. Trees cover it. The satellite can't see through that, so I can't tell what's around it. We need to go in to take a look."

"You mean a recon mission like the one we did in Jersey?" Mickey asked, now fully awake.

"We aren't going to have to crawl around and blow stuff up as we did before, are we?"

"No, I don't think it'll be anything like that. But we do need to see what we're getting ourselves into. We do like we did before. Go in, look around, and go back later for the rescue if he's still there," James said.

"How about some pictures of Bobby. I can call Darcy and see if Janet has a picture of him so we can recognize him. I'd hate to rescue the wrong person."

"Smart thinking, bro. Call Dee, and see if she can get something. She can email it to me, and we'll print it out."

Mickey picked up his phone and dialed Darcy. She picked up on the third ring. "Hello, Mickey?"

"Hey, Dee. How's everything going? Is Carrie doing okay now?"

"She's doing great now. Janet's looking after her and my two. I've been able to get a lot of work done for the firm and do an entire rundown on those names you gave me. Want to hear about them now?"

"Sure, what'd you find out?" he asked.

"The two Sadowski brothers are small time. They both spent time in jail for petty theft and a couple of burglaries. All penny-ante stuff. Now this Satchel guy, he's a pretty hard-nosed worker. He's been charged with everything from drugs to gun-running and Interstate mail fraud. He's also been charged with dealing in stolen goods. He did five years in the state pen. He's been out for some time and has been keeping a low profile. He's a suspect in two murders, but the witnesses disappeared before the court date, so they can't pin anything solid on him. He's the one to be careful of. If he's involved, watch your back," she said in finality.

"Dee, ask if Janet has a picture of Bobby. We may have found him, but when we go in, we want to pull out the right person," Mickey asked.

"Sure, Mickey. Hold on while I ask her."

Mickey held for several minutes. He sat thumbing thru one of James' gun magazines. Finally, she came back on the phone.

"Yes, she has one. It's one of him and Carrie just before he left. You want to come by and get it?"

"How about you scanning it and emailing it to James so we can print it out."

"I'll do that right now. Have you found him?"

"We don't know. We have a lead, but we really won't know until we know what Bobby looks like. Could you send us that picture? And thanks, Dee. My love to the kids," he said and hung up the phone.

"Dee said Janet has one, and she'll send us a copy. Do you know what we'll need for the recon yet?"

"No, but we should be prepared for anything, so we don't get caught with our pants down like we did the last time. We don't want this to come back on us," James said as he studied the picture.

"We need to get a live look. These satellite pictures take out all the people."

"They take out all the people? Why do they do that?"

"A computer program takes out all the people in satellite pictures, so they don't get sued for invasion of privacy. Only government and military sats leave the people in, and we don't have access to that," James answered, still looking at the photo. "So, we're stuck with google maps."

"Can we get live coverage?"

"Yep. We need a drone to do it."

"Those are easy to get. We can buy those at the local toy or hobby store," added Mickey.

"Nope, not good enough. We need military-grade."

"And you have access to one of those."

"Yep, but they aren't cheap. Maybe we can rent one. I'll check on both options. I have a phone in the back room. Get it for me, Mickey."

"Where is it back there?'

"Master bedroom. Look in the top dresser drawer, left-hand side, and get that screwdriver. Then look in the closet on the back wall. There's a panel. Unscrew it with the driver, and you'll find a phone. Bring it here."

"Wait a minute. You cut a hole in the wall of this apartment. I own this building, and you're making modifications to it. Without my knowledge or permission?"

"Yep. Got a problem with that?"

"No. I just…never mind. I'll be right back with the phone," Mickey said as he headed toward the bedroom.

A few minutes later, he returned with a phone in his hand and handed it to James. "I've never seen one of these, but this is a satellite phone, isn't it? Not just a regular cell phone."

"Correct. Now get out for a few minutes while I make a call and get a drone," James ordered. "Go get us a pizza or something. I'll be done when you get back."

Mickey said nothing. He picked up his keys and walked out the door. Getting into his truck, he called the local pizza restaurant and ordered take-out.

When he returned, James was looking at a photograph of a man standing beside Carrie in her wheelchair. As he placed the pizza on the dining room table, he looked at James.

"Is that the picture that Dee sent over of Bobby?"

"Yes, and we can meet up with a drone team leader in an hour. Let's go," James said.

"Put the pizza in the fridge. I'll eat it later."

"Hey, you owe me twenty bucks for the pizza," said Mickey. "What do you mean a drone team leader?"

"She has drones and a team of men that she can deploy to help us with the rescue."

"A team and men to deploy? That sounds expensive. Why do we need them? Can we do it ourselves like we did last time?"

"To answer your questions," James said as they walked out the door, "she has military-grade drones. She has a team of mercenaries on call, and yes, they are expensive. No, I remember what we went through last time, and I don't want that to happen again. They are trained men. You are not, and I can't do it by myself."

"Okay, that's a lot of information you're throwing at me right now. You said she?"

"Yep," said James as they walked to the truck.

"Next, you used the term mercenaries. I suspect you're planning something that you haven't told me about yet."

"That is also true. We'll talk about it when we get there."

"Do you have any idea what this is going to cost us?" asked Mickey.

"I don't have an exact figure but around eighty grand," James said matter of factly.

"How much did you say?" Mickey said as his mouth dropped open.

"Yep, you heard me right. I got a discount because I know the owner of the team. Full military-grade equipment and team. And you can put the pizza cost on my tab."

Mickey's eyes bugged out as he said, "We don't have that kind of money!"

"Yes, we do, and that's a deal considering what we got. Remember, we just had an influx of operating funds, so Satchel's paying for it. Let's get this show on the road."

Mickey continued to cough and clear his throat.

They rode in silence to the diner. Mickey and James got out and asked Pauline if they could use the back party room for a meeting. They informed Pauline that another person would be coming in and would she mind bringing her back here. She agreed to do that.

When Pauline brought their drink order, James asked her to close the party room door on her way out and not disturb them because they had some private business to take care of, and they needed privacy. Pauline nodded her head and left.

When Pauline left, Mickey got up and locked the door so no one could accidentally walk in unannounced. From this point forward, they could afford no interruptions.

A few minutes later, there was a knock on the door. Mickey unlocked the door and James called out, "Enter."

James stood up when the young lady following Pauline walked up to the table. She threw her arms around James and hugged him close. She backed off and looked him up and down. While she was sizing him up, he was also doing the same.

"Wow, girl, you're looking fantastic! What's all this?" he said, waving his hand up and down like a vertical wave. "You look so much different!"

"Better or worse, Jimmy boy?" she said, smiling, putting hands on her hips and jutting them out in a sexy pose.

"Better, for sure!"

She reached up and puffed her hair and said, "For starters, I felt that no longer being in the service, I needed to look a bit more girlish, so I let my hair grow long. Also, you may not have noticed yet, but I bought a couple of other things too," she said, pointing at her chest.

"How could I miss those. Nice and full but not too big," James said. "Turn around. I want to see the backside."

She spun around slowly, smiling and putting her hands in her back pockets. She stood and turned to look at James, swishing her long blonde hair over her shoulders and gave him a pouty look, wrinkled her nose, smiled, and blew him a kiss!

"You've changed so much since I last saw you, Alyssa! How long has it been, almost a year since you needed me?" James asked.

"Thirteen months to be exact, Jimmy boy. I don't go in the field much anymore, so I felt I could have a little work done," she explained. "I mostly sit in the control center and direct the action. If I did need to go, I'm still in the physical condition to do it."

"Seriously, all joking aside, you look amazing," James said. "When did you become a blonde instead of that beautiful raven black hair?"

"As you know, I'm of Latin descent, so I've had black hair all my life. With my darker skin complexion, I thought I'd try the blonde look. I think the contrast looks okay. What do you think?"

"My gosh! It looks absolutely fantastic. You look as sexy as a beauty queen!"

"Why, thank you, James. I take that as a high compliment from you. But if we go on a mission that I must go into the field, I'll change it back to black for the duration."

Mickey sat, silenced, transfixed with this five-foot-five tall goddess-looking girl that was obviously flirting with James. He opened his mouth to speak, but nothing came out. He was struck dumb. He closed his mouth, swallowed again, and made another attempt at speech.

"Hey, James. You apparently know each other. Would you mind introducing me?"

"Oh, sure. Sorry, Mickey. She is an old friend of mine. We were in the same outfit in service. Mickey Ray, meet Alyssa."

She held out her hand to shake his. He wiped his hand on his pants as he stood up and took her hand in his, and shook hands. As soon as she took his hand, she noticed how he was embarrassed at his nervousness. She put her other hand enclosing his in both of hers, saying, "Any friend of Jimmy boy is a friend of mine, Mickey Ray."

"Aly, I've told you a thousand times, I don't like to be called Jimmy boy."

She laughed, "I know. That's why I do it!" she said, sitting down, followed by James and Mickey sitting on either side of her.

"You're the only person in the world that can get away with it," he said to her. "And remember that, Mickey Ray. So don't get any ideas. I'd hate to hurt my best friend."

"Best friend? James, wow, another high compliment from Jimmy!" she said, looking at Mickey.

"Mickey Ray here is almost family. His sister and I are engaged."

"Wow, she's one lucky lady, James. I'm so happy for you."

"No, Aly. I'm the lucky one. All she's getting is a scarred, broken-down ex-soldier with serious problems."

She suddenly got serious and reached out and put her hand on his arm. "James T. Bower, I knew you before the accident and helped you get through the healing. You may be scarred on the outside, but inside you are one of the finest men I've ever met in my life. I don't know her, but I know you, and I say without a doubt, she's the luckiest girl in the world."

James may have been facially scarred, but he blushed as he looked down at the table.

"Okay, Jimmy boy. Why'd you call me? What do you need that I can provide?"

James brought his head back up, composed himself, and started explaining. He started from the beginning. He then produced the printouts of the grounds area, which showed the house and warehouse that belonged to Satchel.

"Seems like you have everything under control. Why do you need my team?"

"The last time we went in on a recon mission, we got caught by cameras. As a result, his sister, my future wife, had to leave town. They kidnapped his girlfriend. To put an end to the whole mess, we ended up killing some people. True, they were all criminals, but that's beside the point. We didn't plan on doing that. It worked out okay, but maybe we could have done it differently. Not quite as messy."

"Wait, you mean a few months ago, those two propane companies that got taken out? That was you two?"

"Yeah, that was us."

"Oh, James. That was awesome. I'd love to have been part of that mission. I saw it on national news. In my book, you two were heroes. You know the saying, 'Kill 'em all, and let God sort 'em out!'"

"I'm out of that business now. That's why I haven't helped you on the last couple of missions. I don't want a replay of that. Will you help us? We have the money to pay."

She turned to Mickey. "Did you go in with him?"

"He helped me with some training, and I kind of backed him up. He did most of it. I shot the tanks. He exploded them."

"He trained you well, Mick. That was one impressive ball of fire!"

"This is what I'll do, Jimmy. As a wedding present, I'll do it at cost. I have to pay my men and miscellaneous expenses, but it'll still cost because my people are the best, and you know how well I pay them. But I don't have to tell you that since you have been one of them since you left the service."

"I understand, and I can't expect you to do any more. First, you see what we have. What do you suggest?"

Mickey interrupted her, "Can I ask, what did you do in the military for the team, as you call it?"

"I did several things, depending on the mission. Sometimes I stayed back and watched from the air. Sometimes I went forward and scouted things out from the ground and directed the men on where to go. That's it in a nutshell. After I got out of the service, I went into the business for myself. Jimmy here has helped me on several of those missions. But as he said, he turned me down on the last two when I called him to help."

Mickey looked from Alyssa to James and said, "So James, when you told me that you were going on vacation or just took a few days to travel the country, you were really going on a secret mission with her?"

James looked at Alyssa and said to her, "I trust Mickey Ray with my life, so I am going to answer some of his questions, Aly. I understand that some of our missions were strictly secret, and I'll not tell him anything that is or was secret."

James turned back to Mickey. "Yes, I did help Aly on some missions during those times. As you have heard me say many times, 'DON'T ASK.' I can't and won't give you any details of those missions. Do you understand that, Mickey?"

"Yes, I understand," Mickey said as his mouth dropped open in amazement.

"I went on secret missions with Aly and her team. That's all I can and will say," stated James.

"Are you satisfied with that, Alyssa?" he said, turning back to Alyssa.

"If you say Mickey's okay, that's good enough for me, as long as you understand those boundaries, James," she said.

Mickey said, "I understand, she understands, James understands, we all understand, blah, blah, blah. Can we move forward now, or do I need to leave the room so the two of you can reminisce about old times and decide if I'm trustworthy?"

James ignored Mickey's sarcasm and continued reading Mickey in on Alyssa's skill set.

"She was our hawk in the sky and radar on the ground. Her superpower was her sight. She was the one that flew the drones overhead if they couldn't redirect a satellite view, which they usually did when they couldn't get live feeds," said James. "She used state-of-the-art equipment to be our eyes. With her keen eyesight and tiny size on the ground, Aly could quietly crawl into a position undetected and direct us from there. By seeing hidden men in places we couldn't, she saved our butts many times. She was also very deadly with a rifle."

"Hey, gentlemen, I need to go to the car to get some stuff to show you, then we'll get started."

"Sure, we'll get some drink refills while we wait," said Mickey as she got up and started walking away. As she walked off, Mickey leaned over and whispered to James. "She's gorgeous. How did you ever keep your mind on the mission, with her around?"

Alyssa stopped, turned around, and called back. "I heard that, Mick. Thank you, but get Jimmy to tell you about my other superpower!"

James took a deep breath. "She's not kidding. I didn't even think to tell you. She has almost super hearing. I mean, she can hear things even a dog can't hear."

"Really?"

"Yes, she's a freak of nature. It wouldn't surprise me if she can hear us all the way out to her car right now. But to answer your question. When we were on the team, she didn't look like that. Her hair was cut very short. She didn't have these," he said, pointing to his own chest. "She was almost flat-chested. To add to all that, she dressed in camo gear all the time. I never saw her in anything, even the least bit feminine. She was almost one of the guys. She went out of her way to be unattractive. Even then, she had a beautiful face but nothing to add to it. She was just one of the guys to all of us. She's done a total about-face. I guess she was like the ugly duckling that turned into a beautiful swan."

"Wow, you can say that again. Shhhh….here she comes," said Mickey.

"Well, boys. I didn't hear everything you said, but my ears were burning, so I know you talked about me while I was gone," she said, smiling.

Now it was Mickey's turn to blush and say nothing.

"We were. Mickey is quite stricken with you. Compared to what you used to look like, you've blossomed, my very dear friend. You wear your beauty very well."

"Thank you, James. Now that we have my looks out of the way, let's get down to business. Here are some of the pieces of equipment we might be using. I'll take several, and we'll deploy as necessary. The first is my headquarters van. As you can see in this photo, it looks very innocuous. I have several drones with various flying times, transmitting ranges, cameras, including thermal imaging and infrared. I can fly several hundred feet off the ground without being seen unless you're looking for it, and even then, well out of small arms fire. This particular one has practically a six-mile radius transmitting range and forty-minute flying time. I have another one that has even more capacity, but in this case, I want to remain close as possible to retrieve you if you decide to go in immediately. Do you plan to do that, James, or do you want a basic recon run and return later for a pickup?"

"If it isn't too heavily guarded, I want to make it all in one run. If it is heavily guarded, we can come back later."

"Do you want to do it in daylight or night?"

"I don't know. What do you think, Aly?"

"Both have advantages. In daylight, we can see exactly what's going on. My drones have the latest technology cameras, and we can see more detail. We can see the men at night, but it's much more difficult to tell their armament. You know, we can't tell if they only have handguns or heavy artillery like automatic weapons or if we can tell that, we can't tell what kind. A shotgun and an automatic will look the same in infrared. My suggestion is if it's not too heavily manned, go in daylight. There may not be as many people there during the day. At night, after things shut down, more may be bedded down for the night. Sure, you have an element of surprise, but higher numbers mean higher risk. Last is, those guys will most likely not be military trained, so skill as well as surprise is on your side."

"You're right. They probably won't be trained, but we don't know that for sure, and that's why we called you, Aly."

"I realize that, and we'll be prepared for the worst," Ally responded. "Just the two of you going in?"

Mickey blurted out, "Yes."

At the same time, James said, "No."

"Okay, which is it, boys?"

"I'm going in, James!"

"And I said, you're not. You're not trained for this kind of mission," said James looking at Mickey.

"I did fine last time. You're the one that got injured, not me."

"True, but my injury was shrapnel, not a gunshot wound. Besides, it was night. There was no hand-to-hand combat. You shot from a distance, and no one was shooting back. Except for that one time, and I took care of that for you. I'll go in with the team. Not you. Now, I said NO, and that's final."

"Mick, I have to take James' side on this. If it went down as he said, he's right. You aren't trained for this. I have two more guys at the ready that can fill in. You can stay back and scout from the cover of the trees just like you did last time. Sort of being a backup, maybe create a diversion if one's needed. You can still take part, just not as one of the men going in front. So, I'm stepping up on this. You'll do what I say, even if you are NOT one of the team. For this mission, you are, and you'll listen to me, understand, Mickey Ray?" she said with a profound air of authority.

Mickey sat silently and sullen.

"Say yes, Mickey, or I'm out," Alyssa said.

"Say yes, Mickey. I'm with Aly on this. You'll do what she says. We all did as she said when we were on a mission because she could see and hear what we couldn't. She wasn't on the mission when we were ambushed, or maybe my team would be here today, and I wouldn't be scarred from head to toe."

"Okay, okay, I'll do what you say."

"Promise me, Mickey Ray, you will NOT go off on your own on this one," said James. "Promise me, bro...."

"I promise."

There was a knock at the door. When James answered, it was Pauline. "Excuse me, guys, I hate to interrupt, but we need to close. If ya'll aren't finished with your business, we open at seven in the morning."

"Thanks, Pauline. We understand. We'll be leaving. We're done here, tonight."

As they walked out to their vehicles, James said to Alyssa, "Thanks for helping us out. We couldn't do it without you."

"Yes, you could. Just do the same thing you did in those other places."

"Mickey has a thing against killing people, and we want to get this Bobby guy out alive and back to his wife and little girl. And seriously, you look amazing. If I had just run into you on the street, I would never have known you. As they say, you clean up real nice. You are quite stunning, to say the least."

"Thank you, James. Even with those scars, I think you're a handsome man, and I know that Darcy thinks so too. Now when do you want to act on this?" she said as they walked to her car.

"When can we do it? We can meet at my place and plan it out," said James.

"How about first thing in the morning? Around five AM?"

"Sounds fine to me. I'll let Mickey know. He isn't an early riser like us, but he'll be there."

James laughed and reached down and opened the door to a new fire red Ferrari. "Nice ride, my dear," he said.

"Thanks, I'll give you a ride someday," she winked.

"Sorry, but my almost wife wouldn't approve," he smiled back and gently closed the door. She fired up the car, backed it out of the lot into the road, and sped away.

Mickey sat in his truck, waiting for James to get in. When he did, he looked over at James and shook his head.

"Don't look at me like that. I told you, Aly didn't look like that when we worked together. Besides, if we had something, I wouldn't have met Dee. So don't give me any grief."

Mickey shook his head again and took James back to his place. As James got out of the truck, he said, "Be here at five AM. Don't be late."

"Got it," answered Mickey. He gave James a mock salute and left.

CHAPTER 12

Sunday 5 AM...The Team

Mickey saw Alyssa's Ferrari as he pulled into the parking lot. When he went into James' apartment, James and Aly were talking next to the kitchen table.

They looked up at Mickey and, in unison, said, "Good morning, Mickey."

James added, "Grab a cup of coffee, and we'll get started. We've been talking strategy. I think Aly here has some pretty good ideas. We'll go over them as we look at the aerial map."

James placed the taped together map on the table. "As you both can see, I blew the picture up and printed it on several pages and taped them together. It's the best I could do with a regular printer."

"It'll do just fine, Jimmy," Aly said.

Mickey poured some coffee, and since both Aly and James were drinking theirs black, Mickey didn't ask for cream and sugar. He looked at the map. He noticed that James had put various marks and notes on the map in multiple locations.

James started, "Okay. As you can see, I've marked the compass headings at the top of the map, right here," he said, pointing to the various designation of N, S, E, W. "The two large buildings are the main house and the warehouse. There's no farmland here, so they must use it for equipment and trucks. I mean big trucks like semis. The road comes in from the west, over here. At the edge of the map is the road leading to the house. It goes to the main road out here," he said, pointing to an area off the map.

"This building over here we think is a kind of bunkhouse, for hired help or possibly security personnel. We can't see windows from this vantage point, so we don't know what they can see. The same goes for the other buildings. That's where Aly comes in. She can move an aerial drone around the perimeter low enough to see the location of the windows. Also, Aly can pinpoint guards. She can get low enough to see but still stay high enough, so small arms fire can't get to it. Her cameras have high resolution and telephoto lenses with zoom capabilities. She can zoom in and identify people and what kind of weapons they might be carrying. The drones all have the range that she can bring them home and pack up to leave before they can be tracked or followed on the ground if they're spotted. If necessary, someone can take control of the drones from different locations to draw them from the command center vehicle. During that period, the CC, or command center can relocate."

"That's pretty impressive," said Mickey.

"We think so, and that's why we're expensive, at least to others. As I told James, you're getting the family discount," said Alyssa.

Alyssa continued, "We'll fly a drone from north to south and make a return trip just low enough to see window locations and posted security. Then we'll do it again, from east to west and back. Unless they are looking directly up, they won't even notice the drones. At a casual glance, people think they're birds. We can make actual placements of ground spotters from inside the control vehicle as that's going on. Right now, we can decide what the most likely point of entry for the teams is. I suggest two teams of two men each. One for the house and one for the barn. Ground spotters can move men around as they can see, and we'll observe from the air to catch and direct what they can't see. If one team clears an area, they can hook up and assist the other team.

"Around seven, the rest of the guys will be here to finalize the mission. Is that good for you, Jimmy?"

James nodded.

Mickey just stood there in awe of this little lady. He felt like an outsider. James and Alyssa clicked like hand and glove. She knew what she was doing, and James understood that she had the situation in control.

Mickey moved away from the table, and they all took a seat in the living room area.

"So, Mick, how did the two of you meet?" asked Aly as she took another sip and made a face as she looked down at the now cold coffee.

James got the coffee pot and brought it back out, and filled their cups. He started making another pot so it would be ready when the rest of the team showed up.

"James and I met in high school right here in Bridgeton. My father owns this apartment complex, and my sister and I now manage it as well as several others here in the town," said Mickey.

"How fortunate for all of you. So, you knew James before all of this." She made a gesture with her hand up to her face regarding James' scars.

"Yes, James and I used to work out together in the school gym, and after he got out of the service, he needed a place to live, so Pop let him move in here. We just kind of picked up where we left off so many years ago."

She tilted her head in a short laugh. "It wasn't that many years ago, Mickey Ray. Only about eight to ten years, I would say."

"True," he said, "but it seems ages ago."

"That I understand and agree. My high school years seem like a hundred years ago too. Believe me, none of us are the same people we were. Not by a long shot. James tells me that your father's in a rehab facility because of an auto accident."

"Yes, but he's getting better, and we hope that he'll come home soon."

"I hope so too, for you, Mickey Ray," she said as a loud knock sounded at the door.

When she answered it, two guys were standing in the hallway. One was tall and muscular, about 6 foot three, and the other was a midget, barely 5 ft tall.

"Shorty, Stretch, welcome to Jimmy's place. Come on in, gentlemen," she said and let them come inside.

They walked in, stopped, and looked around, inspecting the place.

Seeing no one else but James, Alyssa, and Mickey, the tall one spoke, "Are we the only ones, or are we early?"

"Have a seat. You're early. Meet Mickey Ray," she said. "James' still in the kitchen making some breakfast sandwiches, I think. Hey, Jimmy, come on out here. A couple of the team have shown up."

James came out and stopped, waiting for an introduction.

The tall one stepped forward and put out his hand to shake Mickey, then James' hand. "I'm Shorty, and the dwarf here is Stretch."

Mickey and James shook both their hands. "Could have fooled me, Stretch," James said.

"I know. Aly seems to think it's funny to call us that because he's short and I'm tall. She started calling me Shorty, and the name stuck, same with Stretch down there."

Mickey looked confused, "You mean, since you're tall, she calls you Shorty?"

"Yep," the tall man said.

The Short man spoke up, "Yes, she calls me Stretch for the same reason. And Shorty there insists on calling me a dwarf. I'm not. I'm a midget. A dwarf has a normal body with short arms and legs. I'm a midget, a small or little person. She thinks it's funny. Funny lady, she is," he said in a serious tone.

Mickey said, "I didn't know there was a difference."

"Yep, big difference, Mickey. Look it up sometimes," he said.

"I'll do that, Stretch," Mickey said.

"Yes, she knows I hate being called Jimmy, so of course, that's what she calls me. And just to note, she's the ONLY one that gets to do that. To everyone else, I'm James."

"We understand. 'James' it is," Stretch said.

Alyssa spoke up. "James and Mickey, never, and I mean never underestimate Stretch. I've seen him take down a man as big as a football linebacker. If he can't reach your head, he'll take out your kneecaps, and when you fall, he'll bash your head in. Seriously. I've seen him do it. He's the most brutal man on our team.

"Shorty here is a hand-to-hand combat expert and handgun marksman. They work as a two-man team. Soon the others should be here, so if those breakfast sandwiches are ready, James, let the guys dig in until the others get here."

At seven o'clock, there was another knock on the door. When Alyssa opened it, five more guys came inside and began shaking hands and introducing themselves to Mickey and James. Alyssa told them to grab a cup of coffee, and they'd start going over the plans and each one's part in the mission. There was Brock, a sniper and scout. Adam was also a sniper and scout. Earl was a demolitions expert, and Tom Glassman stayed in the vehicle and helped Alyssa operate the drones.

After a few minutes, the men all found a place to sit in the living room area. James had taped the jigsaw map onto a wall so they could all see it. He moved aside as Alyssa began the briefing and plans.

"Okay, men, the mission is to rescue this man," she said as she pointed to an enlarged photo of Bobby Griffin on the wall beside the map.

She pointed a finger at the map. "As you can see," she started, "there are various buildings, and we aren't completely sure which one he's in, but we'll search every room in every building until we find and bring him out. He's being held as a prisoner and doesn't know that there's a rescue operation in effect to get him out.

"When we find him, he may or may not want to come with you. They took his wife prisoner as leverage for his services as a driver. That's the basic story, and we don't need to know any other details. We have the intel that they plan to kill him and his wife when he is no longer needed. James and Mickey here have already located and rescued the wife. Now we need to get the husband out."

One of the other men that introduced himself as "Brock" asked, "Shouldn't this be a police matter?"

"Normally, I'd say, yes, but in this case, Bobby Griffin might be killed if the police get involved. Also, the regular police need warrants, court orders, and a bunch of other crap we don't have or need. All we know for sure is that the person running this organization is not exactly legal. We can get in and out. If we don't find anything, we leave. If we find who we want, then we take him and leave. While we're there, we'll bug the entire house and barn building."

"Why're we bugging the place? Is there something else there we need to know about?" asked Adam.

"I'm sure there's more, but we don't ask and don't care. Our concern is getting Bobby Griffin unharmed."

At this time, James stood up and announced that this is a NO KILL mission.

"What do you mean, a no-kill mission?" asked Adam.

"I mean exactly what I said. NO KILL. If anyone kills someone, the shooter forfeits his pay."

There was a general overall grumbling among all the men. And again, Adam spoke. "On most missions, I'm scout and sniper. I hide on a rooftop or underbrush and kill anyone that's a potential threat to one of our men. You can't expect any of us to go in without that protection."

"I know what you do, Adam, and I know that you don't have to kill. If you need to shoot, wound the person. We are assuming these are not seasoned guys. Most likely, they're a bunch of bush league rednecks or street fighters with guns. A bullet to the hand, knee, or leg, and they'll be out of commission. They're not like us. If we get hit, we either get up and move away or wait for help. If they get hit, they'll fall and cry like babies. I mean, NO KILL! That's the rule. If you aren't good enough to wound instead of kill, walk out right now. You aren't good enough to be part of this mission," said James.

He scanned the room to see if anyone was preparing to leave. No one moved. "Adam and Brock, if you must shoot, I suggest you aim for their hands or arms. If you hit them in either place, they'll drop their weapon and most likely run away, leaving themselves and whatever they're supposed to be protecting unguarded. If you hit them in the leg, they can still lay on the ground and shoot. Are you good enough to do that?"

"We can do it," said Brock, "but we don't have to like it."

Adam agreed.

"Good. I don't care what you like. You're paid to follow orders, so we understand each other."

Adam spoke again, "You said, 'assumed.' That means that you don't know who we're going against. That in itself is dangerous. It is always dangerous when assumptions are made without proper intel."

"True" said James, "but that's why you guys are here. You're to gather intel, and then if it's feasible, you'll proceed. If not, then leave, and we can put together another plan. Can you do that?"

"Yes," said Adam.

With that, James sat back down, and Alyssa began speaking again.

Alyssa pointed at the map and began by addressing Adam and Brock. "The two of you will take up positions here, as lookouts. There's plenty of foliage to hide. Don't move unless you get orders from Glassman or me. You'll give reports from the ground of anything we may not be able to see from the drone, such as a security guard or any other personnel. We won't be able to see someone leaning against a tree or if some person decides to pretend he's a dog and take a leak on a bush."

She continued as she pointed to the northern side of the map and the south. "That way, you each can see two sides of the area. Together you have all four sides covered by a line of sight on the ground. Stretch and Shorty will check out this small building first. We think it may be personnel quarters. Then take the barn, while Earl and James take the main house. We'll have the infrared cameras on, so we should be able to direct you inside also. Whoever gets Griffin will report and take him outside to one of the spotters, Brock or Adam, so that they can get him away. Then you'll go back in and assist the other team. Disable anyone necessary that gets in your way. As James already emphasized, disable, not kill. Now, if one clears an area or building, notify me for orders. Remember, the main purpose is to extract this man. You'll all take a copy of this picture," she said, handing out a stack of wallet-sized photos of Bobby Griffin. "While clearing the house, discreetly place the bugs in these areas. James and Mickey need to have ears inside. Got it, everyone? Everyone'll be given zip ties for the hands and duct tape to use as muzzles to put on someone when he's down. When we leave, everyone there will be zip-tied and muzzled. No one will be left standing. Understood?"

There was a collective nod from everyone.

"One last thing, if you do shoot someone, you'll delay long enough to put a pressure bandage or tourniquet so they don't bleed out. No deaths here. Wear gloves and face coverings so no one can be identified in the future. If something happens and goes sideways, we don't want the authorities closing in on us. Got that also?"

Another collective sigh and head nod of agreement.

"When do we go, Aly?" asked Tom Glassman. "I need time to charge up the drones and check them and all the equipment we plan on using."

Aly turned and nodded to James, "James, do you want to answer that one? And do you have anything to add?"

"We need to go ASAP. Is tomorrow soon enough?"

"No," said Tom, "I need the rest of the day, and if something needs adjusting or repair, it'll take tomorrow. The day after tomorrow is the soonest we can go."

"Okay, guys, you've got about forty-eight hours to prepare yourselves. Be here at four AM, the day after tomorrow. Be quiet. There're other people in this area. We don't want to wake anyone up. If they see us with our gear and dressed, they may think they're being invaded. Now, everyone get out of James' home," ordered Alyssa.

The men got up to leave, grumbling about the no-kill orders. They accepted the fact they're professionals and would deal with it. They would take it as a challenge.

When they all filed out, James, Alyssa, and Mickey were left standing in the apartment.

"What do you think of the team, James?" she asked.

"If you say they're good, then I accept that," he answered.

"I don't like the fact that I've nothing to do but sit on my hands," said Mickey.

Alyssa turned to face Mickey and said, "What do you do if you have a stopped-up drain in one of your buildings and you don't know exactly where it is, or maybe you don't have the equipment to unstop it?"

"What does a stopped drain have to do with this?"

"Answer me, Mick," she said.

"I guess I'd have to call a plumber," he said.

"Correct. In this case, consider us your plumber. We have the skill, manpower, and equipment to do the job."

"I'd be there watching the plumber while they work to make sure they do it right."

"And you'll go with us and watch us work from a safe distance in the command vehicle. We'll get the job done for you."

Mickey stood looking at her for a few moments, then turned and walked away. He gathered his things, said goodbye to Alyssa, and told James he would be talking with him later.

The Landlord and the Wheelchair Child

When Mickey left, Alyssa and James sat down in the living room to talk.

Aly shook her head and ran her fingers through her hair, and spoke to James. "Mickey Ray was pretty upset when he left. Is he going to be a problem, James?"

He picked up his coffee and sat down in the lounge chair across from Alyssa. "No. He's got a lot on his mind right now. A lot's happened to him the past six months, and he's still getting used to it. He's a team player. He'll come 'round. He doesn't understand exactly what you do and that your guys are experts at it. That was a good analogy you gave about the plumber. He's still young enough that it bothers him to admit he doesn't know it all."

"I know I told the guys that we don't know or care about the bugs, but can you tell me? It's not a national security issue, and even if it was, I have a top-secret clearance. So, will you indulge me by telling me?"

"We went into one of their storage units several nights ago and found some stolen medical equipment. I want to know where it's going, and maybe we can intercept it or find a way to notify the authorities so they can intercept it."

"What kind of medical equipment?"

"Big-ticket stuff. Things like MRI and CT scan machines. Then some smaller things like portable x-ray machines and other medical supplies. I don't have a total yet, but it's several million dollars in street value, even at black market prices."

"Aren't machines like that controlled with serial numbers and such?"

"Yes, that's why we're assuming they'll be shipped out of the country. I don't know where, but it'll be to some country that's loose on records and such that will allow things like that to slip through their customs. Even a portable x-ray machine can be used by antiquities smugglers to view inside findings from archaeological sites to set value for illegal sales."

"There you go with that word, 'assume' again," she said.

"I know," James said, "but you must understand that MRI and CT machines can be quietly sold to small third world country clinics and hospitals. It'll be to areas that are difficult to trace. Serial numbers can be forged and changed. Those machines go for a couple hundred thousand dollars to over three million new. Those machines were new, still in their factory crates. They store the actual equipment off-site from the location where we're going. Binghamton is shady and is subject to search if he's suspected of anything illegal. The large barn, I suspect, is used to store and repair the trucks they use for transporting this stuff. It could be used for a temporary transfer station. They can be brought in one day, back out the next. All this is conjecture on my part, but if we get ears inside, we can find out, and if we're lucky enough to get a date and time of a transfer, we can notify the proper authorities. They can go in and catch them in the act."

Alyssa thought for a moment, then said, "I understand all that, but why do you care what happens to the equipment, especially if it goes to some country that helps people? It won't cost the end customers or hospitals that were supposed to get them. They will be replaced by the supplier or sales company. Even then, they should be covered by insurance. The only ones that lose out are the insurance companies."

"Because Aly, these people are criminals, no matter what they steal. They're smugglers and murderers. They aren't doing this for humanitarian reasons. They're doing it for profit!"

"Well, James, it sounds like you have it all worked out."

"Oh, gosh, no. As I said, it's all guesswork. You know that all we're doing wouldn't be allowed legally. And it would take months to get the info we need to do this. We don't have to jump through all those hoops. We just go in, kick butt and get out. Easy, peasy."

"Yeah, and we both know how that goes. Nothing ever goes as planned. Nothing," she said with a sigh. She reached into her purse and took out a card and pen, then wrote on the back of it and handed it to James.

"This is my private number. If you need anything, call this one," she said.

He took it and looked at her. "How many numbers do you have?"

"Several. There's the number I give to clients that have contracted me to do a job. I call that one my business number. They call that one for updates, etc. Then there's the employee number that the team has for information and instructions. That is the one you usually call me on. The top-level is my private and personal number. You now have that one. There's just a handful of people in the world that has that number."

"Hmmm, I guess this makes me special, doesn't it, Aly?"

"It sure does, James. And if you had gotten in touch with me a long time ago, you'd have had it sooner." She reached up to him and gave him a peck on the cheek. "I still say Darcy is one lucky woman, Jimmy Bower." She turned and walked out of the apartment.

He stood for a few moments feeling the warmth of that peck, then shook his head and said to himself, "Nope. James Bower, you're the lucky one to have Darcy."

As Mickey was leaving, his cell phone rang. It was Glen.

"Hey, Boss. Neal and Carson just left the apartment at eight-ten. Just a few minutes ago."

"You did well. That should be all. The job's over. Pack up all your stuff, and as I said, leave the place as clean as you found it. I'll be by there later and pick up James' equipment.

"Yeah, Boss," said Glen.

"I'll give you a call later as soon as I get the cash for you. You did good, and I'll throw in a few dollars for the good work. Thanks, Glen. Make sure all is locked when both of you leave. We'll be changing the locks, so just dispose of your key in the trash."

CHAPTER 13

Sunday Late Morning...At the Diner and Val

Mickey sat in a booth in the corner of the diner. He hadn't eaten at James' place earlier, and he was hungry. Valerie had brought him the hungry man special platter. He'd eaten it and just sat at the table thinking over what had gone on this morning. They were a rough-looking bunch of men, but he didn't doubt that they could and would do what they needed. He noticed that Val was acting a bit offish today and had been acting more and more distant. He also noticed that she hadn't wanted to go out as much as she used to do. He needed to talk to her more about it. She came over to refill his coffee.

"Hey, Val, are you feeling okay today? You seem a bit down," he asked.

She poured the brown liquid into his cup and gave him a forced smile. "I'm okay, Mickey. I'll bring you some more creamer in just a minute."

"Are you working all day today?"

"Yeah, but I have a three-hour break. I work breakfast till two o'clock, then come back at five for dinner."

"Can I see you when you get off? We can go somewhere for a while until you have to come back to work."

"I guess we can do that. Where do you want to go?"

"I don't know. How about me picking up some chicken and we can have a picnic in the park. We'll spend some time together, and then you can get back to work on time."

"That sounds good. I'll get that creamer for you," she said and walked away to serve someone else.

He drank another cup of coffee and left to go to Darcy's. When he got there, he knocked and walked in when she called out.

"Hey, Dee, are you busy right now?"

"I'm busy. I'm working on a pending divorce case for the firm. This is going to be a nasty case. They have three kids, and they both want custody. The thing is, they're both good and loving parents, and both have good jobs and can afford to support them. The wife isn't even asking for any alimony or child support."

"You're working on business on Sunday?"

"Yes, with all that is happening around here, I have to work when I can. It needs to be done by Monday morning," she said.

"I understand. As soon as this calms down, we can all relax. How's Janet and Carrie doing?" he asked.

"So far, so good. Janet's still concerned about her husband. She says she hates him, but she's still worried about him. A love-hate relationship, as they say," Darcy said. "How're things going trying to find him?"

"We think we may have found out where he's being held. We won't know for a couple of days. James has called in a couple of old friends to help get him out."

"What kind of friends, Mickey Ray?" she said suspiciously.

"A few of his old army buddies."

"James doesn't have any old army buddies, Mickey. What's up?"

"Don't worry about it right now, Dee." As he said this, his phone rang. "Yes, okay. Just be sure to dispose of the keys. Is Sam on-site yet to repair that window in the unit?" Mickey nodded his head as though Glen was sitting in front of him. "Yes. I need to stop and get the cash to pay you and George, or would you rather have a check? I thought so. Give me an hour. I'm serious, that place had better be clean, or I'll take cleaning fees out of it. Fine, I'll see you in about an hour." He disconnected.

"Mickey, who was that, and why are you paying him…in cash?" Darcy asked.

"Nothing. Don't worry about it."

"Yes, I'm worried about it, and if you pay someone in cash, get a receipt from him. I mean it."

Mickey got up. "This guy doesn't give receipts. I don't have time to talk about it right now. I have to go. See you later, Dee."

He heard Darcy call out as he walked down the hall, "Whatever you and James are up to, it better not be illegal, and I need receipts!"

When he got back in his truck, he called James and told him that he needed some cash to pay Glen and George and told him to add a couple of hundred dollars bonus. It would make Glen happy and keep him loyal for future work. James said he would leave the money on the kitchen table, and Mickey could use his master key to come in and get the money.

After stopping to get the cash from James' apartment, he headed to the surveillance unit to meet Glen and George. When he pulled up to the unit, he saw Sam replacing the window on unit 140. Also, he needed to change the locks in the surveillance unit across the street as soon as he could and give the new keys to the office when it opened tomorrow morning. After talking with Sam, he walked over to meet with Glen and George. They were both delighted with the pay and bonus and told Mickey to call anytime. They'd be glad to help out whenever he needed them. They helped him load James' electronic equipment into his truck. Mickey collected the key from them anyway even though he had told them Sam would change the locks. He trusted them only to a point.

After that, it was time to go back to the diner and pick up Valerie for their picnic. Mickey phoned in a take-out order of fried chicken dinners for two, complete with plates, utensils, and two drinks. He got to the diner just as Valerie was walking out.

"Wow, my feet hurt today," she said as she leaned back in the seat and closed her eyes.

Mickey noticed she was drifting in and out of light sleep. He let her nap as he drove to the park and found a parking space near one of the public picnic tables. When he stopped, she quickly woke up but still yawned.

As they sat down at a picnic table, Mickey looked at her and spoke, "You look really tired today. Are you feeling okay?"

"Oh, yes, Mickey. I'm fine. I just don't sleep well anymore. I toss and turn all night long," she answered.

"Why?"

"I don't know, Mickey Ray. Don't ask me so many questions."

"I didn't mean to ask you a lot of questions. I'm just concerned, that's all. If something's bothering you, you can tell me." He sat down beside her. "Let me help you," he said as he took a piece of chicken out of the box and put it on her plate. Then he put a spoonful of potato salad on it.

"No, don't give me so much. I don't want it," she said sternly.

"It's your favorite piece. The breast."

"I know, but I'm not hungry. Just let me sit here. You eat. I'm okay."

"Talk to me, Val," he said, putting his arm on her shoulder.

She shied away from him. "Don't, Mickey. Don't touch me right now. I'm fine, really. I just don't want to be touched now. Let's go home. I want to go home."

"Sure, honey. I'll take you home. No problem. Can I go in and be with you until it's time to go back to work?"

"Yes. That'd be nice. I just want to be alone. I mean no other people. You can be there. That's okay. Take me home. Please," she said as he began putting the dinners back into the box.

"Do you want the drink?"

"No, throw it away."

"Okay. I'll throw yours away, but I'll keep mine just in case you want a sip," Mickey said gently as he got up and picked up the box with one hand and gently took her hand with the other. He drove back to her apartment. While he put the food in the refrigerator, she laid down on the sofa. When he came back into the living room, she was drifting in and out of sleep. He sat down in a chair across from her. She was not her old self. He didn't know why, but she was definitely exhausted. She needed sleep. He sat looking at her sleeping. She wasn't getting better. She was getting worse, and he didn't know how to help her. After about an hour, he looked at the clock, and it was time for her to go back to work.

When he gently shook her to awaken her, she sat bolt upright and let out a little yelp. She shook her head to clear her mind.

"I'm sorry, Mickey."

"No, I'm sorry. Did I frighten you?" he said.

"Yes. I mean no. You didn't do anything. I need to go back to work."

"Yes, that's why I woke you. It's time for me to take you back to the diner."

"Let me get my purse. Did you put the food in the fridge?"

"Yes, you can eat it later."

"Take one of the diners home with you to eat later," she said as she got her purse.

"No, that's fine. You keep it all. I have plenty of food at home."

He drove her back to the diner. She got out and walked in without a word of goodbye.

"Well," he thought, "that was mildly painful." He needed to go see Pop.

CHAPTER 14

Sunday Afternoon with Daniel

James called, and Mickey took him back to the car lot where James had left his Humvee for the modifications. Again, James paid the bill with a sealed envelope. So now James had an armored vehicle. Mickey didn't know all the modifications that James had done to it in the past. He did know about the hidden compartment in the back, and the engine's added horsepower, giving it a higher top speed.

He had the rest of the day and tomorrow before it all hit the fan. He didn't know what would happen, but Mickey believed that the men Alyssa had on her team would be very competent to get in and out. He didn't know how well they'd react to the "No-Kill" order. That was a huge unknown, but Mickey had no choice but to trust Alyssa and her team. He wished he could be part of the team for one day, but in all reality, James was right. Let them go and do their job.

The duty nurse said Daniel was in the sunroom. When he got there, he saw Pop sitting in a chair next to a walker.

"Hey, Pop. How's it going today?" he said as he walked in and sat down beside his dad.

"Hello, son. I'm doing great. See my walker? I walked down here from my room. I'm so proud of myself."

"Wow, I'm proud of you too, Pop," Mickey said, and he noticed that Pop was talking a bit faster today and much more fluid. Also, he used more verbal contractions than he'd used since the accident. That was progress, and all in just a few days. He hoped that this was an opening to a road to healing.

"Hey, Pop, I have the entire afternoon off. Want to go for another ride like we did the other day?"

"Why, yes, Mickey Ray. That would make my day. No, it would make my week complete."

Mickey was overwhelmed at how much Pop was sounding like his old self. He went to look for the duty nurse and get permission to take Pop out again for another ride. When he found her, she arranged for someone to help Daniel into Mickey's truck, and they put his wheelchair and the walker in the back seat in case they needed either one.

"I have an idea. How about going through the drive-thru and get a couple of chicken dinners. We can take them to the park for a picnic. It's almost time for dinner, so it would be nice."

Mickey once again today called for chicken take-out and a drive to the park. Maybe it would go better the second time he was there. Daniel got out with Mickey's help and went to the same table where Mickey and Valerie were earlier today. They sat, ate, and talked. Daniel would sometimes slow down to form the words correctly or think of a word, but Mickey was happier than he'd been in months. Being with Pop was almost like it used to be. He felt rejuvenated in such a short time, and he hoped Pop felt the same. Pop asked him if they had time to return to his home like they did the other day.

"Sure we can. I need to warn you that it won't be the same," he said, hoping not to upset his father.

"What do you mean, Mickey?" Daniel asked.

"Well, Pop, it's like this," he started. Mickey spent the next half an hour telling Daniel what had happened. He didn't include the details of how Evelyn had died. He felt that detail was best left untold.

"I see, son," Daniel said sadly. "I'm so sorry my sister caused you such grief and pain. I'm sorry that she's dead, but there is a reason for everything, and I guess there was a reason she died. We were never really close, and I knew she was irresponsible, but I never thought she was that evil. I would never have guessed that she would do something like that to you and your sister. I'm not glad she's dead, but I AM glad she's gone." Daniel just looked down in shame that the family would treat each other like she had done to his son and daughter.

"Pop, don't feel sad for her. She isn't worth your sadness. Just as you said, I'm not glad she's dead, but I'm glad she's gone. Now, let's go to the house and see what's left."

As Mickey helped him back into the truck, they talked about the future. They spoke about his and Valerie's and Darcy and James' future.

"I want to warn you when we get to the house, it's empty, and so's the garage, but we can buy more furniture and find more cars to replace the other ones. We can even find one to restore together."

"Sounds good to me, son. And I noticed that you're now driving my truck!"

"Yep, at the time, I didn't have the money to buy another truck because Evelyn had fired me and took the work truck. So, I took this one. Are you going to let me keep it when you get better, or do you want it back?" he said in a joking tone.

"Mickey Ray, you keep it. I'm retired now. I don't need a truck anymore. And, I may never be able to drive again since that accident."

"I hope you can, and when you can drive again, I'll give you this truck," Mickey laughed.

"Nope, you won't. I don't want your old hand-me-down stuff. I want a brand-new truck. I might even get a big diesel truck," Daniel also laughed, "just so I can drive it up beside this one and say, mine's still bigger than yours."

Mickey's heart beat with joy. At least for a while, his Pop was back. He just prayed that it was permanent. This was definitely a red-letter day for him and Pop.

Mickey pulled around to the back and helped his father when they got to the house. Daniel wanted to use the walker, but Mickey didn't want him to get too tired, so they started with the wheelchair.

When Mickey opened the big sliding door, Daniel looked around and said, "Mickey Ray, did you ever learn about the inventor Thomas Edison, the man that invented the light bulb?"

"Kind of, but I don't know that much about him. Why?"

"He was a brilliant man, but one night in 1914, some of the buildings in his plant in New Jersey caught on fire. Edison said to his son, 'That's alright, we just got rid of a lot of rubbish.' Later, in a newspaper article, Edison said, 'Although I am over 67 years old, I'll start over again tomorrow.' And you know, Mickey, he did. I'm not nearly as old as Edison was then. We'll do it again, and even more and better. You wait and see."

When Mickey saw his father try to stand, he reached over and helped him. Daniel stood while Mickey steadied him. He looked around the building. "It's all right. We'll do it again together," he said. "We'll rebuild our collection of cars. We'll get better, more interesting ones than we had before. Evelyn just gave us a reason to start over." Then he sat down again. "Take me into the house. I want to walk in, please."

Back outside, they switched from the wheelchair to the walker, and very slowly, with Mickey's help, they walked to the house. Mickey carefully helped him up the steps to the entrance. They took their time walking from room to room. As they passed from room to room, Mickey told him that they had some of the furniture in storage. Wordlessly, they went back to the truck.

When Mickey pulled up to the rehab center, Daniel spoke again.

"Mickey, I may not be this clear tomorrow, but I'm getting better each day. I know that. Now that I see what was done, you, James, and I will restore it. Let Darcy pick out the furniture she wants to keep, pitch the rest, and you can buy new stuff to fill in the blanks. Now get me back inside, and first thing tomorrow, I'm going to go to PT like my life depends on it."

Mickey knew that Pop would be coming home soon.

CHAPTER 15

Monday...Daniel's Silver Seraph

The following morning, Mickey checked on Sam and the progress on the vacant apartments since he had a day before the mission. He met Sam at unit 140, and Sam told Mickey that they didn't forget to take their drug stash even though Neal and Carson had left in a hurry. It looked like they had packed their clothes and just walked out. They also left their car, which seemed to be damaged by gunfire. Mickey told him to have the vehicle towed away and get a clean-up crew. Susan had a waiting list of potential renters as soon as it was ready. Mickey felt it unnecessary to tell him what he and James had done to cause them to leave.

"Sam, do you think you could round up a couple of guys to help Darcy move from her townhouse to Mom and Pop's house, then move my things from my apartment to Darcy's old house?"

"Sure, Mickey. When do you want to do it?"

"As soon as possible. I'll be busy for the next couple of days. Can you help Darcy handle the move?"

"Sure, no problem. What do you want me to do first?"

"First, we need to get Pop's furniture out of storage. If you remember, we took it out and stored it after Mom and Pop had the accident. Then we'll move Dee's furniture into the house also. Last, we need to move my furniture from my apartment to Dee's townhouse. Can we get enough people to do that?"

"Of course, we can do that. It'll probably take a couple of days and half a dozen people. I can maybe get three people. Hopefully, that should do it. How about a moving truck?"

"I forgot that. Sure, you have a company credit card. Call a rental company and get a truck. We should be able to do it next week, maybe next Monday."

"You got it, Mickey Ray. I'll take care of it. What happened to that little girl? Did you find her parents yet?"

"Yes, we'll be getting that resolved in a couple of days, Sam. After that, they'll be leaving the area and moving away."

"Great. I'll get the move arranged for next Monday."

"Thanks," said Mickey as he headed back to his truck. He called Darcy and told her that the move is tentatively planned for the following Monday.

"Mickey, I can't get things packed up and ready to move in that time frame! What were you thinking? It takes time to move. You don't just do that in a week. Especially when there are kids involved. All I can say is, I'll do the best I can."

"That sounds good. Sam and whoever he finds will help you any way they can. Good luck, Dee. Gotta go," he said and disconnected. Just as he placed the phone on the seat beside him, it rang again.

He looked at the caller ID and saw it was James. "Hey Mickey, Logan just called me. He found a Rolls Royce for you."

"You really are obsessed with me getting another car, especially a Rolls," said Mickey.

"Yeah, I really did like your last one, and I'd like to see you replace it."

"I don't know what I want this time. Pop did most of the work on the first one. Another one won't replace that one. That time's gone, and so is that first time feeling that comes with anything."

"I get that, but just look at it. Why not go pick up your father and take him with us. You can get his thoughts on it."

"Fine. I'll go pick him up, and we'll all get together and look at it. Pop did the last one years ago. He may not want to go through that again."

Mickey turned out of the parking lot toward the rehab center.

"Hey, Pop, are you busy right now?" he said when he got to Daniel's room.

Of course, he already knew the answer, but it made him feel better to say it with a feeling that his father was well enough to be engaged in something instead of sitting in a chair watching the television. Daniel turned and looked at Mickey, and a smile appeared on his face.

"Mickey Ray. I was thinking about you and hoping that you'd come by to see me today," he said.

"I was getting a bit lonely without my dad, so I thought I would come by and take you out for a spin. Got some free time, Pop?"

"Even if didn't, I'd make time for you, Mickey," he answered.

Mickey became so happy. His father was still clear-headed today. "Hey, James called and said a friend of his found a Rolls Royce and wants us to go look at it. You want to come along for the ride?"

"You bet I would! What kind is it? Tell me about it. I'd love to see it. If it looks good enough, maybe we could get it and restore it like we did the Corniche."

At the nurse's station, he notified them that he was taking Daniel out for a ride. Off they went to Logan's used car lot and garage.

When he got there, James was already there, and he parked beside the Humvee and got out.

James' eyes got wide, and he said to Mickey, "You gotta see this car. It is a beauty. It is almost perfect. Did you bring your dad?"

"Yes, let me get him out of the truck. Where is the Rolls?"

"It's around back. Logan's bringing it around as we speak. You both'll love it."

Mickey went to help Daniel. When Daniel looked at it, his mouth dropped open.

"Oh my gosh, Mickey, will you look at that beautiful automobile!"

Mickey was facing his father and away from the approaching car. He turned around to look at it. He looked at the car, then back at his father. He knew that his father was falling in love with the car right then.

Logan stopped, opened the door, got out and handed him the keys, and said, "Here you go, Mickey. Take it for a spin."

Mickey took the keys and said to Logan, "Logan, this is my father, Daniel Christianson." He then turned back to his father, "Pop, this is

Logan King. He owns the lot and garage. Logan does all the work on James' Humvee."

Daniel slowly put out a hand to shake Logan's. "It's a pleasure to meet you, Logan."

Logan also extended a hand to meet Daniel. "It's my pleasure to meet you, sir."

Turning back to Mickey, he said, "Why don't you take your father for a ride in your new car?"

"I would love to take it for a test drive, but I'm not sure if this is what I want."

"You take it for a ride and discuss it with your father." He handed Mickey a small piece of paper with numbers on it. "This is the price. It isn't negotiable, but I'll say it's been checked over by a certified Rolls Technician and was gone over by a certified competition Rolls Royce judge, and it's almost perfect. It's a fair and reasonable price. Let me know what you think when you get back. Have a nice ride."

He turned, walked away from them, and started talking to James.

"Wow, Pop. It's a gorgeous car, isn't it?" said Mickey as he pulled into traffic.

"Yes, it is, son. Do you like it?" said Daniel.

"How could I not like it? I don't know if it's what I want right now. You and I built the last one together, Pop."

"Yes, son, but that was another time, another life. It's time to move on now. We can find another car to rebuild. I like this one. It's a few years old. It's a Silver Seraph with a 5.4-liter V12 engine. As your friend says, it's perfect. I see what he's asking for it, and it's a fair price. They didn't make many of these. They were transition cars when BMW bought the company, so they're somewhat rare, and in a few years, will be going up in value. If you don't want it, I'd like to have it. I'll have something to drive since you took my truck!"

"Pop," said Mickey, "are you trying to make me guilty for taking your truck?"

Daniel reached over and touched Mickey on the arm. "Absolutely NOT, Mickey. I'm only kidding about the truck, but this is a super nice car. I know I can't drive right now, but maybe I can in a few months, and if you don't want it, I'll take it. When you decide what kind you want, we'll buy it. One last thing, as bad as my memory is right now, it's getting better. I think we should start expanding the Senior areas as soon as I get well enough. Then we'll need to impress investors and bankers alike. This car will do exactly that. We'll need money from all of them. Have you ever heard the term, 'Dress for success?'"

"I've heard of it, yes."

"That term can also apply here…Drive for success," Daniel said and sat back in his seat to enjoy the rest of the ride.

After a few minutes, they pulled back into the car lot.

When he got out, Logan walked over to him and asked, "Well, what do you think of it?"

"Pop likes it. If buying it makes him happy, it makes me happy. Where do we sign?"

"Trust me, Mickey Ray," said Logan, "you won't be sorry."

"I hope not. Can we see under the hood and trunk? You understand, look the whole car over, kind of, kick the tires, so to speak."

"Go right ahead. Car repairs are in the rear building where you went a few days ago. Car sales are in the front office in that building," he said, pointing at the building in front of the lot. "I'll be in there filling out the paperwork. Take your time."

As Mickey talked to Logan, Daniel managed to get out of the car and walk around to the front using his walker. He waited for someone to open the hood. James saw this, went to the driver's side, opened the door, and pulled the hood latch, then walked around to the engine compartment and looked down at the engine.

"Can't see much, can you, sir?" he said, speaking to Daniel. "Almost the entire engine is covered with shields."

"Yes, James, they started doing that a few years before this model. I don't know why, but it's a pretty boring sight, isn't it? A beautiful V12 engine like this should be left open to admire."

"I agree, sir," answered James.

"Mickey isn't particularly impressed with this car right now, but as we begin to expand our holdings, he'll see the advantages of owning a car commensurate with his position."

"You plan on building even more, sir?"

"You bet I do. I hope you and Mickey will be a big part of it."

"I hope I will meet your expectations, Mr. Christianson," James said.

"You will, son. I know you will. Let's go inside and buy this car," he said. "It's a beautiful color too, isn't it, James?"

"That silver is an exquisite color, sir," he said as he guided Daniel toward the office.

They signed all the papers, Logan put temporary tags on the car, and they drove off the lot with a Rolls Royce Silver Seraph.

CHAPTER 16

Tuesday 4 AM....The Mission

AT 4 AM TUESDAY, IT WAS still pitch dark when Mickey pulled into the parking lot where James lived. In it was a 15-passenger van and a plumbing truck. He assumed that this was the command center Alyssa would have come in. And the rest arrived in the van. When Mickey knocked softly, Stretch answered the door, motioned for Mickey to come in, and silently closed the door.

There were all dressed in camouflage and carried no weapons. They all whispered amongst themselves. When Mickey walked up to Alyssa and James and said good morning, they nodded back at him. He wasn't dressed like the rest, but he did have on all-black clothes. Aly told them to grab a biscuit and coffee from the kitchen, then follow her. She led them out to the vehicles. Aly, James, and Mickey got in the plumbing truck with Tom Glassman in the driver's seat. Tom started the plumbing truck and backed out, and the van carrying the rest of the team followed. They drove down the road with James sitting in the passenger's seat and giving Tom directions. Mickey and Aly sat cramped behind the passenger's seat of the truck. The entire back was packed with several drones of various sizes. Since the back where Mickey and Alyssa were sitting had no windows, he didn't know where they were at any given time. Finally, in about half an hour, they pulled to a stop. Tom motioned for them to get out. Alyssa opened the door, and they started taking equipment out of the back of the truck. The men in the van were getting out and strapping on belts with tools and equipment Mickey had never seen. Last came the guns.

Brock and Adam had sniper rifles with large scopes mounted on the top. Each man had a different type of rifle and a handgun in their belt. They also had tie wraps and a roll of duct tape hanging from their belts. Aly handed each one an earbud. They put it in their ear and said a familiar word to test it. She also handed out small things Mickey guessed were the bugs they would plant at various places once inside. She had a small map and went over each man's area to station himself and where they were to enter and exit the site. Last, Alyssa pointed to a place on the map to meet up if they had to move from this location. Finally, they all lined up, and she bid them good hunting, and they all disappeared into the woods. First in a line, then just before they went out of sight, Mickey saw them split off to the left and right.

Aly judged that it would take them six minutes to get to their stations. She told Tom to get the drones in the air while she put the drones on the ground in the open, got into the truck, and turned on the monitors. She took a position at one desk with a joystick, and Tom took place at the other.

There were six monitors in the truck. There were two on the left side that were used to see drone camera videos. There were four smaller monitors on the truck's right side to be used to view the videos attached to someone's body, helmet, or a stationary surveillance camera. Mickey watched as the drones left the ground and into the air. One drone went forward and left, whereas the other drone went forward to the right. He looked on the monitors in front of Aly and Tom. He could see the treetops on the monitor. It was still dark, so he didn't totally understand what they saw onscreen.

In about a minute, he saw buildings appear on each drone screen. Aly and Tom each moved the drones overhead. Since it was still dark, the drones couldn't be seen from the ground. After it got light, they would move the drones to the side of the compound just above the treetops, and probably no one would notice. If someone did spot one of the drones, they could quickly back off, go higher, and come back into view. They let the drones hover for several seconds, checking with infrared cameras, and when they didn't detect any people outside, they lowered the drones into the yard area and moved around the buildings. Aly and Tom each took a different side of the building, looking for windows where personnel could see a team member approaching. Aly radioed to Adam, and Tom radioed to Brock where every window was located and told them where to change their locations so they couldn't be seen. It would be light in a few minutes, and they would have to raise the drones into the air to get them out of sight. They also would get a better idea of the number of men from their heat signature on infrared sensors. The bunkhouse was on the side that Aly and Brock were monitoring and had no heat signatures, so maybe it was a tool or supply shed, but that didn't make sense because there should be plenty of space inside the big barn building. Stretch and Shorty could check that one out on their way inside the yard area.

Mickey heard Aly say into a microphone, "Stretch, go into the bunkhouse, check it out. Shorty, cover him. Report back." She waited while they moved into position outside the building. She saw them grab the knob, and it opened. Interesting. It wasn't locked. Stretch stepped inside and immediately back outside. "It's a powerhouse, a generator. It's probably used for backup power to the house and barn," said Stretch softly.

Aly says, "Stretch and Shorty. Ten people in the barn, northwest corner. They're armed but don't know with what. There's a lot of activity in there. It looks like a big truck with the engine running, probably getting ready to leave. Let it go for now. It makes fewer men to deal with now."

Tom said, "Earl, James, difficult to get an accurate number of people in the house. It's well-insulated, making infra-red ineffective. Go back and help Stretch and Shorty. When the barn is secure, move to the main house."

Aly again, "Adam, coming around the front of the barn, single person sighted from drone."

Adam, "I see him. Unarmed."

"We'll get him," says Shorty. And then, in the monitor, Mickey sees both men approach from the rear, grab and take the man down. They watched her men put zip ties on his wrists, tape up his mouth, then drag him to a corner of the woods.

"One down," thought Mickey.

Stretch and Shorty took a position on each side of the sliding door of the barn. It was getting light now, and Aly moved the drone higher to get a better overall view of the area. Tom still had his drone on the other side down low, watching the house. "There's a single door at the corner of the building and another one in the back. Earl and James line up at the corner door."

Aly says into the com unit, "Adam, watch for someone running from the back door."

"Got it," he answered.

Tom says, "Guys, we have heat signatures on occupants. Earl, one is headed for your door. Let him come outside and take him quietly if possible. Others stand by. The truck is slowly moving forward."

Earl and James stood by, waiting for the man to exit at their door. James grabbed the man by the arm as the door swung open, and Earl closed the door again. James slammed the man on the ground, flipped him over, and put zip ties on his wrists in one swift movement like a rodeo rider roping a calf. Then James turned him back over and put his hand on the man's mouth.

"You mutter one sound, and you're a dead man. Understand?" James said to the man.

He shook his head as James removed his hand and placed tape over his mouth. James dragged him away from the door a few feet away. Earl stood waiting at the door for another one to come out.

Tom's voice came over the com unit again. "Two are heading to the back area of the building. I don't know what they plan on doing but be prepared. Get ready to breach the building. Adam, watch the back door for runners."

"Back door in sight, boss."

Aly says, "Shorty, watch the front door. Someone's approaching it. He may be getting ready to open and let the truck out. Don't let it go."

"Got it. It's not going anywhere," Shorty answered. He motioned for Stretch to move back and let the door open.

"Wait for the big doors to open, then breach," came Aly's voice to everyone.

Slowly the huge doors began to slide back. Stretch was on one side and moving back, staying close to the door. Shorty did the same as Stretch, as the door he was standing beside was also beginning to slide open. When both doors were open about ten feet wide, Shorty and Stretch stepped into the opening with guns aimed at the general direction of the interior.

"Everyone, down on the floor. NOW," they yelled.

Two men next to the truck froze like deer in headlights. Shorty pointed his gun at one, and he dropped to the floor. The other one followed. Neither man was armed.

One man ran for the side door and almost ran into Earl and James as he went through the opening.

Tom's voice came through the com units, "And we have two runners. Adam, take care of them."

As the men ran out the back door about thirty feet away, Adam was standing, pointing his rifle at them. "Halt, or I'll drop you."

One man stopped, but the other one continued to run. Adam took careful aim and put a bullet in his thigh. He dropped to the ground.

Adam called out again. "I told you I'd shoot, ignorant S.O.B.! Now, you," he said, pointing to the first man, "get up and go check on your friend."

"NOW!" Adam yelled.

The man got up and ran over to his friend and called out, "He's bleeding. You shot him."

Adam called over his com unit. "Got them. All's contained."

"We saw," called Aly. "Go tend to his wound and secure them."

He walked over to the one that was standing. "Here, take this zip tie and tie his hands behind his back."

"What about the bullet in his leg?"

"Do I look like a doctor to you? Do as I tell you! Tie his wrists!"

The man did as he was told. Adam handed him a roll of duct tape and told him to turn the wounded man over and wrap the tape around the wound tight enough to stop the bleeding, then tape up his mouth so he would quit whining like a baby.

When he had done that, Adam told him to tape up his own mouth and lay down on his stomach. When he did that, Adam tied his wrists also.

As this was going on, Earl and James were doing the same to the others in the barn. No one noticed the truck beginning to move forward. Suddenly there was a roar, and the truck lurched forward, almost running into Shorty, who was standing guard near the front of the building. As the truck moved forward, Shorty managed to raise his gun and fire a dozen rounds into the truck's radiator. It kept moving forward out of the garage and started around the house and into the exit driveway toward the main road.

"What's happening down there. We can't see. Turn your cameras on, everyone."

James said to Aly, "The truck drove off. Shorty put some rounds into the radiator so that it won't get far. A couple of miles at most."

"A couple of miles puts him about our location."

"Okay, if he comes your way, can you take care of him?"

"I guess we can. But I said not to let it go," Aly said.

"Aly, you weren't here. Shorty almost got run down by the monster. It happened too fast."

"If he had shot out the tires instead of the radiator, it'd still be sitting in the yard."

At that moment, shots rang out in the garage. The entire team dropped to the floor as they looked around for the shooter. High up in a corner loft area was a lone gunman with a rifle aiming at Shorty. Stretch shot in that direction, knowing he couldn't hit the man but all he was trying to do was stall the shooter long enough for another team member to take a shot. The shooter quickly slid around inside a booth area.

"Aly. Do you see what is going on in here?" called James loud enough to be heard over the com units.

"No. No one has their body cams on yet. The drones didn't pick any other heat signatures. What's happening in there?" she asked.

"Shooter in a booth in loft area in the rear of the building. He's got us pinned down. Can one of the spotters help?"

He heard her say, "Adam, Brock, take positions on each side of front sliding doors. We have a sniper in the upper left loft area."

"We copy, command. Moving now. In a new position in ten," came Adam over his earbud.

Each man alternately fired a round near the area in the sniper's location but didn't take the time to aim. All they wanted to do was keep him in his booth until Adam and Brock moved into position.

All was quiet for a few very seconds. Then came the voice of Adam, "In position. Left door."

Brock followed, "In position. Right door. Aiming to kill."

Aly looked over at Mickey, who had suddenly turned pale. "Your call, Mickey," she said.

"I can't order the death of a man, Aly."

"I understand, but in this case, it's self-defense. Him or one of my men, and by the grace of God, it won't be one of mine." She turned back to the microphone on the console of the truck. "Shoot to kill, Brock."

The silence seemed to hang over the airwaves. Finally, the sound of Brock's voice came over the earbuds that everyone was wearing. "Copy that, command."

A few seconds went by, and everyone heard the crack of Brock's rifle. "Done," came the voice over the earbuds.

Everyone on Aly's team got up and began zip-tying the ones that had been in the garage.

Tom called out, "Adam and Brock, back to your original position. I see two runners that came from the back of the building. Earl, stop them."

Tom had his eyes on the monitor watching the two men run across the area to the main house. He saw they were carrying automatic weapons.

"James, back up Earl. Those men are armed to the teeth. They have heavy artillery."

James answered. "Copy that, command. I'll give support."

James ran out of the garage leaving the others to wrap up things in the garage. He saw both men duck into the house just as he came around the corner.

"Can you give me interior location, command?"

"Negative, the house is too well insulated. You're on your own now. Be careful."

James backed against the outside wall of the building. Earl came around the side of the house and joined James.

"Got any flash bangs on your belt?" James said to Earl.

"Always. Standard equipment," he answered.

They both knew the use and results of using flash bang grenades. Its primary purpose was to stun, temporarily blind and disorient an enemy. The British first developed it in the late 1970s and it was less lethal than regular explosive grenades.

They both moved to the door, and Earl crossed to the right side of the opening. James backed up and kicked the door open from the left side, and backed to the side. Earl stepped forward and threw in a flash bang, and also backed away. They both closed their eyes as the grenade went off with a loud explosion sound and bright light. James went in first, followed closely behind with guns raised to his shoulder, ready to fire. James moved to the right while Earl aimed to the left to cover the entire room. Laying on the floor in the right corner of the room were two men. Each man was lying on the floor in a fetal position, eyes closed and hands over their ears. Their guns were lying next to them.

James called out, "Move, and you die!"

The men didn't move. James and Earl bound and taped the eyes shut of each man and got up to move further into the house. Shots rang out, followed by bullets tearing the walls, barely missing both James and Earl, who also dropped to the floor and blindly returned fire at the bullet hole-riddled portion of the wall. They heard someone grunt and heard a thud as the man's body hit the floor.

They looked at each other, knowing they had just broken the no-kill order again. They also understood that it couldn't be helped and things don't ways go as planned. After waiting a few more moments, hearing no more response, they rose and proceeded into the other room and down a long hallway with their gun on their shoulder and ready to fire. James went to the right and Earl to the left into what looked like bedrooms at the end of the hallway. They searched the entire house until they found what appeared like a safe room.

Outside, Aly and Tom were watching and directing the rest of the team until Aly heard the truck coming up the road outside the command center vehicle.

She turned to Tom and said, "Keep the drones in the air. I'm going after the truck!" Then she turned and grabbed an automatic rifle out of the locker at the rear of the command truck. She jumped and started running down the road toward the entrance to the driveway. When she got about a hundred yards away, she jumped into a ditch and dropped down, and waited for the big rig to appear at the entrance.

As it pulled up, she could already smell the heat of the engine from her position. The truck was going slow, but the weight of the trailer kept it moving. She took careful aim and took out the two front tires, and it started swerving. She continued to move back, hitting the truck's back tires to cause it to lose traction. Finally, it came to a stop. The driver's door popped open, and she stood up with her gun aimed at the driver's head.

"Stop right there, or you'll be dead before you hit the ground."

"Who are you, lady?"

"Shut up, get down slowly and look down at the road. Do not look up, or whatever you see will be the last thing you ever look at. Now start walking forward." As Alyssa got near the command truck, Tom notified the others that the big rig was stopped. When she got to the command vehicle, wordlessly, Tom handed her a zip tie and a roll of duct tape. She turned the driver around, tied his hands, and put tape over his eyes and mouth.

As she got back into the command truck, she said into the mic, "No more names, guys. The driver is here, and he can hear everything."

"Has anyone checked out the house yet?" Tom asked.

The answer came, "Yes. We did that while you were playing with the truck driver. It seems they have a safe room and locked themselves inside it."

"Can you get it open?" she asked.

"Don't know yet. We can try. We didn't bring the proper ordinance to blow something like this open."

"Do what you can, using what you have," she said.

"With what we have, we can't guarantee no casualties," came the answer.

"Do what you can WITHOUT any more casualties," she said.

"Got it. Will report results. They probably have cameras outside to monitor the situation and know when it's safe to come back out."

"Exterior cameras would be my guess," came the voice that was unmistakably James. "We're going to try to get the safe room open."

Earl set up explosives in locations outside the area they had deduced was a safe room. He placed them in locations that he felt would do the least damage inside the room. After setting the charges and backing out of the area, he set them off. When James and Earl re-entered the area, they saw a wall blown open, but no one was inside the room.

"The house is clear. No one here," came James' voice back to the command center.

James and Earl returned to the garage and joined the rest of the team.

"We're going to interrogate the men here and see if we can get any info out of them," James said.

"Copy that," said Aly. "We'll talk to the driver we have."

She turned to Tom, "Okay, bring the drones back and put them away. We don't need them in the air anymore. I'm going to talk to the driver."

"Bringing them back, boss," Tom said and turned to the monitors. He took one out of automatic hover mode and started turning it back to the command vehicle. As Alyssa got out of the truck, she heard Tom say, "Come back home to mama and papa," as he moved the joystick around.

Just as he did this, a shot rang out in the forest. There was radio traffic originating from the compound and the command center.

"What was that? Who fired that shot?" asked James over the com unit.

"Did anyone see where it came from? It wasn't one of us," said another voice.

Mickey jumped up. "How do they know it wasn't one of us?" he asked Tom.

"Our men know the sound of all the weapons we use. No one has one that sounds like that. I don't know, but I would say it's some kind of hunting rifle. Definitely not military," he answered.

Tom called over the airways, "Find that shooter and neutralize him!"

"Copy that" sounded over the radio from two different men.

"Can you see it from the air?" asked one voice that sounded like Adam.

Aly jumped back in the truck and took the controls of one of the drones. She began sweeping the area just above the treetops.

They all heard another shot. When that happened, one of the monitors Aly was controlling went blank. She said something unintelligible under her breath and told Tom to keep looking.

She called out over the com unit. "Everyone. One drone is down. Be careful. Repeat, one eye in the sky is down. Northeast corner. Concentrate search in that area."

She got out of the truck again to talk to the truck driver. She pulled him into a sitting position. She reached down and rapidly ripped the tape off of his mouth. His lip started bleeding where the tape had stuck to it.

"Ouch," he called out as blood trickled down his mouth. "What the…"

"Shut up, scum. And talk only when I ask you a question.

"One of your men just shot down a forty-thousand-dollar drone. Who is that man, and where's he hiding?"

"What do you want from us?" he asked.

She kicked him in the side. He fell over and grunted. "Did you hear what I said?"

"Yeah, I heard," he said as he sucked in air because of being kicked in the side.

"I don't know who did it. I'm just a truck driver," he said breathlessly now.

Aly kicked him again, and he curled up into a fetal position.

"I don't know, lady. I swear to God. I don't know. I don't get involved with all that stuff. I'm a truck driver. That's all I do. Please don't kick me again," he pleaded.

"Pay attention and answer my questions and when we're done here, we'll let you go unharmed. Understand?"

"How do I know you won't kill me after I answer your questions?"

She kicked him again, and again he grunted with pain. "You don't know that. You just have to trust me. Listen to me. I don't want you. I don't even know you. All I want is some information from you. I have absolutely no reason to kill you. If you do what I ask, I don't even have a reason to hurt you. Now, will you cooperate, or do I have to beat it out of you?"

"Okay. What do you want to know?"

"Who shot my drone?"

"I don't know. I can't tell you what I don't know!" he said as he coughed up some blood.

"You were in this truck, and they opened two doors to let you out. Where were you going with this truck?"

"To the marine terminal in Portsmouth."

"What's in the container you're pulling?" she said.

"I don't know."

She moved her foot up to his side and gently rubbed against it like she was getting ready to kick him again.

"Wait! Don't kick me! I mean, I don't know exactly what's in it."

"What kind of answer is that? What's your name?" she asked.

"It's Randy. But they call me Bubba."

"You loaded it up. What do you mean you don't know what's in it?"

"I don't do the loading. All I do is drive. Honest, lady. I'm a driver, that's all."

"You mean you don't have a clue what you're hauling?"

"I asked once, and they told me it's better that I didn't know. All I know is it's some kind of medical equipment. It's being shipped out of the country. I don't even know what country. Honest. Those are some really bad dudes. I don't ask questions. I saw them shoot a man once because he asked too many questions. Just shot him for asking questions. I don't know anything, and I don't wanna know. Now, will you let me go? I can't help you."

"Do you know Bobby Griffin?"

"I've heard of him, but I don't know him personally. He's one of the other drivers. He left here earlier this morning before I did. Now, will you let me go, lady?"

"We're about finished here. What was he driving?"

"He was driving a Freightliner with a trailer on the back just like me."

Tom called out of the back of the truck. "Hey, they got the man that shot the drone. He was just a local redneck out hunting at dawn for deer. He didn't even know what he was shooting at. We have him in custody. Do you want to hold him?"

Aly thought for a moment. "Yes, we have to hold him. No matter what he says, he heard the shooting at the compound. Find out what he knows or thinks he knows. Keep him in the dark about what's going on.

We'll drop him off somewhere else later. Be sure to get his identification. We'll check him out later. Don't hurt him if he's not involved with this group."

She turned back to the truck driver. "Do you have the license plate number of his truck?"

"No, why would I know that?"

"What color is it, and where's he going after making that delivery?"

"What color is what?"

"The truck, stupid. The cab of the truck," she said, getting a bit annoyed.

"I don't know. Wait. I think it was blue. Yeah. It's blue. It was a blue cab with an American flag on the antenna mast. That's all I know, honest. Are you going to kill me now?" he said. "Please, lady, don't kill me. I didn't do nothin' to nobody. All I do is drive a truck for these crazy people, and I mean it. They're crazy."

"Where's he going after he makes the delivery to the marine terminal?"

"He brings the truck back here. He stays here. They don't let him leave the premises. He's due back around noon, I think. I helped you. Are you going to kill me now?"

"No. I'm not going to kill you. We had a deal. You talk, and I'd let you live. If they're so crazy, why do you work for them?"

"For the money. The pay's a lot more than we could make anywhere else. And we keep our mouths shut. As I said, lady, I saw them kill a man because he walked around the back of the trailer and looked inside. They just shot him dead. Just for looking and asking a question. I swear I don't know nothin' else."

"Why are you talking to me if you are so afraid of those guys."

"Because you also said you'd kill me if I didn't talk. Either way, I'm a dead man. You know, dead man walking. That's me right now."

"I'll tell you what I'm going to do. You did good by talking to me. I can let you go back to those guys, or you can come with us, and I'll let you go when we get back to town."

"Okay, I'll do that. You let me go when we get back to town. Do you promise me that?" he pleaded.

"No. I don't have to promise you anything. It's not like we're friends or anything. You do what I tell you, and I'll let you go when we get back to town. And one last thing. You never come back here to drive for those guys. Just to be sure, I'm going to tell them you ratted them out. If you leave town and never show your face here again, you'll be fine. If you come back, they'll hunt you down and kill you. Deal?"

"Please don't tell them I said anything. Please," he pleaded.

"No deal on that part. I tell them, and you leave town never to return."

"Okay, I'll leave. I Promise."

"We still have to wrap up a few things here, so you have to wait until we're done."

By this time, Tom was bringing the drone home and landing it in the road. He moved it from the road to the back of the truck. He got back inside and contacted the team that was still waiting for orders from either him or Alyssa.

Alyssa called to the men, "Did anyone see where the other drone came down?"

Brock's voice came over the com, "I saw it. Want me to bring it home?"

"If you can. If it's lodged in a tree or will take too long, leave it," she said.

"Not a problem. It's on the ground in a small clearing. Just lucky where it came down, I guess."

"Bring it home," she said.

"Will you take the tape off my eyes now. And untie me?"

"No. That's for your safety. If you look at me, I might have to kill you anyway."

"I didn't get a look at you. I wouldn't recognize you if I saw you again. Honest."

"Good, let's keep it that way. Now I'll take you a few feet from the truck, so my partner and I can talk, and I'll tape your feet so you can't walk away. If you try to get free, I'll be forced to shoot you. Are you clear on that?"

"Yes, I won't try to get away. I promise."

"Stop promising stuff. Just shut up. Don't say anything. Deal?"

He nodded his head. She led him about twenty feet from the truck, he sat down, and she taped his legs and feet together. He sat still and quiet. She went back over to the truck and picked up the microphone.

"James, we can talk now. I've moved the driver and turned down the volume, so he shouldn't be able to hear you. Is everything still secure?" she said.

"Affirmative. We're awaiting orders. No one here will talk. They're terrified of Satchel. Even more terrified of him than us. We hit a dead end. That is unless Mickey gives permission to shoot someone, so they know we're serious."

Alyssa looked over at Mickey, who hadn't spoken a word for the last half an hour. He shook his head NO.

She said that Mickey wouldn't agree. He'd heard her interrogating the driver. The driver had spilled everything he knew, so they have enough to work from here. She then told James to move all the prisoners to one room, lock them in if they could, exit the compound, and meet back at the truck.

James turned to the prisoners and said, "We're going to move you to the bunk room and lock the door."

The team herded all the men into the back bunk room and then went inside to make sure they couldn't use any equipment or weapons to escape or call for help. They found and destroyed numerous cell phones, a couple of knives, and one pistol, which they handed over to James.

"I'm going to put a hand grenade on the handle, so if you manage to get yourself loose and turn the handle, you'll blow yourselves up."

He reached onto his belt, held up an old-fashioned World War Two grenade that everyone was familiar with, and showed it to the men the team had secured. He pulled the pin and placed it between the doorframe and the knob to demonstrate how it worked. He turned the knob, and the grenade fell. He caught it and replaced the pin.

"If I hadn't been here to catch it, it would have blown up. Now I show you this, so you'll understand how it works and know not to kill yourselves. It'll be on the outside of the door, so you can't see it when it falls. Understand me?"

Everyone shook their head yes.

"When someone comes, they'll see it, and if they know what to do, they'll let you out. If they don't, they'll blow themselves up and maybe some of you also. I don't know when someone will come looking for you, but you can work that out when it happens. Right now, Satchel is locked in the house. We don't know when he'll come out. By that time, we'll be gone. Last chance before we exit the building. If someone wants to help us, we'll let them come out with us, and they'll live. We won't hurt them. All the others will stay in here and take their chances. No one? Okay. Goodbye, and good luck. Alright, team, let's go."

They all filed out, and James jiggled the handle a bit and made a sign for them to leave. He put the grenade back onto his belt.

After they all walked out, Earl asked James, "Is that antique thing still good?" he asked, referring to the grenade.

"Nope, but it sure scared those guys. And if you noticed, I jiggled the knob so they'd think I was setting it." He looked at Earl with a smile.

They looked across the grass and saw the driver of the disabled truck sitting quietly bound up in tape as they got back to the command vehicle.

They unloaded their gear, put it into the van, and then helped power down the truck and electronics inside. Then they put the drones inside.

"Are we just going to leave him sitting there like that?" someone asked.

"No, we're taking him with us," Aly said.

"I thought we don't take prisoners, boss," said Stretch.

"He's not a prisoner," she said.

Someone else chimed in, "Oh my, the boss has picked up a plaything."

"We're letting him go when we get to town."

"That's the deal we made. He talks, and we let him free. He rides in the van, so watch what you say. He has no idea what's going on, and we don't want him to know. Who's driving the van?" she asked.

Earl spoke up, "Me."

"We'll also take the hunter you guys got. He destroyed an expensive piece of equipment. I guess I chalk it up to the price of doing business. Load him into the van along with the truck driver," Aly said.

"Drop the guys off, and take Bubba and the hunter to a back road somewhere and drop them off. Don't remove the tape from their eyes. You can untie the hunter, but give him strict instructions not to take the tape off his eyes for five minutes. Then he can release Bubba. That'll give you time to leave and get out of sight. The hunter might be fine, but Bubba's a dork and a coward, so he'll follow your orders."

"Let's rollout. Meet me tomorrow at nine AM at headquarters."

They put Bubba and the hunter in the van, and the rest of the team piled in and left. James got in the truck with Mickey and Alyssa, and Tom drove again.

"You still need us for the takedown of the truck with Bobby?" asked Alyssa.

"No, Mickey and I can handle it from here. The team did great. We couldn't have done it without you, Aly."

"I know," she said smugly.

When the command center truck pulled up at James' apartment, James told Alyssa that he would get with her in a day or two and settle the bill. They needed to get ready to head out again.

James went into the spare bedroom and returned carrying a battery-powered chain saw, two rifles and changed into fresh camo gear. He threw a camouflage jacket at Mickey, "Here, put this on. Let's get on the road now."

"What's the plan, James. I have a few ideas, wanna' hear them?"

"Sure, I can listen while I drive," said James.

Mickey almost had to run to keep up with James as he walked to the Humvee. He walked behind James and started talking. "I think that if we go back to Satchel's place, we can go down the road and wait for Bobby to return and stop him and get him out."

"And you think it'll be that easy, right?" James said as he got into the Humvee.

"Sure, it won't be that hard. It's only been about an hour since we left there. Those guys may not even be out of that room by then. If they aren't, and Bobby shows up, we can get him and be gone before anyone even realizes it."

"What if they're out of the room by then? What do we do? Those guys will tell Satchel that we want Bobby, and Satchel will definitely have him killed," said James.

As he pulled to the entrance to the apartment complex, he saw Alyssa's truck sitting there. He pulled over, and she got out. Smiling, she had a large case at her side and was still dressed in camo gear. She grabbed the door handle, opened it, pitched the case inside, and jumped in the back seat.

"I knew you'd be heading out again and thought the three of us could spend the afternoon together. I guess the plan is to intercept Bobby driving that truck on its way back to the compound."

James nodded his head. "Mickey's catching on fast. He already had that same plan, which is the one I had planned to do before either of you said a word. And for your information, I knew you'd be waiting somewhere out here for us."

"Oh, so you think you know me, Jimmy boy," she said.

"Of course, I know you. You'd never let anyone go into a situation unprepared, and all it takes is one little screwup, and the last part of this mission dies, and maybe one of us goes down with it."

Mickey once again felt out of place with these two. They think and act almost as one. He could see how they worked together in combat. "Would you tell me the details of the plan, James?"

"Sure, Mickey. The most likely road Bobby will take is the same road we took coming this morning. Just in case he comes from the other direction, we have this chain saw. We cut down some leafy saplings and lay them across the road, and it'll look impassable. That should stop traffic from coming in that direction. Then from the direction he should be coming, we also cut down some more saplings to get the truck to stop. When it does, we step out of the brush with guns drawn like we're hijackers. When he stops, we take him and leave. Simple."

"And if someone's with him?" asked Alyssa.

"The same thing, we take Bobby and leave."

"Good plan," Mickey said. "That's basically what I had in mind, except without the tree cutting to get them to stop. I thought we could shoot out the tires."

"That would work too. If he doesn't stop, we may have to do that anyway," Alyssa said. "I agree with James. You're catching on very well. If you want to join our team, with a few months training, I'd consider it."

"No, thanks, Alyssa. I'm good with just fixing up houses," Mickey said, and he sat back in the seat, looking forward, as James drove.

CHAPTER 17

Tuesday Afternoon...At the Compound to Get Bobby

They turned onto the road that led by Satchel's private driveway. James pulled to the shoulder a quarter-mile down the road, stopped, got out, and took out the chainsaw.

"Why did you get a battery-powered one? The gasoline ones are much more powerful," said Mickey.

"Yep, and you could hear it all the way to town from here. This one's a lot quieter, and we aren't cutting down giant redwood trees, just a few saplings. Now go over there and cut some branches about two to three inches in diameter. I'll pull them out and lay them across the road. Aly is going to go down the driveway and check out the house.

"Wait," said Mickey. "Remember the security post. If she passes that on the road, it'll notify the house. She needs to cut through the woods like we did this morning."

"Right, little bro, good thinking. I'll go tell her." James left.

As Mickey started cutting down saplings, he could see James pointing to different locations, and finally, Alyssa began to move into the woods. He continued cutting until they made a pile of brush about three feet high. It wouldn't stop the big truck if they tried to drive through it, but it looked daunting enough to make them stop to check it out.

James came over to him and said, "Fine, now move down the road to the other side of the driveway, and we'll do the same thing, just in case they come from that direction."

As Mickey was cutting and James was piling the brush, Alyssa came back from the woods. They both stopped working when she walked up.

"All's quiet there. So, Satchel's still probably not there. I checked the back bunk room. I could hear noises, so no one's gone to check on them or let them out. I know it isn't locked, but they still believe you put that hand grenade wedged in the knob. That was genius," said Alyssa as she looked around, scouting out the area.

"Yeah, it was. Wasn't it?" James said with pride. "We're done piling the brush. All we need is to wait for the truck."

"And what'll you do if Bobby tries to make a run for it instead of coming back here?" Aly asked.

Mickey spoke up. "He has three reasons for not running."

"And what would those be, Mick?"

"The first two would be his wife and child, that sweet little girl in the wheelchair. That's why he got into this mess in the first place. The third is the person Satchel sent with him to make sure he came back," said Mickey.

"How do you know he sent someone with him?" James asked.

"As insurance. Satchel's no dummy. The driver said that they shot someone that asked too many questions. That's cold. So, he wouldn't take the chance that Bobby wouldn't come back."

"Sound logic there, little bro. I believe you're right."

"Shh," said Aly. "I hear a truck."

James pointed to the other side of the road and told Mickey to take his position there. He told Aly to take her position on this side, and he'd move in front behind the brush. The sound was coming from the direction they had anticipated. They took their positions and had guns in hand, ready to shoot the tires if the rig didn't stop. As it approached, it began to slow down. James pulled a mask over his head so he couldn't be identified, and as the truck slowed to a stop, the door opened, and the driver got out. When he did, they could see it was Bobby. The man in the other seat slid into the driver's seat and revved up the engine, and the truck started to move. Bobby quickly ran to the side, and Mickey began shooting the back tires. Aly started shooting the front tires. With no back tires for traction and flat front tires meant no control. The truck slid and sluggishly moved sideways in the road. James was sending multiple rounds of ammunition into the front of the giant truck, and finally, the engine died. Bobby was running straight into Alyssa's position. She jumped up and knocked him down with one blow to the chest. The man in the cab threw up his hands in surrender. Since James was wearing a mask, he moved forward to the side of the truck, opened the door, pulled the man out, and threw him on the ground. The man didn't say a word. Neither did James. He zip-tied his wrists, and put duct tape over his mouth, then proceeded to push the man's eyelids closed and put duct tape over his closed eyes. The man was lying face down on the pavement. James motioned for Bobby to move out. Mickey and Alyssa followed James with Bobby moving along with Alyssa's help each time he stumbled and grabbed his chest.

When they all got into the Humvee parked down the road out of sight, they felt free to talk. James took off his mask, and Bobby groaned with his hand on his chest. Aly just sat with a Cheshire cat grin on her face.

"What did you hit me with, lady? It felt like another truck," he said. "I think you broke some ribs!"

"Shut up, Bobby!" they all said at the same time.

"She just saved your life!" said James.

"Who are you people, and what do you want with me?" he said, sounding a bit concerned as well as annoyed.

"I'm James, and this is Mickey. Never mind who the woman is sitting beside you, and she hit you with her bare hand, so don't try to mess with her. We don't want anything with you. All we want is you. We're taking you home to your wife and child. Sit back and thank God and that woman sitting next to you that you're still alive. We couldn't have done it without her help," said James as he drove down the road toward Darcy's house.

By the time they got back home to Darcy's house, it had been a very long day. It had been a long and stressful day. Mickey told them he would be back first thing in the morning, and they would work out the logistics of getting them out of town to a safe location. James was going to meet with Alyssa later tomorrow to settle up her bill. The three of them, James, Aly, and Mickey, again got into James' Humvee.

CHAPTER 18

Wednesday Morning...Darcy's House with the Griffins

THE FOLLOWING MORNING MICKEY AND JAMES rolled up at Darcy's townhouse. When they went in, they saw a haggard group of people. Darcy, Janet, and Bobby were all sitting at the kitchen table sipping coffee. James and Mickey grabbed a cup of coffee and also sat down.

Mickey spoke up, "It looks like no one here got any sleep last night."

"We didn't get much, Mickey Ray," said Janet. "Bobby and I had so much to talk about. We're so thankful for what you and James did. We'd like to know all about it."

James cut in, "No, you don't want to know the details, but we did find out that Satchel would've killed you both if we didn't get you out of there. So, we did it."

"Really? He told me that as soon as I made a few runs for him, he would call it even, and I could leave," said Bobby.

"Well, he lied. He was never going to let either of you leave. You knew too much. One of the other drivers told us that he had shot someone that just looked in the back of the truck. I don't know why he didn't kill you right up front, but for some reason, he needed you to make a few more runs, so he let you live to do that."

"Sometimes the authorities do a random search of a truck, and if they did that and found what we're shipping, the driver would go to jail, and so would the shipper and, in that case, Satchel. He's always short on drivers. I worked for him years ago when he was legit, so I thought he would let me work for him again. When I saw what he was shipping, I knew we could all go to jail, so I told Satchel I wanted out. He said since I had worked for him in the past, he would let me go, and the money he had loaned me would call it even. All I had to do was do eight to ten more runs. He promised me."

James shook his head. "He lied. We heard them say that as soon as you finished your last run, you would both disappear. He didn't want to take a chance on you. We did some background checks on you, and we know you have a problem with the bottle."

"Not anymore. I swear. I haven't had a drink in months. I needed to get straight to drive, pay Satchel back and make some money for Carrie's operation. I'm clean."

"Maybe you are, but that might be the reason Satchel didn't trust you. You could easily fall off the wagon and turn on him, and he didn't want to take that risk," James said, looking Bobby straight in the eye.

Bobby looked back at him and shook his head, "NO. I'm clean."

Janet took a sip of coffee, then asked as she placed the cup back on the table, "James and Mickey, may I ask a few questions?"

"You can ask anything you want, but I can't guarantee that we will answer them," said James.

"Fair enough. First, why are you doing this for us?" she asked.

"I'll field that question, James," said Mickey as he pulled his chair closer to the table.

"We did it for Carrie. We both have a soft spot for children. James here, as you can see, has some problems getting close to children. He feels that they are afraid of him because of his facial scars."

James silently reached up and placed both hands on his face in acknowledgment of Mickey's explanation.

Mickey continued, "I've known a few people that grew up in the foster system. The government tries to find good people to care for the children they are entrusted with, but sometimes those families are often only in it for the money and don't care for the children. Each child is a gift from God. I believe that children should be loved and cared for. I also believe that their natural biological parents should do it, so we set out to help Carrie find her parents to prevent her from going into this flawed system we call foster care. We did it to help and protect Carrie."

"We're so thankful that you helped us. I don't know how we could ever repay you, so maybe we should just go and get away from here before you get in trouble," Janet asked.

"You can go. We aren't holding you prisoner here, but we don't think it's best that you leave yet, because Satchel and his organization will hunt you down and kill you," James answered her.

Bobby shook his head and stated, "Yes. You're correct. We'll be dead before we get to the county line. I don't know what we're going to do. And how can we repay you? You've gone to a lot of trouble to help us."

"Okay then, here's what we are going to do. If it's acceptable with Dee, you can stay here for a couple of days while we sort this out," James said.

"Just for a couple of days, James. I want to help them, but it's a bit crowded in here right now," Darcy said.

"I know, and if you can just bear with it, I'll take care of everything, and they can leave. Right now, they can't go to a hotel because Satchel may be watching them. We need to keep them safe until they get out of town."

Bobby said, "We don't have any money to go anywhere, but we'll leave. We appreciate everything you've done, and we don't want to be any more trouble than we've already been to you."

James continued. "I know. Be patient. We'll get it sorted out. I don't want to be rude, but could I ask the two of you to step outside while I talk with Mickey Ray and Dee?"

"Yeah, sure," Janet said as she motioned for Bobby to get up.

When they walked out the back door, Darcy looked at James with an "Are you crazy?" expression.

"James, I understand why you brought them here yesterday, and I wasn't prepared for that. They spend the night here. You tell them they can stay for several more days. James, I'm not running a boarding house or a safe house for any stranger you decide to bring here. That is NOT acceptable to me. These people need to leave. Do you hear me?"

Mickey just sat back in his chair and folded his arms. He was a bit amused at this situation. James hadn't seen Darcy like this before, and Mickey wanted to see how James would handle it.

"Dee, we had nowhere else to take Bobby. What could we do?"

"Did you know that you were going to find him yesterday?"

"Well, yes…" James said hesitantly.

"Then you could have made some arrangements in advance. Did you ever think of that? I don't like strangers staying in my house. First, I admit that Mickey found this little girl, and she ended up at my house. Alright, I accept part of the blame for that, but then you two show up with her mother. Yesterday afternoon, the two of you showed up with her father. Who will be next, the circus? No, they can't show up! They're already here! James, and you too Mickey, get them out of here. I don't mind helping people out, but this is ridiculous!" Now, Darcy sat back in the chair and folded her arms in defiance.

"Can we have one day? I promise, we'll make some arrangements by tomorrow, and they'll be out of your hair."

"What do you plan to do, James?" she asked.

"We'll find them a hotel to stay in for a few days until we can get them safely out of town. Then we'll set them up in another city far from here, and they can start a new life. I kind of have it worked out."

Darcy sat with her arms folded, just staring at James. She looked over at Mickey and back at James, then spoke again to James, "What do you mean, 'you kind of have it worked out?' That means you don't have a clue what to do now, doesn't it? And where's the money coming from to get them out of town and set up in another city? James, WE DON'T HAVE THAT KIND OF MONEY. Since Evelyn took all the available cash, we're just barely making payroll. It'll still take us months to build up an emergency fund. Right now, this situation may be an emergency for them, but we aren't responsible for them. We can't support them!"

Mickey got up and turned to walk out of the kitchen.

"Hold it right there, little brother, you ARE NOT walking out right now. Sit back down, Mickey Ray Christianson."

There she started, using all three of his names. He knew he was in trouble. He turned and sat back down.

"I was just going to check on the others outside," he said.

"They can wait. It's not like they have anywhere else to go. So, sit!" Darcy looked from Mickey to James, "Someone is going to tell me what's going on here. James, I know you have, or at least had some money because you gave me some a few months ago, but what you are talking about is moving them, and setting them up. That will take several thousand dollars. I don't know if you have that much stashed away, but you can't go around just handing out thousands of dollars to every waif and homeless family you meet."

James turned and looked at Mickey.

Mickey shrugged his shoulders and said, "I think it's time to tell her. If not, she may try to beat it out of one of us. At this point, I wouldn't put it past her. She's totally ticked off right now, dude."

"Yes, I am," she said with her arms still folded.

"I really think I should go out and check on the Griffins."

Darcy looked and him and said, "Go!" Then she turned to James, "You, talk."

Mickey got up and walked out.

James started telling Dee what had happened and how they found out where Janet was being held.

"So, when you went to the wrong storage unit, you found all this money."

"Yes."

"And you stole it?"

"No, we didn't steal it. It's profits from a criminal enterprise!"

"It's still stolen money, James."

"Yes, but it's not like we stole it from a legitimate business or some private citizen. It's like stealing money from the mob, something like that."

"And you think they'll just let it go and forget about it?"

"They don't know we took it. That's the beauty of it all." Then James told Darcy that they had let Neal and Carson go with enough of the cash to get out of town and hide from Satchel.

"And this Satchel Binghamton will blame those two idiots."

"Exactly. Neal and Carson are criminals, and they're the ones that kept Janet prisoner in that storage unit, drugged and tied up, laying in her own filth."

"Why was the money being kept there in the first place? There are a lot more secure places to keep that kind of money."

"We don't know why the money was there. I do know that that kind of medical equipment is worth millions on the black market. I did some research and estimated that retail price for that equipment is almost 15 million dollars in that one storage unit.

"It's all being shipped out of the country. By the time you buy an MRI or a CT machine, pay the authorities to allow it in the country, and set it up, it costs almost double. So, they purchase the machine black market discount, then use the additional funds for pay-offs. I checked into it, and it's a very lucrative business. It's kind of like selling organs on the black market. Same principle.

"That's for big machines. Even small portable X-ray machines can be used and hidden in small third world villages and run with a portable generator."

"Okay, now how do we launder the money you stole," she asked.

"Let me straighten you out on this. We didn't steal the money from a legal, legitimate business or person. We stole it from a murdering criminal. He took it from people buying stolen or hot medical equipment.

"Right now, if we turn it in, we have to explain how we found it. Everyone involved with them is a criminal. We'll use it to help people. People like the Griffins," James said.

"How do we launder it and make it legal?" She repeated.

"We don't. We just use it on a cash basis, no paper trail. No questions, no explanations. If we give money to help the Griffins, will they ask how and where we got it? I don't think so!" James said and then sat back in his chair, satisfied with his explanation and answers to Darcy's questions.

Mickey walked back in and sat down, and asked, "What do you think of what happened?"

"I think you're both a bit crazy and have some big ones," she said.

"Big what, sis?"

"You know what I'm talking about!" she said sarcastically. "Now, you've told me how you got this huge wad of money. Tell me what your plan is to get the Griffins out of town safely."

"Can I offer some thoughts on this one?" asked Mickey.

"Sure, bro. The money's as much yours as it is mine. We found it together," said James.

"To get them out of the house, we need to move them out of this area. Probably at least to Richmond, while we decide where we want them to go," and he gave them his thoughts on getting them out of town.

James said, "I got to know a lot of doctors that I could call that are now in private practice. Maybe they could give us some leads on good hospitals to help Carrie. That would also determine where we'll move them."

They also agreed to take some of the money to pay for Carrie's operation and get Janet and Bobby out of debt so they could make a clean start. After they had some basic plans worked out, Mickey went back to bring them inside to explain the new plan.

When they came back in and sat down, Mickey told Janet and Bobby what they had to do.

Mickey started, "Janet and Bobby, here's what we'll do, and this's what we expect from you. We have a bit of money to help people like you. We'll pay your moving expenses to a city where Carrie can get the medical care she needs, and we'll help with Carrie's medical expenses. We'll help you get set up in a house and pay for a rental car for a short time until you can buy a car while Bobby looks for a job with a good medical plan. If you keep straight for 12 months, we'll match whatever you've saved for a down payment on a house. Now, we expect Bobby to stay clean and sober. We'll have people watching over you. If you screw up, all deals are off. We're offering you a second chance. DON'T BLOW IT! Do you understand what I've said?" He looked at both of them.

Janet sat crying, and Bobby had his arms around her. They were both nodding their heads, yes.

"Oh, thank you so much, that's all we need. A second chance. We won't let you down. We promise," Bobby said.

"Okay, we still have a lot to do. James, let's go and start getting things ready to get them out of here. Dee, can you get them a room in Richmond. We'll come back and get them this afternoon."

"Sure, Mickey. I'll make a reservation for tonight," said Darcy.

Mickey dropped James off at his apartment and drove to the diner. He was sure that Valerie would be working. Martha, the owner, told him that Valerie had taken a couple of days off when he got there. He asked if anything was wrong because she hadn't mentioned it to him, although he did admit he hadn't talked to her for a few days.

"No, Mickey Ray, she didn't say anything specific. She just said she wanted a few days off, that's all," said Martha.

He went to see his father. When he went to Pop's room, he wasn't there, and he knew the next place to go was to the solarium. That is where he found him, sitting in a thickly padded chair, and his walker was right next to him. Daniel turned to greet Mickey when he came into the room.

"Hey, son. Glad you came by. The doctor was here about an hour ago, and he said that a few more therapy sessions and I should be able to go home. I'm so looking forward to that. Have you driven the new Rolls anymore since you bought it?"

"That's great, Pop. Sorry. I've been so busy that I haven't had time to drive it, but I'm looking forward to it. Thanks for buying it, and as soon as you're able, it's yours! And, yes, Dee's starting to pack so she can be ready for you too. We'll call the movers to come and start moving things next week. Will that be soon enough?"

"Oh, sure. I guess I'll be in the downstairs guest area. I never thought that I'd be a guest in my own house."

"Pop, you aren't a guest. It's still your house. For the time being, it'll be easier for you to get around downstairs," Mickey said.

"I know. The more I remember, the more I miss your mother," Daniel said sadly.

"Yes, we'll all miss her forever, Pop. She would want you to go on and get better to help Dee and me continue what you started. James told me you want to continue with that expansion to the Senior area you were planning last year."

"Do you think you can do it, son?"

"Not without your help. The two of us can do it together," Mickey said proudly. "I was thinking. Instead of hiring outside contractors, we could do it ourselves. You know, start a construction company and call it 'Christianson and Son.' How's that sound?"

"I like it! I think a better name would be 'Christianson's Construction,'" said Daniel.

"Yep," Mickey was thinking, "Pop really is getting back to his old self. In a few months, he'll be good as new."

They talked a few more minutes, and Mickey had to leave. This was the best day he'd had in months! "Pop's almost back!" he said to himself as he walked to his truck.

His phone rang, and when he looked at the caller ID, he saw it was Valerie.

"Hey, Val. What's up?" he said into the phone.

"Can you come over for a few minutes, Mickey Ray? I'll fix dinner for you if you can."

"Sure, I would love that, Val. I just left the rehab center. I stopped by to see Pop again today. I'll be there in about ten minutes."

"Okay, I'll put something on the stove, and it should be ready shortly after you get here. See you then," she said, and the phone disconnected.

The hair stood up on the back of his neck. He was glad that Val had invited him over, but he just had the feeling something was wrong. He couldn't quite put his finger on it, just the way she sounded. He drove toward her house.

Since his apartment was at the other end of the building where she lived, he parked in his usual parking space and walked to her unit. He heard her call out to him to come on inside when he knocked.

When he got there, he put his arms around her as she turned a hamburger patty in a frying pan. She didn't turn toward him but motioned for him to get a plate to put the burger patties on.

He tried to pull her to him, but she resisted with the excuse that she wanted to get the burgers done, and on their plates before they got cold. She continued to get dinner ready and on the table. She did all this in silence, so Mickey went back into the living room area, sat on the couch, and turned the TV to the news.

After a few moments, she came out with a plate with a fully loaded burger and potato chips. She put a cola on the coffee table. She then served herself the same as they watched television in silence.

As Mickey finished his last mouthful of food, he said, "Hey, Val. What's wrong? I know you asked me over here for a reason. Can I help you with it?"

"Not quite yet, Mickey. Let's finish eating. Please?"

"Honey, did I do something wrong? I don't know what I did, but whatever it is, I can make it right if you let me know. I promise. I don't like you upset like this," he said gently.

"Please, Mickey. Let me finish eating first," she pleaded and again lapsed into silence.

Mickey turned back to the television and absently watched the news.

Valerie picked up the dirty dishes, took them to the sink, and came back and sat down in the stuffed armchair at the end of the coffee table beside Mickey. She picked up the remote and turned off the television.

She took a deep breath and said, "Mickey, we need to talk."

He turned from the television and looked at Valerie. "I know, dear, but I don't know why. I don't know what I did to upset you."

"I need to know what you are doing to help that little girl in the wheelchair?" she asked.

"We were trying to find her parents. That's all."

"Have you found them yet?"

"Yes, Val. We did get them, and the whole thing was a success, and no one was hurt. They are all safe right now at Darcy's house."

"The last time you did something like that, I was taken, Darcy had to leave town, and all hell broke loose in this sleepy little town."

"It all worked out, and all those people are gone now. Problem solved," Mickey said.

"Mickey, I don't feel safe here anymore. I'm scared all the time. I'm afraid when I go to my car to go to work. I'm so scared when I drive home at night. I'm afraid when I'm here alone, anytime day or night. I can't deal with it anymore," she said as the tears ran freely down her cheeks now.

"Everything is fine now. No one is going to hurt you anymore. You have my word on that. You know that if something did happen, I would walk through hell and back to keep you safe."

"How did you find them?"

"What kind of question is that. We found them. That's all there is to it, Valerie!" he said, getting a bit annoyed.

"I don't know what you and James were doing, but it was something dangerous, wasn't it? Don't lie to me, Mickey Ray Christianson!" she said adamantly.

He knew she was very annoyed. Mickey also knew that, like Dee, when Valerie started using all his names, she was extremely upset with him.

"Dear, don't get so upset. You are overreacting over this entire situation. What are you talking about?" he fired back.

"Don't play games with me, Mickey Ray! I don't know what's going on, but you've had secret meetings at the diner, at James' house and coming and going at strange hours. I don't know what you're doing, but I don't like it. James is a wonderful man, but both of you are involved with something dangerous," she said and began to cry. "You're scaring me. You are getting involved with something, and I can't deal with it."

"You can't deal with it, you say? It's nothing. It's over. Well, it's almost over. It will be soon. I mean it," he said defensively.

"So, it is dangerous, and you refuse to tell me," she continued.

"I can't tell you right now. Give me a few days, and I'll tell you everything."

"You'll tell me now!" she demanded.

"No, I won't. It'll upset you needlessly. I don't want you to overreact about this either."

"So, whatever you're involved in this time, you won't walk away from it?"

"I can't walk away. Not until I finish it. People's lives are on the line here!" Mickey said.

"That's what I thought. If it wasn't dangerous, then people's lives wouldn't be at risk. Your life wouldn't be at risk. That is exactly what I am talking about, Mickey Ray. You're involved with something dangerous. Here's how I am going to 'react' as you say." She sat back in her chair and took a deep breath.

"It is nothing like that last thing. I promise. The Griffin's need help," Mickey added.

"I know, but as long as someone needs your help, you'll help them. I can't deal with it again. I need to get away from all this. I can't live my life in fear all the time."

"You won't. This is just a one-time thing. It's nothing like the last thing. Nothing like that will ever happen again," he said, pleading now.

"We can't get married. I love you, but I can't marry you, Mickey Ray! I have to leave. I'm moving next weekend. I've already made arrangements."

"What do you mean? Where are you going? Is it permanent?"

"I put in an application for culinary school, and I was accepted. It's in Oregon, and to get there in time for the next semester, I need to be there in one week. I need to move this weekend. Yes, it is permanent. I love you, Mickey Ray Christianson, but I can't stay here."

"Please, Valerie, can't we work this out? You're the only person I've ever loved."

"No, Mickey. I've made up my mind. I've already sent in the first installment on my tuition. You're my first and only love, but I can't deal with what happened to me anymore. I can't live in a town that everywhere I go, I feel horrified and afraid. I love you, Mickey Ray, but I'm leaving," she cried. "We can't get married. I don't feel right about all this. Things are different now. I'm different. You're different. Nothing is the same."

Mickey stood, walked around the table to her, gently pulled her to her feet, and embraced her. She cried with her head on his chest. He gently ran his fingers through her hair and held her close.

"Can I do anything to help you, Val?" he asked.

"No, just let me go. Let me leave."

"Do you need any money to help you with your moving expenses?"

"No. I still have enough money from the insurance claim from the fire a few months ago." She pulled away from him and looked into his eyes.

"I want to do something to help you," he said.

"Can I just leave and leave the furniture here? You can give it to someone else that needs it. Actually, you could use it. You haven't completely refurnished your own apartment since it was trashed a few months ago. Besides, I don't have any way to take it with me."

"Sure, I deal with things like this all the time. Take what you need, and I'll take the rest. Will I ever hear from you again?"

"Of course. When I get there, I'll call you and give you my address, and we can talk on the phone all the time. I still love you. Maybe someday, we can each get our lives together, and we can pick up where we're leaving off."

"I look forward to that day, my dear Valerie," he said.

"I'll never forget you or the time we spent together, Mickey Ray."

"What day are you leaving, Val?"

"Saturday. I'm catching a plane out around noon. Can you see me off?"

"You bet. Wild horses couldn't keep me away," he said with a smile that he didn't feel at this time.

"Good, I'll need you to be there, so I'll have the strength to get on the plane. Now go home before I break down completely."

He kissed her slowly and passionately, pulled away, turned, and walked out the door. He wanted to cry. In the past few months, he had seen so much happen that, as much as he felt like it, he knew that he would never again shed a tear for anything or anyone. He hadn't felt this empty for many months. He walked down the building's sidewalk to his apartment.

He got in his truck and drove back to the country roads he had driven so many times since he was old enough to drive. It was early spring, and the leaves were sprouting as the trees came awake from their winter hibernation. He thought back to when he last had a drive like this. It was also one that filled him with sadness. He was in his Rolls Royce Corniche. Those times alone with nature, the car he loved so much that he and Pop had restored together, were terrific memories. He treasured his time alone on those back roads. He thought about how he had envisioned his future back then. That future was today, and it was so different than the one that played out in his mind those years ago. He had wonderful happy dreams of a remarkable young life of fun and carefree days. No, it hadn't been like the days he dreamed of at all. It had not been a dream. The past months had been a nightmare. His mother gone, Pop out of commission but at least getting better. Now, the girl he planned to marry was leaving. Reality is so different from our dreams. He drove on with the music from his father's teen years blaring through the truck's speakers. On and on, he went with the memories playing and replaying in his mind.

CHAPTER 19

Thursday Morning…Darcy's House, Hotel, Future Plans

MICKEY KNOCKED ON THE BACKDOOR OF Darcy's townhouse at eight o'clock the following morning.

"Do you have a pot of coffee yet?" he asked.

"Yes, we do, Mickey Ray."

Everyone was in the kitchen, with juice, milk, and coffee. Then Cyndi and Joel ran up to him and gave him a big hug. Carrie was trying to move her chair when Mickey held up his hand to stop her. He walked over to her, bent down, and gave her a big hug. He greeted Bobby and Janet.

"Dee, can we talk privately in your office," he said.

"Sure, but if it concerns our guests, you can talk here. I'm sure that whatever you say that concerns them, they can take it."

"No, it's a personal matter," he said, nodding at Bobby and Janet.

Mickey stepped aside as Darcy walked past Mickey and headed toward her office in the back.

Mickey sat down in the chair in front of her desk. Darcy walked around and sat in her desk chair.

"What is it, Mickey?" she asked, waiting for him to begin.

He sat for a few moments to collect himself. "Valerie and I won't be getting married. She's moving away in a few days," he said.

"Oh, Mickey, what did you do this time?" she said softly.

"Nothing. I didn't do anything this time, Dee. It wasn't me. I swear!"

"You did something stupid, didn't you, Mickey?"

"No. I didn't do anything. Val said that because of what happened and being kidnapped, she just doesn't feel safe around here anymore. And she believes that what happened before could happen again sometime."

"No, it won't happen again. Did you tell her that?"

"Of course, I told her, but she thinks that since we are trying to help Carrie, something like that might happen again. She doesn't want me to get involved. Dee, I love her so much. I never realized it until a few months ago. When I finally got my head together about her, that happened. I don't know what to do."

Darcy got up and walked toward Mickey and reached out her arms to him. He got up, and they hugged.

"I know you love her, but maybe this is best for both of you."

"I don't know how, Dee. I don't know what I'll do without her. She's always been here since high school. I almost can't remember life without her. It's like we almost grew up together."

"I know, little brother, but as much as you'll miss her, life will go on. You'll get over her in time. You'll be okay. James, myself, the kids, and hopefully soon, Dad will help you get through it. I promise you," she said. "Maybe it'll only be temporary. When she gets herself straight, she'll come back home. Does she want you there when she leaves?"

"Yes, I'll meet her at the airport when her plane leaves. She said she wants me to see her off."

"Fine, let me know when her plane leaves, and we'll all be there." She backed away, patting him on the cheek like he was a child. "You'll be fine. I promise."

"It just seems like one thing gets fixed, and something else falls apart."

"I know, it does, Mickey. It sure seems that way, but it'll work itself out. I know it will."

"Yeah, I guess it will, but it seems so bad right now."

"Come on. Head up. Chin up. Shoulders back. Let's go back out there, and help that family!"

"Yes, let's do that," he said unconvincingly as he turned and walked out of her office.

When Mickey and Darcy got back into the kitchen, Darcy announced that she had gotten a reservation at a local hotel near Richmond for them to stay in for a few days. James was going to make a few calls, and when he had gathered more information, they would discuss possible places for them to move. Then she'd purchase plane tickets for them to leave. They left for the Richmond Hotel. When they got there, Darcy checked them in, James and Mickey took Bobby aside to talk.

"Janet, if you and the kids will follow Dee, James and I need to talk to Bobby for a few minutes," said Mickey as they headed for the sitting area outside the hotel lobby. "Just have Dee bring Bobby the key to the room when she gets you checked in, please," he added.

James, Mickey, and Bobby walked out to a little park area in the front of the hotel and sat down at one of the wrought-iron tables. James started first. "I made a few calls to some people I know. They're doctors in a couple of cities. They're in private practice now, but they used to be military doctors treating wounded veterans like myself. They have agreed to look at Carrie's medical records and see if they can help her get out of that chair. We'll discuss that later, but I wanted you to know that we're working on it. The problem is, you will have to move to where they're practicing, so your choice of relocation is limited."

"I don't care. We'll go wherever you say we need to go."

"First thing first, Bobby. What is your background? James has found some doctors that can help Carrie, but what are your job qualifications? That'll be useful to know so when you move there, we'll know what kind of jobs you've had in the past so we can arrange for good references if a prospective employers calls."

"Well, let's see," Bobby said, rubbing his chin. "I trained as a machinist in jail for two years, and…"

"Wait," said Mickey. "You spent time in jail? We didn't know that. What for?'

"Robbery. I got drunk one night and held up a convenience store on a bet," he said hesitantly.

"On a bet? You are a bigger idiot than I thought you were," said Mickey.

James sat quietly, then shook his head disgustedly at Mickey. Mickey continued, "What were you thinking?"

"That's the problem. I was drunk, and I wasn't thinking. Like I told you before. I'm clean. I haven't had a drink since the accident that put Carrie in the wheelchair. I swear!"

"I'm beginning to agree with Dee and Val. Maybe we are making a huge mistake. Maybe we should have called the police and social services to put Carrie in a decent home."

"No, please. I don't want Carrie to go to some strangers. I'll do whatever you want. I'll stay clean. I promise."

Mickey thought for a moment, then began with more questions for Bobby. "Fine. You are a machinist. What else can you do?"

"As you know, I can drive a truck, and I have a degree in accounting."

"You went to college?" asked James.

"Yes, when I got hooked on the bottle, I began making mistakes in my record keeping and was fired. Then after I spent time in jail, I couldn't get a job in any accounting firms, and machine shops wouldn't hire me because of my record. The only thing left was truck driving. If you have a good driving record, most of them will hire you. That's how I met Satchel. After a couple of years working for him, we moved to North Carolina to a trucking firm there. I got on the bottle again, and then the world fell apart," he said, hanging his head.

"Yep," said James, "you screwed the pooch on that one. I'll try to work with it, but you don't exactly have a stellar background for me to work with. Janet said she had a job. What did she do?"

"She worked in the same accounting firm I worked for. We met there. She was moving up in the firm until I went to jail, and they didn't feel comfortable letting her work high-powered accounts, so that kind of killed her chance of advancements."

"You pretty much tarnish everyone you come in contact with, don't you, Bobby?"

"Right now, we have a more urgent problem, that's Satchel Binghamton. You know he's going to come after us, more specifically, you. We need to get him in jail. He doesn't know about us. That is

Mickey, myself, and the team we hired to get you out, but as long as he's on the street, he'll be looking for you."

"Why would he be looking for me? I think as long as I disappear, he'll know I'm gone and write me off," Bobby said.

"Because, as James said, he doesn't know us, but he does know you, and you're the link to us," Mickey spoke up. "Trust me, Bobby, he has several million reasons to look for you, as well as a few other people he thinks stole some money from him."

"What money? None of the drivers handled any money as far as I know," Bobby questioned.

"Don't be concerned about that. Trust us, Satchell will be fuming mad, and the less you know, the safer you are, and so are we. Now, we helped you out of there. Now we need your help to put him away," James said.

"I don't know what I can do to help you, but I'll do anything you want."

"It could be dangerous. That's why we aren't discussing this around the ladies and children. You can't tell them anything we discuss now, except the part about moving to another city for Carrie's treatments."

"You have my word on it. I won't say anything."

James continued, "I mean it. This is one of those situations if you were in the military and they tell you that you can't discuss your job, you can't do it. Not even your wife! Understand? We said we would help you with medical bills and money until you get back on your feet. If we find out that you told anyone, we mean anyone, we'll drop you like a hot coal, and you'll be on your own."

"I swear, I won't tell anyone."

"We're serious. You don't even tell God in your prayers! Not now. Not next year. Not even on your deathbed!"

"I got it, you guys. I won't tell anyone, ever," Bobby said exasperatedly.

"Do you know the times and dates of the runs from his house or the compound or whatever you call it?" asked James.

"Kind of."

"That's not an answer, Bobby. Do you know or don't you know?"

"It's different. Some weeks it's regular, then times it isn't. Also, it depends on the load and whether it's a pickup or delivery or load to the shipping terminal."

Mickey cut in, "We need you to explain that in more detail. We aren't familiar with the whole business, so we need you to explain to us what all that is."

"I don't understand it all myself," Bobby said, getting a bit flustered at these questions.

James reached over and placed his hand on Bobby's hand that was on the table. "Calm down, Bobby. We aren't your enemy. Now, we need your help to prevent Satchel Binghamton from hunting you down and killing you and your whole family. We'll not hurt you. You have my word."

"Okay. Okay, but you two are scaring me. I don't know you. How do I know, you may only want to steal stuff from Satchel, and you're using me to do it?"

James took his hand back and thought for a moment. "That's an excellent question. If we wanted to use you, wouldn't we do the same thing Satchel did and hold Janet and little Carrie to pressure you into helping us?"

"Yeah, but maybe you're doing that already. Maybe you're going to keep them if I don't help you."

"Another good question. The way I see it is, you have two options. One is you trust us, help us, and take your chances that we'll keep our word and help you get away to a new life. Second is not to help us, and we walk away right now."

"Since I don't know what you'll do, I might just take my chances on my own. No, I won't help," Bobby said, sat back, and folded his arms in defiance.

Just then, Dee walked up and handed Bobby a key with a room number tag on it.

James stood and said, "Thanks, Dee. Go back to the desk and tell the manager that we're canceling payment on the room and that Bobby and Janet Griffin will be responsible for payment."

"What?" Dee said.

"Bobby here thinks he's better on his own without our help. That includes paying for their hotel room, plane tickets, meals, and relocation," said Mickey.

As Mickey was talking, Janet walked up to the table.

"What's going on here?" she asked.

Mickey turned to her. "We asked Bobby to help us put Satchel and his men behind bars. He doesn't trust us to keep our part of the bargain to help you with Carrie's medical expenses and move you out of town to a safe place. So, we're parting company here."

Janet furrowed her brows, walked over to Bobby, and shoved him so hard he almost lost his balance sitting at the other side of the table.

"You lowlife, piece of dirt. Sometimes I wish they hadn't found you. When those men took me, I almost died locked in that storage unit. Mickey and James risked their lives getting you out of that crap and offered us a whole new life."

"We don't know them, Janet. They could be using us like Satchel was using us," Bobby said.

"Just a few hours ago, you called them our saviors, and now you're saying this! I ought to shoot you myself. You ungrateful slug! I don't know what they asked you to do, but I will do it if I can. I appreciate what they've done for Carrie and me, and you should too!" she said and stormed off crying into the hotel.

Mickey, James, and Darcy stood for a few moments, then Mickey said, "Let's go. We'll do it without him. Janet's right. He doesn't deserve our help."

They turned to leave when Bobby called out, "No, wait, guys. I'm sorry, Janet's right. I didn't mean what I said. I'll help you. I'll do whatever you say. I promise."

Mickey looked at James, "What do you think? Should we give him another chance?"

James looked at Darcy, "What do you think, Dee?"

Darcy shrugged her shoulders, "I guess so. We started this whole thing to help Carrie."

"I'm not positive Bobby will carry it out. He might bail on us when we need him most. James and I'll talk about it. We need a few minutes," said Mickey, and he motioned for James to follow him into the hotel.

They went into the hotel restaurant and sat in the back corner far away from other patrons. A server came over, and they both ordered a soda.

"James, I'm tired. I'll be glad when all this is over," said Mickey.

"Me too, Mickey. What do you want to do about Bobby?" James answered.

"Let him sweat for a while. We'll help him, but let's not make it too easy. I don't like his wishy-washy attitude. One minute he's with us. The next minute he wants to walk away. He's not reliable." Mickey took a sip of his drink.

"I agree. He's not stable. I don't know how we can depend on him. But we need him for this plan to work. We need to get Satchel and a confession out of him so that we can put him away. If we don't get a confession, the most he'll get is a few years for theft and smuggling. We need to get him on a murder charge, so he'll spend the rest of his life in prison," said James. "Since he knows Bobby, Satchel will talk more freely to him."

"True. If we can keep him straight long enough to do that. Now, we need to address what happened the other day at the compound."

"What do you mean? What happened?" asked James calmly.

"You know what I mean. I said no-kill, and we killed two people, James! That was against all the rules."

"It couldn't be helped. We were under direct fire. It was kill or be killed!"

"Couldn't you just withdraw?"

"No, we couldn't. Trust me. It was kill or be killed, literally. There were no alternatives."

"That makes me a murderer!" Mickey said, so no one around them could hear.

"No, it doesn't. It wasn't you. It was the team," said James.

"I got us involved in this whole affair, which means I'm responsible for the death of those people."

"Get over it, Mickey. They're murdering criminals, and the world's better off without them," said James.

"Get over it, you say? I woke up half a dozen times last night and almost vomited my guts out over this entire thing. I wish I had called the police and let them handle it."

"You could have done that, but then you would have that little girl's foster care on your conscience as well as the blood of Bobby and Janet," James said, taking a sip of his soft drink.

"I don't want to hear that. The police are trained for that stuff, so is the FBI or whoever would have gotten this case."

"I'll end this conversation with this. You're doing the right thing. In some circles, you'd be a hero. In this particular case, you weren't there, so you can't say what could have or should have happened. Things rarely go as planned, so suck it up and deal with it, Mickey Ray."

Dee came up to the table and sat down. "Alright, boys, what are we going to do? Are we going to walk away, or are we going to finish the job? Bobby and Janet are waiting outside."

Mickey got up, followed by James and Darcy, "Let's get this over with."

Outside they saw Bobby and Janet in a heated discussion.

"Alright, we'll help you, but you have to do everything we tell you to do. If you do, we'll keep you safe," said Mickey.

"Dee, go back into the hotel. We have to talk to Bobby, man to man," said Mickey.

"You don't want me to know what you're about to do. Do you?" Darcy inquired.

"True," he said.

"It's dangerous and probably illegal, isn't it?"

"Yep."

"I won't like it, will I?"

"Again, correct."

"Oh, Lord, help me. No, Lord, help the three of you. I kind of understand why Val's leaving," Darcy said, walking away.

"Do you guys do stuff like this all the time?" asked Bobby.

"Yes," James.

"No," said Mickey. "This is just the second time."

James turned to Mickey, "What did Dee mean by Val's leaving, Mickey?"

"What do you mean, this is just the second time, Mickey Ray?" asked Bobby. "What happened the first time?"

"I want to know what she means by Val's leaving," persisted James.

Mickey put his hand up in a stop motion, "Both of you, be quiet for a minute. James, we'll talk about Val later. Bobby, never mind what happened the first time. That's none of your business. We helped out some other people, that's all. Besides, that's another secret that we don't talk about, not even to God! Now let's move forward with the information and plans for this situation."

They sat back down at the table again. James tried to pick up where they left off.

"Bobby, what do you mean by these different routes?" he asked.

"All I know is they steal medical equipment and ship it around the world, to mostly third world countries. They get it from various sources and move it from truck to truck, so it's harder to track. They move the money the same way, but they use storage units. One person leaves the cash, another picks it up, and they change units and facilities for the same reason. It's all high-end equipment. Some shipments may only be a few hundred thousand dollars. Others could be several million. Portable X-ray machines are the most common but also the lowest price. CT and MRI machines are the really high-end stuff. They don't sell many of those, but when they do, it's big bucks. Satchel has the entire East Coast. Somebody named Coswell is in charge of the West Coast. I don't know anything about him."

"Right now, we don't care about Coswell. We want to get Satchel, and we need your help," said Mickey Ray. "When we get him, we'll keep our promise."

James asked Bobby, "Do you know the transfer points?"

"Yeah, they're pretty much the same. Why?"

"We want to steal one of their trucks," answered James.

"That's simple. A driver pulls into a rest area, usually at a state line or State Welcome Center, and the drivers trade keys. They trade an empty truck for one that's loaded."

"Why do they trade? Why doesn't one driver take it all the way?"

"It's a way of not letting the right hand know what the left hand's doing. It's a security thing. The drivers don't know what they're carrying."

"They just pull into a terminal, hook up a trailer and deliver it to another location. They don't know, and I would take a guess, they don't care. Why is this any different?" asked Mickey Ray.

"I don't know exactly, but the beginning and the end of the line are the weak points. As you said, drivers usually go to a terminal to pick up their trailers. In this case, they go to Satchel's barn, maybe to unload at a storage unit like the one where Janet was kept. Someone has to drive the truck, someone runs the forklifts that load and unload, and so they keep changing drivers, so no one knows exactly what's going on."

"How did you find out?" asked Mickey Ray.

"I used to work for Satchel when he was legit, and I kind of found out things by accident. They didn't plan on telling me as he got into this stuff. When I found out what they were doing, I quit, and Janet and I left the area. You don't just quit on Satchel when you know something. As long as you're totally out of the loop, you can leave. There is no leaving once you're on the inside. So, when I caused Carrie's accident, I came back to him and borrowed some money. I sent the money to Janet. Then they wouldn't loan me enough for Carrie's operation. When I threatened to report them, they told me I could work out my debt and leave. Apparently, they didn't plan on letting me leave as they promised."

"Ya think," said Mickey Ray, as he shook his head.

"Hey, man, I worked for him before. I never thought he'd be like this. He used to be a different guy," said Bobby defensively.

"Well, he's like it now, and it sounds to me like you're in real deep. You're lucky we got you out when we did."

"You're right. How can I help to pay my debt to you?"

James broke in, "We need to get one of those trucks. One that has a load."

"Why?" asked Bobby.

"The less you know, the better we all are," said James.

"You don't trust me?" asked Bobby.

"Look at your track record, Bobby!" said James.

"Hey, I find that very offensive."

"Bobby, I don't really care what offends or doesn't offend you. We're helping you, your wife, and your daughter, so don't push my buttons. We aren't getting anything out of this but the satisfaction that we've helped someone. You got a problem with that?" James said.

"No, I guess not, but...."

"The more you open your mouth, the less I like you...." added James.

Mickey stood up and placed both hands, palms down, on the table. "Hold it. Both of you. You're acting like school kids on a playground."

Mickey turned to Bobby. "James said, we have a lot to lose here, so you don't get to ask questions since we are the ones that are putting ourselves on the line. We helped you. Now you can help us."

Then Mickey turned to James, "You, my good friend, need to get over your personal feeling about Bobby here. We need to get this job done and get them out of here. Let's just do it, okay?"

"You're right," James said, then looked at Bobby. "I'm doing it for Carrie."

"We have that straight. Now let's get on with it, please," Mickey said and sat down again.

Mickey turned to Bobby, "You'll help us get a loaded truck. Tell us how we can do that."

Bobby took a deep breath and said, "We need to do the exchange at one of the rest stops."

"Do they have any regular schedules, like a certain day or time?" asked Mickey Ray.

"Kind of. Sometimes they have some electronic equipment coming in, but that doesn't bring in as much money as the medical stuff going out. Electronics comes into this country at the Portsmouth terminals. Medical goes out. They try to send drivers out with a load, but they have been known to send a truck out empty if they think government officials may stop it. Oh, yeah, I almost forgot, sometimes they send out cash on a truck loaded with bricks."

"Bricks? Why bricks?" asked James.

"It's easy to transport bricks because of the weight. They can put one thing on the lading or shipping paperwork bill if it's a closed container. And the weight must correspond to whatever is supposed to be inside. Can you imagine the raised eyebrows if the paperwork lists a load of appliances that should weigh five tons, and the actual weight on the scale doesn't match up because it is a small box of money? Do you realize how small the size of a box of one-hundred-dollar bills is?"

James and Mickey looked at each other. They remembered the size of the briefcases of money they found in the storage unit, and the light went on in each one's head.

"We have a rough idea," said James as Bobby continued talking.

"They would catch that and open the trailer to inspect it. They can put several million dollars inside a refrigerator packed inside a cardboard shipping box, and inspectors won't open every box in the trailer. If it's an open trailer or flatbed, they put a box of money in the middle of a load of bricks. No one's going to break steel bands and manually take apart a load of bricks."

"We just need to figure out when the next load goes out and take the truck at the exchange point," Mickey said.

"Yeah, but how're you going to do that?" asked Bobby.

"We'll work on that and get back to you," said Mickey Ray.

"Give us the schedules as you remember them. What days do they go out?"

"They go out on different days, depending on if they have a load or not. Maybe they didn't get something that week. Sometimes they need to hold onto stuff for a week or two until the heat cools down on stolen merchandise, especially the medical stuff. Most of the time, they take orders and steal to order. Know what I mean?"

"No, we don't. Tells us more. How did you learn all this stuff? You sound like you're pretty familiar with the entire operation," said Mickey.

"Yeah, I am. That's why they didn't want me to leave, but I insisted I needed to get back to Carrie and Janet. Before he got into the illegal stuff, I helped with the scheduling and arranging of the shipments. Sometimes I even drove a truck when someone was out. When I came back a few months ago, he wouldn't let me do anything but drive. He changed how the trucks move, but I know how he does it all, know what I mean?"

"Go on with more details."

"Okay, they have stuff coming from the terminals, then if they can swap electronics from the terminals with medical stuff going out it costs them less money. A driver makes a round trip and only gets paid for one trip. If he goes out again, he gets paid twice. They get paid a lot of money for each trip, empty or full. The money keeps them happy and quiet. Sometimes a person gets drunk and maybe says too much or starts throwing his money around. Those drivers are terminated, and I don't mean fired, if you know what I mean!"

"We get a general idea. Is that how you got in their spotlight?"

"Yeah, I got drunk one night and said a bit too much. I convinced them I'd keep my mouth shut and work to pay off my debt, and they promised not to fire me, at least not in the usual way, if you know what I mean!"

"We get it," Mickey and James said together.

"And stop saying 'if you know what I mean!' If we don't know, we'll ask, for heaven's sake!" added James.

"Okay, okay. Don't get so testy!" said Bobby.

"We get the basic gist of the operations. We need to know when a shipment goes out, Bobby. Right now, we don't care about all this other crap," Mickey said. "Do you know all the drivers?"

"Usually, if they have something, it's on a Wednesday. It gives the men two days to load or unload shipments and get ready for another in the same week."

"We have an idea how things work. We'll be in contact. DO NOT, I mean it, DO NOT LEAVE THIS HOTEL. Let Carrie play in the pool, order room service or food delivery, whatever. DO NOT LEAVE, and don't make any phone calls. Do you understand? Your life may depend on it. I think it's time for us to get out of here. When you go back inside, would you tell Dee that we're ready to leave?"

"Sure. Thanks for helping us," Bobby said as he got up from the table to go back into the hotel.

As he walked away, James turned to Mickey. "I DO NOT like him, and I don't trust him."

"I agree. The more we're around him, the more I feel the same way. We need to be very careful what we say around him. And even after this is all over, it wouldn't surprise me if he and Janet aren't together for more than six months."

"If they're together that long," James added. "But we got into this to help Carrie, and we'll finish what we started. Now, what's this about Val leaving? You didn't tell me that. What's going on, bro?"

"Val told me she's leaving in a few days. She's going to some cooking school in Oregon."

"How long will she be gone?"

"Permanently. She's moving away."

"Is the marriage off?"

"Yep, everything's off. Val said she couldn't handle this stuff anymore. She's afraid that something like what happened before could happen again. I tried to convince her that everything will be fine, but she won't accept that. Of course, it didn't help that we got involved with this. She'd explode if she knew what's happening right now. I don't dare tell her."

"I don't blame you there. Nothing like this has ever happened before. All the years your father was buying and building the business, it went smoothly, didn't it?" James asked.

"I guess it did. Pop ran into some objections from city councils and other competitors like builders and investment companies, but nothing like what happened with his sister."

"Then it shouldn't happen again."

"I know that, and you know that, but Val doesn't understand. Maybe she does, but I think it might be a bit of PTSD like a person gets after some traumatic event."

"Now that, I can relate to, Mickey," he said.

"You can relate to what, James?" asked Darcy as she walked up to the table.

Mickey looked up at her, "We were just talking about Val and why she's leaving the area."

"That's sad. I feel so bad for you, Mickey," she said, massaging his shoulders.

"Oh, now that feels good, Dee, keep it up," said Mickey as he rolled his head around to loosen his neck.

Darcy lightly smacked his head and said, "Don't get used to it, little brother!"

"Dee, do you have enough things packed so we can begin moving from your house to Mom and Pop's house? I think Pop will be discharged sometime next week."

"We can move some things. I called a temp agency, and they'll send two people over tomorrow to help pack. James said he could get a rental truck and trailer in the morning."

"Sounds good for tomorrow. James, if you can come over to my place this afternoon, we can discuss more strategy on getting this thing moving."

"I'll be there as soon as we get back to Dee's house and I get the Humvee. See you then. I've got some ideas we can talk over."

Darcy spoke up, "Please, guys, don't get your selves killed. Let's get this thing over with and get on with a normal life."

Darcy went back inside, got the kids, and they all headed home.

When Mickey got home, he got on his computer and pulled up satellite photos of all the rest areas in Virginia's main interstate roads. James got there about half an hour later.

James walked in without knocking on Mickey's door. He saw the maps spread out on the kitchen table.

"James, as far as I can see, these are the most likely to be used as transfer points. In these two," he said, pointing to the first two on his left, "the trailers are parked at angles which make it easier for drivers to park and switch without other drivers taking notice. The ones on the right have better locations but aren't as easily concealed to other drivers. My thought is, if we hide off in the wooded areas when a driver comes out, we take them and pull them back into the cover of the brush and wait for the other truck. We can decide which one to take depending on our intel about the actual load. I'm sure that international shipping of stolen goods is a federal crime much more severe than just electronics that'll stay in this country. Theft of something coming into the country is a felony, but moving items out, is smuggling which is a more serious crime."

"I agree, Mickey, but how do we get this information?" James asked.

"Easy, peasy. We initialize those bugs we left in the warehouse barn at Satchel's place when we went in looking for Bobby," Mickey answered.

"I can do that. It should be simple unless you want to do it."

"Nope. That's not my job. You're the technical support on this team," said Mickey.

"So, now we're a team?"

"Yep. I'm making it official. We're now a team."

James looked at Mickey and rolled his eyes. "A team, my gosh. What'll you think of next? Do we get secret decoder rings? Hey, how about this, we get t-shirts with our team logo on them!" he said sarcastically.

"Don't be such a jerk, James," Mickey said with obvious agitation.

"Alright, don't get so upset. I was just joking," James said seriously.

"Getting this guy Satchel isn't a joke. I'm serious, and you're cracking jokes. If we aren't careful, we could be killed, or if we're lucky, end up in jail right beside Satchel."

James leaned over the table and placed his hands palm down on it. "I know what we're getting into, Bro. I've seen more crap than you can imagine. I also know when things are getting really tight. And right now, you're assuming that I don't know what can happen. Yes, I'm joking about a dire situation, but I also know there's a time to let off steam. And you need to learn that also. I can joke but be aware and serious about the situation at the same time. You got that, teammate?" James emphasized the last word, teammate, as he looked straight into Mickey's eyes.

Mickey turned and walked over to the coffee pot. "The coffee's cold, but I can put a cup for you in the microwave along with mine."

"No. I'm good right now," James said.

"Can you fire up those bugs?"

"They're already on and listening. All we need to do is get a receiver and start listening."

"How long will they last?"

James thought for a minute. "About another three days. I have a repeater at my place. We need to go back to the compound and place the repeater close enough to pick up the transmission from the bugs. Then that unit will transmit it to our receiver at my place. When do you want to go in and place the repeater?"

"Tonight?"

"Sounds good. I don't need backup. I can go in, place the unit, and you can be at my place to make sure it's working properly," said James.

"Can it handle all the bugs Alyssa's men placed? And will it record all of them?" asked Mickey.

"Yes, and a lot more."

"I guess that's about all we can do until we have more intel. I'm going to go see Pop and see if he knows when he'll be discharged."

"I've got nothing to do until I go set that repeater. Want some company to visit your dad?"

"Sure. You're always welcome to come with me. Let's go. I'm going to go by and check in with Dee to see how her packing's coming along."

"If I won't be in the way, I'll go with you there, too."

"Come on, let's go," he said as he started for the door.

As they pulled out of the apartment parking lot in Mickey's truck, James asked when he and Daniel would look for a new car to restore.

"Good question, James. I haven't had time to do anything lately. Maybe after all this crap's done, Pop and I can go looking."

"Do you know what you'll look for?"

"No, not really. Pop likes Rolls Royces, but we've already done one of those, and we just bought the Seraph. I'll let him decide. Besides, he'll be doing much of the work. I still have a job, remember?"

James laughed, "Yeah, things like jobs really get in the way, don't they? You and Darcy have taken over managing all the property. Your dad doesn't have anything to do. He'll get bored. Getting involved in a hobby like another car should help him. It gives him a reason to get out of bed."

"We have that huge garage sitting empty now. Pop did say he wanted to start all over. He doesn't give up. That's my Pop! Maybe as soon as things calm down a bit, we can look for a project car for him. That might be fun."

"I bet he'll like that," said James.

Mickey nodded. They listened to the radio tuned to a channel of 1960s music that Daniel used to listen to as they rode. When they checked in, they walked back to Daniel's room.

"Hey Pop, how're you doing today?" asked Mickey.

"Hey, son. I'm doing great. How about you?"

"I brought James with me," said Mickey.

James stepped into the room and extended his hand towards Daniel. "How're you doing, sir?"

"Hello, James. So glad to see you. How're the wedding plans coming along?"

"A bit slow, sir."

"Slow? Why's that, son?" Daniel said.

When James heard Daniel call him son again, he stood a bit taller. He always stood almost at attention when he talked to an older person, but Mickey knew that when his father called James "son," he was pleased and very proud of it. James had grown up without a father in his life. When he was just a little boy, his father and mother had divorced, and his father had left the state. James had not had any contact with his father since that time. All he knew was that his father had honored the court ruling of child support and alimony until he was eighteen, and his mother passed away of cancer three years ago. His father had sent payment for the funeral but didn't attend. So, when Daniel called James son, he felt that he was becoming part of the Christianson family, and he was looking forward to that.

"Well, sir. We don't want a big ceremony, but a lot's going on right now. We just haven't made plans. Dee is working on that as she has time from her job at the law firm."

Daniel looked at James for a few moments, then said, "James, my boy, when I get a bit better, we'll look at the finances and see if there's a way for her to leave that firm and come to work for our company full time!"

"That would be nice, sir, but I don't want her to support me. I want to support her!"

"We'll work that out later. Besides, we do need a good property manager, and she's a top-notch accountant and legal researcher."

They talked a few minutes more, and Daniel's physical therapy aide came in, and Mickey and James left and once again headed for Darcy's townhouse.

When they pulled into the driveway in the back of the home, Mickey saw a pickup truck backed up to the door. Darcy was stacking boxes into the truck bed.

"Hey, sis, where'd you get the truck?" Mickey asked.

"I borrowed it. It belongs to the husband of one of the women that work at the firm," she answered, dropping a box onto the tailgate.

"Great. James and I can put a few things in the back of my truck, and we can make a double load over to the house."

"Alright, you two, take the beds apart and put what you can into your truck while I fill this one with boxes. Joel and Cyndi are bringing small boxes they can carry from their rooms."

They all continued loading until both trucks were full. They unloaded the trucks into the foyer area just inside the front door. James asked Mickey to drop him off at his apartment to go back to Satchel's house, and he could place the repeater in a location to transmit. He needed to wait until it got dark to get in and back out without being detected.

CHAPTER 20

James Sets the Transmitter

JAMES WENT INTO HIS APARTMENT TO get the transmitter, his night gear, and a sidearm, just in case he got cornered. He also got his night-vision headgear to see in case he couldn't see enough in the moonlight. He called Alyssa to be online to set up the connections to the bugs when he placed the transmitter.

He drove to the road that entered the compound that Satchel's home and truck transfer station was located. He moved his Humvee carefully into the woods and underbrush. Since it was matte black, it was almost invisible when he backed it just beyond the edge of the road unless someone was looking for it. He got out, locked it, and set the transmitting alarm on it, so if anyone tried to enter the vehicle, it would notify him. He took his equipment and carefully started his way through the woods toward the house. After about ten minutes, he came to the edge of the forest and the perimeter of the compound. Laying quietly in the brush watching through his night-vision goggles, he waited to see if someone would come out. After a quarter of an hour, he crossed the compound to the barn building. A pile of old bricks and debris looked like it had not been disturbed for months. It was a perfect spot to hide the transmitter. He placed it and slowly stood up. As he turned around, someone walked around the building.

The man was startled and stood motionless for a few moments. James and the man stood looking at each other, then James jumped into action and gave the man a roundhouse punch knocking him off his feet. James moved over the man and punched him again when the man hit the ground, knocking him unconscious.

James was dragging the man over toward the trees when another man came out the door of the building. The man called out, "Hey, George, while you're getting yourself a beer, bring a six-pack for the guys in the shop." The man stopped and looked around, then saw James. He yelled, "Hey, you! What're you doing?"

James dropped the unconscious man, turned, and ran toward the man that had come out of the building. As he lunged toward him, he punched the man in the stomach knocking the wind out of him so he couldn't speak. As the man bent over, James gave him an uppercut in the jaw, bowling him over like a blow-up clown punching bag. The man crumpled to the ground. James grabbed his collar, pulled him beside the first man. He then grabbed each one by the shirt collar and dragged them both to the edge of the trees. After pulling them inside the tree line James zip-tied their hands and duct taped their mouths. He moved away to get enough distance to whisper on the phone to Alyssa.

"Alyssa, you have an audio on the transmissions?"

"Copy that, James. Loud and clear on the ones in the bunk room and the lounge kitchen. Nothing in the shop area. I think that's because no one is in there at the moment. The men placed them as close to a phone as possible, so we should hear this side of the phone conversation but not the other end. We're good to go on audio. Want me to start auto-recording?"

"Affirmative, Aly. I'm done here. I did run into a couple of men here. I subdued them, so let me know if someone suspects any kind of bug. I don't think they have any idea what my mission was here, so it shouldn't be an issue."

"Got it. I'll keep you informed," Alyssa said.

"Okay, clear channel," James said into the cell phone and disconnected as he walked over to the unconscious men. He looked them over to make sure they weren't injured. When he was satisfied, he walked away in the opposite direction of his vehicle. As he cleared the area and went into the woods, he heard alarms go off around the entire area. He began running toward his Humvee. As he ran, he heard gunshots and the crack of tree branches as the bullets zinged around him. Since the team was here, apparently Satchel had his men place sensors around the premises.

What he didn't know is where the sensors were placed. He also didn't know if it was a general alarm or if the sensors could pinpoint his location or the location of the Humvee.

He kept on running. It was dark, and running with night vision goggles isn't as easy as portrayed in the movies. They were bulking and only had a viewing area of thirty degrees, making it very confining. They were great for stationary surveillance. He tore the goggles off his head to increase his sight area. As he ran, he took his sidearm from its holster. He stumbled and dropped the goggles. He heard more gunshots as he ran. Trees he could see in the darkness, but tiny sprigs and saplings were invisible to him in the almost total blackness of the forest. He wished he hadn't dropped the goggles. He slowed down and hid behind a tree, hoping the men looking for him didn't have night vision goggles. He waited breathlessly and listened to the sounds in the distance.

He heard men talking. "You go that way. I'll take this direction," he heard one of them say. "And shoot to kill," he added.

James leaned against the tree. He peered around the tree and saw a glow of light sweeping the night looking for him. He watched as the lights got closer to where he was hiding.

"How stupid," James thought.

James had the advantage. The man didn't know where James was hiding, yet he made himself a target for everyone to see with that flashlight. These men were ignorant street thugs. If James wanted to, he could take that man out, and no one would know where the shot came from. They also wouldn't know if one of their men was shooting at him or he was shooting their man. James would quietly wait for the man to come to him. As time passed, he could see slight glimmers of moonlight glistening through the trees. It was just enough for him to get his bearings. James knew that one shot and he could kill the man, but he knew that even though Mickey would never know, he couldn't betray the trust of his best friend. He continued to wait for the man to get within personal combat range. He listened to the footsteps of the man as he trudged through the underbrush of the trees. James breathed slowly and quietly without moving.

James saw the edges of the light glow on each side of the tree where he was hiding. He knew the man was a few feet behind the tree. As soon as the man stepped beside the tree, James jumped out and put a well-placed fist on the man's lower jaw. The man's head tilted back with the force of James punch, and he fell backward to the ground with the light flying from his hand. As he did, the gun in the man's other hand went off, sending a bullet into James' upper arm. At least, it was his right arm, and James was left-handed. He grabbed the man with his left hand and slammed the man's face into the ground until he stopped moving. James felt his neck looking for a pulse. He found one and knew that the man was only unconscious. He picked up the flashlight and the man's gun and started running toward the Humvee.

As he ran, he heard several other sounds in the woods as a result of the gunshot. He heard several voices call out.

"Who shot? Report in. Who shot? Did you get him?" the voice asked.

James stopped for only moments. He called back over his shoulder. "We have a man down. All units disengaged the hunt."

A voice called out, "Do not disengage. That voice is not one of us. Continue the search. Shoot to kill. I repeat. Shoot to kill."

"Oh, crap," thought James. He had hoped they wouldn't realize that his voice wasn't one of them. He wanted to throw them off his trail so he could gain more distance while they stopped the search. He kept running. When he got back to the vehicle, he checked it over to make sure someone had not placed any explosives and found it untouched. It took him only a few seconds to look under the vehicle, but it was valuable time he lost trying to get away. He unlocked it and got in, and pulled onto the road in a hail of gunfire. They had found his Humvee, were waiting for his return and set up an ambush. His arm felt like it was on fire. He was bleeding, and if he didn't stop it, he would lose consciousness from blood loss. He had to get out of here. He heard bullets hitting the sides of the vehicle and was glad he had the armor plating installed. Still, he needed to get away from here so he could stop and tend to his wound. The side armor only stopped small arms fire. At least all the glass was bulletproof. He continued to pull onto the road and pushed the gas pedal to the floor. The Humvee lurched forward just as he felt bullets hitting the tires.

"Go ahead, you jackasses, the tires are run-flat and bulletproof also. Keep on shooting as I drive into the dark of night," he thought as he drove. He knew they would be coming after him, so he had to keep moving until he felt confident he had lost them. After a few miles, he pulled off a side road, then another side road. He called Logan and told him he needed to come in with the Humvee.

"You got serious problems to be calling me in the middle of the night, James," Logan said calmly.

"Yeah, I do, and could you get someone that could help with a medical situation?" asked James.

"What kind of medical situation? Cuts and abrasions or gunshot?"

"Gunshot. I gotta go and stop the bleeding right now, or I won't make it to your shop."

"How far out are you? Want me to meet you halfway?"

"As long as I can stop the bleeding, I should be able to make it. I'm about fifteen minutes out," James said weakly.

"We'll be ready for you," Logan said and disconnected.

James got out and went around to the back, where he kept a first aid kit. He took out some rags and twisted them into a rope to make a tourniquet. He put a tight compression bandage on the entrance to the wound and gave himself an injection of morphine for the pain. After giving himself first aid, he got back into the driver's seat and started once again toward Logan's garage.

As soon as he pulled up to one of the garage bay doors, the door began to rise, and he drove inside. When he was inside, he slumped over the steering wheel and passed out.

Logan closed the door, another man ran over to the vehicle and pulled James out. They both put him on a gurney and wheeled James to a room in the back of the garage.

Logan went to a filing cabinet and looked through the drawer until he found James' medical file. The man looked at James' records.

Logan looked at the man and said, "Doc, I took some compatible plasma out of the freezer. It isn't quite thawed out yet, but I'm a match, so if you need some blood now, I can let you have some of mine."

"Fine. Sit down, and I'll get a kit. We'll need some of your blood. He's a little low right now. We probably won't need the plasma, but let it thaw just in case," the man said.

As the man began hooking Logan up to a blood donation bag, he said. "Logan, after all these years, you still never fail to amaze me. You keep all those peoples' medical records and have a basic first aid room in the back of an auto garage. And it's complete, not just with medical records, but everything a person needs to do elementary operations. And how in the world do you get prescription drugs like antibiotics and the painkillers you stock in that cabinet?"

"Every time you ask me that question, I'll give you the same answer. That's privileged information. As you can see, we need some of those things right now. James needs either blood or plasma, and you need to take that bullet out of him. He'll need the painkillers during and after the operation and antibiotics when he leaves here."

Logan took a deep breath, "Doctor, as usual, you must keep quiet, and you'll be well paid. Once again, I assure you that what we do may be illegal, but we aren't criminals. We're the good guys using our skills to stop criminals. So, I respectfully ask you to please take care of my friend."

Logan sat back in the chair and let the life-giving blood drip out of his arm while the doctor administered painkillers into James' arm. When the doctor felt confident that James was no longer in pain, he began removing the bullet.

After a few minutes, Logan heard the drop of the bullet into a small pan. He knew that the doctor had completed the operation. He looked over at the doctor and asked, "Will he be okay?"

"Yes, he'll be fine. Luckily the bullet didn't hit anything that will affect the use of the arm. He'll be in a sling for a while, but other than that, I predict a full recovery. Someone did a great job of putting on that tourniquet. That probably saved his life. Did he say who helped him with it?"

"Yes, he stopped on the side of the road and did it himself, doc," Logan said.

"I've met a lot of your people, but this man is amazing to perform first aid on himself in such a competent manner. As I said, he saved his own life. Here, let me take the needle out of your arm. I think you've given enough this time. If that plasma is thawed now, I'll give him some of it. We usually don't need plasma in situations like this, but it doesn't hurt, and he may get his strength back a little sooner."

"Can you tell me what he did to get shot?"

"No. You know I can't do that!"

"Will I see it on the news?" the doctor asked.

"Possibly."

"Okay, he's stable now. I'll get some antibiotics and some painkillers out of the cabinet to take with him. When he wakes up, he'll be a bit unsteady but okay to go. You have some slings in your cabinet of goodies. Make sure he knows to keep that arm in a sling for several weeks. If you need me because of some complications, you know how to get in touch with me."

"Thanks, doc. I appreciate you coming and helping out. We'll settle up later."

The doctor gave a mock salute and walked out the side door of the garage.

Logan got up and walked back out to the garage area to look at James' Humvee. In his opinion, it was a mess. It was riddled with bullet holes. There were bullet holes along the side and back, even a couple in the windshield in the driver's area. He was glad that James had commissioned him to add the armor plate kit. Logan didn't know if James had planned on a significant shoot-out or if it was just luck that James had asked him to install it at the right time. Either way, it saved James' life.

One thing he did know was that James would need it repaired as soon as possible. He'd better get started on it while he was waiting for James to wake up. It was still the middle of the night, but it wasn't the first time someone on Alyssa's team needed quick repairs on themselves or a vehicle. He was the one that had made the custom changes to her drone surveillance truck. His used car lot and auto repairs were just a front for his custom work for black ops teams and operations like Alyssa's. He started by rolling over his toolbox so he could start the repairs.

In about two hours, he had the doors off, the windshield out and taken apart. He had already ordered a new windshield and back glass from his supplier. It was also open twenty-four hours a day because it supplied people like him. He ordered a new gas tank also. He noticed a tiny hole in it, and James was lucky that he didn't run out of gas before getting to the shop. The new one was armor-plated.

As Logan wheeled himself out from under the Humvee, James staggered out of the back room. His arm was dangling, and he looked haggard from his ordeal. Logan pulled a chair beside the Humvee and helped James get to it and sit down.

"Is it morning yet, Logan?" James asked.

Logan looked at his watch. "It'll be getting light in about half an hour."

"When can I leave?"

"Anytime you want to, but I wouldn't suggest it until you clear your head a bit more," Logan answered as he slid back under the Humvee.

"Did the doc get the bullet out of my arm?"

"Yes," Logan answered from under the vehicle.

"How long will it take to repair Betsy here," he asked, referring to the Humvee.

"She took a significant beating this time. You're lucky you had me install that armor plate kit, or you'd be dead as we speak, James. The bullet holes I can repair quickly enough. The gas tank got a hit, so I ordered a new armor-plated one for you and a new windshield. The present one did stop the bullets, but it's cracked now. It has to be replaced."

"Good. When can I have it back?" James said, shaking his head to clear it.

"The repairs will be done in a few hours. The new paint needs time to dry, but I can push it with some drying agents. I would say around two o'clock this afternoon."

"Okay, I'll be back around noon. Did the doctor leave instructions?"

"Yes, he did. Put that sling on your arm, take the painkillers and antibiotics on the table over there by the door, and don't come back any sooner than one thirty, or you'll be leaving here with wet paint on this thing! Got it?"

"Got it."

"Your phone is over there with the meds. Call someone to come pick you up, maybe that friend of yours, Mickey Ray."

"Thanks, Logan. I owe you big time," said James as he walked to the table for the meds and phone.

"Yes, you do. And take care of yourself. I want to get paid!"

James got his things and sat in a chair outside the garage building. After calling Mickey Ray to pick him up, he sat back and watched the sun come up over the rooftop of the office building at the front of the car lot.

In a few minutes, Mickey rolled up to the garage. "What in the world happened? Did this happen to you when you were activating the bugs?"

"Yes, and I don't want to talk about it."

"I don't care what you don't want to talk about. You'll tell me."

"No, I won't," James said.

James got up and walked to Mickey's truck, and got in.

Mickey got in the truck, sat there for a few minutes, then turned to James. "You'll tell me or get out of my truck and find your own way home. I care about you, and you'll tell me right now, or I swear to God I'll not move from here."

"Promise not to tell Darcy if I tell you?" James said.

"I promise. The truth is, I won't have to tell her. She'll see it, so tell me, James."

"I'll tell you. Now take me home so that I can get some rest."

James told Mickey the entire episode. When James finished, Mickey asked him why he didn't call him when he got to the garage.

"I would have, but I passed out as I drove into the garage. I barely remember the door opening to let me in. The next thing I remember was waking up in the treatment room, and walking out to the garage area, and talking to Logan."

"I get that. In the future, if we are going to be a team, we need to help each other, which means keeping in contact, etc. We call each other when we need help. I understand that when things started going down, you couldn't call me, but when you called Logan, I should have been the next phone call. If you had passed out on the road, I would have known where to begin looking for your dead body. Logan didn't. Now, I agreed not to tell Dee, but that arm will be one big magic trick to keep secret. When she finds out, she's going to explode, and you know it."

James leaned back in the seat and gently rubbed his arm. "I know. You're right. We need to keep it secret until we finish the mission. Life can be short, bro, I know. I've stood at death's door too many times. Seize every moment you can, while you can," his voice trailed off as he spoke.

Mickey drove on, letting James get some much-needed rest. When Mickey got to James' apartment, he helped him out of the truck and into the apartment. Just as James got home and into his bed, his cell phone rang. It was Alyssa.

"James, I got some audio you may want to hear. They found the men you ran into. They're now on full alert. One of the bugs is near an intercom system. They're having fits. They know that someone tried to get into the building. Since we went in before, they think someone, being us, is getting ready for another attack. Right now, they're arming themselves to the teeth. If we are planning on going in again, they'll be loaded for bear."

"Well, we aren't going in again, so they can load for elephants. We don't care. All we need's info. We can do that with the listening devices we hid. I'd like to know when and where Satchel's going. He may not announce that to his crew in the garage," James said.

"Too bad we didn't get some devices in the house or on his phone," she said. "As well as the house was insulated, I believe that it was faraday protected against transmissions. That's why we couldn't get any transmissions from inside the house."

"Let me give you an update on what happened after I set the devices and we got them online last night," James said.

James told her the entire story right up to Mickey bringing him back to his apartment.

"Are you totally out of commission now?" Alyssa asked.

"For heavy work, I am, but we'll work with what we have. Mickey will help, and I think we can do it adequately. If I need help, I may have to call you."

"I'll keep the recordings going on. I was headed for bed when I heard this and thought I'd give you a call. See you soon, James."

"I was already in bed, but thanks for getting me up for the update. Later Aly," he said, then disconnected.

CHAPTER 21

Friday Morning...Satchel

James got up, got dressed, and called Alyssa. "Hey, did you get anything new that I need to hear about?" he asked when Alyssa answered.

"Nope, not a thing. I got up a while ago and did some speed listening, and nothing noteworthy happened last night," she answered.

Speed listening was when you could speed the recording to a level where the people sounded like chipmunks. It was easier to do on old vinyl records and recording tapes, but it took special equipment and computer programs on newer digital recordings. He knew Alyssa had programs and equipment to do it. It was like fast-forwarding on visual recordings, only on audio versions. After disconnecting with Alyssa, he called Mickey Ray.

"Hey, Mickey Ray, anything new on your end?" he asked.

"Not really. We're still moving. We're packing the trucks again. We should have about everything here moved, and then we have some help at the storage unit moving some of Mom and Dad's things back into the house. We should be done by the end of the day. Are we getting anything we can use from the transmitter?" asked Mickey.

"Yes, we're getting clear reception, but nothing's happening that affects us. They're all on high alert. There'll be no more surprise visits to the compound."

"Not a problem. Until then, I guess we can keep on moving the stuff into the new house. Are you coming over to help?"

"Sure. I'll be there as soon as I can. Have you heard from Valerie since she broke it off?"

"I've called her a couple of times, but she really won't talk to me. She answers her phone and goes through some pleasantries, but then finds a reason to hang up," said Mickey.

"Sorry to hear that, Mickey," said James.

"It's okay. I'll be fine. You know that when Val finds out what happened to you last night, she'll freak out, don't you?"

"I know, but we won't tell her, will we, Mickey Ray?" said James.

"Not on your life. That's one secret we'll never tell. When Dee finds out, we need to insist she not tell Val," said Mickey.

"See you in a while," he said and disconnected.

James got in his Humvee and headed for Darcy's house. When he got there, he took his arm out of the sling and tried to make excuses why he couldn't help with the move.

Finally, Darcy grabbed James' arm, and he winced.

"James, come clean with me. What is wrong with your arm. I've noticed you favoring it since you got here. What happened? And you better tell me the truth," she said.

"Let's go in the house and sit down, and I'll tell you," he said walking toward the door.

He went inside, sat down in a kitchen chair, and rubbed his arm. Mickey heard Darcy's question and knew that it was about to hit the fan, so he followed them into the kitchen and sat beside James in emotional support.

James and Mickey sat silently in their chairs.

Darcy spoke up, "Talk."

James looked down at his lap, saying nothing.

"I said, TALK, and I mean right now, James."

Mickey spoke first, "Listen, Dee. You see James was...."

"You shut your mouth, Mickey Ray Christianson. I want it straight from the horse's mouth, and that's James. Tell me what happened to you?" she said, turning her attention back to James.

"It was an accident, Dee. A freak accident," James continued, telling the entire story, being sure to explain how the gun fell out of the man's hand and as he fell, the gun went off, wounding him in the arm.

"In that case, I see it was an accident. It could have killed you, not just wounded you. It would never have happened if Mickey had not gotten us involved with this whole holy mess. I understand more each day why Valerie feels the need to leave to get away. You're both becoming a liability to everyone who loves you. James, you fought for this country, and you see what happened to you. I love you with all my heart. I don't want to lose you. You did your part for this country and for us a few months ago. Step away. Retire. You don't need to help everyone in the world.

"And you, Mickey. I understand that what happened last year you needed to do to protect us. As my brother, I love you also with all my heart but keep yourself and us out of other people's business. We can't go around trying to protect and change the world. Mom and Dad worked very hard to give us an easier life than they had. Let's enjoy what they worked for. I don't want you or my future husband killed. I don't want to be a widow."

"Do you both understand me?" she said.

Mickey and James just sat there like two chastened children saying nothing.

"Do you understand me?" she repeated.

James nodded. Mickey just sat looking blankly at her.

Darcy furrowed her brow. "Mickey, DO YOU UNDERSTAND ME?" she said slowly.

"Yes," he answered.

"James, you will put that arm back in its sling and go over there and sit in the corner while Mickey and I load these trucks," she said, pointing to a chair in the corner of the room.

Mickey and Darcy continued moving furniture onto the trucks, and they drove to the new house. While they were unloading the furniture into the house and setting it up, James' phone rang. Alyssa's ID showed up on the cell phone screen.

"Jimmy, sorry to bother you, but we had some intel we needed to act on. Satchel was leaving the premises, and I had two men near the location, so they went out, intercepted the vehicle, and subdued him. Earl trussed him up like a turkey, and they're holding him for you. They took his car with them. I told you that I'd take no profit from this one, but these guys are charging me by the hour. They'll keep him on ice as long as you want, but the clock is ticking, and they're expensive. What do you want me to do?" she asked.

"Hold him, text me the address. We'll leave now to pick him up," James said into the phone. He then called Mickey. "Hey, Aly got a couple of her guys to pick up Satchel. They're holding him, so we gotta pick him up now. Tell Dee, we're sorry, but we have to leave."

"You bet," Mickey said as he turned to find Darcy.

As they were pulling out, James asked, "What did Dee say about us leaving?"

"She said, GO! She's totally behind us. She wants us to get this over with," Mickey said. "What're we going to do when we get him?"

"I don't know. He's muzzled and blindfolded. I guess we can take him to one of your empty apartments. We don't want to take his blindfold off. Everyone in town knows me, and most of them know you."

"Yeah, sounds like a plan," said Mickey.

James drove on and finally spoke up again. "Have you thought any more about what kind of car you're going to get when your dad gets well enough to help you work on it?"

"What brought that up?" asked Mickey.

"Nothing. I'm just wondering. That's all."

"You're really concerned about what car I'm going to get, aren't you? We got the Rolls. Now you are nagging me to get a car to work on?"

"I'm just thinking about your Pop, that's all. He'll need something to keep his mind busy," said James.

"Here we're going to pick up a dangerous criminal that some black ops guys that we don't know have kidnapped, and you're thinking about what kind of car I'm going to buy for my father to play with? You're one strange dude, man," said Mickey shaking his head.

"Yep, that's me, alright. Strange!" James said and laughed.

They pulled into a dusty gravel lane and drove almost a mile that ended in the front of an old-looking log cabin. James honked the horn but stayed in the vehicle until someone came out holding an automatic

The Landlord and the Wheelchair Child

rifle. When he saw James, he lowered his weapon and motioned for them to exit the vehicle.

"Hello, James. We've got your guy inside. Hey, what happened to your arm?"

"Long story, maybe I'll tell you sometime," James said.

"That old guy in there is a feisty old man. We put tape over his mouth to shut him up! After being around him, I absolutely do not like the guy. Please take him off our hands."

James laughed and said, "Lead the way to him. We'll do exactly that."

Sitting in the corner of the cabin was a thin man looking in his mid-sixties. His hands were bound behind him, and he had duct tape over his eyes and mouth. The area over his eyes bulged out under the tape.

"Why are his eyes bulging like that?" asked Mickey.

"That keeps the adhesive on the duct tape away from his eyes, so he doesn't get blinded," a man standing beside him said as he punched the man on the arm.

The old man made a grunting sound under the tape.

"I don't think he likes us," said the man beside him. "To be honest, I don't care because I don't like him either. Now, if you would do the honors of getting him out of here, we at least can go home. I have a cookout to get to with my kids."

"Sure, be glad to oblige," said Mickey. "Would you mind loading him into our ride?"

"You bet. Get up," he said as he kicked the old man's chair. The man just sat there.

James reached down and ripped off the tape in one smooth, tearing motion. "Did you hear the man? He said, get up! Now move!"

The old man spat in front of himself, hoping to hit someone with spittle, but James sidestepped it as it whizzed by.

"You do that again, and you'll be spitting blood and teeth," James said.

"Who are you, and where are you taking me? What do you want?" he asked.

James said, "Ask me no questions. I tell you no lies. Now, shut up before I put the tape back on. Get up and let the men here put you in our vehicle."

Mickey noticed James didn't say car or truck or Humvee. He said only vehicle.

The man stood up. The men moved to each side of him, grabbed his arms, and then walked him to the Humvee. When they got there, they put him in the back seat and motioned for Mickey to get in beside him. James got in front.

James turned to one of the men and said, "We'll settle up with you later, okay?" to which the man silently nodded as James did a U-turn in the gravel road and headed out the way they came. They rode in silence as they drove to the apartment complex where James lived. Mickey wrote on a slip of paper asking if James could keep him at his place until they had a better place. James nodded affirmatively. They were cautious not to call names or addresses to keep Satchel Binghamton from identifying either of them. They drove to James' apartment.

Satchel had said nothing as directed during this time, but they knew he was trying to make mental notes to identify them later.

"Hey, Satchel, do you need to use the bathroom?" asked James.

He nodded yes.

"Let me go in and make sure there is nothing inside that you can hurt yourself or try to hurt one of us."

James went in and brought out a few things in a small bag. He led Satchel to the bathroom when Mickey spoke.

"Hey, why don't one of us go in with him and help him, so we don't have to unbind him?" said Mickey.

"I don't care, but it'll be you. I'm not taking another man into the bathroom and help him with his business."

"Flip you for it?"

"No, I'm not going in. You do it!" said James.

"All right. Come on, Satch," said Mickey, abbreviating his name.

"It's Mr. Binghamton to you," he said.

"Yeah, right," Mickey said as he cut the ties holding his hands behind his back. Mickey then pushed him into the bathroom. "Do it yourself. I'm going to stand here at the open door. If you try to take the tape off your eyes, I will punch you out. Got it? I'll aim you at the toilet before you let go. You better hit it, or I'll make you clean it blindfolded."

Satchel did as he was told, and Mickey told him to stand still in front of the toilet while he put a new zip tie on the man's hands behind his back again.

"I'm thirsty too."

"Too bad. You'll get a drink later. We have a lot to talk about right now," Mickey fired back at him.

They sat Satchel in a chair in the middle of the room. James and Mickey sat on the couch in front of him.

"Now, Satch, we want to know when you have the next pickup?" asked Mickey.

"How do you know my name?"

"We know a lot about you. Now answer my question," repeated Mickey.

"You know where you can go, don't you," he said.

James got up, but Mickey stopped him and pulled him back down into the seat.

"We have a lot of time here, and we have food and water and a bathroom. You can have these too unless you decide not to give us what we want. Now I suggest you talk!" Mickey said.

"I don't have anything to say. Who are you two?"

"I am the Mongoose," said James.

"What's a Mongoose?"

"It is a small animal that loves to kill poisonous snakes. You, Satchel Binghamton, are a snake," James said.

"I don't know what you're talking about."

"We don't want to go back and forth like this. We know you deal in stolen goods, especially medical equipment. Legitimate hospitals need that equipment. You steal it and smuggle them out of the country to third-world countries."

"So, what. It's called capitalism. Besides, I help people. If it weren't for me, people in those countries would not get the medical help they need, and some would die."

"You are a thief and a smuggler."

"If those countries weren't so corrupt, they'd let the equipment in, and it could be sold legally."

"But you don't buy it legally. You steal it. Then you sell it to the highest bidder regardless of need."

"Yeah, and it's called capitalism."

"In this situation, it is called theft and smuggling. Now, tell us when you expect the next shipment."

"Over my dead body."

"That can be arranged. Go get the pliers in the toolbox in the back room," James said, but shaking his head NO to Mickey.

"Don't mind if I do. I haven't crushed any fingers in several months," Mickey said, understanding James was using this as intimidation.

James pulled one of the kitchen chairs over and set Satchel in it. James tied his arms to the wooden chair. Mickey just stood and watched James secure the blindfolded man. James walked back to the bedroom and came back with a rope and a pair of pliers. He wrapped the rope around Satchel's torso, then a few wraps around Satchel's wrist to secure and tighten it to the arms of the chair. Mickey stood mouth open. Was James going to crush some fingers?

The man squirmed and protested. "Hey, you can't do this to me. I'll have you killed, I swear."

James lightly tapped the pliers on one of the man's fingers. "You have ten fingers. It won't disable you too much if I crush just a couple."

James shook his head reassuringly at Mickey to let him know he wouldn't really do it.

"I mean it, I'll have you killed, both of you!" he said.

"Who'll you have killed. Do you know who we are?"

"We'll find out. I have connections. I know people. I'm serious," he was beginning to sound a bit desperate.

"If you don't tell us, we might have to kill you. A mongoose kills snakes!"

"What's a mongoose? I don't know what you're talking about."

"If we let you live, you can look it up when we let you go. If we let you go. Now when is the next shipment transfer?"

"Do you know what the trapezius muscle is, Satchel?" James asked.

"No. Why should I?"

"It's the muscle that extends from your neck down your back. If I squeeze it, it really, really hurts. If it gets damaged too much, you will lose the use of your arm. Can you imagine if I damage both of them?"

James grabbed the muscle that extends from the backside of Satchel's shoulder and extends up to his neck. He pinched it, and Satchel screamed. Then he did the other side. Again, Satchel screamed. Then James motioned for Mickey to follow him into the backroom out of earshot of Satchel.

"Mickey, you saw where I pinched him, right?"

"Yes, and I know how it hurts when someone does that," Mickey said.

"Correct. It hurts like the devil, but it won't injure him. I'll do it a few more times. It's a very childish form of torture. Kids do it all the time. When a kid starts crying, they quit. We'll not quit, and he won't know how childish it really is. In about half an hour, it'll be fine, maybe just a little bruised and sore, but no permanent damage. I just wanted to let you know that I am not actually torturing him. He doesn't know that it'll be fine, but it'll scare the crap out of him. I may make a few other threats, but I promise, not real torture. I'm not into that. Got it?"

"Yes. I get it. I don't want to get into torture for any reason, as long as you promise me it'll not cause real injury!"

"Promise. Now, let's get back in there," James said and walked out of the room back toward the living room.

"Are you ready to talk now, Satch?" said James.

"No!"

"Okay. I hate to do this, but you're forcing me to get a bit more personal. James took the pliers and slid them up the inside of the man's thigh and into his crotch. As soon as James got into that area, Satchel jumped in the chair, almost causing it to fall over.

"Okay, now we're getting a better understanding of what can happen." He grabbed Satchel's trapezius muscle again and squeezed harder. He leaned his head over against his shoulder and brought it upwards in a reflex action to the hard pinch. He let out another yell. James moved to the other shoulder and pinched again with just two fingers. Tears began running down Satchel's face.

"If I do this a few more times, it will separate the nerve endings in your arm and shoulder, you'll continue to be in pain, and it'll paralyze your arms. You don't want that, do you?" James looked at Mickey and shook his head NO. Mickey understood what James meant. No real injury was done, and it was a painful bluff.

"No. No more. It'll be the day after tomorrow, at the rest area on Interstate 95 near Richmond. Now, will you let me go?"

"Not yet. Not until we intercept that shipment," Mickey said.

"Hey, if you let me go, I'll pay you. How much do you want? I can give you a hundred thousand dollars," Satchel said.

"Ha, surely you jest!" James said, circling him.

"Two hundred!"

"Nope."

"How much?"

"All of it. We want it all, Mr. Binghamton," James said.

"All? You've got to be reasonable. I have a business to run. I need capital to operate. I can't let you have everything."

"Too bad. I guess we intercept that shipment and take what we want."

"I already have buyers lined up for it. They'll kill me if I don't deliver."

"We don't care. Heck, we may decide to kill you."

"Hey, listen, I don't know who you are, so I can't hurt you. Let me go, and I'll give you a million dollars cash."

"Now that sounds more reasonable."

"Yeah, let me go. I'll get it and deliver it where ever you say. I'll deliver it personally. You have my word on that."

"Sorry, your word's no good here," Mickey said.

James laughed, "You think we're that stupid, Satch. If we let you go, you'd send some goon to kill us. Nope. Here's what we're going to do. We'll let you call one of your goons to deliver the money and then go away from the drop point. When he's safely away, then we'll retrieve it, and then we'll let you go. How's that sound?"

"Sound's okay. We can work that out. You promise to let me go?" he said with a small sigh of relief.

"Sure, we promise. Here's what we'll do. First, we put you on the phone with one of your guys. You'll tell them where to leave the money. Then they'll leave. Got it?"

"Yeah, I got it. Then what?"

"We get your truck, put you inside, then leave, and one of your guys comes to get the truck, and you and all your contraband will be inside.

We'll not touch the stuff inside. You can have it all. We'll leave quietly, and you'll never hear from us again. Deal?"

"Yeah. Your word, you'll let me go and not take the cargo in the truck?"

"In all honesty, you aren't really in a position to be trying to negotiate, but we'll do it," said James, and he began cutting the ropes loose from his hands and arms.

James said to Mickey, "Keep a watch on him. If he tries to get up, shoot him in the foot. That'll stop him. I'm going in the backroom and make arrangements for a pickup. Then, we'll let him make a call."

James left the room to call Alyssa and use one of her team members to make the pickup.

When James left, Mickey started talking to Satchel. "How did you get into this line of work anyway."

"What's it to you?"

"Nothing, I was just wondering. A criminal such as yourself has to be pretty smart to be successful, even in illegal operations. If you had been totally above board, you most likely would have done pretty well."

Satchel thought, for a minute. "Are you aware of all the government regulations for everything? No matter what business you're in, they have so many rules and regulations that it's nearly impossible to be profitable. What kind of business are you in besides kidnapping?"

"Hey, this conversation isn't about me. Let's keep talking about you until he gets back. I'm sure you could have done well legally. That's all I'm saying."

"Maybe yes, maybe no. Even if I did, taxes alone would eat me alive."

"Now, on that, we both agree," said Mickey.

"You sound like a reasonable person. How about I give you three-quarters of the million dollars, and you let me go?"

"No. I'll not turn for ten times that much. Now it's time for our little talk to end. Sit there and be quiet."

They sat in silence until James returned.

After almost twenty minutes, James returned. "Now, this is what you're going to say to whomever you choose to call. You'll tell them to get the one million dollars and put it into a plain box, then go to the marina in Bridgeton. There'll be a man wearing a red watch cap. Your man will open the box, show my man the parcel, and let him inspect it for tracking devices and maybe even some explosives. Then he'll leave exactly as he came. Now, I'll tell you, if someone is tailing or around that looks even a little bit suspicious, then my man will shoot him, as well as your courier. My man is a trained sniper, so don't think that your guy will get away. My partner will leave here and meet my courier to retrieve the box of money. When he gets back here, we'll make arrangements to meet your truck. When we meet your truck, we'll put you and the driver inside. As I said before, you'll never hear from us again."

"Your word, you'll not hurt my men or me?"

"I said before, you aren't in any position to insist on anything, but yes, you have our word. Now, we have a cell phone here. Give us the number, we'll dial it, and we'll let you make the arrangements. For your information, it's a burner phone, so trying to trace or get our names will be fruitless."

When Satchel gave him the number, James dialed it and handed him the phone. "When you talk, don't try any funny stuff or code words. We know all those tricks. Straight forward instructions, or you die right here. Got it?"

"Can you at least take the tape off my eyes? I'm about to go crazy in the darkness here."

"No!" James and Mickey spoke in unison.

"When does my man meet yours?" he asked.

"An hour and a half from now," James said, looking at his watch.

"Hello?" came a voice from the phone.

"Jack, don't talk. Listen. Go to the safe and get out a million in cash and put it in a plain box. Take it to the Bridgeton Marina. There'll be a man in a small fishing boat wearing a red watch cap. Let him check out the box thoroughly. Nothing funny, just give him the money. Then leave. Don't try to follow or do anything. Just leave and keep the phone with you for further instructions. You must get to the Marina in less than ninety minutes. GO. NOW," he said, then handed the phone back to James. "Good enough?" he asked James.

"Fine. Now we wait for a call telling us that the money has been picked up." James once again wrapped the rope around Satchel's arms, securing him to the chair.

Mickey silently motioned for James to follow him to the back room.

"James, I assume that one of Aly's men is doing the pickup, right?"

"Aly is doing it herself. She trusts her men, but only so far, and a million dollars in cash is a big temptation even for them. But I trust her, so it'll be okay. She'll bring the money here."

"As beautiful as she is, how's she going to pass as a man?"

"She knows how to dress down to fit the part. A bit of dirt, ragged clothes, and hair pushed up under that cap, and no one will take a second look at her, trust me on that, little bro," James said with a wink and a nod.

"If you say so. Now, are we really going to let him go?"

"Yes, I gave him my word. If you don't have your word, you have nothing, my friend. But I have a few extras up my sleeve. Just wait. It'll all work out."

"Why are we taking more money?"

"We don't know how much it will really take to get Carrie's operations, and we also promised to take care of her medical needs. I want to be sure we have enough."

"What do we do with any leftover money?"

"We do have a big bill to pay for Aly's services. As I said, her time is comped, but not her expenses, and those guys are cold-blooded mercenaries. They'll be paid, and very generously, I might add."

"How much is generous?"

"About a hundred grand, give or take...." James said as he walked out of the room. "And that's the friend and family discount."

"Holy crap, I should have been a mercenary," said Mickey under his breath, as he followed James back out of the room.

Back in the living room with Satchel, James asked if he wanted something to drink.

"Yes," was the one-word answer.

"I'll fix you a hot dog if you want something to eat. That you can eat with one hand and tape over your eyes," said James.

"I hate hot dogs."

"Okay, that's your call. I don't care," James said.

Mickey went to the refrigerator and took out a bottle of water while James untied one arm. Then Mickey opened and handed him the bottle.

"How do I know you haven't poisoned it or something?"

"You don't. Drink it or not. We don't care, either way."

Satchel drank every drop. Then dropped the bottle on the floor.

"You're probably going to kill me anyway, so why not take this tape off my eyes and let me confront my killers."

"We gave you our word. The truth is, we don't trust you, so the tape stays on, now shut up!"

"When I get out of here, I'll have both of you killed. That's my word. I promise."

"Now that we believe, so the tape stays on. I said, shut up," said Mickey.

They sat there in silence, each reading a magazine until James' phone rang. He answered, "Yes. Got it. Here." He disconnected.

James took a notepad and scribbled on it, "Aly got the money. Bringing it here."

Mickey nodded his head in understanding.

Satchel spoke up, "Was that your contact?"

"Yes."

"Did he get the money?"

"Yes. Are you letting me go now?"

"Not yet. Later, when we get the truck," Mickey answered.

In a few minutes, there was a knock on the door. James let Aly inside. She looked over at Satchel and said in a low and deep voice, "I had his man check it and did some random checks for counterfeit cash. What we checked was okay. So, I can reasonably assume it's all okay. No trackers, so it should be untraceable."

James reached into the box, took out a stack of bills, and handed it to her, "Okay?"

She nodded, "Yes," then turned and walked out the door again.

James, after dialing the contact again, gave Satchel the phone. "Tell him, got the money, continue business as usual until you hear from me. Then hang up, that's all."

Satchel did this without comment.

James spoke, "We need to leave now. We're going to move you to another location until we get the rest of this transaction complete."

Out of earshot, James said to Mickey, "We're taking him to your father's garage. We can secure him there while we make other arrangements. But we need to make a quick stop on the way."

James drove to an electronics store and went inside while Mickey sat in the back with Satchel. He pointed to the bag when he got back out, indicating that Mickey could look at its contents. Mickey looked inside and saw a home security camera and base station. Mickey looked questioningly at James.

James just said, "I'll explain later."

They drove wordlessly to Mickey's father's enormous garage. Mickey sat and waited until James got out and opened the large sliding door. James silently pointed to the back room of the garage, where Daniel had a small parts room and office to do auto research and rebuild auto parts. They sat him in a metal chair, put some chains on his wrists and feet, then secured him with large padlocks. They locked the door when they walked out.

When they got out, Mickey asked why they had brought him here.

"We can secure him easier here than we can at my place. Also, it's easier to look after him with food and water.

"We need to get Bobby down here so we can intercept those trucks. While we're doing this, we can help Dee straighten up the house. We have the rest of the day and all day tomorrow to kill. I don't want to sit around looking at him. Do you?" James said.

"Not even a little bit. Let's go in and see what Dee's doing now. Her car was around the front, so we know she's here."

They walked into the house and called out to Darcy.

"I'm upstairs," she called back.

They walked upstairs. She was in the master bedroom putting clothes away in the closet and the dresser.

"Did you get whatever it is you left to get?"

"Yes, and he's out in the garage," said Mickey. James stood behind him, saying nothing.

She stopped putting the clothes away and turned around to face them. "What do you mean, he's out in the garage? Who's out in the garage?"

"Satchel Binghamton's out in the garage tied up and secured in Pop's garage workshop."

"Mickey Ray, tell me you're joking. You brought a murdering thieving criminal to our home?" she said astonishingly.

"He's secured. He won't cause any trouble. I promise, Dee!"

"Sure, until he gets loose and comes back to murder us all! Are the two of you insane? What were you thinking! You have both lost your minds. Get him out of here, and I mean now!"

"Calm down. He's blindfolded and fully secure. He doesn't know who we are or where he is. Come on, and we'll show you."

"No. I don't want to see him. I want him gone. Get him away from here and away from my children. It's like keeping a wild animal here. I want him gone. Do you hear me? DO…YOU…HEAR…ME? James, that goes for you also. Both of you. Leave and take that person with you!"

"Now listen to me, Dee…We're…"

"No! No! No! You listen to me! Get him out of here!" she screamed. "I can't believe you brought someone like that into our home. First James gets shot, then you bring the boss of the man that shot him into my house?"

"Calm down. I told you, Satchel doesn't know where he is."

"You're on a first-name basis with him now! No wonder Valerie is leaving. I don't blame her. The two of you have lost your minds! Get him out of here!"

"He doesn't know who we are. He's tied up and blindfolded."

"My gosh, I don't know how we even got involved in this mess. If he doesn't have you shot, I might do it myself," she said, losing some of her anger.

"He'll only be here for a day or two. The day after tomorrow, he'll be gone. Promise."

She sat down on the bed. "I don't like it. I don't like it one bit. You're going to get us all killed. Both of you. Especially you, James. I'd expect something like this out of Mickey Ray but not you."

"I'm sorry, Dee. I didn't think you'd be so upset. I truly believe we're safe. You know I'd do nothing to put any of you in danger," James said apologetically.

"You didn't think I'd be upset! The problem is, neither of you is thinking at all. What have the two of you been smoking? You've lost your minds. I'm getting tired of this. It better be over soon or I'm leaving with Valerie. James, you say that you wouldn't put any of us in danger! That is exactly what you've done. We're smack in the middle of a murderer's gun sight, and you're both acting like it's a Sunday stroll in the park. When this whole thing's over, we're sitting down and having a long talk, assuming we live through it. You boys need some boundaries. Now get out of here before I get really mad. GO. LEAVE MY SIGHT!" she almost screamed.

James got up to leave, but Mickey had to have the last word.

"We need a safe and secure place to keep him until we can turn him over to the police. That'll be the day after tomorrow," sighed Mickey Ray.

"I guess it wouldn't do any good to move him now since he's already here. If he knows, it's too late. If he doesn't, it's up to both of you to keep him in the dark about where he is. Just make sure he can't get loose," she said, sitting down on the closest chair, looking exhausted.

"We will. We promise. It'll be fine. Where are Joel and Cyndi?" asked Mickey trying to change the subject.

"They're in their rooms putting their stuff away also. Why don't you go say hi to them and leave me alone right now?"

As they walked out, James said to Mickey, "I've never seen her so mad. What're we going to do?"

"Just keep doing what we planned. We're in too deep now to quit. We have to finish this thing."

When they got back to the garage, Mickey went in first in case Satchel had managed to get the tape off his eyes. James came in behind him when Mickey saw that Satchel was still sitting in the chair with the chains and blindfold on.

"Hey, what kept you so long, and when are you going to let me go? You promised," Satchel called out.

"We promised to let you go unharmed, but we didn't promise when we'd let you go," said Mickey. "We have a few more things to take care of before we cut you loose."

"What stuff?" he asked.

"Never mind. Just sit still. We're going to leave, and we'll be back in a couple of hours. We have you on camera, and we'll know if you try any funny stuff, so don't try anything. If you do, we might still let you go, but you may be missing a couple of fingers, or maybe we could break a foot so you can't walk away. It all depends on how well you behave. We can monitor you wherever we go, and we have someone just outside also monitoring you so that they can be here at a moment's notice." He reached over to a radio sitting on a shelf in front of the chair where Satchel was seated.

James took the bag he had gotten from the store, and he took out a small base station and set it on the counter. He also took out a small camera about the size of a child's wooden toy block. He quietly pulled up another chair, stood on it, and stuck it on the wall with the sticky backing tape on the camera base. He then stepped outside of the room and set the base unit on a shelf near the exit door. He put something in front of the base unit to make it less evident for a casual person to see. He then placed another small camera facing the garage entrance door and another one facing the workshop door. In all, James placed five cameras around the room, with two in the room where Satchel was secured. Mickey watched in silence. Finally, when James was done, he took out his phone and downloaded an app, and set up the system so they could call up any one of the cameras and see what was happening in the viewing area of each camera.

They were standing in the front area at the other end of the garage from where Satchel was secured. James said, "We now have video and sound in all the cameras. They're motion-activated and have two-way sound communications. We'll download the app on Dee's phone so that she can keep an eye open also. If something happens, she can see it, and we're the primary ones to be notified. She'll be the secondary, and the system will inform both of us of any activity. If we see something happening, we can speak to him and let him know that we can see what he's doing. That might be a deterrent for him to misbehave. Now we need to move things out of his reach that he can use to free himself or use as a weapon."

They went back into the room and moved things around and out of his way. He questioned what they were doing, and they answered him with almost honest answers. Of course, they didn't tell what they were moving, but they were moving items out of his reach. They told him of one of the cameras but neglected to tell him of a second backup camera.

"So now you know we have eyes and ears on you. Behave, and all this will be over soon enough. We'll leave you a couple of bottles

The Landlord and the Wheelchair Child

of water. Just remember what goes in must come out, and we won't be here to hold your hand or anything else you might need to hold when it needs to come out. Sorry about that. We'll give you a couple of towels to mop up any spilled liquid. Just remember that Janet Griffin was in the same situation. So, what goes around, comes around," James explained.

"Is that what this is all about, the little jerk, Bobby Griffin? I'll kill him too. You'll see. He's a dead man. I may not know who you are, but I know where he is, and before he dies, he'll tell me who you are, then I'll kill you too. Both of you. Do you hear me? Do you?"

"If anything happens to him, you'll be a dead man. That subject is closed," said James. James threw two grease-covered rags in his direction and walked out of the room back into the main garage area.

Mickey closed the door and locked it. When he turned around, James was looking straight at him. Mickey knew exactly what James was thinking.

"Do you think Bobby ratted us out?"

"I doubt it, but it crossed my mind. I don't think Bobby's done anything yet, though I can't say what he may do in the future if he gets in trouble again. I shouldn't have said that. That was my error. I should have kept my mouth shut. Another reason he wouldn't tell is we promised to pay for Carrie's medical bills. Why would anyone sell out someone that's trying to help them? Let's go and set up Dee's phone, then get out and talk to Bobby and tell him what he needs to do so we can get that truck."

When they finished, they told Darcy that the cameras were motion-activated and there was two-way voice communication. If anything happened, they could talk to Satchel, and he could answer them. She would be safe, but she would have enough warning to leave the house if worse came to worse.

Mickey suggested they go by the rehab center and visit a few minutes with Pop on the way out.

"Sure, Mickey. We need to visit him. Maybe he has some information about when he can go home. Is the downstairs ready for him yet?"

"Good question. I don't know. While you drive, I'll call Dee and find out. We need to get to Richmond and check on Bobby. You drive, I'll make some calls. Head to the rehab," said Mickey. Mickey called

Bobby and told him they would be there in a couple of hours to go over the situation and when they could leave the area.

"Hello, boys. How's my son and my almost son doing?" Daniel said cheerfully when Mickey and James walked into his room.

"Great, Pop. We're doing fine," answered Mickey.

James smiled, moved toward Daniel, and put out his hand to shake it. "You're looking well, sir. We hope you're ready to go home."

"I am ready to go home. The nurse told me that the doctor had approved my discharge tomorrow morning, right after my last physical therapy treatments. If I pass all the tests, I'll pack my clothes and be waiting at the front door for pick up. How's that sound to you?"

"Oh, Pop, it sounds wonderful," said Mickey as he bent over and hugged his father for the first time in months.

James moved over and patted him on the back, but as he did, Daniel looked up at him and said, "Son, bend down, give me a hug."

So, James bent over and also hugged his father-in-law-to-be.

They talked for a few minutes, bid him goodbye, and promised to be near the phone when he called for pick up. James turned on the radio to an oldies channel and sang to the music all the way to Richmond. They pulled into the parking lot of the hotel and saw Bobby. Carrie was on a swing with her wheelchair nearby, and Janet was pushing the swing to Carrie's laughter.

Mickey looked over at Janet and her daughter after he and James sat down beside Bobby.

Mickey said, "Bobby, you screwed up a while back, and it costs all of us here a lot of time, emotions, and heartache. That doesn't even include the money we'll be spending to set this whole situation right. When it gets straight, you better not mess it up again. Do you get that?"

"I do get it. I'll never mess up again. You don't know how much I appreciate what you guys are doing for us."

James spoke up next, "Now, it's time to step up and do your part. We have Satchel, and we need to intercept one of his trucks. We need you to talk to him and make him admit to the theft of electronic equipment and the millions of dollars of medical equipment and shipping it illegally out of the country. If you do that, then he'll go to jail for a long time. A good lawyer will get him off if you don't, and all of our heads will be on his chopping block. A few hours ago, Satchel promised to kill us all. He meant it. If he goes free, we're all dead men. Is that understood?"

Bobby bobbed his head up and down in understanding. "Yep, and he will too. I know that man. He's as dangerous as a crazy man."

"First, we need to know what time of day is the hand-off of one truck to another?" asked James.

"Usually around noon. That gives both drivers time to get to the rest stop in the middle and get back to the parking space by evening."

"Do they use the same drivers? Do you usually know the other driver?"

"Most of the time, but sometimes drivers just disappear, you know, they get to know too much or just quit and leave without notice."

"How do you recognize the other truck?"

"Our trucks have Bridgeton shipping on the outside of the cab. The trailers are different, but the truck itself is always a Bridgeton truck. He uses a shell corporation to insulate himself from ownership in case someone gets caught."

"We understand. How do you know so much about his business?"

"I told you, I worked for him years before he turned crooked. Different company names, different personnel. Stuff like that," Bobby said.

"So, you know how important it is that we get a complete confession out of him. If we just handed him over to the police, he'd be out in an hour. We need him admitting to the operation and killing people. You talk to him and get him to admit that. We can't get ourselves on the recording. We live in this town. If someone recognizes our voices, then we might be connected to him. You don't live here. No one knows you and your voice. Got it?" James insisted.

"Yeah, I understand. After I do this for you, when do we get to leave?"

"I've already made some calls. There is an excellent hospital in Denver, Colorado. I talked to a doctor I know that's retired military, and he can do whatever surgery that Carrie might need. He's agreed to do it for me as a favor pro bono, but there are still many medical things, hospital charges, physical therapy, and so much more, which we will cover. You'll need to look for a job like I talked to you before."

"Denver, Colorado? Isn't there some other place we could go?" he asked.

"Nope, not unless you have enough money to pay the medical bills."

"Okay, I'll do it. When can we leave?"

"As soon as you get the confession from Satchel, hopefully the day after tomorrow, you can leave. We'll come by and pick you up around seven that morning. And we'll go to someplace to be alone, and you can talk. Then when we get the truck and move it, we'll get you out pronto and on a plane to Colorado. Deal?"

"Deal," he said.

Mickey and James got up and headed back for home in Bridgeton. It was going on midnight, and they were both tired from a full day.

CHAPTER 22

Saturday Morning....Daniel Goes Home

MICKEY CALLED DARCY AND INQUIRED ABOUT Daniel's living area downstairs in the house. She told Mickey that it was almost ready and should be prepared for occupancy by noon. She would work on it until Daniel called, and they could both go to pick up their father and bring him home. She had ordered a cake to be delivered early today, and she would have it set up in the dining room to give him a welcome home party. She had also called Valerie, who would be standing by to come when they called. The rehab center said most discharges were before noon, and they expected the doctor to sign the discharge papers in an hour or so. Daniel's last physical therapy was scheduled for ten in the morning. She had also called James and told him to be on the alert for the discharge call. Darcy wanted everyone there to welcome her dad home.

James called Mickey, and they agreed to meet at the diner, so Mickey showered, shaved, dressed, and headed out to the diner. When he pulled up, he saw the Humvee was in the lot.

Mickey went in and saw James sitting in a booth in the back. James told him he had already ordered for both of them when he walked over and sat down.

"We need to discuss what we plan to do with the money we found and the additional million we got yesterday from Satchel," said Mickey.

"We can't just turn it in because they'll ask where and how we got it. When we explain that we got it as ransom from kidnapping Satchel Binghamton, we to jail. If we give it anonymously, the government will keep it. We can do some real good with it. Besides, you don't know how much it cost to call Alyssa and get her team here to help us. Mercenaries are expensive. That's why they're mercenaries. If they wanted to work for dirt wages, they'd be in a regular army somewhere. Without that money, Carrie wouldn't get the much-needed medical care. We wouldn't be able to put Satchel out of business. You need operating capital to do things like that. We don't need the money personally. At least I don't. I have very few needs and wants, so I'm good financially. Because of your family business, you have a comfortable income. You don't need the money. We can do real good. I mean, really help people with it. I vote we do that," said James.

"I don't know about you, but I don't plan on going into this kind of business regularly. I just want to stay in the real estate rental business. Now that Pop is coming home, I want to spend some time with him and just take care of our property."

"Good, you can do that. What if something like this happens again?"

"It won't. All these years, it hasn't happened. I don't think it'll happen in the future."

"Maybe not, but if it does, you or we have the funds to help. And if one of your tenants gets into dire straits, you can anonymously help them with their rent until they get back on their feet."

"Yeah, there is that, but most of them are just too lazy to get out and work. When they get behind, they just skip out and trash the place."

"You said, MOST, so that means that some of the people have real legitimate problems, right?"

"Yes, some, but that's a small percentage," said Mickey.

"Okay, then those you take a bit of money and donate it to pay their rent. Also, what about some of your worthy tenants, that maybe have kids that are smart but they don't have enough money to pay for college? You can help with financial help for college tuition. Didn't you offer to help Valerie with tuition for her cooking school?"

"That was different. I offered to help out of my own pocket, not from stolen money."

"I keep telling you. We took it from murderers and thieves. They're the criminals, not us, Mickey Ray. They'd use it to fund more illegal transactions. They're not helping others. We'd be doing that. We're the good guys!"

The waitress brought the breakfast and filled their coffee. "How about a Danish and coffee to go when you boys are ready. Mickey, I'm so sorry that Valerie has decided to leave and go back to school, but she'll make a great cook. Maybe when she graduates, she'll come back here, and the two of you can still get married."

"Thanks, Polly, a Danish and coffee would be nice. Yes, I'll miss Val very much. Maybe we can get together when she graduates," Mickey answered. Then Polly turned and walked away.

"Just think about it, bro. We can install a safe in the garage, and we'll both have the combination," James said as he ate.

"I'm not worried about where the money is kept. I just want to be able to sleep at night. I still have nightmares about what happened a few months ago. That's the whole reason Val is leaving. I don't want any more of this kind of stuff. She broke our engagement, and I doubt if we'll ever get married even if she decides to come back to Bridgeton," stated Mickey.

"You have a classic case of PTSD, and so does Valerie, but you're dealing with it better than she is. She's running away, and you're staying and dealing with it like a man," James said, with a mouth full of food.

"Maybe you're right, but I don't like it."

"You don't have to like it, but you do have to deal with it. Let's get out of here. Hurry up and eat. We need to check on Satchel. He might need more water and at least something to eat. I don't want to be deliberately cruel to the scum bag. Do you have a camping toilet?"

"No. Why would I? I don't go camping."

"I thought I'd ask. Satchel might need one, that's all. We can stop by a store to get one on the way to the garage."

Polly came back with a pot of coffee and filled both cups. "I see that you wolfed that food down. Do you want your checks now?"

James spoke, "Yes, ma'am. Put both of them on mine. And two Danish would be good. Add that to the check also."

When she came back, she had two cups of coffee and two Danish wrapped to go. She placed the check on the table. James laid some bills on the table, got up, thanked Polly, and told her to keep the change. James told Mickey he would meet him at the garage in a few minutes because he'd stop at a camping store.

Darcy was setting the table when Mickey got to the house, and in the middle sat a huge cake that said, "Welcome home, Daddy." Darcy said the rehab had called and told her that their father would be discharged in about an hour. The paperwork was being prepared. Darcy told them that someone would be there to pick Daniel up. She suggested that Mickey and James pick up their father, and she would continue decorating the house and getting the kids ready for Grampy's return. Mickey told her that James would be here in a couple of minutes so they could check on Satchel in the garage, and then they could leave for the rehab center.

In the meantime, Mickey went out to the workshop room in the garage to check on Satchel. He opened the app on his phone to see what was happening before he unlocked the door. He saw Satchel sitting in the chair, with his head resting on his chest, apparently asleep. He unlocked the door and called out at a distance to awaken him. After calling out several times, his head bobbed up, and he answered Mickey.

"I'm here. Where would you expect me to be, you little SOB!" Satchel called out.

"I was just checking on you. My partner will be here in a few minutes with some food and additional water. Also, he is bringing you a toilet so that you can take care of that business."

"Yes, I'm about to split my bladder. I'm not too keen on wetting myself," he scowled. "I didn't drink any of that water so I wouldn't fill my bladder. I just took a few sips to keep my mouth moist."

"Smart thinking, Satch. I wouldn't have thought of that. Most people would have drunk all of it and peed on the floor."

"Yeah, well, I'm not most people. I wouldn't have lived this long or be this successful if I didn't have good sense. That's why when I get out of this, I'm going to kill both of you personally."

Mickey stood looking at the man for a moment, then said, "Be nice, or shut up! We might just kill you anyway."

"Nope, not you. Your partner gives me the impression that he could kill babies and not lose sleep, but not you. You have a weakness for being NICE, as you put it."

"That may be true, but even I can only be pushed so far. So, I think you should shut up now."

"I agree," said James as he entered the room. He had a bag and a medium-sized box in both hands. Putting the box on the floor, he opened it and took out a camping chemical toilet. Then he took out a key and unlocked the padlocks securing the chains wrapped around Satchel's arms and legs.

"Now, use it if you need to. We'll be outside the door, but the cameras are running, and we'll be watching, so don't try anything stupid. Specifically taking off the blindfold. If you do, we may have to kill you for being able to identify us."

"If you have cameras, it's not like I have any privacy anyway, so why are you leaving? You might as well stay and get a close-up live view."

"You may not have privacy, but we want some, so we'll step outside to talk and still keep an eye on you. In the bag are more water and a couple of hamburgers. I remember you said you don't like hot dogs, so I went with burgers."

"I don't like hamburgers either. It's mostly dog food," Satchel spoke sarcastically.

"Then starve. We don't care," James said as he motioned for Mickey to follow him outside the room. He closed the door behind him. They stepped over to the monitor hanging on the wall near the base station to see Satchel.

"Dee called me. I'm ready when you are to go pick up your dad," James said.

"As soon as we finish with Satchel, we can shackle him. When we get back here, we should let him move around and walk even if it's just around the inside of the garage," suggested Mickey.

"That's a humane thing to do, so I agree. When we get your dad home, I can sneak out and walk the old man. He's more trouble than a little puppy," James said as he looked up at the monitor and saw Satchel reach into the bag, grab one of the hamburgers and start eating it.

After Satchel stuffed one burger down, he reached in and took out the other, and shoved it in his mouth also, then washed them down with the bottled water.

"For a man that doesn't like burgers, he sure is stuffing his face!" laughed James.

"One more day, and he'll be gone. I'll be glad when this is over so we can get back to a normal life," said Mickey.

"Me too, but you know, I haven't had this much fun since I was in the military."

"Fun for you, a nightmare for me," Mickey said exasperatedly. "When he's done, meet me at the truck. I'll tell Dee we're leaving," he said. After letting Darcy know they would pick up their father, he waited in the truck until James came out and got in.

"Darcy and the kids had originally planned to come with us to pick up Pop, but she still had some things to do to get ready. She is also waiting for a rental wheelchair to be delivered in case Pop needs it," said Mickey.

"I'm glad I can be with you to pick him up," said James. "I think I'm going to like having him as a father-in-law."

Daniel was sitting on a bench outside the front entrance of the rehab center. He smiled as Mickey and James walked up.

"My two sons have come to get me. I'm a happy man today," he said, and he pushed a button on a small box hanging around his neck.

Soon, a nurse came out and said to him, "Looks like your ride is here, Mr. Christianson. Let me help you into the wheelchair, sir."

"Yes, Lucy, you just help me. After all, this will be the last time you'll be helping me."

"I'm glad you're going home, but all of us here will miss you, sir," she said.

"Ah, yes. I'll not miss being here, but I will miss all of you. Everyone's been wonderful to me," he said.

It was only about twenty feet from the bench to the truck, but insurance required that he be wheeled all the way to the vehicle. She also helped him get into the truck, and they drove proudly out of the rehab center that had been Daniel Christianson's home for several months. Finally, Daniel was going home.

When they pulled into the driveway, Darcy and the kids were waiting on the front porch. Darcy and the kids followed the truck to the back of the house. It was closer for Daniel to get out and into the house. He looked around at the family that was gathered around and smiled. He held on tightly to the walker and everyone moved in to put their arms around him and hug him. Darcy kissed him on the cheek, then held both kids up to hug his neck and also give him a peck. Mickey stood on one side while James stood on the other side to make sure he was steady.

Daniel turned from side to side. He reached up and put his arms around both Mickey Ray and James and pulled them in close. "I am a blessed man to have such a wonderful family and two wonderful boys. No, I mean wonderful sons. James reached up and discreetly wiped away a small tear from his eyes. He, too, felt that he was blessed to be a part of this family.

Daniel walked slowly to the steps. As he walked, he looked around at the house. He remembered when it was being built. He wanted it to look like an old southern Manor house. It was all white with large columns and a wrap-around porch. On comfortable evenings he and Eleanor, his wife, the mother of Darcy Jean, and Mickey Ray could sit on the porch and watch the kids play in the yard.

All the trees were just saplings back then, but now there was a tall oak tree in the back yard, but on each side of the front lawn were two weeping willow trees that would sway back and forth in the breeze. Other shrubbery was planted to flower and bloom at different times of the year. Eleanor was no longer here to enjoy it, but she would be pleased with how it had all turned out. He would miss her, but at least he would be around to see the children and grandchildren enjoying the fruits of his labors. Sometime soon, he planned to talk with Mickey Ray so they could buy and restore another car. This time, Mickey could do more than just hand him the tools. He could do a lot of the work also.

"Are you okay, Pop?" asked Mickey.

"Sure, I am, son. I was just reminiscing about the time we spent here. And I'm looking forward to the coming years with all of you. Let's go inside," he said with a smile on his face.

Mickey and James, once again, stood on each side to steady Daniel as he slowly walked up the steps to the back door. James stepped ahead to open the door for his father-in-law-to-be. Daniel winked and said, "Thank you, son," as he walked inside.

Daniel walked into the kitchen, through it, and into the area to be his living area. It was a large room he could use as a sitting room, complete with a couch, side table, and large-screen television hung on the wall. Beyond that was a large handicapped bathroom and a bedroom with a walk-in closet.

"To all of you, this is wonderful. I'm going to spend many happy years in this house. Thank you all so much. As I came through the dining area, I didn't miss the place settings on the table and that huge cake. I assume that's for me. Let's get to the celebration!"

He walked back into the dining area, and he saw Valerie walk into the house. "Hello, Valerie. Come and join us. We've been waiting for you to arrive so we could get started," Daniel said.

"Hey there, Mr. Christianson. I wouldn't miss this for the world," she answered. She walked over to him, gave him a gently hug and a kiss on his cheek.

They gathered around the table with Daniel at the head, as they had done since the house was built. He asked that they all bow their heads and give thanks. As the group bowed, Daniel started: "Dear heavenly Father. We gather together around this table to thank you for all your blessings. I personally want to thank you for the soon-to-be additions to our family like James. Valerie will be leaving, but we wish her well and happiness in her journey and new life. I thank you for my kids, Mickey Ray and Darcy Jean, for their love and support. Last but certainly not least, I wish to thank you for my grandchildren, Joel and Cyndi, who will someday become adults and continue the Christianson line. They are a blessing from you, and we dedicate them to your care and service. Bless this gathering and food as we partake. In Christ's name. Amen."

Darcy began bringing a feast of food. Valerie took the cake from the table and sat it on the kitchen counter until dessert was served. Everyone ate until they were stuffed. And finally came the cake. They cut it, and then retired to the rocking chairs on the porch. And it was a wonderful day for all.

James quietly moved from the group and went to the garage to check on Satchel during this time. He was still there, shackled and getting very cranky. James knew that he was getting cramped from not moving for so long, but right now was not a good time to unshackle him. So, he gave him some food and additional water and let him loose long enough to relieve himself into the toilet.

After that, it was getting dark, and everyone went back into the house, and Daniel started telling stories about Darcy and Mickey's childhood. Daniel sat next to Valerie. At the end of one of his stories, everyone laughed and talked amongst themselves. He leaned over and asked her, "Valerie, when are you leaving? Mickey said it was in a few days but didn't tell me exactly when."

She looked down at her lap at her empty cake plate. She got up and placed it back on the dining room table. When she sat back down again, she took a deep breath. "Mr. Christianson, I'll be flying out first thing Monday morning. The day after tomorrow. I hope you won't hate me for leaving Mickey."

"No, dear girl. I understand. No, I can't say that. I don't understand, but I understand that you must live your life as you see fit. If leaving Bridgeton is what it takes, then you must do it. Mickey loves you, and so do all of us. You've been here so long, you are almost part of the family, and if you decide to ever come back, then you'll be welcome here. Mickey will get over it in time. Time moves on, and so do we. I wish you only the best, dear."

"Thank you, sir. That means a lot to me. I guess at least one more thing I can do, is help Darcy Jean clean up the mess here."

"No, you don't," Daniel said. "Let them do it. You sit here with me and enjoy your last time here. I insist."

"Thank you, sir," she said and quietly sat while the others took plates and dishes to the kitchen.

The party went on into the early evening. Darcy could see that her father was getting tired, so she asked everyone to leave so he could get some rest. Mickey walked out to Valerie's car, and she kissed him good night. James and Mickey went once more to check on Satchel. They did let him out into the garage for a few minutes to stretch his arms and legs. Then they trussed him back up in the chair, hopefully for the last time. After securing him, they got into Mickey's truck and left.

CHAPTER 23

Sunday Morning...Bobby Gets the Big Truck

James was sitting at Mickey's apartment at five o'clock on Sunday morning, waiting for him to come out. Mickey came out holding two cups of coffee and handed one to James as he got in the rented box truck James had picked up last night on his way home.

"Wow, nice truck. Did you secure a couple of chairs in the box to put Satchel in?"

"Yes, I did," answered James. "I also put some recording equipment in it, so we can record every word they say. We need to prompt Bobby some more to make sure we get everything that the FBI will need to prosecute."

"I thought that we were going to call the police," said Mickey Ray.

"True, but this is actually an FBI case. It involves high-end theft, crossing interstate lines, and out-of-the-country smuggling. So yes, the FBI. I have their number. We'll call them after we're done. If we call and tell them ahead, they would be there before us, and either we would be included in the arrests, or they would mess it all up. Either way, we would be shut out or charged with a crime. A bad scene all around."

They got to the garage, woke Satchel up, and loaded him into the truck. They strapped him in the box truck, in the back despite his threats.

The Landlord and the Wheelchair Child

"I guess when we get to Richmond and pick up Bobby, we can sit in that parking lot and get Bobby together with Satchel. When they talk, and we get what we need, then we can head out to the interstate rest stop and wrap this thing up," Mickey said.

As James drove, they talked about what they would do when this affair was over. They talked cars and other trivial stuff until they got to the hotel, and Bobby came out.

James told Bobby what he needed to get Satchel to admit doing.

"Okay, is that all I have to do, just talk to him and make him admit to taking all that stuff and killing some people?"

"Yep," said Mickey. "We'll help you a bit by asking leading questions if you get stuck. He's blindfolded, so he doesn't get to see our faces. And he won't know he's being recorded, so don't mention anything about that. When you get in, say his name, first and last, but not your last name. We don't want any authorities to identify you. Act like you're a prisoner, too, then he may open up to you. You know, talk about stuff he may not talk about around us. Let him think you're also tied up. Act like the two of you are alone. Do not under any circumstances let him know we're in the truck with you. Got it?"

"Um, yeah, I think so," Bobby said.

James had backed the truck into a parking space near the playground area. It was still early in the morning, so they assumed no children would be coming out to play at a playground this early. When they opened the door, Satchel called out.

"Hey, what's going on now. When are you jerks going to let me go? I gave you the money, and you promised to let me go! Hey, you lied to me! Talk to me," Satchel yelled.

Bobby looked at James and Mickey and said out of Satchel's hearing, "What money is he talking about?"

"We got him to give us some money that we will use to pay for Carrie's bills. Don't mention it to him, or he will know we made a deal with you, and he may clam up," said Mickey. "We told him we wouldn't kill him if he gave us some money. Make him think that we are going to kill you! We need him to believe that so he won't try to find you to kill you himself. Got it?"

"Got it, Mickey," Bobby answered.

"Shut up and keep your voice down, Satchel. We brought a friend to visit with you," said James. He made sounds like he was shoving Bobby inside. He quietly got in himself and slammed the door, so Satchel would think the two of them were alone.

"Who's here. Talk, so I know who you are."

Bobby climbed up into the box and sat down on the floor inside. "Satchel Binghamton, it's me, Bobby."

"Is that Bobby? Bobby, I thought they took you days ago," Satchel said.

"Yeah, they got me too. I thought you sent them to kill me."

"If I had sent them to kill you, you'd be dead!"

"Well, someone told me that after that last run, you were going to have me killed like you did that other driver a couple of months back," Bobby said.

"Who told you that?" asked Satchel.

"Never mind who. Were you really going to do it? Have me killed I mean."

"Maybe, maybe not," Satchel said.

"You had that Ralph driver killed, didn't you?"

"I'm not saying anything to you. Besides, you sold me out!"

"No, I didn't. I just know you had Ralph killed because he found out you were stealing medical equipment and shipping it out of the country and selling it on the black market."

"Shut up, boy, you talk too much."

"Yeah, I know what you're smuggling, and I know the drivers. I know that you're selling stolen medical equipment."

"What if I am? What's it to you? I paid you well. And the others wanted a bigger piece of the action."

"It's true that you're stealing and selling that medical stuff, isn't it?"

"Yes, it's true, but you'll never live to tell. If those two guys don't kill you, I'll have you killed myself."

"Yeah, that's probably true. That's probably why drivers only stick around to make a few trips, and then they just disappear," Bobby said. "You really are a huge piece of slime. You're a disgrace to the human race."

"Maybe I am, but at least I am a rich piece of slime. You came to me looking for a job, remember. I don't ask anyone for money. You're a pathetic little man."

When Satchel said that, Bobby stood up and pulled back his fist to punch him. James silently grabbed Bobby's arm and shoved him back onto the floor. He then put his finger to his lips in the sign of silence.

"Can't take the truth?" Satchel continued.

"You're a killer, a thief, and a smuggler, Satchel, and you make me sick. You prey on the weakness of others."

"I guess I am all of those things you said, but at least I am a few degrees above those that deal with me, and you're one of them. Now, I don't know what's happening here, but the two thugs have given me their word they'll let me go. I don't know if they will keep it or not. If they do, then if they also let you go, I'll have you killed. If they don't keep their word, I have the satisfaction of knowing that you'll be just as dead as me. Either way, you're a dead man. I at least have a chance at living."

Bobby huffed a few times, then said, "Satchel Binghamton, I hope you rot in hell."

"If I do, I'm sure you'll be right there beside me," Satchel answered.

James got up and walked over to the back door, opened it, and got out. He turned and called to Bobby.

"Come on, Bobby, let's go. We got what we need here," James said.

"What're you talking about, you crazy jerk. What did you get? I want to know what you got. Are you going to let me go or not?" Satchel called out.

"Yes, we're going to let you go, but not quite yet. Maybe in an hour or so. Just sit tight."

Bobby climbed out. And James closed the door. "Did I do okay?" he asked.

"Couldn't have done better myself," said James. "Now, get in the front, and let's get to the rest stop and get that truck."

Mickey was sitting at the picnic table and saw the two men get out. "Did you get what we need?"

James held up a small digital recorder. "Yep, we sure did. Bobby here gave an Oscar-winning performance. Now we need to get on the road so we can get there ahead of the other truck."

The three men got into the cab of the box truck headed for the rest stop on Interstate 95 at Richmond. They got there about eleven-thirty. Bobby looked around and didn't see any trucks that had the name of

Bridgeton shipping on the cab door, so they sat down and waited. They made one last check on Satchel and told him that it wouldn't be long now. In a while, they would transfer him to another truck, and then they would leave.

Satchel once again threatened to kill everyone he could think might even know about what was happening to him. James just slammed the door and walked away. They parked the truck at an angle to open it and take Satchel out without anyone noticing. Finally, Bobby pointed out a truck with the logo painted on the side. When it parked in line with the other eighteen-wheelers, the driver got out. He was looking for someone or something.

Bobby said he knew the driver. It was Dave. He had been with Satchel for almost a year. He knew almost as much about the operation as Bobby, but he also knew enough to keep his mouth shut and play dumb and happy with whatever they threw at him.

Bobby threw up a hand and called out to him. "Hey, Dave! Over here."

"Where's your truck, Bobby?" he answered as he walked to where Bobby was standing.

Mickey and James had slipped a pullover mask on and waited out of sight behind the box truck. Bobby motioned for Dave to come around to the back of the truck. When Dave stepped around, James and Mickey caught the man from behind and clamped a hand over his eyes and mouth. Dave struggled a few moments but knew better than to try to resist much because he knew the dire situation he was in at that time.

He went limp as James and Mickey put him inside the back of the box truck. Then they put zip ties on his wrists, ankles, and duct tape over his eyes and mouth. They shut the door so that casual onlookers wouldn't become suspicious. They pulled off their masks.

"Bobby, can you pull the truck up close enough for us to take both men out and transfer them to the back of the big truck?" Mickey asked.

"Yes, but you better be quick before another truck pulls in behind and sees inside the open door."

As Bobby went back to the eighteen-wheeler, Mickey pulled the box truck parallel to the curb so Bobby could pull up beside it with both rear doors side by side. It would only take thirty seconds to pull the men out and transfer each to the other truck. James watched the roadway to make sure another truck wasn't pulling in to park. They waited while two trucks entered the rest stop. Finally, no one was coming into the ramp leading to the rest stop. James, Bobby, and Mickey opened both doors and moved the men from one truck to the other, then closed the doors and locked them.

As Bobby pulled the semi-truck forward into a parking position, Mickey moved the box truck into a small parking space for camping trailers.

While they waited for Bobby to move the truck, James turned to Mickey and said, "Did you take a look inside the big truck. It's loaded almost to the back door with medical equipment. Satchel will get some serious jail time for all that stuff."

Mickey smiled back at James, "I did see it, and I know that we have done a good thing!" Mickey then put up a hand, palm out, the signal for a "high five."

James put up his hand and slapped Mickey's, and gave him a wink. "You bet we have, little bro!"

James told Bobby that they were going back to Bridgeton next. Bobby was to go to the Bridgeton Mall and park under the light at the south end of the parking lot. Mickey would drive the box truck, and James would ride with Bobby. They would all meet at the parking lot and abandon the truck and trailer there. They pulled out together, and Mickey followed the big truck to Bridgeton without trouble. When they got there, it was late afternoon. The three of them got out and opened up the back of the truck. Bobby had parked it, so the back end was facing into an area that was difficult to view from the rest of the parking lot.

James told Bobby to keep quiet, and they would tell Satchel and Dave that they had felt it prudent to dismiss him. In other words, they would make Satchel think that they had killed Bobby. That would keep Satchel from looking for him. Besides, Satchel thought that they were killers anyway, so it was acceptable to give Bobby a slight edge on his escape. When they put Satchel and Dave into the trailer of the eighteen-wheeler at the rest stop, they laid them on the floor in haste to get the door closed again. Mickey started opening boxes and crates. There was a variety of medical equipment worth several million dollars.

"Hey, Satch. What are you asking for this CT machine?" asked Mickey.

"None of your business," he answered.

James said, "I would guess that it sells in this country for about a million dollars installed."

"So what," Satchel said.

"Hey, Dave. Do you know what he charges for one of these machines?" asked Mickey.

"No, and I don't care," he answered.

"Smart man, Dave," said Satchel.

"I don't know what it's worth in American currency, but I'm sure it'll bring you a lot of years in a federal penitentiary."

"What do you mean? Are you guys cops?" Dave said.

"Nope," said James. "I'm a mongoose."

"I still don't have a clue what you mean by that name," Satchel spat out.

"I don't know either," said Dave, "but a mongoose is a little animal that kills snakes."

"Bingo, Dave. You get the prize. Your boss here is a snake, and I'm not going to kill him, but I will turn him over to the FBI, and they can do whatever they want with him. My guess is it'll be a long stint in jail, and you'll probably join him for at least a few years. We promised not to kill you, and we'll keep our promise. We promised to let you go. We're going to do that also, but we're going to lock you in this trailer until the FBI gets here. So, gentlemen, if you'll stand up and turn around, we'll take the shackles and zip ties off of you. But you're not to move until we close the doors. If you turn around before then, I'll personally shoot you. Got it?" James said.

Satchel and Dave nodded.

"Hey, Mongoose, or whatever your name is, I'll hunt you down and kill you! Got that?" said Satchel.

"Yes, I got it, and I'm shaking in my boots. Just don't turn around, or you won't live long enough to go to jail."

They got out of the truck and slammed the door. The two men didn't move a muscle.

"Would you really shoot them?" asked Bobby.

"No, I don't even have a gun. Not here anyway," said James.

The Landlord and the Wheelchair Child

They walked back to the box truck, and Mickey drove them out of the parking lot and back on the road to Richmond to drop Bobby off at the hotel.

"What did you do with the digital recorder, James?" asked Mickey.

"I put it on the seat on the driver's side and locked the keys inside. I left a note saying that it had an admission of theft and murder, then I signed it as the Mongoose."

As Mickey drove, James dialed the FBI and reported a stolen truck with two men locked inside. Several men were seen putting them inside and leaving something inside the cab. Next, he called the local television station. He reported that the FBI had an anonymous tip on a stolen shipment of medical equipment and an abandoned tractor-trailer truck in a local mall parking lot. Last, he called Darcy and told her to turn on a news station and record any news story about a stolen truck or medical equipment. He hung up and stomped the phone on the floor, and threw the remains out the window.

They drove on for a few miles, and Bobby asked James, "Do you guys do this stuff all the time?"

James said, "Yes."

Mickey chimed in afterward and said a resounding "NO!"

All three laughed, and Mickey drove on. They told Bobby to have Janet and Carrie ready to leave first thing in the morning. He and James would make sure they were on the plane safely at the Richmond International Airport.

When they got out of the truck at the hotel, Bobby went inside. Mickey said to James, "Why don't we get rooms here to save ourselves the trouble of driving back home and the return trip in the morning?"

"Sure, sounds like a good plan to me. Bobby and Janet's plane leaves at seven tomorrow, and we have to be here early anyway. That will still give us enough time to get home and back to the Newport News airport to see Valerie off. Yeah, let's get a couple of rooms," James answered as they both walked toward the lobby.

"Mickey, why are we going to two different airports?" James asked as they checked in and walked to the elevator to their rooms.

"Valerie made reservations at the Newport News airport, and I didn't have anything to do with that. We made hotel and flight reservations here because it's where we stashed Janet and Bobby to keep them away from Satchel. Since we told Satchel we killed Bobby, I hope he believes us and won't look for him. Just a coincidence, I guess, but hopefully, it's safer that way. Maybe we'll see something about the FBI finding the truck on the news. I hope so. See you in the morning. My room is on the floor above yours."

"This has been one long day. See you in the morning," said James.

CHAPTER 24

Monday morning...Catching Planes

The following morning, they met the Griffins in the lobby of the hotel. They put their bags in the back of Mickey's truck and drove to the airport.

Bobby said to Mickey and James, "Did you see the eleven o'clock news last night? They picked up Satchel, the driver, and found the recorder with the confession in the cab. I'll bet Satchel goes away for a long time."

"I hope so," said Mickey, "but you need to remember, even in jail, Satchel may have influence outside, so you must stay hidden to keep safe."

"We will," chimed in Janet. "If Bobby so much as sneezes outside the city limits or makes any contact with his old friends, I'll kill him myself."

"You say that as a joke, but I'm serious," said Mickey.

"Yes, he is," added James. "It's like you're in the federal witness protection program."

James handed them an envelope thick with papers. "Here's some paperwork you'll need. It contains new identities for all three of you. Also, the address of your new home and rent is paid for three months. There's the paperwork you need to pick up your rental car. The rental fee is paid for six months. If you wreck or damage it, you're on your own for the costs. Included is the information on the doctor I contacted. He'll look at Carrie and make arrangements for her operations. Whatever charges are incurred will be taken care of anonymously. There's also a preloaded credit card that should hold you for about two months for food and incidental expenses. By then, you should have a job and can take care of yourself. You have a completely new beginning with no debt. I suggest you start looking for a job immediately. There's a list of job references. If a prospective employer calls these numbers on the sheet in the package, you'll get a good reference in your new name. Don't blow it. If you do, you'll be on your own."

"We've done all we can do for you. It's up to you from here," added Mickey.

Janet moved to Mickey and hugged him, then to James, "You're both saints. We don't know how to thank you. We owe our lives to all of you, even Darcy. Please thank her for us."

"We'll do that," Mickey said. "Now, you'd better get on that plane before it takes off without you."

They watched them go through security, and Mickey and James left.

"Hey, man, what's with you and this mongoose thing. You mentioned it several times. You think you're a superhero or something, and you have special powers?" he asked.

"What do you mean?" James asked.

"I mean, Mongoose. What do you mean by that? I know what a mongoose is, but why do you keep referring to yourself as the Mongoose?"

"When I was in the service, each team had a name, like Cobra, Panther, Lion or some type of animal. My team was the Mongooses. We liked it because we called the head of a criminal sort the snake-head. Mongooses kill poisonous snakes like Cobras."

"You mean like mongeese?"

"No, not mongeese. The plural is still mongooses. Now, you're my team. We are Mongooses!" James said.

"We're not some superhero team. We're two regular guys helping a family. That's it. Nothing more, James."

"True, but sports teams have names, so we can have a name. It's Mongoose."

"We aren't going to continue doing stuff like this. This is the last one, and we need to get rid of that extra money we have. We can donate it to some charity or something."

"We'll see. When word gets out, people will come looking for us. You watch."

"No, I will not watch. I don't like putting my life on the line like this. I want a plain simple life. I want a life where I just follow in Pop's footsteps. I want to be a landlord. That's all I want. Live and let live."

"Okay. I say just give it a few months. If nothing happens, then we'll find a worthy cause to donate the money. In the meantime, let's build a safe in your dad's garage."

"Fine, we'll build a safe. But the main use will be for important papers, like a lockbox at a bank."

"Okay, a safe for papers and cash." James resigned himself to that answer.

Mickey dropped James at his place, and he drove home. He walked to the end of the building to his apartment. At the other end of the building was Valerie's apartment. He wanted to walk down to her apartment and try to convince her not to leave, but he knew it wasn't the right thing to do. If she got herself straight, maybe she'd come back. If she didn't, she'd move on, and so would he. He sat in a chair and pondered over the past few months. So much had happened. The world had changed, and so had he. He finally drifted off into a fitful sleep in the chair. When he woke up, it was time to go to the airport and see Valerie off. He dreaded this, but he had to go. He wished it was all part of his dream. But it was real. He got up and drove to the airport.

When Mickey got to the airport, he looked around for Val. He saw her sitting against a wall with a soft drink in her hand. As he got close, he could see she was looking at a brochure about the culinary school she had accepted. He walked up to the bench where she sat.

He sat down and put his arm around her shoulder and kissed her on the cheek. "Good morning, my love," he said.

She turned and looked into his eyes. She saw a glint of sadness. "Please don't feel sad for me, Mickey Ray. You know I still love you. I have to do this. Please be happy for me."

"I love you too much to be happy you're leaving me, dear," he said softly into her ear.

"We'll keep in touch even when I leave. I promise to call you and to email you."

"Are you sure you can't stay a little longer? We can work it out. I know we can," Mickey almost pleaded.

"No, Mickey. We can't. I'll not force you to change. You're a good, wonderful, and kind person. I love you just the way you are. That's what makes you Mickey Ray. I don't ever want you to change. But I can't handle that kind of life."

She reached into her purse and took out a key. "Here's the key to my apartment," she said, handing it to him. "I tried to leave it clean. I scrubbed the stove, and took everything out of the fridge, and cleaned it. I wiped off the counters and cleaned the bathroom, took out all my trash, and…"

He put a finger to her lips, "Shh. Don't worry about anything. Cleaning up apartments is what we do almost daily. It's fine."

"I didn't want to be like most of your tenants and leave it a mess, Mickey Ray. All the furniture you can have. What you don't want, throw it away, or maybe you can find someone that needs it. Here are the keys to my car, and I signed the title over to you. I left it on the kitchen counter in my apartment too.

"Please don't hate me, babe," Val said, almost breaking down into tears.

He wrapped his arm around her and pulled her closer to himself. "I could never hate you. I'll always love you, and the time we spent together was some of the most wonderful times of my life."

The loudspeaker crackled with static, "Gate 19 boarding now for Flight 4216."

Down the hallway running came Darcy and the kids with James in the lead. They came up to Valerie, and they had a tearful group hug, then she broke loose and gave each one an individual hug.

Everyone was in tears, including Joel and Cyndi. "Aunt Valerie, don't go. Please!" both children said almost in unison.

She bent down to them and stroked Cyndi's hair and kissed her on the cheek, then turned to Joel and did the same. "I have to go. I'll be in touch. I'll give you my email address, and you can both write to me, and we'll always be true friends."

"But you aren't going to be our aunt," Joel cried.

"Yes, I will, Little Joe. I'll be your aunt forever right here," she said, placing her hand over his little heart. "I'll be your aunt forever, and if you don't call me your Aunt Valerie, you'll hurt my feelings."

Joel looked up at her sincerely and said, "I would never hurt your feelings, Aunt Valerie."

"I know you wouldn't, little one. And that's why I love you both," she said, pulling both children to her side.

Valerie stood up and gave Darcy a huge hug also and said to her, "You'll always be like a sister to me, Dee. I'm so sorry things didn't work out for Mickey and me."

She turned to James and took his hand to shake, but he pushed her hand away, reached out, and pulled in for a family hug also. "Valerie, we'll all miss you. I hope you come back to see us and keep in touch." He reached into his pocket and took out a fat envelope, and handed it to her.

She took it and opened it, and her mouth dropped open. "James, I can't take this money from you!"

"It's not just from me. It's from all of us. We managed to scrape a little bit together to help you start your new life."

"But there must be, well, I don't know how much, but it's all hundred-dollar bills and a lot of them!"

"How much it is doesn't matter. We all want you to have it. We all love you like family."

Once again, she broke down in tears as she put it in her purse and more hugs all around. Again, the loudspeaker crackled.

"Final boarding call for Flight 4216, final boarding call for Flight 4216 at Gate 19."

She turned to Mickey, and they embraced, one last kiss, and she whispered in his ear, "I'll always love you, Mickey Ray Christianson."

Then, she waved goodbye to them as she walked toward Gate 19. They all stood and waited for the plane to fill up with passengers, then back from the terminal. A few minutes later, they saw the plane rev up the engines and start down the runway to take off.

As it took off and rose into the air, Mickey thought, another chapter of his life has come to an end, and with all the ups and downs, it was good.

He waved at the large plate glass window knowing Valerie couldn't see him, and he said to himself, "Goodbye, my love."

The Landlord's Dead Body

PROLOGUE

About six weeks before today:

AT ABOUT ONE IN THE MORNING, two people got out of the car at the recently cleared land behind the Senior Village apartment complex owned by the Christianson Company.

The driver opened the trunk and immediately took out the light bulb to keep the area dark while unloading the body.

"Hurry up and get her out," he said as he dragged the body out of the trunk of the car.

"I'm doing the best I can," she answered. "I never realized a body was so heavy. They don't have this much trouble in the movies."

"Right, because they aren't this heavy in the movies, you twit. Be quiet and help me."

"You did this by sleeping with her, so don't blame me!" she said snidely.

"She said she was on birth control, and besides, I didn't kill her. You did, so don't blame me!" he said, dragging the body away from the car. "Get the shovel."

She reached inside and took out a tool, and he called to her, "No. Not that one. That's a garden spade. Get the shovel. That's the one with the long handle, and come over here and help me."

"I don't know one tool from another. They all dig, don't they?" she said.

"Keep your voice down. Someone'll hear us."

"It's dark. We're all the way across this empty field from the closest building, and if someone did see us, they couldn't tell who we are or what we're doing," she answered.

"Just dig, okay?"

"How deep?" she asked.

"I don't know. Most graves are six feet deep."

"I'm not staying out here all night digging this stupid grave," she said as she picked up the spade and handed him the shovel.

"How about four feet? We want to cover the body, so no one finds it, but I agree. I don't want to be here all night."

They dug in silence until they were several feet deep. Then they pushed the body into the shallow grave along with her purse. They forced the dirt in the grave covering her body, gathered their tools, got in the car, and left the field.

As they slowly drove away from the open field, she turned and said to him, "When are they going to start construction? They took months to clear the land."

"I don't know. But they're still trying to secure the financing. They need investors for the down payment and then banks for the rest of the money. Commercial real estate is a complicated business. The Christianson's have come a long way in the past few months. When Daniel, the old man, was in the hospital, they thought he might never recover. Now, he's good as ever. Now his son, Mickey Ray, has joined up with his father, and they're roaring ahead. A few months ago, it seems that Mickey Ray was a kid. Now he is Daniel's right-hand man. He's become a shrewd businessman for his age."

"Do you think they'll find the body?" she pondered.

"Probably not. It depends on where all the underground things like utilities and building foundations are located. I guess it's possible, but there's always lots of open space in apartment complexes. Maybe they will, maybe not. Still, in a few months, it'll be decomposed, so they may not even be able to identify her, so we should be in the clear."

"Yeah, and if you behave and keep it in your pants, we can put all this behind us and go on with life. I'll say this. If I ever catch you doing something like this again, I'll not help, nor will I ever forgive you! Do you understand me on this?" she said with finality.

"I understand, now let's go, and never look back," he said as he pulled onto the road.

CHAPTER ONE

Monday, The First Day of Construction

Two men, business partners, Father and Son, Daniel and Mickey Ray Christianson, looked over the vast field that had been cleared and ready to break ground for the next real estate project. It would be the largest residential project in Bridgeton, and it had been a long, tedious road to get to this point.

Both men had hired engineers, architects, land use, and environmentalist experts. They had spent endless hours wining and dining potential investors, talking to city officials, and attending numerous city council meetings. Last of all, they had presented the project proposal to bankers to get the forty million dollars needed to build the project that was beginning this morning.

The land was cleared, and they were beginning to dig the footings for some of the buildings marked out on the map attached to the wall in the construction trailer parked on-site behind them.

Daniel's arm was resting on Mickey Ray's shoulder while he steadied himself by holding a cane with his other.

"Son, this is the proudest moment of my life," he said as he continued looking over the site.

"Yes, Pop. It's mine also," Mickey answered.

"I wish your mother were alive to see us working together on it."

"That would be the icing on the cake, wouldn't it Pop?"

"You bet. They know where to start, don't they, son?"

"Yes, I talked to the site foreman yesterday afternoon. He didn't like talking to me on a Sunday, but I explained that we needed to start on Monday, today. So, we got it all straight. They're going to start on building five, digging the footing. The plumbing company will follow them as well as the underground electrical utilities. Let's go inside the trailer and take a look at the construction schedule," said Mickey Ray.

The project they were starting was on the edge of the township of Bridgeton. It was a small town between Williamsburg and Richmond, Virginia. Daniel had grown up in the town, left the area when he went into the air force and met a young lady, Eleanor, and got married. When he had served his term in the military, he returned to Bridgeton and began investing in rental real estate. Eventually, he sold his single-family homes and began investing in apartment buildings and later, building apartment complexes.

Mickey, at the time, was in his mid-twenties but quickly matured, dealing with problems and maintenance situations. Mickey was handsome, had a trim physique developed from his regular visits to the gym, and most importantly among the ladies, rich. Daniel and Mickey Ray paired up and organized this project. Mickey Ray attended almost all business meetings and became quite familiar and popular with the town's officials. The young ladies were coming out of the woodwork, hoping to be noticed by Mickey. He was considered the "most eligible bachelor" in Bridgeton.

As they walked to the construction trailer, Mickey said, "They got the trailer set yesterday afternoon and hooked up all the utilities."

They walked up the steps to the office trailer and went inside. Even though it was early morning, it was cool, but the morning sun was already heating the trailer, so Mickey turned the air conditioning on to keep it at a comfortable temperature while they had their first meeting of the day. He also put on a pot of coffee so that it would be ready when everyone showed up.

One by one, men filed into the trailer and looked around at the decorations on the wall. Mickey stood behind a table sitting in the middle of the room covered by a cloth. Finally, he called everyone to order.

He began by saying, "Men, this will be the first of many meetings we'll have here. I hope that they will discuss the future progress, not problems, but with every project comes some problems. Now, I will say this, when you come here with a problem, please try to come with a suggested solution. We'll discuss every detail and work out a solution."

Mickey pulled the cover off the table, revealing a three-dimensional architectural model that showed what the entire project would look like complete.

He pointed to one corner of the model. "You already know that we are starting in this corner. The backhoe was unloaded just minutes ago and should already be starting the foundation on this building," he said, pointing to one of the tiny buildings on the model. "As that progresses, others will be working on the underground utilities in this area. We have to run power, water, sewage, and natural gas lines through the entire area, and of course, under the roadways throughout. I think you have all met Randall. He is the site supervisor. He will coordinate the work with all of the line foremen. There'll be several different contractors working on various jobs, and he'll hopefully keep things running smoothly and each of you out of others way. No stepping on each other's toes. You report to him. He reports to me or my father here, Daniel. We have a schedule and barring any unforeseen circumstances, we should get this entire thing complete in the next eighteen months. Let's go to work, men!"

They all looked at the model and discussed various job topics amongst themselves. Randall made the rounds introducing himself to those he didn't already know. As one would ask him questions, he would sometimes go to the map on the wall and discuss their questions and give them an answer or make notes to get back with them later with the answers.

As Mickey and Daniel were talking to one of the line foremen, the door to the trailer opened, and a burly man stepped inside. "Mr. Christianson?" he called out.

Daniel and Mickey both turned and answered the man. "Yes, can we help you?" they said almost in unison.

"The backhoe operator has run into a problem, sirs."

"How can he have a problem? He's only been digging for ten minutes."

"I'm sorry to tell you this, sir, but he dug up a body."

"Oh, crap!" said Mickey. "This isn't a good way to start a construction job. Pop, if you'll stay here and answer any questions the men might have, I'll take care of this."

He followed the man across the field and over to the backhoe. In a hole, about three feet deep, were some clothing and body parts. The operator stood several feet away from his machine, obviously pale and throwing up his breakfast. Mickey walked over to the man. He looked to be in his early forties and very upset.

"I've been doing this for all my adult life. I've never had anything like this happen. I didn't know what to do when I saw it," he said.

Mickey placed his hand on the man's back. "Are you alright? Why don't you go over there and sit down? You didn't do anything wrong. You stopped and reported it. You did good. It's okay. Take a breather. What's your name?"

"Al. My name's Albert, sir," he said.

"I'm Mickey Ray. My Pop and I own the project. You calm down. Take some deep breaths. Go sit down. We'll call the police and let them take it from here. You just sit. I'll have someone bring you a bottle of water. Would you rather have a cup of coffee?"

"Yes, sir, that would be good," he said.

"Just call me Mickey Ray. Coffee or water, Al?"

"Water's fine, sir," he said. "I thought I would pass out when I saw what I did."

"You don't have to call me 'sir.' Call me Mickey Ray, or if you prefer, Mickey. You didn't know anyone was buried here. No one knew. It's fine," he said and looked over at the burly man. "Would you get Al a bottle of water? We have some in the trailer where you got me."

"Yes, sir," he said, turning around to walk away.

Mickey called out, "And call me Mickey…not sir!"

The man put his thumb up in acknowledgment as he headed for the trailer.

Mickey gave Al the water and told him he needed to stay until the police arrived and tell them what had happened. Then he could have the rest of the day off.

"Bob, I told Al he could leave after he gave the police a statement. It shouldn't take long. All he did was put the bucket in the ground and find the body. And Al gets a full day's pay. He's had a pretty big shock. Don't let anyone around this area, and don't touch anything. Tell the police I'm over there in the trailer," he said, pointing to the trailer as he walked away.

Mickey said, "I need a tall cup of coffee. This's going to be an awful day."

"Tell us about it, Mickey," said Daniel.

Mickey walked over to the coffee pot, poured a large cup full, grabbed a doughnut and chewed it up along with a few sips of coffee. Daniel and Randall stood patiently waiting for Mickey Ray to speak.

"I can't add much to what Bob, the foreman that came in here, said. The backhoe operator dug up a body. I called the police, and they should be here in a few minutes. Needless to say, that part of the area will be shut down until the police release it. Randall, if you'll get another operator to run that machine after the police leave, I'd appreciate it."

"Sure thing, Mickey Ray. I'll have them move over to the next building. He might be able to get that one dug today, and we'll continue around the ring. Then we'll get back to that one," Randall said, then left the trailer to find another operator.

A few minutes later, there was a knock on the door, and Detective Peter Reynolds walked in. "Hey Mickey," he said. "You haven't really got started, and we get a call from you."

"Yeah, you're right, Pete. What do you think of it?"

"I called a forensic team to get on it. They'll take most of the day, and we might need to cordon off the area for a couple of days until we can make sure we don't miss anything," he said.

"Can you go with me back over to the sight so we can talk about it?"

"Sure, Pete. Can Pop come along?"

"Both of you can come. You're more familiar with the site and maybe can shed some light on what's happened the past couple of months. How're you doing, Dan?"

"Doing great, Peter. I see you're still limping from that wound you got a while back," said Daniel.

"Doctor said I may always have this limp. Getting shot in the leg and shattering my thigh bone just didn't heal as good as new like they said it would."

"Let's take a look at the dig site. Mickey told me about it, but I have seen it yet."

The Detective opened the door and held it while Daniel carefully descended the steps. He held it open for Mickey to go next. He closed the door and again took the lead to the backhoe as he came down. They lined up and looked into the shallow hole when they got there.

Detective Reynolds shook his head then pointed at the body. "It's definitely female since she had on a dress. It looks like it was a simple cotton dress. I think the ladies call it a sun dress. The backhoe operator tore it and her body, so beyond that, I can't tell much. We'll know more after an autopsy. My guess is she hasn't been here very long, only a few weeks, because of the level of decomposition. It looks more like a young girl, but I can't say."

"I know that you've had heavy equipment in this area for months, but like I said, the decomp's not too extensive," said the Detective.

"Yes. We started clearing the land months ago. So, you're right, we've cut down a lot of trees, graded the land, turned up a lot of soil to dig out stumps, and level the entire acreage. We would've dug her up sooner if she'd been here more than a few weeks ago. Do you think someone wanted us to find her body?" asked Daniel.

"No, I doubt it. If someone wanted the body found, they wouldn't have buried it in the first place. My guess is, the soil was easy to dig. They just picked a spot where you happened to dig. There are a lot of areas that you'll not disturb during the entire construction. Bad luck for somebody. The problem is, identifying the body and clues. When you bury somebody, you lose a lot of clues along with it. Nature erases a lot. If there was physical trauma, that might be difficult to separate from the damage done by the backhoe. Sad. It really is so sad. We'll do what we can, but in all honesty, chances are, we'll never find her killer. I wish I could be more positive, but you understand. We, no, I'll do my best to find the SOB that did this. Sorry I have to shut the site down. I hope you understand."

"Of course, we understand, Pete. You have a job to do, and we don't want to interfere. We'll work around it. Let us know when your people are finished. We do have a schedule and an order that we have set to make the job progress efficiently," said Daniel.

"Thanks, Dan. We'll do our best to wrap it up and get out of your way," said Pete as he reached out to shake hands with Daniel, then Mickey Ray.

As Detective Reynolds limped back to his car, Mickey turned to his father and shook his head. "Pop, he seems like a pretty decent cop. I hope he's true to his word about working to find that lady's killer."

"He will, son. Pete is one of the best in the Bridgeton police department. If he says, he'll try, you can count on him to do it. I've known him since he joined the force."

"Well, Pop, let's have a real breakfast. I'm starving."

"Where do you want to eat, Mickey Ray? You do know you're buying, right?" Daniel said.

"I wouldn't have it any other way, Pop. How about the old stand-by, the diner? My truck or your car?"

"Let's take the Rolls, boy. We've been working so much lately we haven't had time to buy a new truck for me to drive."

Later:

"I've got to get back to the jobsite. See you later."

Mickey drove back to the jobsite. As he pulled through the gate, he saw a city vehicle sitting by the area where the backhoe had found the body. He parked his truck, got out, and walked over to see two people in the hole with brushes brushing dirt away from the body. He stood there watching for a few minutes before one of the workers looked up and saw him. The man stepped out of the hole and came over to Mickey.

"Good morning, sir," he said.

"That depends on your viewpoint, I guess," Mickey answered.

"I guess that's true," he responded. "Are you Mr. Christianson?"

"I'm one of them. Call me Mickey Ray. My father's over there in the construction trailer. And you, sir, are?"

"I'm Baker, Clyde Baker, but everyone calls me Baker. Sorry, I can't shake," he said, showing his gloved hand.

"I understand, Clyde. What can you tell me?" said Mickey.

"Not much, sir. Ongoing investigation, you understand."

"Yes, I understand; however, I see that you found a handbag. It's lying right there next to the body. Can you tell me her name? There was identification in the bag, wasn't there?"

"I'm sorry, sir, but…"

"Baker, I'm not asking for anything that might jeopardize an investigation. It'll be all over the news in a few hours anyway. All I'm asking for is her name."

"Um, I guess that might be acceptable. Let me look in the bag and see what's in there," he said, turning back to the body in the shallow hole.

He picked it up, opened it, rummaged around, and took out a case containing several credit cards and a Virginia Driver's license. He came back and held it up for Mickey to see. Mickey looked at it, and his mouth dropped open.

Baker looked at Mickey and said, "Do you know her?"

"Yes, I do, Baker. I went to school with her, and she lived in one of my apartments."

Baker took an evidence bag and poured the contents of the handbag into it. Then sealed it up with tape. He then handed it to Mickey.

"Please don't open it up. You might contaminate it. You can look at it with me standing here. Then I must get to work," he said, looking around. He noticed the others working, looking up at him.

Baker took her jewelry, her watch, something in her hair like a hair clip or barrette, and put it in another bag.

Mickey took a quick look and snapped a picture of each clear bag with his phone, then turned them over and snapped a picture of the other side. He then made a motion of zipping his lips and nodded.

"Between you, me, and God. Thanks. I'll put in a good word for you if I have the chance," said Mickey as he walked back to the trailer.

Daniel called out from the office when he entered, "Is that you, Mickey?"

"Yeah, Pop. I stopped by the hole to check the progress there. She was buried with her handbag," he said as he walked into the small trailer office and sat down in the chair across from his father.

"What did you find out?" asked Daniel.

"In her handbag was her driver's license. She was Betty Duncan. I went to school with her, and she lived in one of our apartments. Pop, she was a real sweet girl back then. If Detective Reynolds doesn't find her killer, we have to," Mickey said sadly.

"Pete will do his best, Mickey, because he is the best."

"I know, but I just can't understand what anyone would have against her to want her dead. She was in the same graduating class as Dee. She lived in one of our apartments with her mother. When we were in school, she worked at a grocery store in town.

"Her father was a mechanic and worked on city vehicles at the motor pool. She had two brothers. When they all grew up and graduated, one brother joined the service, the other got married and moved out of town, somewhere out west, I think. Anyway, Betty wasn't particularly pretty and not popular in school. She worked and helped support her mother when her father died a few years ago of cancer. She and her mother were quiet and never caused any problems. I had forgotten all about them until now."

Mickey reached across the desk, picked up the phone, and dialed Darcy at her new office. "Hey, Dee. It's me. Hey, we have an ID on the female that was dumped on our construction site. You'll never guess who it is!" he said.

"Right, I'll never guess, so tell me," she said.

"Betty Duncan."

"Really? The Betty Duncan we went to school with?"

"Yes, the same one. Someone killed her. She was buried with her handbag, and it had her ID in it. She and her mother moved into one of our units a few years ago. Are they, or I should say, is her mother still living there?"

"I don't know, but I can find out. Give me a few minutes to make a couple of calls and dig into our rental records. I'll call you right back."

Mickey hung up and asked Daniel to call Detective Reynolds to see if they can notify Mrs. Duncan.

Daniel called Detective Reynolds and explained the situation to him. The first thing he did was ask how Mickey had found out before he did.

Daniel tried to smooth his ruffled feathers. "Pete, your people didn't do anything wrong. I know it is an ongoing investigation, but it happened on our property, and all they did was give Mickey Ray the girl's name. That isn't a crime and doesn't release any confidential information. Baker, the forensic man, was very good, polite, and professional, so don't take it out on your team."

Mickey could hear the Detective on the other end of the phone was very upset that Mickey had interfered with his people.

Daniel kept talking and trying to calm the Detective. "Do you want to tell that lady her daughter is dead? Mickey knows her and can help her through this, and she'll be more prepared to answer your questions. So, you see, we're doing you a favor, Pete."

Read the entire story in the next installment of the "Landlord" series, soon to be in print. Available at amazon.com, barnesandnoble.com and terryjoegunnelsbooks.com.

Terry Joe Gunnels

CPSIA information can be obtained
at www.ICGtesting.com
Printed in the USA
LVHW110057141122
732905LV00003B/83